THE LIAR

THE LIAR

Steve Cavanagh

First published in Great Britain in 2017
by Orion Books,
an imprint of The Orion Publishing Group Ltd
Carmelite House, 50 Victoria Embankment
London EC4Y 0DZ

An Hachette UK Company

1 3 5 7 9 10 8 6 4 2

A CIP catalogue record for this book
is available from the British Library.

ISBN (Trade Paperback) 978 1 4091 5237 8

Typeset by Born Group

Printed in Great Britain by CPI Group (UK) Ltd, Croydon CR0 4YY

MIX
Paper from
responsible sources
FSC® C104740

www.orionbooks.co.uk

For Chloe

'I do solemnly swear that I will support the constitution of the United States, and the constitution of the State of New York, and that I will faithfully discharge the duties of the office of attorney and counselor-at-law, according to the best of my ability.'

Section 1 of Article XIII of the New York State Constitution; oath of office for a new lawyer.

'A liar is full of oaths.'

From Le Menteur *by Pierre Corneille*

PART
I

August 2nd 2002

Upstate New York

The child had been screaming for twenty minutes. She had been fed, changed, winded, rocked, sung to, even held. Julie had read half a dozen books during the latter stages of her pregnancy and that day she was attempting, for the fifth time, "controlled crying". The book said to leave the baby to settle down on its own. This was an important part of sleep training, according to the author. It was tough, and Julie hadn't managed to last the recommended two minutes without going into the nursery and picking up the baby. In the hazy recesses of her memory, Julie could not recall ever being held by her mother. When her baby was born, she'd felt awkward at first; holding that precious life in her hands felt wrong. It felt like she shouldn't be trusted with something so new, so pure, and so fragile.

Julie pushed open the door to the nursery and began to make "cooing" sounds as she approached the cot. The child settled almost immediately. The blackout blinds were pulled down, and only the night light gave a muted glow to Julie's face. It was enough for the child to see her mother, and hear her voice. Julie continued to hum, softly, smiling all the while as the baby gently drifted to sleep.

Silently, Julie began retreating from the nursery, first making sure the baby monitor was switched on before she left and closed the door.

The clock hit ten oh five.

Julie made her way to a makeshift studio in what would have been the utility room of the house. A half-finished canvas stood, accusingly, on an easel. Tucking the portable speaker from the baby monitor into her jeans, she looked around for her apron. She found it lying in a corner, put it on and began to work. The first half-hour went well, then, as the

3

shakes began, her brush strokes became stilted, heavy. Where before she could produce smooth, delicate lines, they became jittery and uneven. The tremors got worse and she felt that familiar, guilty hunger. The day before she had painted the red roof tiles in a single, smooth stroke, but now they came pitter patter, awkward and skewed.

Julie needed a fix.

She took off her apron, threw it into the same corner of the studio where she'd found it earlier, and went in search of relief. Down the hallway, opposite the nursery. She reached the den, opened the door, closed and locked it behind her. A switch on the wall ignited the ceiling fan, and she set it to the highest speed and opened the windows. From the desk, she took a glass pipe and filled it with small white rocks that were kept in an old tobacco tin.

She lit the pipe. Inhaled.

Another hit.

That sweet, saccharine ecstasy flowed through Julie's body. Her heartbeat quickened, and the wave of euphoria brought heat with it — like being smothered in a warm blanket.

The sound of the front door closing startled her. At last, Scott was back. Crack made her sweat, pretty much instantly, and she wiped her forehead. She placed the pipe on the study desk and opened the door to the hallway.

But there was no one there. Her senses were muddled. Noises seemed both louder and muted. As if the source of the sounds were closer to her but she was now underwater and listening through a fog of liquid. She listened, hard. And there it was again. A soft creak from the loose floorboard in the nursery. Julie crossed the hall, and slowly opened the nursery door.

Light from the hallway spilled into the room.

A man stood in the nursery.

A stranger. Dressed in black. Standing over the cot. The room tilted. With the curtains drawn and the blackout blind pulled down for the child's nap, the man's features were not clear. The more her eyes became accustomed, the more of him she was able to see.

He wore black gloves. Shiny, leather ones. And his face and head were somehow misshapen. She stepped into the nursery and saw that he was wearing a mask.

4

The vision before her had been so arresting, so violating, so unreal and yet so visceral, that at first she hadn't noticed the scent. It came to her now. Strong. Overwhelming. All too familiar.

Gasoline. The entire room had been soaked in gasoline.

Before panic, all of her senses kicked into high gear. And in that same paralyzing moment, she realized that her child's cries had ceased.

For a moment, Julie thought she was falling. The dark in the room seemed to rush toward her. And then she *was* falling. Just before she hit the floor the pain in her forehead kicked in. She felt something wet in her eyes. Something stingy. She wiped her face and looked at the blood on her hands. Julie scrambled to her feet and instantly the darkness took her again. Black gloves took her shoulders and pushed her backwards out of the nursery, across the hall.

Julie couldn't scream. She wanted to scream. She needed to scream. Her throat had closed in panic and her heart was thumping like a football in a washing machine. One of the hands let go, and Julie wriggled, trying to free her other arm.

Something very hard came down fast on top of her head. This time she felt the pain instantly; the fire inside her brain spread over her skull and she felt the pinpricks of agony spilling down her neck and into her shoulders. The figure in black let go of her other arm and for the briefest of moments, she thought it was all over. He was letting her go. She was wrong.

She felt strong hands thump against her chest. Julie catapulted backwards and heard the thump from the side of her head meeting the corner of the desk. The darkness had followed her and all turned black.

Silence. Stillness. Sleep.

Something inside Julie woke up.

It sounded like someone pounding on a door. The noise grew louder. A dull pain began in her head and quickly got worse and worse. It felt like someone turning a dial, increasing intensity until it became ice-hot agony.

Her eyes opened and her body lurched. She didn't know if she was standing or falling. Dizzy. Julie's hands found the floor beneath her and she pushed up onto her knees. She tried to take a breath but there was no air. Just thick, black smoke. As the coughing fit took her, Julie used the desk to climb to her feet. Two words were on her lips.

My baby.

She managed to turn around, and saw that the door was closed over, but not fully shut. She opened it to a wall of angry flame. The heat hit her skin with incredible force. It was like running into a flaming brick wall. The fire was roaring out of the nursery. It had taken hold of the hall ceiling and the carpet. Julie held up her hands and pushed into the hallway, but she could not get into the nursery. She couldn't see inside. The nursery was an inferno. Even with the smoke choking her lungs, and her tears evaporating on her cheek from the heat, Julie screamed. A long, scorching scream.

She didn't know how long she stood there with her flesh searing and the noise of the burning house drowning her voice. The ceiling let out a fierce crack and plaster, dust and then a heavy beam fell from the floor above and landed on top of Julie.

She lay there, drifting in and out of consciousness. The blood seeping from her scalp cooled her skin. She knew that before the beam fell on her she had a strong desire to go somewhere in the house, to get something, but what that was she couldn't remember. When the fire truck pulled up outside, Julie knew that she was upset, that she had lost something or someone.

And then Julie fell asleep.

CHAPTER ONE

Past midnight, fairly sober, I stood outside my office building wearing my best black suit, white shirt and green tie, my shoes polished and hair brushed, as I waited for a car to take me into the middle of a living nightmare.

West 46th Street seemed quiet with the bar on the corner already closed up for the night. Any restaurant stragglers that remained were avoiding the outside tables. Instead they stayed inside, praising God for the invention of AC. I'd only been on the street for five minutes and the back of my clean shirt was soaked through. July in New York City meant that everything and everyone on the street was hot and wet.

Crime went up in the summer as people went a little crazy. Usually people who weren't crazy any other time of the year. The dip in the crime figures for the regular offenders, who were often too damn hot to do themselves or anyone else serious damage, was made up for by the regular men and women who lost it in the terrible heat, their hands wet with blood and sweat. One human being for a flashing red moment does something unthinkable to another. And July was the crazy season.

We were two weeks into a record-breaking heat wave and even the darkness brought no relief.

Unlike most lawyers, I didn't carry a briefcase. Or a notepad. In fact, I wasn't even sure I had a pen with me. In my jacket pocket was a single document. Four pages long. Single spaced. My retainer agreement. There was a space at the bottom of the agreement for the signature of my new client. I didn't need anything else. The benefit of being a one-man law practice was that I didn't have to keep a lot of notes in case somebody else had to pick up one of

7

my cases. Witness statements, police interviews, court dates, juror selection – apart from the odd scribble, I kept it all in my head. The exceptions were those cases that we all try to forget.

As I sweated it out in my suit, I wondered if the case I was about to take on would be one of those that *I'd* try to forget in years to come.

The phone call came around twenty minutes ago, direct to the office landline, not my cell phone. So I didn't pick up at first. Only a select few had my cell. My best clients knew it, together with a couple of friends and the desk sergeants in half a dozen precincts who gave me a heads-up on any juicy arrests that came in.

It was after midnight so I knew it wasn't my wife or daughter. Whatever the caller wanted, it could wait.

I let the answer machine kick in.

"The office of Eddie Flynn, Attorney at Law, is now closed, please leave a message . . ."

"Mr Flynn, I know you're listening to this. Please pick up the phone." A male voice. Not young, maybe in their forties of fifties. An effort was being made to enunciate properly and hide an old, working class New York brogue; Brooklyn Irish.

A pause while he waited for me to grab the receiver. I poured a little more water into my bourbon and sat on my bed. I slept in a small room in the back of my office. With a couple of recent, really good paychecks I was getting closer to saving enough for a deposit on an apartment. For now, the pull-out bed in the back room sufficed.

"I don't have much time, Mr Flynn. Here's what's going to happen. I'll tell you my name and you'll have ten seconds to pick up the phone. If you don't I'll hang up and you will never hear from me again."

From the sounds of it, this guy I could do without. He was messing with my nightcap. One drink a day was all I allowed myself these days. My gut wanted it at six o'clock, but I found that I needed it just before I turned in for the night. A large glass, taken slowly, helped me sleep and sometimes even took the edge off the nightmares. No, I'd decided no matter what this punk said his name was, I would not pick up that phone.

"Leonard Howell," said the voice.

The name was instantly familiar but at that time of night I wasn't thinking straight. A long day in arraignment court, client meetings, and not much to eat in between meant I was punchy at this hour. I might not remember my own name.

After four seconds I remembered how I knew the caller's name. "Mr Howell, it's Eddie Flynn."

"It's good to hear your voice. You probably know why I'm calling."

"I've watched the news, and read the papers. I'm so very sorry for . . ."

"Then you'll know I don't want to talk on the phone. I want to know if you might be available later? I think I'm going to need some legal advice. Sorry to be so blunt, I don't have a lot of time," he said.

I had a million questions. None I could ask over the phone. An old family friend needed help. That was all I needed to know for now.

"You available at four a.m.?" he said. He didn't need to spell it out. Something was going down.

"I am. But I'm not coming at four. If there's something I can do then I'd rather come see you right now. Like I said, I've been following the news. I remember you from the old neighborhood, running football bets for my dad. He always liked you. Look, I'm really sorry about your daughter. If it's any use, I've been there. I know what you're going through."

He didn't say anything. He hadn't been expecting this.

"I remember your dad. And you. That's kind of why I'm calling. I need someone I can trust. Someone that understands my situation," he said.

"I understand. I wish I didn't, but I do. My daughter was ten when she was taken."

"And you got her back," said Howell.

"I did. I've played this game before. If you want my help, I need to be there, now. Where are you?"

He sighed and said, "I'm at home. I'll send a car. Where do you want to be picked up?"

"My office. I'll be waiting out front."

"Driver will be there in a half hour," said Howell, and with that, I heard the click as he ended the call. I thought about Lenny

Howell. He didn't like anyone calling him Lenny these days. He was a lot older than me and his reputation was well known in my old neighborhood. He'd been a hoodlum at first. Petty crimes and burglaries. His family were poor and he grew up hard. His old man used to beat him on the front steps of his building. Until my dad saw it happen one day and took Lenny's father to one side for a man-to-man conversation. Lenny never got hit again. He never committed another burglary either. Instead he worked as a runner for my father's illegal bookmaking business. Lenny learned how to run a book from my father. I knew him a little; Lenny was the first person to ever teach me a con. One day Lenny got a little too rough with a marine that couldn't pay his Tuesday blues – the debt from a bad bet on Monday night football. The marine kicked Lenny's ass, then told him he should join up. The marine liked young Lenny, and took him under his wing. Joining the navy saved Lenny from the life. He'd left his old ways behind. I knew the feeling, I'd been a con artist in my early twenties and gave it up for a career in the law. But what I'd begun to realize in the last few years was that you can never truly leave your past behind.

Three days ago I'd watched Lenny Howell give a press conference. All the major news channels carried the story. The chief of police sat on his left, his new wife, Susan, sat on his right, wearing a wedding ring barely four years old. The rock that she wore below that ring sparkled for the camera flashes and considering the size of the thing, I wondered how she managed to wear it without breaking her slender finger. If I'd been advising Howell I would've told him to go on TV alone.

He'd barely spoken. No need, really. When he took off his glasses and looked straight into the camera the ravaged look in his eyes had said it all. When he did speak, his voice was broken and strained. His words had stayed with me, because I'd been in his situation and I knew that pain.

"Whoever has my daughter, my Caroline, please don't hurt her. Give Caroline back to me and nothing will happen to you. I promise. We just want Caroline back."

Caroline Howell was seventeen years old. She'd been missing for nineteen days. There had been regular press conferences but this was the first time her father had appeared. Howell knew more about missing people than almost anybody. He'd served in the marines and completed tours of duty in every major conflict for the past twenty years. He'd returned a war hero and switched careers to law enforcement. For the last ten years he'd been making a fortune running Howell's Risk Management. A security firm that offered personal protection, hostage negotiation, hostile territory evaluation, and threat assessment.

Few people in the country knew more about kidnapping, hostage retrieval and negotiation. Now, his daughter was the victim.

I remembered watching him deliver a plea to whoever had taken Caroline – he said all the right things, stuck to his script word for word. He'd repeated her name, over and over, but I could see it in his eyes. I could hear the echo of loss in his voice. Once, I'd sounded exactly the same. My daughter had been taken a few years before. The ordeal had only lasted for two days, but those days still haunted me. I wouldn't have gotten her back from the Russian mob if I hadn't had a lot of help.

Every time I saw Howell's face on TV, or pictures of him in the paper, it sent a burning, hollow feeling into my chest. It was like looking at an old photograph of myself. I'd been that man.

I had to wipe a fine sheen of condensation off my watch face to check the time. Twenty-four minutes since I got the call. A red Volkswagen Sedan pulled up outside a bar called Brews. The driver leant over the passenger seat and eyeballed me. This wasn't the kind of ride I was expecting. I'd anticipated a Mercedes, or a high-end BMW to come pick me up. Howell wouldn't have sent something like this.

The guy got out of the VW and put on a white ball cap. He wore a faded red tee which read "Arnac Deliveries" on the chest. From the back seat he picked up a package wrapped in brown paper and set a white envelope on top. He closed the car door and made his way across the street toward me with the package and envelope under one arm and a clipboard in the other.

"Eddie Flynn?" he said.

I tensed up. It was a little late to be making deliveries, and this guy had nothing to do with Lenny Howell. Looking left and right quickly, I saw there were no pedestrians on the street; so this guy didn't have any buddies backing him up. He was no delivery boy, I knew that for sure. I turned to my right, giving him less of a target in case he had a knife tucked into the back of his jeans.

He was smiling, but not a real smile. It was for show. My hands were loose and ready to fly into this guy's face if he made a sudden move.

"I'm Eddie Flynn, I'm not expecting any kind of delivery."

Setting the package and the clipboard on the sidewalk, he picked up the envelope. As soon as he did that I knew exactly who the guy was.

He held out the envelope. I didn't take it. He came forward slowly, stood just a few inches from my face, planted the envelope on my chest and said, "You've been served."

I took the envelope.

The guy was a process server. People in that line of work spent their days tracking men and women and when they found them, they handed them envelopes that they didn't want; so they posed as delivery personnel, tourists looking for directions or new customers or clients. I wasn't expecting any papers. If he wanted to find me he could've come at a sociable hour – like most process servers. No, the timing of service had almost certainly been requested by whoever employed this guy. They wanted me to get this late, so it would keep me up all night. As I ran my hands over the blank envelope I thought that it could only be one thing – divorce papers.

I opened the envelope. It wasn't from my wife, Christine. It was a subpoena for all of the files and paperwork on someone called Julie Rosen. The subpoena required the files to be deposited at the process server's office within fourteen days. From what little I could glean from the document, it seemed to relate to an appeal in the matter of The People v. Julie Rosen.

It meant nothing to me. I was pretty sure I'd never represented anyone by that name. The subpoena said it had been prepared by counsel for the appellant, but as usual the subpoena didn't identify the lawyers acting for Rosen.

"Hey, who are Julie Rosen's lawyers?" I asked.

He said nothing and simply turned his back to me. An unwise thing to do in the circumstances. I put the subpoena in my jacket pocket and paid attention while the process server bent down and picked up the package and the clipboard.

With his back to me he said, "That was a piece of luck, I was going to call at your office and do the whole delivery routine. You saved me a couple of flight of stairs. Sleep well, pal."

"Who are her lawyers?" I said.

The process server didn't turn around, he just started walking to his car and said, "That's confidential. You know I can't tell you that."

"Don't you want your wallet back, Brad?"

He stopped, felt his hip pocket and spun around.

"How did you . . ."

I held his open wallet in one hand, his driver's license in the other.

"You should be careful not to turn your back to strangers. Now I know where you live, Brad," I said, slotting the license back into the wallet. "You want this back you gotta' tell me who gave you the subpoena; who's representing Julie Rosen."

His face folded into a snarl, he threw aside the dummy package and the clipboard. He drew his hands into fists.

"I'm going to beat the shit out of you," he said, striding toward me.

He raised his hands, wrists held straight and tucked under his chin like a brawler from an old movie. I knew then that Brad wasn't a trained fighter. First lesson I learned in Mickey Hooley's gym, twenty-years ago in the ass-end of Hell's Kitchen, was how to punch someone without breaking your wrist. Mickey taught us to angle our wrist to about 45 degrees, so the index-finger knuckle is in a straight line to your elbow. That angle engages all the little muscles around your wrist, giving you a solid punching base.

I could've demonstrated on Brad. Put my fist through his angry face. In a way, I wanted to. Brad probably thought he was tough. I could teach him otherwise. But I didn't. I figured he would be easier to talk to if he still had all of his teeth. Instead, I stopped him in his tracks with something a lot more powerful than a straight right hand.

I slid his license back into his wallet, swiped a C note from my billfold and held it up in front of my face.

His pace slowed and his hands began to drop. I took advantage and asked him a couple of questions.

"What's the going rate for time-specific personal service these days? Two hundred dollars? Two-fifty? When you take out your firm's cut, taxes, gasoline, insurance, what do you get? I'd say eighty dollars. Am I right?"

He stopped a few feet away. Looked me up and down, then stared at the hundred dollar bill in my hand.

"Eight-nine fifty," said Brad.

As an attorney I'd used process servers all over Manhattan. I knew the cheapest, I knew the best, and I knew exactly what they charged and how it broke down.

"I can do one of two things, Brad. It's your decision. Either I can make a call to a friendly court clerk I know, first thing in the morning, and she can tell me who issued the subpoena and all it'll cost me is a box of donuts next time I'm in court or you can save me the trouble and I'll put this hundred dollar bill in your wallet before I give it back. Your choice," I said.

Brad wiped his mouth, stared at the money.

"What if it comes back to me? I could get fired," he said.

"Look, it won't come from me. I'm not going to tell anyone I got this from you. They'll assume I charmed a clerk, is all."

I prised open the sleeve of the wallet which contained Brad's cash. He kept a neat wallet. It wasn't bulked out with old receipts or business cards. His driver's license and a couple of credit cards poked out of individual pockets that were stacked neatly on top of one another. A hundred and forty-seven dollars in cash was arranged in an orderly fashion in the wallet. The hundred dollar bill at the back, followed by a twenty, a ten, three fives, and two ones. I turned the wallet toward Brad, slid the tip of my hundred in between his hundred and the twenty.

"Last chance," I said.

"Copeland. The lawyer is Max Copeland," he said.

An electric chill prickled at my back.

I let Brad see me slip my hundred into his wallet, which I then flipped shut and tossed. Brad caught it, put it in his front pocket. He wouldn't carry his wallet in his hip pocket again. Not until he bought a chain for it. I watched him pick up the dummy package and clipboard, get back into his car and drive away.

Brad didn't check his wallet before he left because he saw me take a hundred from my pocket and put it right in there with the rest of his cash. I opened my right hand, unfolded Brad's hundred dollar bill which I'd swept up with my fingers and expertly palmed only moments ago. Brad didn't see it because I didn't want him to see it. My hand was in his wallet to put *my* money *in*, but he didn't see me take *his* money *out*. I stared at the hundred, and thought about Max Copeland.

Until three years ago, give or take a few months, very few people outside of the legal profession knew anything about Max Copeland. He didn't advertise, he wasn't listed in the yellow pages, he didn't have a website or even a sign outside his office. Lawyers knew him by reputation only. Max Copeland exclusively represented the worst kind of clients imaginable and he did so with a bloodthirsty relish. Only after an article appeared in the *Washington Street Journal* did any of the public come to know the name.

The article was entitled, "The Devil's Advocate." A pretty accurate summary, despite the cliché. Max represented pedophiles, child murderers, serial killers and rapists. He did this with a single goal in mind – get them off and get them back on the street. I'd never met him, and had no desire ever to do so. Guys with his rep didn't sit well with me.

In the end, it didn't matter – I'd never represented Julie Rosen, and I was pretty sure I had none of her files.

A set of headlights came around the corner. They were from a custom built, stretched Lincoln; black, beautiful, nineteen-inch chrome alloys and a polish that made the damn thing gleam like the rock on Susan Howell's finger.

The car pulled up in front of me. I put the subpoena in my jacket pocket and realized, too late, that I would've been better off not answering that call from Leonard Howell. Maybe it was the subpoena, maybe hearing Copeland's name – I didn't know exactly what it was, but I had a strong urge to ask the driver of the Lincoln to tell Howell that I was sorry, that I'd changed my mind.

The night had started badly and I knew, somehow, it would only get worse.

CHAPTER TWO

The driver's door opened and a man got out of the car with some difficulty. He wore a black suit that was a little too big for him. Gray hair, and his heavily lined face contrasted with sharp blue eyes. It was hard to discern his age. Either he was well into his fifties, or he had spent a lot of time on the street. The street does that to people. It ages you like nothing else on earth.

I heard a rasp from a hard-soled shoe scraping along the road. He dragged his right leg with what looked like an awkward and painful limp. Coming around the hood of the car, toward me, I could see that his right foot turned inwards, and bent as he dragged it along the blacktop. His left leg then shot out and stood straight to let him bend his torso and shimmy along. His head was bent down and he leaned on the hood to steady himself. While his head was down I glanced at his foot and saw that he wore a leather brace on his ankle. The strapping led to a steel plate that was probably built into the arch of the shoe, right next to the heel.

"Mr Flynn?" he said, in a light, somewhat sing-song voice.

"Thanks for picking me up," I said and held out a hand.

He hopped forward a little and took my hand in his. The grip was stronger than I'd expected.

"I-I-I'm G-G-George," he said. "Mr How-How-Howell sent me to . . ." His lips froze together and quivered as he tried to bust out a word beginning with p.

My grandfather on my mother's side had a stutter. When I was six or seven years old, I would go to his house and play with him. He always had candy stashed somewhere in the kitchen and we would play a game where I had to hunt for it. He could shake or nod his head while we looked for the candy, to tell me if I was getting close to the hiding place or further away. It was his favorite game because he didn't have to talk. If we did talk, my mom constantly scolded me for finishing my grandfather's sentences. Eventually I stopped, and learned to be patient.

I waited for George to finish, still holding his hand. With every passing second his grip became stronger, and it was beginning to hurt. His face turned a deeper shade of pink and a fine spray of spit machine-gunned from his lips as he got closer to delivering the elusive word. Eventually, he wound back his sentence a little and took another run at it.

". . . sent me to PICK you up," he said.

"Thanks, George," I said.

He released my hand, shuffled and scraped around the car.

"Let me g-g-get the door," he said.

"Don't worry about it, George. I've been opening car doors on my own since I was twenty-seven," I said.

George laughed and wagged a finger at me. He turned, awkwardly, and began loping around the car to get back into the driver's seat.

I got in the back before George even got as far as the driver's door. George had the AC on full. It was delicious. Like stepping out of a sauna and being wrapped in chilled silk. Leaning in between the front seats I couldn't help but take a look at the pedals. The accelerator looked normal but the brake pedal had been lowered and specially adapted with a thick rubber block to make it easier for George.

Lenny Howell was still a good guy.

George got into the driver's seat, started the motor, and reached into his pocket for a handkerchief. He wiped the sweat from his face and said, "It's one of those ni-ni-nights."

He sure got that right.

We drove along the north side of Manhattan on the Henry Hudson Parkway, with the AC blasting and the moon on the river to my left. Past Washington Heights, Harlem and then the freeway moved further inland at Inwood while the city boiled. George took the exit for the Cross Country Parkway headed toward New Rochelle. He didn't speak, other than to ask if I was comfortable. I was glad to be out of the humidity and my hair was almost dry.

I thought about the name Julie Rosen, and nothing came to mind. My former partner, Jack Halloran, and I had worked closely together. If it had been Jack's case I would've recognized the name. The only other explanation was that it was a dead file sitting in storage from a law firm called Ford and Keating. I got into the law because of a chance meeting with the then part-time judge Harry Ford. We'd become friends, and when I hung out my shingle with Halloran and Flynn, Harry got a full-time judicial position and gave up his partnership in Ford and Keating. Harry's old partner, Arthur Keating, retired around the same time and Jack and I bought their few remaining live cases. With the twenty or thirty live cases we also got their old files to store. Because we were taking the dead wood we got a discount on the cases that could still make money.

Could Julie Rosen have been an old client of Ford and Keating, attorneys at law? I checked my watch. 12:40 a.m. Far too late to call Harry. Even if it was one of his old files, I didn't want to call him at this hour. It would wait until the morning. Whatever it was, the fact that Copeland was involved made my gut twitchy.

"I-I sure h-hope you can help Mr Howell," said George.

"I do too. How's he holding up?"

George simply shook his head. That was enough.

"And the rest of the family?" I asked.

"Not so bad," said George, after a pause. "There's only M-Mrs Howell. And she ain't the g-g-girl's blood, you know?"

"I read it in the paper. Mr Howell got remarried."

When George replied, there was weight in his words, despite the stutter.

"M-Maybe it's a blessing, you know? The girl's real mother is in the ground? N-N-No parent should lose a ch-ch-child," said George.

The *Post* had mentioned, in one of the first articles, that Caroline Howell's mother had been deceased for some time.

We came off the freeway and found Main Street quickly. There was little traffic at this hour. We were headed for Premier Point, New Rochelle. A sister community of Premium Point. Whereas Premium Point held fifty of the world's billionaires in a highly secure, gated community – Premier Point was the poor cousin. It was still a gated living space, with private streets and armed security guards, but you could buy your way onto the bottom rung of the Premier Point property ladder with only seven or eight million dollars. You didn't get a helicopter pad, or your own private golf course, but Premier Point still had its attractions.

I could tell we were getting close to the entrance by the presence of news channel vans and the assortment of satellite dishes scattered along an open lot opposite the gate. In fine, entrepreneurial tradition a coffee stand and a taco van had decided to pitch on the same open lot to keep the news anchors and reporters wired and fed. Dark figures tossed coffee and scrambled for their cameras. They managed to get a few flashes at the car as we drove into the private lane and pulled up at the gatehouse. A warm glow came from inside the gatehouse, and we sat there waiting for the guard to come out. George put the car in park and folded his arms. I guessed he was used to waiting for the night watch guard to haul his ass away from the TV in the gatehouse. Night watchmen never do anything quickly, that's why they're night watchmen.

My cell phone vibrated with a call. It was Harry Ford. The late call could only mean trouble.

"Hi, Harry. I'm kinda glad you called—"

He cut me off, "Eddie, I just got served with a subpoena duces tecum for the file in an old case. I'm just giving you fair warning, you might get handed one of these." Harry was well into his sixties, one of the first black superior judges in New York's history and a man who enjoyed half-a-dozen glasses of bourbon before he hit the pillow at the end of the day. I could hear the whiskey in his voice.

"Too late. I already got mine. I was going to call, but I didn't want to wake you. Is this something to worry about?"

"It's an old case I dealt with about fifteen years ago. A bad one. Julie Rosen was convicted of murder. She burned down the house with her baby daughter asleep in her cot."

There was something in his voice. But it wasn't booze. Regret, guilt maybe.

Most trial lawyers, if you buy them a drink, will tell you all about their greatest victories. War stories. Lawyers love war stories: how they were up against the odds, how they outsmarted their opponent and won. Knowing what I know now, I wouldn't hire one of those lawyers for my worst enemy. You get a *great* trial lawyer talking about their career, and they won't blow smoke up your ass about their wins – they talk about the cases they lost.

Everyone loses, sooner or later. It's the verdicts that got away that stay with you. Why do the losses mean more for others? Why do they stay with the best lawyers? It's easy. They give a shit. They care. Give me a lawyer that's haunted by a guilty verdict on a shoplifting charge that got their client a month in Sing Sing, twenty-five years ago. Those are the lawyers you want in your corner. Harry had been one of those lawyers. And I'd been lucky to learn at his side. I wouldn't have a career without Harry; he took me on as a clerk and then set me up in practice. Without him I'd still be hustling on the street instead of hustling in the courtroom.

Harry had a few cases turn bad. He told me about most of them. I couldn't remember him ever discussing a case like this.

"I'm on my way to see a client. Listen, Harry, I don't want to worry you but the process server was working for Max Copeland."

He said nothing.

"You took the case all the way to trial?" I said.

"Sure did. Julie told me a man dressed all in black set fire to her house. She said she either didn't see his face, or he didn't have a face. She was kind of fuzzy. Had a bad head injury. Jury didn't believe her."

"Any trace of the guy?"

"Nothing. Nobody saw him. You think Max Copeland has found the guy?" said Harry.

"I don't know. He's got something though. Listen, I have to go, but I'll call you in the morning."

"Call me later, I'll be up reading a case for tomorrow," he said, and disconnected. Lawyers and judges keep odd hours, but it was a long time since I'd known Harry to stay up all night reading a case. He'd probably read it already or he didn't need to read it for the morning. I got the impression Harry just wanted something to take the subpoena off his mind.

I knew he was worried about this subpoena. Copeland had a habit of attacking his client's old attorneys. Whatever new evidence, or maybe new witnesses that Copeland had to launch this appeal didn't matter much. The target for criticism would be Harry. He would seek to prove the conviction was unsafe because Julie Rosen had a poor lawyer; he always pleaded ineffective counsel. He'd ruined careers to win appeals in the past. Harry would be his target.

That made Copeland my target. I wasn't about to let Harry get sucked into a shit storm by a low-life like Max Copeland.

George held up a friendly hand at a security guard that eventually emerged from the gatehouse dressed in a dark, short-sleeve button-down shirt. He wore a Glock, and a ball cap with a company logo that read – "Howell's Security."

A torch shone on my face briefly, obscuring my view of the guard's features.

He turned his back, killed the torch and waved us through.

A two-lane road, with tall, white picket fences on either side, took us further into Premier Point. I wound down the window so I could smell the salt from the East River. After ten minutes we turned right into a single-lane private road. A stone wall sat on either side of the mouth of the road, and there was something else. At first I thought it was a sign pointing out the name of the property; I'd seen other signs like it on the private road like "The Manse," "The Lodgehouse" and "September Rest." The signpost outside of Howell's property didn't bestow a name on the spread. When we got closer I saw the blue lettering on the sign – "For Sale."

As we drove along the lane I wondered what would break first, the Lincoln's suspension or my spine. The road was littered with potholes. Some small, some huge and George, despite his best efforts, was hitting every Goddamn one of them. I thought that with the property being up for sale, Leonard Howell didn't want to start resurfacing the road if he could get the house sold without the added expense. After a minute or so I could see a huge house in the distance. Lights were on in almost every window. It was too big to call a house, and not quite big enough to qualify as a mansion in this part of town.

Maybe a half dozen vans and cars were parked on the gravel drive outside the house. The cars were Fords; all the same make. There were two vans in all. One carried the livery of the NYPD. The other – Federal Bureau of Investigation.

George pulled up outside the house. I could see a figure standing in the open doorway, nothing more than a silhouette. I could tell it was a woman by the shape of her legs and her hair. There were no lights outside, just the warm spill from the windows.

I got out, turned to face the car and closed the door.

A voice said, "Freeze, FBI. Hands on the roof right now!"

CHAPTER THREE

The voice was female. Young. So were the hands that shoved my cheek into the polished roof of the Lincoln.

I heard George grunting and failing to spit out an explanation. A male voice told him to stay back.

"Take it easy, my name's Eddie Flynn. I'm a lawyer. Leonard Howell invited me . . ."

"Shut up," said the male voice. I felt hands searching me. They found the unsigned retainer, the envelope containing the subpoena, my cell phone and wallet.

"What kind of lawyer doesn't carry a briefcase?" said the female voice, as she released her hands from my skull.

I got my head up but didn't turn around.

"The kind that's going to see a new client and doesn't have a file of papers yet."

"Face down. Hands on the roof," came the command from the male and he forced his hands onto my shoulder blades, pinning me.

I put my head down on the cool roof of the Lincoln and kept my hands still. Last thing I needed was some twitchy fed putting a slug through my gut. Whoever stood behind me lit up a flashlight. The beam fell on my face, then moved away as I heard the rustle of paper.

"Those documents are confidential," I said.

"Let him go," said the woman. The hands holding me fell away. The first thing I saw was George with a pitiful look on his face. Then I saw the woman. She was just over five feet tall, brunette, short hair, wearing a green shirt tucked into a pair of blue jeans. The lace-up boots on her feet were almost as big her. She read the retainer agreement, the torch light shining through the paper. She muzzled the beam from the torch by tucking it under her arm, then folded the retainer back up and handed it to me. I guessed she was in her early thirties, with a soft, oval face, although her expression was anything but soft. She was pissed.

The guy beside her was my height and wore a suit and tie. His hair was short and razored into a neat line. Another fed. He handed her the envelope and my wallet and said, "ID matches. He's seems to be who he says he is."

She ignored the wallet and opened the envelope, bringing the flashlight up to read the subpoena.

"The wallet you can check, but the envelope is confidential."

"Sure it is," she said, reading the subpoena. She shook her head, bundled the wallet, envelope and subpoena together and thrust them into my chest.

"You're not cleared to be here. George knows all visitors come through us. The guard on the gate didn't mention a passenger name so we had to check you out. Now, you mind telling me why you're here?" she said. For the first time I noticed the accent. Midwest and educated.

"I mind," I said.

Hands on her hips, her right little finger stroked the butt of the Glock on her waist. She looked at the other fed. I got the impression she was considering whether to arrest me or play this another way. Her partner swung away to the right and raised a hand.

"Why don't we start over? I'm Special Agent Joe Washington," said the fed in the suit, this time holding his large hands across his chest. He twisted to his right and looked at the female agent and said, "This is Special Agent Harper."

I held out a hand toward her and said, "You got a first name, Agent Harper?"

"Blow me," she said, and kept her hands by her sides.

"Name like that would've made you popular in college," I said.

She lifted her chin, looked me up and down and said, "At least *I* got laid in college."

She backed away and turned toward the house. Washington was trying to stifle his laughter. I could no longer see her in the dark, but I heard the furious thump of her boots on the gravel. I looked at the house and saw that the female silhouette remained standing at the front door, casting a long shadow into the drive.

"Look, I'm sorry, pal. We're all a little wired. Your driver should have let us know he was bringing you in. Look, we're here for Mr Howell, we're not in the habit of interfering in his personal business. You go ahead, and if we need to, we can talk later."

"Why do I get the impression this isn't the first time you've had to apologize for your partner?" I said.

"It's part of my job. I've got her back. That's how it works."

"Is it worth it? Is she good at her job?" I said.

"She's the best," he said, like he meant it.

They were tight. It was only natural. The FBI was still overwhelmingly staffed by white males, and an African-American agent and a female agent would naturally bond. The good-old-boys Bureau club would treat them as outsiders, and for that same reason, they'd probably found each other. I was an outsider too. There weren't too many former con artists from Brooklyn with a license to practice law. So even though they'd crossed the line, I didn't complain.

It wasn't the first time I'd been rolled by law enforcement and it probably wouldn't be the last.

In truth, I was more confused than angry. If Caroline Howell was either a missing person or a person whom they suspected had been abducted, there would be a sole family liaison officer who would visit once a week, and because the Howell's were millionaires they'd get an occasional visit from a senior officer in the missing persons division. The FBI would not be here. The NYPD wouldn't have a van here. They wouldn't be this tight-assed about security and there certainly wouldn't be FBI agents backed up by tactical officers in full gear with guns in their fists on the front lawn.

Something else was going on here. Something bad.

CHAPTER FOUR

I walked with George toward the house. He'd told me to go on
ahead, and not to wait on him, but I didn't want anyone else
jumping out of the dark and pointing a gun in my face. I figured
I was safer with George. Besides, I liked him.

He'd produced a foldable cane from a shoulder bag, flicked it and
let it clunk out into a solid walking stick. He leant on it heavily as
we made our way, slowly, along the gravel driveway. Even with the
benefit of the walking aid, George's foot dug a trench in the loose
gravel as we made our way through the dark.

"Don't they have outside lights?" I said.

"They do," said George, aiming his cane at an unlit, mock
Victorian street lamp. I looked around and saw a few of them,
standing dark and unused. "But ss-sss-sssssomebody ka-ka-cut the
lines," he said.

"Who?"

He shrugged his shoulders.

The female figure that had been standing in the doorway was
gone. Instead, a very different kind of shadow stood there. It blocked
out almost all of the interior light from the entrance hall. I had to
do a double take, because at first I thought somebody had closed
the damn door.

It was a man, well over six-and-a-half feet tall. We took our time
coming up the steps, and the closer we got to the door, the bigger
the guy looked. His head was almost square, and sat on what looked
like the curves of somebody's ass, sitting on top of his shoulders. I
then saw these were his massively overdeveloped trapezius muscles.
His shoulders were well rounded too. This was a guy who spent
many hard years in the gym, and probably followed it up with a

26

truckload of steroids. The huge, almost comically overgrown torso led to a narrow waist and legs that looked like they were full of balloons. I nodded at the man. He didn't move and for a second I wondered if he was real – or some kind of dummy people placed in their window to scare off intruders.

Up close, I could make out a chin like a shelf and a long fat nose, but the man had no discernible eyes. Only small black slits sitting above bloated cheeks.

"Mr Howell is expecting you," he said, in a voice that was too high for his size. I'd been right about the steroids. He stood aside and let me in.

I took a minute to look around. White marble entrance hall, curved staircase and doors to the left and right. And, of course, a huge chandelier right above us. It was expensive, but somehow lacked taste. I didn't pay much attention to the furnishings or the rest of the house. There was something that took my mind from it.

Tension.

It was as if the house itself was wound tight. I could practically hear the floorboards above me creak with the atmosphere. It reminded me of going to an Irish wake with my father in the Bronx when I was maybe ten years old. I'd been to plenty of wakes before that one, and they were usually fairly raucous affairs with beer, sandwiches, whisky and poteen flowing along with the heartfelt, often hilarious stories about the recently deceased. An Irish wake wasn't that dissimilar to a house party on Saint Patrick's Day. The only real difference was that somebody died before the party started, not during it.

The wake in the Bronx that day was different. The dead man had been in his early twenties, and there were no funny stories. The women and the men had cried into their Bushmills, and the whole house seemed dark and thick with death. Howell's mansion felt just the same. I sensed the pressure in the air.

The mountain turned and expected me to follow him.

"You go on, Mr Flynn, I-I-I'm go-going to get sss-ssssss . . ."

"Come on, we don't have all night," said the big man. I ignored him and stood beside George, waiting for him to finish.

". . . SOME tea. See you . . . you-later," he said.

"I'm sure I will. Thanks for everything, George."

He disappeared through an alcove. The big man stood below the staircase and beckoned me.

I followed him as he broke right and went through a large oak door. Beyond the door was a lounge filled with cops, some in full SWAT gear and others in suits. The suits studied me as I walked by. In the corner I spotted a pair of FBI agents wearing bullet-proof vests over their shirts. Law enforcement were using the lounge as some kind of incident room. They sat in front of open laptops, or stared at a map displayed on a fifty-inch TV screen affixed to the wall and everywhere there were coffee cups and food wrappers. Muted conversation and the tap of fingers on keys punctuated by the occasional metallic slap and click from a SWAT officer loading an AR-15 assault rifle.

They were prepping. Something was about to go down, but I'd no idea what that might be.

The noise level diminished as I followed Bigfoot through the lounge and into the corridor beyond. Just before I left the lounge area I spotted Harper nudging another female officer and looking at me. I ignored them both and turned my attention back to the big guy.

At the end of the corridor he took me through an identical oak door. We were in a large, spacious study. The blinds were pulled shut and a couple of lamps lit the room, but not too brightly. On my left was a brown leather couch and matching armchairs. A small dark-skinned man in a navy suit occupied the chair closest to the window. He didn't register my arrival.

On my right, behind a mahogany desk, sat Leonard Howell. His head bent low over the desk, his fingers locked behind his head. He sucked in a long breath, unlaced his fingers and sat up. On the desk in front of him was a nine millimeter Beretta and a magazine. Behind him I saw the same figure I'd seen silhouetted in the light of the doorway when I'd pulled up in the town car earlier. She was attractive. She had that poise and the expensive perfume that comes from being married to a guy like Howell. I'd read somewhere that her first husband died of carbon monoxide poisoning, and that she and Howell hooked up after his first wife passed away. Strange how death can bring two people together.

Her ash-blonde hair fell about her shoulders in a carefree manner as she leaned down and kissed Howell on the cheek. There was no tenderness in that kiss. It seemed perfunctory.

"Are you sure about this?" she said.

"It's the only way," said Howell.

She nodded and made for the door. As she passed me her gaze lingered. I caught the smell of booze. The big guy closed the door behind her, returned and flapped his big hands underneath my arms.

"Hands in the air, I have to search you," he said.

I put my hands up and waited while he patted me down.

"I've already had the FBI searching me. You've got enough law enforcement here to invade a small country. What's happening?" I asked.

No one responded.

I felt the big man taking my phone and wallet. He placed them on the desk in front of Howell.

"Make sure it's turned off," said Howell.

For a second, the big thumbs struggled to find the power switch. Eventually he seemed satisfied and I watched the screen turn black. Howell checked the phone to make sure it was off.

"Thank you for coming, Eddie. I'm afraid I owe you two apologies. First, I insist on security and privacy – so please forgive Marlon here. Second, I will answer all your questions in time, but I'm sorry to tell you it's going to be a very long night."

CHAPTER FIVE

Howell looked a lot worse than when I'd last seen him on TV. His skin held a gray tinge, with dark patches around the eyes. The eyes themselves looked strained, raw, and painful. For a guy in his late fifties he looked remarkably thin and yet you could still see the outline of a much younger, and more defined, physique through his white silk shirt. Broad shoulders and chest, well developed arms. Black hair, probably assisted by a two-hundred dollar dye job.

His hands shook just a little, and I put it down to physical and nervous exhaustion.

"The gentleman who escorted you here is Marlon Black. He handles security at the house," said Howell.

I turned in the direction he pointed and locked eyes with Marlon's chest.

"He's not the best at introductions," said Howell.

I held out a hand. Marlon nodded at it.

"And behind you is Mr McAuley. He's my associate."

I didn't offer a hand to McAuley. The dark-skinned man in the navy suit lit a cigarette and simply smiled at me.

"Please, sit down," said Howell.

The chair facing Howell looked like an antique. Gingerly, I took a seat.

Elbows on the table and hands beneath his chin, Howell looked me over. The gun on the desk was all for show. For whatever reason, Leonard Howell wanted me to know that he was in charge.

"How was your ride over here? George isn't much of a driver, or a conversationalist. But he has a good heart and I trust him. You can't buy that in an employee," he said.

"The trip was fine. I like George. He seems like a good man."

"Good men are hard to find. When you get one like George you hold on to him and treat him right. I learned that from your father. I was sorry to hear he passed."

I nodded.

"Everybody in the neighborhood knew Pat Flynn. Hell of a cannon, and ran a straight book. He worked his crew like a pro. If you were in, you were made, but give Pat one reason to doubt you and you were out. He was big on trust. I respect that. Your father was good to me when I was a kid. I know he would've been very proud of who you are now."

"He never wanted me to go into the life. Didn't want to teach me the grift. You helped persuade him otherwise," I said.

I remembered a lazy Tuesday afternoon in the back of the Irish pub my father used to run his book. He was out collecting. The pool table was busted, and I was bored. Lenny passed that afternoon for me by teaching me three-card monte. My first con. My dad came back to the bar around four, and watched me work the cards. Lenny told him I was a natural, I'd already taken twenty bucks off of the regulars. So my dad agreed to teach me. He taught me the cons, the street hustles, the techniques and skills for the life of a cannon.

Lenny smiled, but it didn't last. I could tell the smile felt unnatural to him. He wiped it away with the back of his hand, then spun the Beretta on the table. It was an idle distraction. I got the impression that the small talk was more for Howell's benefit than mine. It struck me that he was warming up his voice. I could hear the cracks in his throat. There was a dark pain eating away at Howell and he was doing his best not to let it show.

"What can I do for you, Lenny?" I said.

"I'm going to need a lawyer. I want you."

"I'm sure a man like you has a long-standing relationship with a law firm. Why do you need me?"

He leaned back in his chair, let his arms fall into his lap and studied me. For a second, I saw him glance at McAuley before returning his stare to me. I could smell McAuley's cigarette.

"I heard you don't drink too much any more. I can understand that, but it's late and I could use one. Care to join me?" he said. He got up and made for a drinks cabinet behind his desk. He selected two low-ball glasses and filled one halfway. The decanter was poised over the second glass.

"It's twenty-year-old Scotch," he said.

"No, thanks. Maybe later," I said.

His lips turned down and he shrugged, set down the decanter and returned to his seat. He placed his glass right in front of me, inches from my seat and a good three feet from his.

He took a sip from the glass and placed it back down.

"Caroline didn't like me drinking in the house. I hadn't touched this stuff in a . . . well, when she didn't come home that night . . ."

Another hit from the glass emptied it. He drank like I used to: not for the taste, not for the pleasure, booze was the medicine that numbed the pain. He refilled his glass.

I said nothing. The Scotch propped him up enough to get through another sentence.

"As you are probably aware from the press, the NYPD and the FBI believe someone has taken my daughter."

From the papers and the news, I knew Caroline was in her senior year of high school, a straight-A student who already had great offers in for college. As far as her parents and her friends knew, she didn't have a boyfriend. Her picture had been on the news for days. She was every high-school boy's dream – blonde, captain of the school cheerleaders and apparently very kind with it. Her interests were slightly unusual; she loved comic books. Instead of hanging out in the mall with her friends, she spent most Saturday afternoons rooting through baskets of old comics in second-hand bookstores.

Nineteen days ago she set off in her car to go pick up a comic book she'd ordered from Zero Comics, on Hudson Street. She never got there. When she didn't arrive home that night, Leonard tried calling her. No answer. He called Caroline's friends. No one had seen her. Howell called the cops and they checked out the bookstore and her friends. An APB went out on the 2015 VW Golf that Leonard had given to her on her birthday. The car was never found. Her cell phone didn't register at any cell towers that day. Girls like Caroline disappear all too often. But everything was good at home. Nobody who knew Caroline ever thought she would run away. What was there to run away from? She hadn't packed a bag, she left money in her room and her cell phone charger.

The working theory for law enforcement was abduction. A couple of the papers announced this theory a few days after she'd been missing in their initial reports on her disappearance. No doubt Leonard Howell knew it within hours of her disappearance. The media attention proved fierce. NYPD press liaison briefed reporters every twelve hours. In the days that followed her disappearance specially trained NYPD officers questioned nearly every kid in her school. Twice.

No suspects. No reason to believe she up and left on her own. Her debit card showed no withdrawals.

Abduction.

But no ransom demand. Which was a bad sign. For the last two weeks one word had been on everyone's lips. You could tell the papers were hinting at it. The TV too. You could see it in the cops' eyes.

Murder.

The press conference I saw three days ago confirmed my suspicions about Caroline Howell. Leonard was reaching out to whoever had taken his daughter. That only meant one thing: no contact from any supposed kidnapper. The longer a person was missing without a ransom demand, the more likely it was that they weren't taken for ransom – they were simply taken for someone's pleasure, and they won't ever come back.

This was a last roll of the dice for Howell. Go on TV and hope she was still alive. The fact that Howell specialized in the kidnap and ransom retrieval for some of the biggest insurance companies on the planet meant that it was possible someone was giving him a taste of what it's really like when your child is taken from you.

A thought occurred to me that if Caroline Howell had been a girl who'd come from a family that didn't have a million dollars in the bank, a family that struggled on welfare in the projects, the media would not have given one inch of column space to her.

"I know it looks like kidnapping. I heard your appeal on TV. I'm sorry for you, and your family," I said.

He took the glass from the center of the desk, swallowed in one shot and put it back down in front of me. His face was twisted.

There were two emotions fighting for control of Howell – fear and hope. When you find out your kid has been taken, it feels like a knife in your stomach and with each passing second, time itself twists that blade deeper into your guts. People think that hope keeps you going; that wishing and believing, somehow, it will all turn out okay actually helps. It doesn't. It makes the pain from that blade a thousand times worse, because it reminds you of what you've lost and all that there is yet to lose.

"Thank you. The thing is, I thought she was dead. When I gave that press conference, I didn't think anyone still had my girl. I'd hoped, you know . . . but I knew she hadn't run away."

He put his hand inside his shirt and drew out a crucifix on a gold chain. The chain was thin and the cross looked tarnished.

"This belonged to her late mother. It was the only thing she had belonging to her mom. She kept it in a jewelry box in her room. She never would've left without it."

Rubbing the cross between his thumb and forefinger, his gaze fell away and he stared into nothing. I knew that look. He was thinking of all the times that he'd spent with her, the good times. Holding her, playing with her, Christmas mornings and the weight of her on his lap as they watched old movies.

I shook my head and realized I was projecting. I'd done the same when my daughter, Amy, had been taken. I was thinking about the times I'd spent with her. I wanted to see her right then, but I'd have to wait. I'd arranged to visit the next day.

Howell let the cross fall onto his chest, and then tucked it back under his shirt.

"I thought she was gone. We had no contact, no demands for ransom, but then everything changed."

CHAPTER SIX

He was about to tell me more. I could see it brewing in his throat as his Adam's apple bobbed.

"The retainer," said McAuley, behind me.

"He's right. Before I go on, I need to ensure confidentiality. Did you bring the retainer agreement with you?"

I produced my retainer from my jacket but didn't place it on the table. Instead, I held on to it.

"I'm not entirely sure I can help you. Tell me what you want me to do, before you sign this."

He nodded to McAuley.

"In short, I need a lawyer to help me deal with the ransom. We got a legit ransom demand after the TV appeal. Photos of my daughter held captive. The FBI think it's solid. Caroline is insured, and there are a lot of hoops I have to jump through to get my insurance company to make the ransom available. The FBI is all over this too, so I need a legal mind in my corner. And not one of those Harvard pricks. I need a lawyer I can trust."

I took a moment to think it through. While I turned over every thing I'd heard, he flipped around a framed picture on his desk.

"That's my daughter," he said.

She sat on a grass bank surrounded by her friends but the photographer only had eyes for her. The others were merely background scenery. She wore black and white striped leggings, denim shorts, ugly black boots and a pink tee sporting the name of a punk band that I vaguely recognized. Over her shoulder was a leather biker jacket, with pins on the collar. I knew the band names on the pins; The Stones, Thin Lizzie, Pearl Jam, The Black Keys. My eleven-year-old daughter once had a denim jacket just like it; covered in pins.

It reminded me of the time I spent trawling flea markets with my Amy. A couple of stalls sold tee-shirts, bandanas and every kind of rock merchandise you could think of. Amy wanted a vintage Black Sabbath pin, and it took us months to find one. We had ice cream the day she found it hiding under a belt buckle on a junk stall. She stared at it, and took a long time to decide where to place it on her jacket.

"She decorate the jacket herself?" I asked, examining the photo of Caroline.

He nodded.

"I think I'll take that Scotch now," I said, handing him the retainer agreement.

Marlon took Howell's glass and refilled it. Grabbed a fresh one for me too. He placed them both on the table and I took a sip while I watched Leonard scan the retainer. He patted his pockets and said, "Where the hell are my glasses?"

Neither Marlon nor McAuley did anything to help him find his spectacles.

"I'm sure it's fine," he said. He took a pen off the table and signed the retainer, slid it back to me.

"This means you're my lawyer now, right? Client confidentiality?" he said.

"Right. Anything you say to me is treated in the strictest confidence. Attorney client privilege, it's completely confidential," I said.

"Good. I'm glad," he said, picking the Beretta off the center of the table and slotting the magazine into the receiver. "Because, I'm about to commit a major felony."

CHAPTER SEVEN

The Scotch may have been well aged, but it tasted bitter.

"I should tell you, Lenny, that if I'm given information that leads me to believe that someone is in danger then I have a duty, as a lawyer and officer of the court, to report that to law enforcement. If I didn't I'd be breaking my oath, and I'd become an accessory. So be careful what you tell me. But you'd better tell me why you really want me here or I'm going to tear up this agreement, call a cab and send you a bill for my time this evening."

"Fair enough, I'll choose my words carefully," he said.

From the chair behind me, I heard McAuley say, "I told you."

I didn't turn around, and I watched Howell shake his head and put the Beretta in the back of his pants.

"Without wasting your time or mine, I know who you are. I know what happened in the Chambers Street courthouse; somebody kidnapped your daughter and you got her back. That's why you're here. You can handle the pressure, you're a father, you've been in my situation and you come highly recommended. We've had contact from the man holding my daughter. I want to pay the ransom. Technically that's illegal."

"But wait a minute, won't the feds turn a blind eye to the ransom payment? Isn't that normally how things work?"

"It is. The kidnap and ransom game is based on the economics of human life. It's the same all over the world. If the kidnapper is paid, and the hostage returned safely, the kidnapper will go straight out and do it again. Paying the ransom facilitates that crime, it gives it a business model. Official US policy is that we do not negotiate with kidnappers. Unofficially it happens every damn day. I make my living dealing with kidnappers."

"So why do you need a lawyer this time?" I said.

Howell leaned forward and placed both hands on the table.

"In most domestic kidnappings the FBI deliver the ransom. They can justify the ransom being paid because they get their chance to follow the kidnappers and make an arrest. It's like baiting a hook. This time, the feds are fishing in the wrong pond. After the press conference we got a ransom demand with proof of life photographs. They wanted two million. You may have noticed the SWAT guys and the feds getting organized for the drop. It goes down in two hours at the Rochelle train station. Three a.m. sharp. While the drop is going down I need you to cover my back."

I felt a prickle of heat on my neck and said, "What do you mean, *cover your back?*"

"It's a con. One hour after the kidnapper sent the pictures of Caroline to the FBI, he also contacted me on a secure email system and told me the train station is a decoy. He sent me the same photos of Caroline and a demand for ten million. It's good proof of life. The photos are definitely Caroline and they are recent. The exchange goes down tonight – same time as the FBI are chasing their tails in the train station, I'll be dropping the money off at the real location. The kidnapper doesn't want to get arrested – he wants the feds and the cops miles away from the real drop. He's smart. The feds want to capture the kidnapper and take Caroline alive – in that order. My daughter is not their priority, they want their arrest. I want my daughter back – I'm not interested in anything else."

His voice had just about held together, but the more he talked the heavier it sounded, like there was a tidal wave of desperation and fear that he was holding in check.

"You have any idea who might have taken her?"

"No. I've dealt with kidnappers all over the world, it could be any of them or none of them. There's no clear MO here. But it doesn't matter who took her, you're going to help me con the feds and the NYPD so I can get my daughter back alive. I've played this game many times, all over the world. I know how to retrieve a hostage – alive. The only way it works is with one man, no police and a bag full of cash. She's my daughter and I'm calling the shots. Thing is, I don't have ten million. I've only got two," he said.

"So where are you going to get the ransom?" I said, and instantly felt that was a question I shouldn't have asked.

"My insurers are sending the ten million. I contacted them privately. The feds think the insurance company are bringing two million. When the insurance bondsman arrives, I'm going to bring him in here, alone, stick my gun in his face and take him hostage. I'll tie him up and keep him here. I know the man, so I don't want to hurt him if I don't have to. I'll give the feds my two million and wave them goodbye – then I'll go get Caroline. I *will* get her back. And when I do, I'll be arrested for kidnapping and perverting the course of justice. The FBI have an unwritten rule not to prosecute families who pay ransom. But I'm doing a lot more than that. I'm committing a felony kidnap and colluding with the people who have my daughter to help them evade capture. There's no other way to put it. They *will* prosecute me for this – you're going to defend me. Also, I'm breaking my contract with my insurers. There's a clause that the ransom becomes repayable, in full, immediately, if I refuse to co-operate with law enforcement."

My eyes closed, my teeth ground together and not for the first time that night, I wished I hadn't picked up the damn phone. What Howell was proposing was way off the reservation. The FBI and the NYPD were all over this. It didn't matter if he saved his daughter, the feds wouldn't see it that way. What Howell was about to do was highly illegal, and would end with him getting arrested and sued for ten million.

For what seemed like minutes on end, I explored every inch of Howell's face. Behind the pain, there was determination.

I had a duty to go out into the lounge and tell the first cop I saw exactly what Howell had just told me. It was the only exception to attorney client privilege: if a client tells you they are about to commit a crime that could put someone in danger, you must break confidentiality and report it. On my first day as a lawyer I'd taken an oath to the court and the Constitution in front of Judge Harry Ford. As I spoke that oath for the first and last time, I saw Harry's beaming smile. He was proud of me. I owed him a debt that I could never repay. With Howell's proposal if I kept my mouth shut I was an accessory before the fact and I was breaking my oath. I would be disbarred and sent to jail for ten years. What he asked me to do essentially required me to commit professional suicide. There was no amount of money that could persuade me to say yes.

"I'll do it," I said.

39

CHAPTER EIGHT

Howell had played a dangerous game, hiring me. But he'd called it right. If it was my daughter, Amy, I would kill, lie, cheat, steal, and then do life in prison for it if it meant taking her home in one piece. And I did a lot of those things when Amy had been taken by the Russian mob a few years before. I got her back and I'd relied on people to help me. Howell knew what he was doing. He'd been in the hostage game for ten years, he was a talented negotiator and his company was world renowned for getting people back alive from kidnappers in Afghanistan, Central America, China, Brazil and a half dozen other places whose black market economies thrived on ransom money.

If anyone could do this, it was Howell.

I asked myself, after I'd told him I would do it, why the hell I'd agreed. It didn't take much time to analyze that decision. I would do whatever it took. And if Caroline came back safe and sound, then whatever happened after that didn't matter – it would be worth it. But I wasn't doing this for Howell alone. I was doing it for the little girl in the photograph with the badges on her jacket.

As soon as I'd said yes, Howell stood and shook my hand.

"Thank you. Father to father. Really, thank you," said Howell.

I nodded.

He released his grip and disappeared through a door in the back of the study. I turned and stretched my back. I felt tired but adrenaline was keeping me going. I wouldn't change places with Howell for all the world and I felt for him. Anything I could do to ease that burden, I would do in a heartbeat.

Even though I'd said I would help him, a growing sense of unease took hold in my gut. Taking an insurance bondsman hostage was risky. So much could go wrong. What if he fought back? What if he got hurt? What if he got out of the office and tipped off the law? And then there was private security to consider. Nobody travels on their own with ten million. If the bondsman came with guards then they might have to be dealt with too. They would be armed.

Shit.

"Welcome to the team," said McAuley.

I turned around and shook his hand too. He was much smaller than Howell, about the same age, but there was something else about McAuley that I couldn't quite put my finger on. I could get a pretty good read on most people – you have to when you're a grifter. There was a smile that wasn't really a smile.

"Mr Howell has just gone to get a few things together. We're glad you're on board, but we don't want you to worry. None of this is going to come back on you. We're going to need you when Mr Howell is arrested. And just so we're clear – it was my idea to hold back until the retainer was signed. Mr Howell wanted to be upfront from the start. I persuaded him otherwise. So don't judge him," he said.

"I've got to say though," he continued, "I wasn't convinced Mr Howell had chosen the right man. I thought you'd go running to the feds. My bad. That's why he runs the show."

"Have you known him long?"

"A very long time. We've saved each other's lives more times than either of us can count. I normally run the drops and Mr . . . well, Lenny, backs me up. So yeah, he's more than a business partner. I owe him. Say, Marlon, will you go and get Mrs Howell?"

The big man left through the door I came in.

When the oak frame shuddered from the door closing shut again, I saw McAuley's mask slip. The pretense of the smile fell away, his face hardened and he gave me a once-over.

"This whole thing stands on a knife edge. I need to know, can we rely on you?"

McAuley was close buddies with Howell which meant he was probably very close to the family. He looked exhausted, excited and nervous about the drop. And the nineteen days that Caroline had been gone would've taken their toll on him too. Even in this great old study, the stress was still cloying the air around us, just as it had filled the entire house with the same smothering, mortal intensity.

"I won't let you down," I said.

"Good."

"Do you have any idea who might've taken her?"

McAuley pursed his lips, and stared just over my shoulder while he debated what to say.

"No. He didn't give a name. He just sent a photo. We don't know who it is, but all things considered, I'd say it's something personal. I've done this for a long time. Over the years I've dealt with Somali pirates, Al Qaeda, even a few of the South American cartels. It's hard to explain; sometimes you just get a feeling – and then you know."

"Know what?"

"You know that whoever it is you're dealing with is fully prepared to kill their hostage."

From his jacket pocket he produced his phone, and after a couple of swipes of his finger across the device, he flipped it around. It was Caroline Howell all right. I'd seen maybe three different photographs of her in the papers. This was her. She was bound hand and foot, wearing a pair of blue jeans and a white sweater – just like the description. Her leather jacket was missing though. I thought she was asleep. He swiped the screen and said, "This is the other photo."

I guessed that the first photo being taken had woken her up. In this shot, she was awake and the look on her face was pure terror; her eyes were wet and frozen in panic. Her face dirty with tears and I saw dried blood on her wrists where she'd struggled against the cable ties. I studied the background in the photo; it was the same as the first. It had been taken on a camera with a flash – the area surrounding Caroline was black and the only thing visible was the concrete floor. Wherever she was, it was a large dark room, maybe a basement or an abandoned building.

"When Susan arrives . . ."

The door behind me opened, strangling the words in McAuley's throat.

In the doorway stood Susan Howell. Her face looked slightly vacant – like she'd been anaesthetized to get herself though this. I could smell the anesthetic on her breath – gin. Lots of it.

"Thank you, Marlon," she said and dismissed him by running a hand down his back. Her hand lingered – finding the contours of his muscled back with her fingers. I didn't like it. It was a display of affection and control. Marlon walked out of the room and closed the door behind him.

Susan Howell said nothing to me. She simply raised her eyebrows at McAuley.

"He's gonna defend Lenny," said McAuley.

Without another word she folded her long legs into an armchair and rested her chin on a delicate hand. People react to extreme stress in different ways. Some crumble, some power through it with sheer will and others go a little nuts. I thought Susan Howell was in the latter category. Either that, or she just didn't give a shit about her stepdaughter. I decided to give her the benefit of the doubt.

"Why the difference in the ransom amounts?" I said.

"I don't know. Best guess is the kidnapper is playing with us. But he also wants the fake drop to look real. We'll be giving the feds two million. That should be enough to throw them off the scent," said McAuley.

Lenny came out of the back room, into the office, carrying a roll-on briefcase in one hand and a stack of cash in the other. He put the case on the desk, opened it and put six stacks into the case before closing it up. The case was large enough to hold ten times that amount of cash.

McAuley bent down and retrieved a small black bag from below a chair. He kneeled, opened the bag, and spread out a mini-assault rifle, magazines, a gag, cable ties and more equipment.

That vague sense of unease quickly turned into a lead weight in my stomach. This wasn't going to work out. I stared again at the briefcase on Lenny's desk. It was big, cumbersome. Not easy to haul around if he needed to move fast.

"Why the big case for that amount of cash?" I said.

Lenny looked at the briefcase and said, "This is a bulletproof, bomb-proof case that the insurance company uses. The insurers are my clients. I've had to use their cases in the past to transport ransom, so I bought one. I need the feds to see the same briefcase coming out of my office as the one that went in. This has to look real."

I rubbed the back of my neck. Susan Howell looked up at me from the armchair, a worried look on her face. I felt McAuley's hand on my back.

"Susan is going to help smooth things over with the feds. Make sure they don't come in here. I can handle the bondsman's security detail," said McAuley, lifting up his jacket to reveal a pistol strapped to his waist.

Howell poured himself another shot, threw it back and shook himself. He was fighting the adrenaline. The more I thought about this, the more certain I became that the plan would fail. And if it went south, Caroline would end up dead.

I thought about that afternoon in the bar, when I was just a kid, sitting on a bar stool beside Lenny Howell, watching his hands move the cards.

"This isn't going to work," I said.

McAuley looked at the ground, his lips tightening. Howell shook his head, poured another drink and said, "It has to. There's no other way."

"Yes there is. Taking the insurance bondsman hostage is just far too risky. It won't work. And it means even if you get Caroline back, no matter what I do you'll probably go to jail," I said.

"If I get her back then I'll live with that," said Howell.

"What if there was another way? A way to get the money, lead the feds on their wild goose chase and not hurt anyone?" I said.

McAuley and Howell exchanged glances.

"How?" said Lenny.

I walked back to the desk, put my hand on the briefcase and said, "Three-card monte."

August 2001

Upstate New York

Julie Rosen felt uncomfortable sitting on Rebecca's couch. She'd worn the same jeans for about a week, including one night when she'd slept rough. If her pants left a stain on the floral patterned couch there would be hell to pay.

Rebecca returned from the kitchen carrying two steaming mugs of coffee.

"Grab a coaster," said Rebecca.

From a box on the table, Julie selected two coasters and laid them out. They were cork coasters with pictures of puppies on the laminated veneers. The mugs were placed carefully, and Rebecca took time to turn the handle of Julie's mug so that it faced her.

"How are you feeling?" said Rebecca.

The sun felt hot on the back of Julie's neck; the heat coming through the sash window was somehow intensified.

"I'm okay. Taking one day at a time, you know how it is," said Julie.

Rebecca nodded. Julie knew Rebecca didn't have the first clue about what it was like to go through drug detox. The shivering pains that seemed to spread over your body, the rattling of your teeth so loud you can't sleep, and the sweats that always seem to be the precursor to vivid, strange, dark hallucinations.

"You look so much healthier," said Rebecca. "I've seen what drugs can do to people. Some of the customers I get . . . well, they're practically skin and bone. They're not even people any more."

Julie nodded and shifted forward on the couch, feeling even more uncomfortable. She'd heard Rebecca talk about her customers before and it always made her skin crawl. Rebecca worked as the county medical examiner and her customers were corpses.

45

"I've seen burn victims, murder victims, just last week I . . ." Rebecca paused, her eyes searched the floor. It seemed to Julie like Rebecca was rooting her vision in the present, so that perhaps she wouldn't catch a glimpse of whatever horror she was recalling.

". . . last week they brought in a baby. Just a few weeks old. Two police officers found it in a dumpster behind a tequila bar. You know, I almost felt relieved. Child born to a mother like that had no future anyway. That child wouldn't have had a life. Not really. Baby was already an addict. Born into it. You are so lucky to be out of that now, Julie."

Julie took a sip of coffee, looked around the lounge at the soft furnishings, the paintings hung on the wall, and the cushions which had no doubt been selected to match the scenic artwork. It seemed strange to her for Rebecca to say such terrible things in a house like this one. Julie didn't want to think about drugs, or addiction. She was trying to put that life behind her.

"This is lovely," Julie said, continuing to look around the room.

"Thanks. It's a big house for just the two of us," said Rebecca.

"I can imagine," said Julie, not really being able to imagine it at all.

They sat quietly, drinking their coffee, and easing the tension with quick, false smiles.

"I know this is none of my business, but I wanted to know how you're doing financially," said Rebecca.

Taken aback, Julie said, "Oh, well, I'm working part time. It's just waitressing. Paint costs money, you know. I'm working on a few canvases at the moment, hopefully when they're done I can sell a few."

"Great," said Rebecca, behind glassy eyes.

She continued, "It's just, that, ahm, I think I can help you. You know, with money."

Carefully setting down her coffee on the coaster, Julie stood up and smoothed down her tee-shirt.

"I don't need your charity," she said, and took a step toward the hall.

"Wait, it's not charity. I want to help. And . . . this is so hard . . . I think you can help me," said Rebecca.

Julie stopped, sighed, turned and said, "What can I do? You want to buy a painting, is that it?"

"No, yes. Sorry, not exactly but a painting would be lovely," said Rebecca, looking at the carpet, unable to meet Julie's eyes.

Julie realized Rebecca was crying. False tears – maybe.

"What's wrong?" said Julie.

"I need you. I need your help. There's no one else I can turn to. I'll pay you. I promise. Ten thousand dollars, right now. Another ten when it's done."

"What are you talking about? What are you asking me to do?"

Rebecca stood and embraced Julie.

"It has to be a secret. Just between us. Do you promise?"

"I don't know what you're . . ."

"Do you swear?" said Rebecca, a desperation creeping into her voice.

"I promise. Just tell me what it is you want."

"You haven't seen Scott lately? You're not with him any more, are you?"

Julie sighed, and lied, "No. I haven't seen him. We're not together."

Rebecca nodded, cupped Julie's face and said, "Good, because no one can ever know. If anyone finds out, we'll be ruined."

CHAPTER NINE

I made my way through the lounge, Marlon in tow, and he showed me to the small kitchen which sat directly off the north end of the room. I guessed this wasn't the main kitchen, because there was no stove, but it was a pretty big kitchen by any standards. Just as when I'd first made my way through the room, the bustle seemed to dim especially for me. That was law enforcement for you, they wouldn't trust a lawyer to walk on a carpet without trying to rip it up as he went along.

"Just wait in here, Mr Flynn. I'll bring your retainer fee right out," said Marlon, loud enough for the senior feds and cops to hear. At least he didn't mess up. He did what I told him to do.

I took up a bar stool at the kitchen counter and helped myself to coffee. There were two SWAT guys in the kitchen, filling their water bottles. They soaked their bandanas, wrung out the excess water and then tied them over their scalps. It would get real hot in the back of the SWAT van when they were wearing full tactical gear.

I could see most of the lounge from my seat. This kitchen was more of an extension of the lounge with a white tiled floor delineating the two areas. A dining table sat in the other corner. I needed to stay within earshot of the law. My attention was drawn there by a pair of raised voices. One was familiar, one was not.

Agent Harper was arguing with a man in a gray suit, white shirt and red tie. An FBI badge hung around his neck on a chain. They stood apart from the little groups huddled around the computers, checking maps or making calls. Some of the cops and other agents were trying to listen to the argument, even as they pretended to go about planning for the drop-off.

You're making a mistake," said Harper, "this is some crackpot who saw Howell on TV and either wants to make a quick buck or wants to get himself killed by the police. It's got suicide by cop written all over it. And if I'm wrong about that, then you still shouldn't go, because that can only mean it's some kind of sick hoax."

The agent she was addressing stood with his arms folded, and occasionally picked at his teeth with his thumbnail. He was listening, because others were listening, but I could tell he'd already made up his mind to ignore Harper.

"We've got proof of life, Harper. Now, either you get in on this or you get the hell out," said the male agent.

"Lynch, you're wrong about this. I know it. The drop is all messed up," said Harper.

"I'm the SAC here. Have you forgotten that?" he said.

Their eyes met and something unspoken passed between them. I noticed Harper almost dancing on the balls of her feet. Her lips were set tightly, ready to blow out whatever she didn't want to put into words in front of the rest of the team. SAC stood for Special Agent in Charge, which meant Lynch outranked Harper. The air around these two seemed to bristle with more than a mere professional disagreement. I couldn't be sure but I guessed there was personal history there.

Given what I knew, it was easy to tell who was smarter; Harper for all her volatility was the one with the sharpest tools in the box. She knew the rail station was somehow off.

"I haven't forgotten," she said. "I know exactly who you are."

Lynch put his hands on his hips and stuck his chin toward the ceiling so he could look down his nose at Harper. She looked at him like he'd just pulled down his pants and taken a dump on the front lawn. That look remained on her face as she walked away.

That's when Lynch noticed me.

I nodded a greeting. It was his turn to look disgusted, and he joined a group of agents who were examining a digital plan of the Rochelle rail station on the big screen TV affixed to the wall. All the entrances and exits were marked with blue dots. There were small red dots marked on the plan, with letters and numbers beside them. I guessed the letters and numbers represented surveillance operatives, scattered around the station at various points to cover all the possible angles of view. A green dot on the map sat beside the rows of benches. This dot had a name – "Lynch." I guessed this denoted the agent who would deliver the money.

"What are you looking at?" said a voice.

I turned and saw SAC Lynch behind me. I'd been so engrossed in looking at the plans that I hadn't noticed him peeling off from the group of agents and cops.

"Nothing," I said.

"You're the lawyer, Flynn, right?" he said.

"That's me, good to meet you," I said, extending a hand.

He ignored the gesture and said, "I heard you had a run-in with Agent Harper. That right?"

"We met," I said, standing. I didn't like the idea of Lynch towering over me. As I got to my feet I saw, in the corner of my eye, Harper standing at the edge of the lounge. She must've heard somebody using her name. I turned my back to her so I could address Lynch.

"From what I've heard it was more than that. It's been reported to me that Agent Harper was extremely physical with you; pushing your head into the roof of a car? If that's correct then I'd like to hear it from you. The Bureau doesn't stand for that kind of behavior from our agents."

"You must've heard wrong. Agent Harper was courtesy personified."

"I find that very difficult to believe," he said.

"Ask Agent Washington if you don't believe me. I'm sure he'll verify my account," I said.

He was getting nowhere with me, and decided to cut his losses. As he walked away he said, "I'm sure we'll talk again, Mr Flynn."

He almost bumped into McAuley. The two men eyed each other and Lynch went back into the lounge.

"Agent Harper," said Lynch. "We've had a complaint in relation to your conduct with a representative of the family. You're off the property effective immediately. Go back to the field office and write out a statement in relation to your encounter with Mr Flynn. I'll expect it on my desk in the morning."

I tried to interject, but Harper held up a hand. She'd heard me denying it. She lifted the shoulder strap of her laptop bag off the back of a chair and walked out of the room with all eyes on her.

McAuley handed me a black leather roll-aboard trolley case and said, "Your retainer, Mr Flynn." I extended the handle and wheeled the case behind me as I walked through the lounge, flanked by McAuley. The case bumped into a table, almost knocking it over. I swore, then switched hands and felt another tug when the wheels got stuck on the edge of a thick carpet.

When I was satisfied I'd attracted enough attention with the case, I left the lounge. In the hallway that led to the front door, I saw Washington waiting with his hands clasped together in front of him.

As Harper strode toward the front door Washington held out his right hand. They shook hands and she stepped out of the house into the dark.

I wondered if anyone but me had noticed the slim black device that Washington had palmed to Harper in the handshake. Probably not, I thought.

Then I wondered if anyone had figured that the case I dragged behind me carried two million dollars. Again, probably not.

CHAPTER TEN

I stood on the porch and watched Harper get into a car which I guessed was her personal vehicle. A red Dodge Charger with a black racing stripe over the hood. She spun the wheels and sent a shower of gravel over the lawn as the torque bit down. The rear lights disappeared into the distance, down the single lane that led to the street.

McAuley and Howell joined me. They didn't speak, just put their gaze to the stars while the SWAT team clambered into the back of their van. The feds came next. And soon the half dozen cars in the gravel drive were all warming up.

"Mr Howell, can I speak to you for a moment," said a voice behind us. It was Lynch.

"Of course," said Howell.

Lynch crunched through the driveway, then stopped when he noticed that Howell hadn't walked with him. He wanted a quiet word away from McAuley and me.

"You can say anything you like in front of these gentlemen," said Howell.

Reluctantly, Lynch dragged his feet back to the stone porch and said, "Very well. We'd like you to reconsider our advice, Mr Howell. It really would be better if you stayed here with your wife. We know you're a professional, but we can handle this. The last thing your daughter needs is a conflicted father rushing the drop and . . ."

"Getting her killed? Is that what you were going to say?" said Howell.

The FBI agent's eyes found his feet.

"I was going to say we didn't want any surprises, Mr Howell. With the greatest of respect we'd like you to think on this matter again. And stay here. If you're worried about the two million—"

"Look, I hear you. It's not the money. It's Caroline. I'd be giving the same advice if I was in your shoes. And at the same time I would understand the father's insistence on being present at the exchange. I'll think about what you've said, agent."

"If it comes to it, Mr Howell, my men may have to put you into protective custody. We don't want to jeopardize the transaction."

And with that, he left and got into the front passenger seat of a Ford and started making calls. It had been Howell's idea to pretend he was going to the Rochelle drop. It would be what the feds expected him to do. Howell was going to allow them to persuade him otherwise, eventually.

Headlights in the distance. Coming this way. A finger tapped at my wrist; McAuley telling me this was the car we'd been waiting for.

I hefted the suitcase and let my eyes roam the driveway and the half acre of lawn in front of me. For the next ten minutes I decided to assume that there were still cops and feds out there in the dark – watching my every move. The headlights arced to the right and came around to stop in front of the house. The vehicle was a security van, and two armed men in uniform got out. They opened the rear of the van and a third man in a light-blue suit leapt down onto the stones. He carried a large briefcase identical to the one I carried. According to Howell, the insurance company bought these cases in bulk. They were light, tough, and looked exactly like the case at my side. Only difference was the case was attached to the man's wrist with a pair of steel handcuffs. In his other hand he held an iPad.

Howell made his way down the steps, greeted the man in the suit and guided him back toward the house. Agent Lynch got out of the Ford. He'd been waiting for the ransom in the vehicle. I saw him introducing himself to the man in the suit with the briefcase.

"Let's go into the office," said McAuley.

As Howell, Lynch and the man with the case walked up the steps toward the house, I saw McAuley knock on a door in the hall. Susan Howell came out, her face streaked with tears.

Fake tears.

Her job was to collapse as the three men came into the hall. She would fall into Lynch's arms and break into hysterics. When Lynch calmed her down, she would insist on speaking to him about the drop. She would tell him she needed reassurance. We needed Lynch out of our way.

McAuley's best guess was this would take around five to six minutes. More than enough time for Howell to take the insurance agent in the nice suit in back, complete the paperwork for the handover of the money and get him the hell out of there before the FBI asked questions about how much was in the case. By the time Lynch made it out of Susan's clutches, he would be handed the identical roll-aboard suitcase in my hand with two million dollars inside.

On no account could the law realize there were two separate ransoms. Caroline's life depended on it.

I watched Susan Howell as she wiped her face, smearing her make up even more, then she strode up the hall. She had a drink in her hand, probably more gin. The ice fell over her lips as she put her head back and drained the glass before placing it on a table. She stood at the end of the hall, waiting on her mark.

The three men came through the door in silence. Howell was flanked by Lynch on the left, and the insurance bondsman on his right. They walked past McAuley and me, headed for the study.

I felt an escalating unease the closer the three men got to Susan Howell. She swayed a little, pressed her fingertips into her forehead. I got the impression that either this was all too much for Susan Howell, or that there were problems in her marriage that the kidnapping brought to the fore. Howell must have spotted Susan's demeanor too, because he slowed his pace.

"Shit. I hope she doesn't choke," said McAuley.

Susan Howell shook her head, covered her mouth with her palm and walked away.

McAuley and I exchanged a look, and he said, "I knew she couldn't do it. She's taken too much of the hard stuff."

The party ahead of us turned the corner, and McAuley and I broke into a run.

CHAPTER ELEVEN

McAuley and I stepped inside Howell's office before he could close the door. I could sense the panic in Howell.

I whispered to him as I walked past.

"We can still do this. Follow my lead," I said. Agent Lynch hung back, putting an elbow on a bookcase in the far corner of the study. The man with the briefcase stood beside Howell at the desk. McAuley and I stood on the opposite side of the desk.

Howell handled the introductions.

"Gentlemen, this is Valter Bergstedt from Dahlquist Equities. Dahlquist's hold my family's K & R insurance and Valter here has the ransom. Valter, you've met Special Agent Lynch, and this is my lawyer, Eddie Flynn. You already know McAuley."

The bag man from the insurance company looked like a guy who enjoyed his money. The suit was tailored, tight fitting, and set off his well-groomed beard and immaculate hair. He was courteous and said hello, but didn't shake hands. One hand still held the iPad and the other was still handcuffed to ten-million dollars of bearer bonds. I guessed the ransom was so large because bonds could not be moved and so easily converted into cash as they used to be. Likely the kidnapper would get seventy-five cents on the dollar.

"I would like my lawyer to witness the handover signatures if that's all right," said Howell.

"Of course," said Valter. His pronunciation was perfect but he couldn't shake the Swedish accent.

I came around the large desk to stand on Howell's right. Valter was on his left and Lynch came forward to stand beside McAuley on the opposite side of the wide, mahogany desk.

With one hand, Valter placed the iPad on the desk and brought the device to life. He flicked his hand across the screen and I collapsed the handle of my trolley case. After a few seconds he brought up what looked like an agreement on the screen.

I touched Howell's hand. He looked down and I discreetly pointed to the floor, letting him get a view of me toeing my suitcase under the table. The cases were hand-cut Italian leather, from the same company that made seats for Ferrari. All of the cases had combination locks, a trolley handle and wheels. They smelled like money and each could probably hold forty or fifty hardback books – or ten mil in bearer bonds.

My idea was simple. Just like three-card monte. It's the oldest con in the book. And Howell had taught me well. The three cards can be anything, but normally it's a queen and two low numbered cards placed side by side, face down on a small table. The only card that matters is the queen and you have to find it. The dealer starts every game with the cards in his hands, face down, cradling the edges of the cards with his fingers. Two in one hand, the queen on the bottom and the ten above it and a single five of diamonds in the other hand. He then throws down the queen, face down, and throws the other cards around it. It's easy to spot where the queen has landed and follow it as he moves them around. A buddy of the dealer will bet on where the queen is, and get it wrong. The mark thinks he's got it all figured out and places a bet. This time, with money on the table, the dealer throws the top card down first, the ten, keeping the queen till last. The switch gets them every time.

We were playing two-card monte. Only we weren't switching cards, we were switching cases. But this time we had to do it with an audience member in the shape of SAC Lynch.

Howell nodded. McAuley too. They got the message.

All Howell had to do was put the damn case he got from the Swede under the desk after he signed for it. Then he'd pick up the two million case and give it to Lynch, and I'd pick up the ten million.

Couldn't be easier. No hostages. No guns. And a better chance for Howell to escape a jail sentence when the feds found out what really happened.

Everything would work out fine as long as the insurance agent didn't mention the sum of money in the case, and Howell got the case off him and under the desk. Howell seemed pretty sure Valter wouldn't mention the cash figure. He said Valter would consider that "impolite."

Valter flicked his thumbs over the number lock on the case, and opened it. Howell took a quick glance inside then closed it and said, "I'm sure it's all there, where do I sign?"

"Digital and hard signature, if you please. You'll find the lock is programed with Caroline's date of birth," said Valter, placing a document on the table. He flipped open his iPad, unlocked it, removed a digital pen from the case and laid it on the screen. Valter then spun the numbers on the case to lock it.

I watched Howell squint at the screen and then the page. Without reading it he picked up the e-pen and ran it across the screen in what looked like a quick signature.

"You can keep the handcuffs by the way, I've got my own," said Howell.

A droplet of sweat hit the screen. He dropped the e-pen, wiped his brow, picked up the ink pen and scrawled another shaky signature on the page.

The only sound was Howell's quick breath and a dull crunch from McAuley grinding his teeth. His jaw muscles were working overtime and his eyes never left the case cuffed to Valter's wrist.

I was ready. Soon as Howell put the ten mil on the floor and shuffled it toward me with his feet, I was out of that room.

I heard the jingle from the long silver chain as Valter placed the case on the desk, then unlocked the cuff on his wrist. I held my breath as Howell reached out to take the handle of the case. Before Howell could react Valter lifted the case off the desk, strode over to the bookcase, put the case on the ground, grabbed hold of Lynch's left arm and slapped the cuffs onto his wrist.

"What the hell is this, Valter?" said Howell. The blood drained from his face.

"I'm sorry, my friend. We've made concessions already. No hostage committee – you want the ransom paid and that's good enough for the old men in Zurich. But you're too close to this. My direct instructions were to place the ransom into FBI custody on your behalf. You've just signed your agreement to reflect this. I take it you have no difficulty with this, Agent Lynch?"

The fed shook his head and was about to say something when Howell interrupted.

"No way, the money stays with me. I won't hand over a cent until I see her alive. Valter, you can't do this," said Howell.

The bagman's features softened as he approached Howell. "It is already done. I am deeply sorry, Leonard," he said, placing a hand on Howell's shoulder.

He shrugged it off and stared at McAuley. Both of them looked like startled goldfish – mouths slightly open, shock and disbelief in their eyes. And I could see the bubble of fear about to explode inside of Howell. Sweat soaked his face and he wiped at his forehead with his sleeve.

Special Agent Lynch was about to ensure that Caroline Howell never made it out of that dark hole alive.

"This is not happening . . ." said Howell, the rage and denial gilding every syllable. His right hand dropped and slowly made its way behind his back. This man was as desperate as any I'd ever met. He knew Lynch was about to walk away with the only chance he had of getting his daughter back and Howell couldn't let it happen – he was going for the Goddamn Beretta tucked into his waistband. My plan was falling apart. This would end in a gun battle if I didn't think fast.

"It's safer, for everyone, if you're not involved in the drop," said Lynch.

"I think what Mr Howell means is that he's agreeable to this happening if I accompany the ransom money to the drop and I ensure that it's in my sight until the exchange. That fair enough with you, Special Agent Lynch?" I said.

Howell's hand locked around the grip of the pistol sitting at his back. Across the table, McAuley dragged the left lapel of his jacket to one side, exposing the butt of a handgun in a shoulder holster.

The gun at McAuley's side was a silent question for Howell. Do we take the money now by force?

Decisions like this cost lives.

I gently, but firmly drew Howell's fingers away. I silently mouthed the words, *trust me*.

Lynch extended the handle on the case. The chain was maybe a foot long, so Lynch couldn't fully extend the handle. He collapsed it, took hold of the leather grip attached to the body of the case and picked it up.

"I've no objection. But Mr Flynn will have to ride with us and, of course, once we're inside the rail station he can't be with me – it's a single man drop. Those are the kidnapper's terms," said Lynch.

"That's up to you, Agent Lynch," said Valter, handing him the key to the cuffs. I watched Lynch take the keys with his right hand and place them into his pants pocket.

"Again, I'm sorry," said Valter to Howell.

Howell didn't shake Valter's hand. I doubt he even saw the Swede extend the courtesy. He couldn't take his eyes off me. Valter gathered the signed papers together, folded them and placed them in the pocket of the iPad cover and made for the door.

"I'll wait in the corridor," said Lynch.

He left along with Valter, and they shut the study door behind them.

"We're screwed," said McAuley, in a wet hiss.

"No we're not," I said.

Both men stared at me like I was dumb. I couldn't blame them. My father had taught me how to be a cannon: how to pick a wallet, or dip for a purse in a bag and more besides. With practice I'd gotten pretty good and my father guessed that I had a natural talent for it. He called it *the touch*. Said it was the same kind of thing that great golfers, or great pool players, or great magicians had too – they all had smart hands. It was a deftness; a light, sure, blindingly fast movement that can't really be learned. You're born with it, and you nurture that talent to get the best out of it. With practice, you get the synapses firing faster, the muscles grow memory and become stronger, and the technique, the speed and form improve.

At one time my father told me he thought I was one of the best pickpockets he'd ever seen. I was older now, and I guessed I was also a lot slower than I'd been at thirteen or fourteen when I had practiced every day.

I wondered how any of that would help me now. Picking a wallet out of somebody's jacket without them noticing was one thing, but switching a briefcase with another that's handcuffed to a federal agent?

Well, that's something else.

"What's your cell number, Leonard?"

He looked at his phone and said, "I'll send you the contact."

"Don't bother – just tell me the number. I'll remember," I said.

He rhymed off his cell phone number.

"Don't you want to key my number into your phone?" he said.

"No need. I've already memorized it. I'll call you from the fed's car. Follow me."

"What are you going to do?" said McAuley.

I picked up the briefcase from beneath the desk and said, "I'm going to get your ten million."

CHAPTER TWELVE

Lynch was as good as his word. He'd waited for me in the corridor outside Howell's study. He held the briefcase in his left hand. His eyes met the case in my hand, but only for a moment.

"Ready?" he said.

I didn't answer at first. My mind was running all kinds of calculations. I guessed there was around a hundred and twenty feet of carpet and marble tile between us and the front door. Add another forty feet from the front door to the car. The average person walks at five feet per second. That gave me thirty two seconds to get the key to the cuffs from Lynch before we got into the car. Once we were in that vehicle I wouldn't have a hope of taking the key.

The FBI man started walking.

I started counting.

The corridor was by no means narrow, but it wasn't wide enough for two men carrying bulky cases to walk side by side without having to occasionally fall back and step to the side to avoid knocking over a table or vase in the hall.

We got to the lounge fast.

Twenty-six seconds left on the clock.

Lynch stayed ahead of me even though I picked up my pace. He nodded to Agent Washington who sat in the kitchen off the lounge. He was sending a text on his cell phone. He put the phone away and put on his jacket. It was time to get moving.

Twenty-three seconds.

At the alcove that led into the lounge, I drew level with Lynch and walked on his right-hand side. The chain on the cuffs beat out a dull rattle against the leather case. The sound of the chain on the case matched the rhythm of Lynch's feet.

Eighteen seconds.

I listened harder as we walked. Far as I could tell, Lynch didn't have change in his pocket. At least that was one blessing.

"Is your car outside?" I said.

He turned to the right, then looked ahead and said, "Should be. Let me just check."

The pace slowed as he raised his left arm instinctively to reach for his cell, and remembered that his wrist was chained to a heavy case. The two million in my case wasn't light either. He reached his right hand inside the right side of his suit jacket. It was an unnatural reach. One which caused him to slow and twist his torso slightly. I stepped in and my right made a sweep for his pocket, but I couldn't get my hand inside. Not with him walking. Fortunately I'd been light enough in the attempted dip for him not to notice.

Fifteen seconds.

He made a call.

"We're coming out," he said.

Turning into the entrance hall I heard the engine from a large sedan outside. Even with the front door closed I could hear the rumble of the tires on the gravel and the low muttering from a three-and-a-half liter V6.

Nine seconds.

I fell back to let Lynch get ahead. Suddenly I was conscious of someone behind me. I turned around and saw Howell and McAuley bringing up the rear. They'd stopped to talk to Washington, distracting him for the final few seconds. Even though I turned, I didn't stop walking.

"Are you going to follow us to the drop point, Mr Howell?" I said, walking straight into Lynch. My case hit him in the back of the knees and I saw his head bump the door.

"Oh, God, I'm sorry, Agent Lynch. I wasn't looking where I was going."

"It's *fine*," said Lynch, through gritted teeth. "Doesn't matter. I'm just glad you're not coming into the rail station," he said, opening the front door.

I remained in the entrance hall and watched him make his way to the car. I needed to see which door he was going to use to get into the Ford. With a case in your left hand, a sensible person would get into the rear passenger side of the car so they could set the case in the middle of the seat, instead of the driver's side, which would mean having the case between them and the car door.

I was right. Lynch entered via the rear passenger-side door. There was one other cop car behind Lynch's vehicle. And I saw Marlon revving the Lincoln behind the second Ford.

Susan Howell came out of a side door in the hallway.

"Goddamn it, Susan," said Howell, behind me.

"Doesn't matter," I said, facing the open front door, my back to Howell and McAuley.

Slowly, I opened my hand, letting Howell and McAuley see the small key that nestled in the cleft of my middle fingers. The pocket dip had been smooth and fast. If he'd only put the key in his jacket pocket or hip pocket I wouldn't have had to hit the damn fool in the back of the knees to distract him. I closed my fist and looked out at my shadow which now covered the lawn, just as Susan Howell's and Marlon's had done earlier.

For some reason the sight of my shadow made me feel uneasy. My eyes closed and I told myself to slow down. I'd crossed the line with this case, early. The image of Caroline Howell was bright and clear in my mind's eye and I knew it would remain that way for a long time. Doing something illegal, so long as I believed it was right, normally didn't bother me. This bothered me. If I came out of this in the next ten minutes without being arrested I promised myself I would take a step back for my own good. I needed some distance on this whole thing, especially if I was going to defend Howell.

"Be ready with your phone. I'll call you or text when I need you," I said.

I enjoyed the sight of my shadow growing smaller and smaller the closer I got to the fed's car. In the distance I saw a flash in the sky, followed seconds later by the low grumble of thunder. The air was a fever and the storm was about to break it.

The darkness had a different quality now. Somehow it felt dense and taut. The rear driver's side door was unlocked and I got into the seat immediately behind the driver. I set the large suitcase in the middle of the seat, on my right. The leather scraped and squealed as it rubbed against the case that Lynch had brought with him.

I closed the car door and we set off.

63

CHAPTER THIRTEEN

It was only me, Lynch and the driver in the Ford Taurus. The car was obviously federal law enforcement transport; it smelled of fried food and gun oil – the two basic food groups of the Bureau.

The driver took us past the house, headed for the single-lane road.

"You must've got a pretty big retainer if you needed a case this size," said Lynch, his left arm resting on top of his case, tapping the leather with his fingertips.

"I earn every cent," I said.

"I'm sure you do."

Soon as the driver turned onto the single lane, I remembered my earlier ride along this road with George and I knew this was my chance. I typed out a text to Howell.

Call me, right now.

The Ford lurched forward and back as the front tire hit the first pothole. My cell rang.

"What do you need?" said Howell.

I pretended to listen to Howell saying something on the other end of the line. In reality I listened to his breath, fast and full of nervous energy.

"I'm glad you're reconsidering attending the drop. I'll put you on to Agent Lynch so you can discuss it further," I said, handing my cell to the fed.

He raised his left hand to take the phone, felt the weight of the cuffs and switched hands. At first, he listened, then began preaching to Howell, telling him why it would be safer for his daughter if he wasn't there when the exchange went down.

Rain began to fall, hard, fat and fast. It was a blessing. More lightning, close this time. Thunder too. Lynch looked out of his window and raised his voice so that he could be heard on the phone over the noise of the downpour on the roof.

With the cases in the back, side by side, separating us, there wasn't too much room left, so he planted his left arm back on top of the case. He held my cell phone in his right hand. I palmed the key in my right hand and placed it on top of Lynch's case.

The second pothole rocked us in the back, rattling the chain on the handcuffs and almost threw the key out of the lock. Lynch was too busy trying to reassure Howell that everything would be fine.

One more twist and the catch would release.

I needed to be quick.

Leaning to my right, I looked out of the windshield. The wipers were a blur and still they only managed to sweep off sheets of water from the windshield for half a second before the glass was filled with rain again. It was like driving through a swimming pool.

Another blink of brilliant light in the sky. Lightning was getting closer all the time. Up ahead I could see two small lakes had already formed in the largest potholes. The first was forty feet away and its larger twin a good ten feet beyond that.

We would roll over both of them quickly.

Lynch's gaze remained fixed out of the window, his head turned away from me.

I didn't have to pretend to be thrown around in the back with the first pothole of the pair – it genuinely hurt and I heard a metallic scrape from the underside of the car hitting part of the road on the way out. At this moment I popped open the cuff that had been attached to the handle of the case. The other end was still safely locked to Lynch's wrist.

Gently, slowly, I took the cuff off the handle, holding it open and ready.

Second pothole – the Grand Canyon – and I felt my whole body pitch forward. The seat belt caught me before I put my face into the seat in front. And at the same time my right hand reached around and tipped the ten million dollar case off the seat, and my left slapped the cuffs on the case beside me.

The fed didn't notice. His head had smacked off the window and he'd dropped my phone.

"Jesus H. Christ, Larry. Slow down – it's like driving on the surface of the moon around here," said Lynch, picking my cell phone off the floor.

"Sorry," said Larry.

Between the two of us, we gathered up the ten million dollar case and I set it beside me. I grabbed the handle of the two million dollar case, and shifted it closer to Lynch, making sure he saw my hands touching the cuffs on the handle. I needed an explanation for my fingerprints being on the case and the cuffs.

"Mind if I talk to my client for a moment?" I said.

He didn't object, and told Howell he was passing him back on to his lawyer.

"Mr Howell," I said, "I think it's time to let the professionals do their job. How about you and I sit this one out?"

"Did you really get it?" said Howell.

"I think that's fair to say."

I turned around in my seat, looked out the back window and I could see a couple pairs of headlights behind us. One of those cars was Howell's.

"Okay, I'll get out. Come pick me up," I said.

The call disconnected.

"My client wants to see me. Can you pull over?" I said.

Lynch ordered the driver to pull over beneath an oak tree on the corner of the private road. The rain beat down on the car like machine-gun fire.

"Do you have a spare umbrella?" I asked.

A satisfied look appeared on Lynch's face. "I do, as it happens, but it's federal property. Sorry," he said.

When I opened the door the interior light came on. Before I swung my legs out I turned to Lynch and was about to wish him good luck anyway when I saw something sitting on the passenger seat.

"Those potholes sure shook a lot of stuff loose," I said, nodding toward the seat.

Agent Lynch leaned over the case attached to his wrist, with two million dollars inside, and saw the handcuff key sitting on the seat. I picked it up for him, letting him see me touch the key.

"Shit!" he said, retrieving the key. "Thank you. If I'd lost that God knows what I would've done."

"Good luck, Agent Lynch," I said. I closed the door and ran beneath the tree, almost slipping on the wet grass.

Even underneath the huge branches of the oak, the short time I stood there was enough to completely soak every item of clothing I wore. My feet were engulfed in water, and rain poured off my head.

The second FBI car passed me by and I got into another Lincoln, driven by Marlon this time. McAuley sat up front alongside him. I got in the back beside Howell and he took the case from me before I could close the door.

He popped the catches.

"Jesus. Ten million. How did you . . ."

"I didn't do anything, Mr Howell, remember?"

McAuley craned his neck to stare at me, just as Howell did. Both men were appraising me anew.

"I can't even begin to thank—"

"Then don't. Drop me off somewhere and go get your daughter."

"I can call George to come pick you up and take you back to the house?" said Howell.

I blew rainwater from my lips. It was running out of my hair, down my face. I really wanted a change of clothes, but I didn't want to go back to my apartment, and I sure as hell didn't want to go to Howell's place. It was a gorgeous house, but the atmosphere was thick with sweat, tension and loss. And I didn't want any more of that tonight.

"There's bound to be a coffee shop or something around here. I can't sleep until I know you've got her, and I don't want to go home. Let me out at an all-night diner and I'll dry off, get some coffee and you can call me when it's over. Then we start negotiating with the feds," I said.

"Do you think they'll negotiate?" said Howell.

"Lynch won't want to admit that he lost ten million dollars of ransom money that was handcuffed to his Goddamn wrist. That kind of thing is a career killer. Somehow, this will all work out. Don't worry, just get her back," I said.

"I will. Look, there's a truck stop just off the freeway. We'll stop there. It's on our way," said Howell.

I didn't ask what way he was headed. Part of me wanted to know. Part of me wanted to keep myself out of this. The line I'd crossed was a blur now, and I wanted to begin drawing it again.

After we left through the security gates of Premier Point, and the photographers got their shots, we found the freeway and Marlon floored it. Howell didn't say anything more. His eyes seemed lost in total concentration.

McAuley was punching numbers into the satellite navigation system built into the dash. Before the screen returned to a map of the freeway with a blue arrow for direction, I saw the destination. It was one of those places that you know, that you recognize, even if you've never been there.

The navigation system would bring the car to the gates of Sleepy Hollow cemetery in up-state New York. Travel time to the destination was forty-two minutes.

The only sound was the steady, reassuring hum from the engine. From the freeway I saw the occasional light from a house a half mile or so away – stark and bright in the darkness. At the first rest-stop sign, Marlon left the interstate and looped around a two-lane slip road that brought us to a gas station with a restaurant tacked on to the side. A giant fiberglass hotdog, that had seen better days, sat on top of the diner with a sign below it that said, "Fill Up At Bob's."

Thankfully, the rain had stopped.

I got out of the car and Howell leaned over his seat for a final word.

"I won't forget what you've done. Thank you."

I started toward the restaurant, and was pleased to see some people inside. There were rigs and haulage trucks in the lot out front.

And a single car.

A car I recognized.

It was a red Dodge Charger, with a black racing stripe on the hood.

CHAPTER FOURTEEN

Before I went inside the diner, I made a call. Rain hadn't fallen for a full five minutes, but the diner's guttering still poured water into drains. Harry Ford picked up after the second ring.

"You still awake?" I said.

"Uh huh. Can't sleep."

"Is it a big case tomorrow?"

He sighed and said, "No. I read it twice already. I'm thinking about that subpoena. I'm thinking about Max Copeland."

"I shouldn't have told you about Copeland," I said.

"You had to. Actually, it helps. At least I know somebody is gunning for me. Copeland is as predictable as he is dirty. His first point of appeal is always to throw the original defense attorney under the bus. You remember what happened to Seth Bozeman?"

I did. Stories like that weren't easy to forget. Seth had been a litigator in a good-sized Manhattan law firm. He had a wife, two kids, and was working on a big mortgage for his brownstone family home. He coached little league on Saturdays and even earned himself a position as a deputy judge. His firm acted for a wealthy realtor named Pollack who got caught with a dead sixteen-year-old boy in his apartment and the partners assigned Seth to defend him. The dead boy was the same age as Seth's son. There was no trial. Pollack pleaded guilty. Two years later he was out, and Seth Bozeman was inside. All thanks to Max Copeland who took on an appeal for Pollack on the grounds that the search of his apartment was technically illegal and that he'd been railroaded into a false confession due to ineffective and coercive counsel. The police search was declared illegal, so the NYPD had no evidence. Pollack walked. And Bozeman walked into a divorce – walked into the unemployment line when he got canned by his firm and lost his deputy judge post – walked onto the street when the bank defaulted his mortgage, but he had to be carried into Sing Sing because he assaulted Pollack on the street.

"You're a superior judge, Harry. That's not gonna happen to you," I said.

"Seth Bozeman never imagined it would happen to him, either. Thing is, I always thought Julie was innocent. I wouldn't have represented her otherwise. But the jury didn't see it that way. She deserves to be exonerated," said Harry.

Nothing hits harder than an innocent client sent away for murder. The client never really leaves you. They are there when you're taking your kids to school, they are there when you're lying on the beach watching the sunset, they are right beside you when you close your eyes every night. Innocence has a way of haunting you like nothing else.

"The jury sent her away. Not you. Remember what you told me? It's the plea bargains and deals that get you into trouble."

The sad fact of criminal law is that a lot of innocent people plead guilty. Happens all the time. In fact, the system wouldn't work if all the genuinely innocent defendants fought their cases. There simply wouldn't be enough courtrooms and judges to handle that volume of work. Why do they plead guilty? Because they'd be fools to turn down a deal. The DA's office makes an offer – you plead guilty, we offer one year jail time and with remission you'll probably only serve eight or nine months, but if you're convicted you'll do eight years. Would you take that risk? Not many defendants are willing to take those odds to a trial. Often, when the defendant is a month into their sentence they suddenly think they didn't get such a good deal after all and they blame their attorneys for bad advice, stating they are innocent people who were pressured into a deal.

"I remember all right. Plea bargains are ticking time bombs for lawsuits. It's just . . . this one had a bad feeling around it the whole time. There was something about her. I'd like to see the files before you hand them over. You still keep your old cases in that storage place in Brooklyn?"

"Same place. If I get a chance tomorrow I'll swing by and get it. Say, have you spoken to Julie Rosen recently? You get any kind of hint she was gonna try for an appeal?"

Harry sighed, "Julie Rosen died in 2011. If she were alive I'd be the first one to support an appeal. The fact that she's dead means only one thing. You don't need me to spell it out."

He was right, I didn't. Posthumous exonerations weren't common. They either happened because law enforcement realized they'd made a mistake and wanted to try somebody else for the murder, or there was the other reason. The reason that applied in this case. Somebody was gunning for Harry. Copeland had been hired to appeal the case, but really his job was to ruin Harry Ford. Didn't matter if you were a Supreme Court Justice, somebody alleges you once messed up a murder trial and your career, personal and professional rep go down in flames. This appeal could finish Harry's career. And he lived for the job. Take away his judicial office and Harry would slide through a liquor bottle and into the grave inside of six months.

"How did she die?" I said.

"Liver failure, I think. I went to the funeral. She was one of the last prisoners on East Brother Island. The asylum shut down not long after she passed. Apart from an orderly and the chaplain, it was just me at the funeral. She deserved better."

"If Julie is dead, who is paying Copeland? Who's got it in for you?"

"I've no idea. Julie didn't have family, not that I remember."

"I'm sure we'll find out soon enough. Just try and get some sleep," I said.

"Not much chance. See you tomorrow."

Harry hung up the phone, and I stretched my neck, pulled the door to the diner and went inside. If the sign outside invited patrons to Fill Up At Bob's, I guessed that they meant beer or coffee. That was all that was on offer. This was explained to me by the waitress/cook/bartender, Macy, who was a big woman in an apron only fit for much smaller frames than hers. She had an expressive face, and I could tell by the way she chewed her gum that she didn't like my wet clothes dripping onto her floor. I guessed the floor was mopped once a day, and it was past due.

Rock Radio played over the smell of stale coffee and bleach. Red vinyl seats dotted around a semi-circular counter. Booths beyond. The place didn't look too clean, despite the smell. Springstein told us he was born in the USA as Macy popped a bubble over her lips.

"We got pie," she said, giving me a look that said she really couldn't face the thought of having to go in back to fetch me a slice.

"Pie and coffee, please, Macy," I said.

"How about a smile for the customer with that," said a bearded man in a ball cap and check shirt, sitting at the other end of the long Formica counter.

The answer to his question came in the shape of Macy's middle finger and a smile that could easily have passed as a stroke.

"I don't know why I come in here," said the man in the ball cap.

Looking around, the booths were all but empty. Two men were reading newspapers in the left corner. And apart from the one-man Macy fan club at the counter, the only other person in the place had her back to me in a booth. She sat as far away from everyone else as possible. Brunette, with the strap of a laptop bag on the seat to her left, closest to the wall. She sat quietly and poured a concentrated avalanche of sugar into a steaming cup.

Agent Harper clearly enjoyed a sweet tooth.

While Macy was safely in the kitchen, I turned to the man at the end of the counter.

"Say, is there a bathroom in this place?"

He looked over his shoulder, then looked at me. It seemed as though whatever helpful energy he had was spent already.

I thanked him and made in the direction he'd indicated.

There was a single room, directly off the diner, which doubled as a toilet and shower. At least there was a hand dryer.

I took off my jacket, then my tie and shirt. Wrung what water I could out of them then tried to dry my shirt on the hand dryer. It was pretty hopeless. Same with my pants. At least when I put them back on they felt only moist instead of soaking wet.

My socks, I put in the trash. Hand towels inside my shoes seemed to absorb the worst of the rain. Putting my shoes back on barefoot felt weird, but a lot better than wearing wet socks underneath.

When I came out of the john, Macy had a hand on the counter, the other on her hip, and she was staring at me.

"You like hand dryers, pal?" she said. Obviously, they'd heard the drier.

"Just trying to dry off a little," I said.

"You know you can buy one of our tees for fourteen-ninety-five?" she said.

Up on the wall behind Macy, nailed to the bare plaster, was a shirt that read, "I Filled Up at Bob's."

"Who is Bob?" I asked.

"Bob's dead. You want a tee or not?" she said.

Politely, I declined. I took my coffee and a slice of pale pie to a booth behind Agent Harper, so she couldn't see me.

The night was still a hot, wet, summer fog and at least the diner had some air con set at a comfortable temperature. Two or three mouthfuls of pie later I still couldn't determine the flavor. It was either lemon and lime or toilet disinfectant. Pushing the plate to one side, I decided I'd be better off not knowing.

At least Bob's had free Wi-Fi. I accessed the court service website from my phone, entered my login details. The subpoena in my jacket was smudged with the rain, but I could still make out the docket number for the appeal. I searched under the reference number and found the appeal filing.

Copeland had gone to town on Harry. Nothing specific, but he'd covered all the bases for the appeal in standard pleadings; incompetent counsel, negligent representation, failure to discharge duty to a client by performing due diligence, ineffective representation and professional negligence. Attached to the filing was an affidavit on the case.

Julie Rosen had been found guilty of the first-degree murder of her infant child, Emily Rosen, in February 2003. The appellant alleged at trial that an unknown assailant had gained access to her house, injured her and then set fire to the place. The fire started in the nursery according to the report from fire marshal. In the cot, the calcinated bones of an infant were found. The fire had been so intense that the bones were practically ash. No witnesses in the area reported seeing any man in black. And then I saw something that gave me a hint of what Copeland's appeal might touch upon. A year after her conviction, Julie Rosen had been declared insane and moved to an old asylum on East Brother Island.

Copeland might argue that Julie wasn't fit to plead in the first place – and Harry messed up by not getting her examined by a psychiatrist. I made a mental note to ask Harry about this in the morning.

My pants were drying nicely, as was my jacket. Half an hour and two refills later, I felt a lot better. That little part of my head that I tried to keep quiet, told me that if I had a couple of beers with whiskey chasers I'd feel better still. Not for the first time, I tried to silence that voice and thought about Howell, and Caroline.

Ten to three.

The truckers thanked Macy, grabbed their gear and headed out to the lot. I looked around and found the diner empty, apart from Harper and Macy. There was a clinical stillness in the air. Thin Lizzy came on the radio and Phil Lynott told us he was waiting on an alibi. Cracking the spine on a paperback with a picture of a woman in a pink ball gown on the cover, Macy mumbled to herself about the cheap tips she'd been left and settled down to read *The Enchanter's Heart*.

Nine minutes until the exchange.

Leaning to my right, I saw Agent Harper had inserted a black plastic device into the USB slot of her laptop. This was the same small, plastic device that Agent Washington had handed to her on her way out the door of Howell's house. Since I'd walked into this place, Harper hadn't turned around. Not even when the truckers left or during my conversation with Macy. Far as I could see it, Harper was in the zone; total concentration. My feet were crossed beneath me, my right foot cradling the left. In my efforts to see what Harper was doing, my foot slipped with a squeak of shoe leather on the polished floor.

"You make a lousy spy, Flynn," said Agent Harper, without turning.

"I didn't think you knew I was here," I said.

She turned around in her seat, gave me a look that conveyed exactly how stupid I felt, and said, "I made you before you even set foot over the door. I watched Howell let you out of his car in the lot. You get fired?"

"No, what makes you think that?"

"Cause you arrived at a mansion with Howell's personal chauffeur, now you're wet through and drinking bad coffee in the middle of nowhere and you seemed to have lost your briefcase."

"I didn't want to wait in the house. You know, for word back about the exchange. I just needed to get out of there. My case is there, don't worry."

"Is Howell at the drop?" she asked.

I said nothing, drained my coffee and settled my back into the vinyl.

"What's the USB stick for?" I asked. "I know it's a gift from Agent Washington, but I didn't get the impression it was that kind of relationship."

Harper ignored me. Turned back to her screen.

"You're a good team. I'm guessing Washington doesn't want to leave you out in the cold. I'd say the device sticking out of your laptop is keeping you in the loop."

She got up, came around and sat across from me. The metal zips from her leather jacket tinkled on the tabletop. It reminded me of the noise the handcuff chain had made.

"You see a lot," she said. "Do you know if Howell is going to the drop or not?"

"I know," I said.

"But you're not going to tell me?" she said.

"The way I see it, I've got information. So do you. Why don't we agree to share?"

"What do you want to know?" she said.

"I want to know what goes down in the rail station."

"In case you hadn't noticed, I'm not at the rail station exchange," she said.

It was my turn to give her a disbelieving look.

"Like I said, Washington is cutting you in. I want you to do the same with me."

"Why?" she said.

I couldn't tell her the real reason. I knew if things went down okay in Sleepy Hollow, Leonard Howell would likely come back to an arrest for perverting the course of justice, fraud, and a host of other charges. Whatever sense of right and wrong I had left – I knew that no father should have to pay a price for saving their daughter's life. That just wouldn't fly with me. Anything Harper could tell me about the dummy drop might help with Howell's defense.

"I want to know that Caroline comes back okay. I'm a father too," I said. "Why do you want to know if Howell went to the rail station for the drop?"

Her eyes took on a keen glow as she moved her body forward, her face inches from mine, she said, "Because I know the rail station drop is bullshit. And I know Howell knows it too."

CHAPTER FIFTEEN

Neither of us spoke. Macy turned a page of her book, the yellow paper whispering against the rough skin of her fingertips, the radio DJ introduced an AC/DC classic that needed no introduction, and the patter of heavy rain began to beat on the roof of the diner.

"I heard what you said to Agent Lynch. Why do you think the drop at the rail station isn't kosher?"

"For the same reasons that your client believes it's not the real kidnapper. First, the location. New Rochelle rail station is covered with security cameras. Every inch of it. If a bag of money goes in there – it's not coming out without a set of eyes on it. There are three exits, and we can cover them all. The station is twenty minutes from the nearest Interstate. The drop is at three a.m., and the station will be practically empty. A train gets in at two fifteen a.m., and the next one isn't until three thirty a.m. No crowd cover. May as well put the ransom in a fishbowl in the middle of Times Square. If you want to collect ransom then either you get it wired or you do the drop in an environment you can control and get out of in five seconds flat without a tail," she said.

"You're supposing the kidnapper is a professional – maybe they're rank amateurs."

"I don't think anyone could be that stupid. Plus, there's also the fact that this ransom demand only came in after your client's face got plastered all over the news, appealing to whoever had taken Caroline to let her go."

"What about the proof of life, the photos?" I said.

Her gaze fell across the table and she shook her head.

"I don't know about those. They looked genuine, but this drop stinks."

"How are the kidnappers communicating with the Bureau?"

"Didn't your client tell you?" she said.

"He told me they were payphone calls. That right?"

"I think I want to know if Howell is going to the drop. I've given you more than enough."

As a defense attorney, it went against all my basic instincts but right then, looking into Harper's eyes I decided I could trust her with this at least.

"Your boss persuaded him to stay away."

She checked her watch, got up and returned to her seat. I got up and slid into the seat beside her. There was no objection, so I didn't ask permission.

A flick of her thumb across the trackpad on the laptop brought the screen back to life. There were four images on the screen split into a grid view. One image in each corner of the screen. It was the rail station. Views of entrances and exits, the main concourse and, selecting a menu in the right corner of the screen, Harper was able to flick between different images of the rail station.

At first I thought they were just pictures. Then I saw a man walking through the station entrance.

"Is this the security camera feed?" I asked.

"It is. The station's video system is being fed into the Bureau's network. Long as you've got the right cypher," she said, tapping the device protruding from the USB port.

The device that Washington had given to Harper. He was doing more than keeping her updated; he was making sure she could watch the drop go down – live.

She'd guessed, correctly, that the rail station was a bust. She had no evidence of that, of course. I thought about what she'd said, and decided that it took a lot more than instinct and a bad drop location for the money for Agent Harper to have been convinced that this was a dummy drop. There was more to this than I knew.

But right then, I did know one thing – Harper was the key.

"Tell me why you're really convinced that this drop is a con."

She stared at me while she considered her response. Weighing me up.

"Why'd you lie to Lynch about me? Why didn't you tell him I slammed your head into the car?"

77

"It wouldn't do my client any good. I took you for one of the smartest in that room. Why deprive my client of a good FBI agent?"

"So you think the train station is a bust too," she said.

I had to be careful. She was being polite, but I didn't trust her entirely. Not yet.

"I think what you're saying has logic. But you've got to remember, kidnapping is a risky business. And criminals aren't always as smart as they might appear."

She took a sip of cold coffee. Those hazel eyes never wavered from mine. Not for a second. Those eyes weren't penetrating. She wasn't trying to read me, she was putting up a shield.

"Come on. There's something else," I said.

The images on the split screens remained unchanged. She checked the rest of the cameras in the mini-view then said, "This kidnapper, he's patient. He waited a long time before he made contact. Most kidnappers panic and get on the phone, demanding money right away before the family even knows their loved one is missing. This guy didn't. And he's done his research: he knows to the cent how much they can raise in ransom in twenty-four hours. See, there's probably a lot that you don't know."

"So tell me something I don't know," I said.

"We found Caroline's car yesterday morning. Your client doesn't know that either," she said.

CHAPTER SIXTEEN

Each of the video feeds remained static. No movement on the entrances to the rail station. It was getting close to three a.m.

"Why didn't you tell him about the car?"

"You know your client has a reputation for doing things his way. He got to where he is now because of that rep. We can't afford to have a father running around town with a gun. Some things your client can't know. For his own good and that of his daughter," she said.

"So why tell me now?" I said.

"Because it doesn't matter any more. Howell is making his play right now, isn't he? That's the real reason why he's not at the rail station."

I didn't answer.

"Don't worry. Nobody else believes me. But they'll believe me when the rail station becomes a bust, and Howell comes back to the house with his daughter. That happens – then your client is in major trouble and he'll need a good lawyer."

"If you really believe that then why aren't you following him?" I said.

"How do you know we're not?" she said.

Was it a bluff? Hard to tell. She let the silence build. And brought her gaze back to the laptop screen.

The way I figured it, Harper was one agent, with no backup. Unless Washington was following Howell? I thought about taking out my cell and texting Howell. But I didn't make a move. I kept my hands on the table, and leaned back.

The overhead light shone on the dark screen, and I saw Harper had angled the laptop to keep an eye on my reflection as well as the screen.

I decided it was either one of two things.

It was a bluff – and the moment I took out my phone to text Howell she would know that he was on another mission and I would just have confirmed her theory.

It was true, or partially true. Only reasons to withhold information from Howell were either to keep him out of the hostage game, or because he was a suspect in his daughter's disappearance.

After a few seconds I decided there was nothing I could do about any of those scenarios without making things worse. I drained the last of my coffee and left my cell well alone.

"So where did you find the car?"

"It was on an old dirt track in the woods, behind a cemetery just over the state line in Virginia. A guy out walking his dog called it in. We hauled the car to the lab. Didn't find anything unusual – not really. No blood. Some hair from Caroline on the headrest. No signs of violence inside the car. But we found something on the back seat. A pair of glasses. There were blood spots on the lens. We're testing the blood against Caroline's DNA profile."

Before I could say anything I saw her sit bolt upright and focus on the computer.

A man in black walked into the rail station rolling a suitcase behind him. She slipped some earphones on and folded her arms.

I asked her if she had another earpiece, and she practically threw a pair of white earphones at me. Placing them into my ears, I then held out the jack and she quickly plugged it into the second audio socket without taking her eyes from the screen.

The man in black strode into the rail station and stood in the center of the concourse, to the left of the unmanned information desk. I heard a phone ring and the man in black answered his cell.

"This is Lynch," he said.

I leaned forward and I was able to make out SAC Lynch a little clearer.

The voice on the other end of the line was low, undoubtedly male and computerized – like he was using a device to disguise the voice. It was lower in volume than Lynch but you could make it out.

"Go to the men's room," said the voice. The device which filtered the speech made it sound disjointed, somehow alien.

The cameras followed Lynch as he walked toward the screen, then disappeared out of shot. Almost as soon as he'd gone from one camera, Harper flicked her index finger over the trackpad and a fresh angle came up on the right corner, replacing the old camera view. No one was outside the john, and as Lynch went inside we lost visual.

But we could still hear him.

His rubber-soled shoes sent high-pitched screeches over the mic.

"Third cubicle," said the voice.

The agent hesitated. I could tell, the squeaking had stopped. Then the sound of a door backing open. Another, then another. My guess was that Lynch tried every cubicle door, bar the third one, to make sure the place was empty.

"I'm here," said Lynch.

"Lift off the toilet cistern," he said.

From the sound of a heavy case hitting the linoleum floor in the men's room, the rattle from the handcuff chain, and the high-toned echoes from a porcelain cistern cover being lifted clear and set down, we knew that Lynch was probably leaning over the toilet bowl and peering into the reservoir of dull water.

The unmistakable noise of a toilet flushing, the cistern draining, and then a rapid drip as something was lifted clear of water.

"Take the key out of the bag and go to the lockers," said the voice.

Five seconds later Lynch appeared on the screen again. He still held the phone in his right hand, and carried the case in his left. He stopped in the middle of the floor, and looked at the banks of lockers on either side of the station. On the left was a free standing bank of lockers, twenty on one side, ten on the top, and ten on the bottom and the same on the reverse side.

"Left side," said the voice.

Lynch began moving in that direction – slowly at first, then faster the closer he got to the set of pine lockers. The station was Saturday-night-church quiet. Not even a station attendant, or a guard, or a cleaner in sight.

"This guy has got to be kidding me," said Harper and she snorted a laugh afterwards.

"He wants Lynch to put the ransom in a locker in a public rail station, covered with cameras twenty-four hours a day. This is either amateur hour or a setup," she said.

So far, the kidnapping hadn't looked amateur to me. The perp had gotten Caroline Howell cleanly, without any witnesses, and so far without leaving any trace evidence. This was wrong. Having their ransom placed in a public locker that they couldn't get near without being seen was pretty stupid in my estimation. It didn't fit with the professionalism of the abduction. It screamed *fake*.

Lynch checked the metal stub attached to the keyring. Probably looking for the locker number.

Before the tip-off, Lynch had walked slow. Having a final destination for the suitcase gave him enough motivation to double-time it to the lockers.

Setting down the case in front of the lockers, Lynch unlocked the handcuffs first. Then put that key in his pocket and held the locker key ready. Harper selected the camera with the best view and moved it to full screen. The camera was around thirty feet away from Lynch, and looking at his right side.

As Lynch opened the locker door it swung outwards, covering his face from our view.

But only for a second.

I expected the federal agent to open the locker door, and then heave the case inside it. Then he would await his next set of instructions, like where he was supposed to drop the key, and when and where he would pick up Caroline.

The suitcase remained on the station's pale tiles.

And whatever the hell Lynch saw inside that locker was enough to make him stop dead.

CHAPTER SEVENTEEN

A quick check over my shoulder told me that Macy had put her feet up on the bar, slipped her earphones on and was gently rocking in her chair while she read her romance novel. It was a good thing too, as Harper was unable to keep the panic out of her voice as she got Agent Washington on the phone.

"What the hell is it?" she said.

I could only hear her side of the conversation. Washington wasn't wearing a mic, like Lynch.

"Hold off on SWAT. Don't break cover. Wait until we know what the hell is in there," she said.

The tall, commanding figure of Agent Washington appeared on three of the screens, from various angles, as he raced toward the lockers and Lynch. Nothing from the SAC. Whatever Lynch had seen, he wasn't talking about it.

Three feet from the bank of lockers, Washington put on the brakes and skidded to a halt beside Lynch. I saw him ask the lead agent if he was okay, then he looked to his right, at the open locker. Washington's eyes lingered on that locker and he ignored Lynch. The image quality was poor, but we could clearly see Washington's eyebrows furrow, and his lips part in a grimace as he fought to understand the sight before him.

"What is it?" said Harper.

I saw Washington register Harper's voice by glancing at this cell phone, which he then swiped at with a finger.

"He hung up on me," said Harper.

"For good reason, look," I said.

Like me, Harper watched Washington flip his phone and hold it up to the locker. We both saw the flash go off half a dozen times.

After Washington took the photos, Lynch gently eased him to one side, so that he could look directly into the locker.

Harper's cell phone vibrated like a power drill. Over and over. The photos that Washington had taken were coming through.

I noticed that Washington remained at a distance from the locker – simply staring at it. From his hip pocket he produced something small, floppy, white: a pair of latex gloves. Never taking his eyes from the locker – he pulled on the gloves. I watched as he smoothed out the fit by jamming his fingers together, hand to hand, so the latex met the webbing between each finger. I imagined that he'd slipped on rubber gloves a thousand times before, and I wondered if he went through that ritual each time.

Harper opened the first of the messages from her partner.

Her phone screen was quite large. Big enough for two of us to see easily. A blue circle rotated on a blank screen, loading the first image.

"What's the meaning of this?" said Lynch.

"Leonard Howell is guilty," said the voice.

"What do you mean Leonard Howell is guilty?" said Lynch.

The cold, distorted voice spoke slowly, and carefully.

"It's up to you now. I've kept my promise."

A click came over the mic. Lynch pulled the earpiece from his right ear. The kidnapper had disconnected.

The blue swirl on the screen of Harper's phone disappeared, and the white canvas gave way to color.

CHAPTER EIGHTEEN

"What the . . ." said Harper.

Inside the locker I saw two items. One was a cell phone. It lay on the wooden base of the locker. Behind it, I saw something else. At once it was familiar and yet strange. As it was at the very back of the locker, the shadows obscured a full view.

The second photo taken by Washington zoomed in closer.

A shirt. It looked just like the white one Caroline had worn on the day she went missing. It was stained red. And below that dark red stain were more red marks. They were a lighter red. And they formed a sentence. Something written in red marker pen, or lipstick.

Or blood.

Howell murdered her in the basement.

A cell phone began ringing. Mine was on silent. I saw Harper check her cell. Nothing. Then we both looked foolish – the distant ring tone was sounding over our earpieces. A phone was ringing in the rail station. At first, I couldn't piece together what was happening on screen. Lynch and Washington were looking at each other, then they stared into the locker. The white call screen had lit up on the cell phone.

I checked the time on the cameras.

3:13

Hitting the call button, Lynch stopped the ringing and brought the phone to his ear slowly. He didn't say anything. Just listened.

The voice that came through the phone, into Lynch's earpiece and sounded in our own earphones, was familiar.

"Where is she?" said Howell.

"Mr Howell? It's Agent Lynch."

The call went dead.

I swallowed down the taste of bile that swamped my throat.

I got up and dialed Howell's cell, walking quickly toward the bathroom. Macy was still rocking gently, back and forth, reading her novel, popping gum in time to the beat pumping from her headphones.

Voicemail.

My pace quickened while I listened to Howell's answerphone message. I wanted to be locked in the bathroom, out of Harper's earshot when I left him a voicemail.

I didn't make it to the bathroom.

The floor shuddered, every window in the diner flexed, plates and cups smashed on the floor, Macy fell out of her chair and I stopped dead in my tracks.

It was no longer dark.

I saw a massive tower of flame in the distance, beyond the trees, in the direction from which I'd come that night. On the crest of the black hill, half a mile away, a big house in Premier Point burned the night into an early dawn.

CHAPTER NINETEEN

I closed the passenger door of Harper's Dodge Charger as she dialed a number on her cell. Her leg straightened as she punched the gas pedal like it owed her money and we were out of the lot and onto the highway before I could peel the back of my head off the seat. The employee of Howell's Home Security who manned the gate of Premier Point confirmed it for Harper over the phone.

Howell's house was a fireball. He'd called nine-one-one, asked for fire trucks and ambulances.

Agent Harper hit the speaker on her phone, and dropped it onto the dash so she could change gears. I put on my seatbelt when she pushed the Charger beyond eighty-five miles an hour. The road was still slick with rainwater and the car had about as much grip as a rattlesnake on a plate glass window. A jerk of the wheel or a half-inch of quick pressure on the accelerator would send us into a slide that Harper had no hope of controlling.

Her face was set with concentration and anger. Chewing on her bottom lip, eyes fixed on the road, I could tell two things: Harper was an excellent driver, and she wasn't really concentrating on the road – her mind was still inside the rail station, still inside that locker.

Harper chewed on that lip. The Charger chewed the road. And the sky got brighter the closer we got to Premier Point.

"Open the gate, we're fifteen seconds away," said Harper.

Sure enough, she let her foot off the gas slow, careful not to brake, and gradually slowed the car by grinding down through the gears. Each gear change came with high revs from the engine, then the protest from the motor being denied the accelerator it craved.

She made the left turn into Premier Point at thirty miles an hour and ate ten feet of drift in the process. I gripped the handrail above the door but I was still being thrown around in the car. Harper could've been a professional driver – she was that good.

"Where did you learn to drive?" I said. I wasn't that interested, I just wanted something to take my mind off the fear that my head was about to go through the windshield.

"South Dakota."

"On dirt tracks?"

"No, Rapid City. I had an eventful childhood."

The gate was already open. Most of the TV reporters were lit up from their cameras, with the orange haze from the fire just above their heads, peering over the top of the tree line.

Once inside the quiet, deserted night streets of Premier Point, Harper let the Charger go and steered the beast slowly, surely, touching the brake to make it through the bends then flooring it on the straights.

"My dad ran an auto-shop. I was doing donuts in the back lot from the age of thirteen," she said.

Maybe because she was talking, or maybe because we were getting closer to the fire, but she misjudged the turning for the single-lane entrance to Howell's place. The back of the Charger lost grip, slid to the right, and no amount of wheel spin from Harper could catch the asphalt before the rear passenger side of the car wiped out the For Sale sign.

"Shit," said Harper, as we hit the first pothole and she lost control – arms pumping to grab a straight line. Nobody could've held it, and she busted through the wooden fence on the right. It turned out to be a blessing. Ploughing the field with the V8 at fifty made better progress than winding through the holes in the single lane at twenty-five.

Five hundred yards before the house we felt the heat. I'd never seen a fire so big. At least half of the damn house was ablaze. A black figure stumbled out of the front door.

"Hold on," said Harper.

Palms on the ceiling, feet planted on the floor, back of my head buried in the head rest and I still managed to bang my head on the window when Harper punched the Charger through the fence again and the wheels took air before landing on the loose stone drive.

She handbraked us to a stop and was already out and running toward the house before I'd gotten my door open.

No sign of a fire truck anywhere.

I caught up with Harper as she reached the silhouette on the gravel drive.

A cop in uniform. He was bent over and coughing, his face black with soot, and what little skin I could see on his cheeks was red and puckered from the heat.

"Is everyone out?" Harper said.

The cop shook his head. He placed a hand on my shoulder and ducked, spitting out a glob of dirty sputum.

"I fell asleep. Woke up when the floor ballooned and broke. The cripple and . . . the . . . the wife . . . upstairs," he said.

I looked at the house, the fire licking most of the ground floor rooms and some on the first floor – lighting them up like a candle in a jack-o-lantern. Every window had blown out, and the breeze was feeding the flames through the entire building. The cop had gotten out through the front door, and the fire hadn't yet taken hold of the entrance. The noise of the blaze was horrific. It sounded like a living thing; like some kind of huge, fierce animal that consumed everything in its path mercilessly.

Over the noise of the fire, I could hear sirens. The firemen would be here any second. I turned to tell Harper that I'd heard the fire trucks – but she was no longer standing beside me. Only then did I hear her boots thumping and I looked up just as she disappeared through the column of smoke that blew out of the front door.

"Shit," I said, as I put my toes to the stone and charged in after her.

CHAPTER TWENTY

It felt like walking through the back door of hell. The marble entrance hall was a swirling black mass of smoke and in the rooms on either side – a wall of flame. I looked up and saw that the ceiling was on fire. The red and orange thing was eating the paint, and spreading like spilt mercury over every single surface.

The enormous chandelier that hung above me was still swinging from whatever explosion had rocked the house. A chunk of plaster the size of a dining table fell from the ceiling and exploded on the tiles beside me. Whipping my jacket over my head, I started coughing and running up the marble stairs. They felt warm under my feet, but they were not on fire. Not yet.

At the top of the first flight of stairs, I called for Harper. The corridor to the left was soaked in flame. Same to the right. It looked like an arbitrary choice between where I'd most like to burn to death. I bent low, and took in some air for the first time. It felt like I was inhaling burning gas.

I had to think or die.

Managing to stifle the cough, I closed my eyes and listened.

Five seconds.

The cracking of timbers, the fizzles and sparks from the electric cables and above it all – the growl from the fire as it ate through the building.

Then something else. Heavy footfalls above me.

I took the next set of stairs two at a time. The second floor wasn't nearly as bad as the one below. Thin streams of flames poured from the electric sockets and the wires in the wall, but the fire had yet to take firm hold. I went right. The footsteps I'd heard from this floor had headed in this direction. Last door on the right of the corridor was ajar. I hit it with my shoulder, then managed to grab the top of the door frame before I fell twenty feet to the floor below.

The center of the floor had given way. I gazed down into the bedroom on the first floor. And through the thick smoke I saw Susan Howell lying face down on a bed of broken, smoking timber. Harper was beside her, trying to get up. She'd fallen through the hole in the floor. In the mass of wood and plaster, I saw George, unconscious.

I turned and ran back the way I came, took the stairs one flight down and headed right, toward the room I'd seen from the floor above. I stopped dead.

I couldn't get to them. The corridor was a red tunnel. My suit was smoldering from the heat.

Think.

The door to my left was open and I saw a sink and toilet inside. I went in and was glad to see the room was not totally gone. The tiles on the wall had split, and a torch burned out of the electric socket on the wall. The drapes over the bathtub were smoking. I pulled them down, ran the faucet and soaked them, fast as I could.

I was really coughing now. My chest was an acid burn.

Swinging the dripping curtains over my head, I came out of the bathroom and sprinted down the corridor to the last room on the right. The door gave way and I came in on top of George.

"Get up, let's get out of here," I said, tossing one of the curtains at Harper. She got Susan Howell up and over her shoulder, pulling the drape over them both with her right hand. I slapped George, got him awake and coughing. Unlike Susan, George's face was white with plaster, and here and there I saw blood spots on his face.

I got him up, but knew I couldn't carry George and the wet curtain. I got him under my shoulder, covered his head with the drape and made for the door.

Harper followed, slowly.

"We gotta run," I said.

But we couldn't. The thirty feet along the blazing corridor to the stairs took far too long. Before we'd made it halfway the drapes had dried out and caught fire.

We tossed them and half tripped, half stumbled and dragged ourselves to the staircase, and some reprieve.

None of us could speak, we choked, huddled together, all four of us at the top of the stairs. We didn't make our way down to the hallway. Harper dropped Susan on the smoldering carpet and cried out.

Below us, a huge fissure had erupted in the marble entrance hall. It was way too big to jump. The floor beneath our feet shifted and fell as the staircase cracked in two.

Susan Howell awoke and spat black blood over the wall. Her face was swollen with the heat, and her eyelids were blistered and bleeding.

Harper patted Susan's face. Held her close.

We couldn't get down. We couldn't get out. No air.

And the flames came closer. I could feel them.

I looked at the ground floor, trying to think, trying to figure out what the hell I should do. The cough was bad now. My body was in agony. It felt like the fire was burning from inside of me, and growing stronger every second, tearing at my skin, my muscles, the soles of my feet. Gasping, retching, I was no longer aware of anyone else. Just the drowning black smoke in my lungs and the hot tears streaming down my face.

Then a pair of black boots appeared on the floor in front of me. My eyes grew heavy, and as I blacked out I felt strong hands pulling at my shoulders.

CHAPTER TWENTY-ONE

I came to on a soft bed. Something was clamped tightly across my face and I sat up, drinking in the air and listening to the shit rattling around in my chest. Another coughing fit and I tried to get whatever the hell it was off of my face.

A firm hand on my solar plexus. Another grabbing my wrist.

"Take it easy, it's only an oxygen mask. You're okay, fire service brought you out. You're out," said the paramedic. He was short and bald, and had a kind face. I lay down and turned my head around. Far as I could tell I was in the back of an ambulance, but we weren't headed anywhere. I didn't hear any sirens, didn't feel the motion of the vehicle weaving through traffic.

Across from me, on an identical gurney, I saw George. He was awake, and breathing better than me. I saw wet dirty phlegm in the nosepiece of his mask, and the steady rise and fall of his chest. Neither of us spoke. We just sucked in as much air as we could, and held our diaphragms tight, stifling the coughs, getting as much of the good stuff as we could. The paramedic must've washed George's eyes. There was a band of pink skin around his eyes, but his cheeks, mouth and neck remained stained with soot.

I wasn't even aware of the paramedic working on me, bandaging a burn to my right hand. Seeing the burn made it sing and I arched my back, willing it to stop; praying to go back in time before I'd seen the burn and triggered the pain receptors in my brain to launch into overdrive.

"I'll give you something for the pain," said the paramedic, disappearing out of my line of view. He returned with a vial and a syringe. He measured a shot, and leaned over me. I felt a tugging sensation and saw that he had an IV set up on my left wrist. The shot was bliss, and instantly numbed my hand and chest.

It was like submersing myself in an ice-cold pool.

Gloriously numb, I tried to speak. The words fell apart and my eyes closed.

What the hell had I done? Running into a burning building? Some would call it foolishness, and they were probably right. But I knew exactly why I'd done it. Same reason I'd agreed to help Howell.

It was the right thing to do.

Images of burning cars and burning houses swam in the morphine. And then I saw a blonde seventeen-year-old, not quite Caroline Howell, nor quite my own daughter at that age – but perhaps a mixture of the two. She sat in a smoke-filled room.

And all around the girl were piles of burning money.

CHAPTER TWENTY-TWO

Around ten a.m. I dressed in a pair of jeans and an old tee-shirt behind the screen of my hospital bed. My throat felt like I'd been sucking on a tail pipe and my hand hurt like hell. Every few minutes I hocked up black spit, and drank more water. I'd been pouring water down my throat for most of the night. First thing I did when I woke up a few hours ago was call Harry. He'd managed to get another judge to take over his docket of cases for the day, swung by my apartment, picked up some clothes and drove out to see me.

While Harry waited on the other side of my hospital bed screen, I'd made a call to my wife, Christine. The hospital had contacted her earlier that morning. She was my next of kin and the call from the nurse scared the crap out of her. I knew it was wrong, but I couldn't help feeling good knowing that Christine worried about me. We'd split up some time ago and she took Amy and moved out of our rented house in Queens.

"I'm fine," I said.

"You don't sound fine. I've been worried sick. What the hell were you doing last night?" she said, urgently.

I heard a voice on the other end of the line. Somebody talking in the background. A male voice. I checked my watch. It was ten-fifteen.

"Is Amy at school?" I said.

"Yes, of course. Why?"

"Just thought I heard her in the background, that's all."

"Oh, no, that's Kevin."

"Who is Kevin?" I said, with a little more punch in my tone than I'd expected.

"He's a friend," she said.

95

I was about to say something when I started coughing. Another paper cup of tepid water eased my throat.

"You still there?" I said.

"I'm here. You were supposed to come see us tomorrow. I made up a bed in the back room. Amy's been looking forward to that boating trip. I don't suppose . . ."

"No. I can't. I'm really sorry. I'll make it up to Amy, I promise."

"I'll tell her. Jesus, Eddie, these cases you take on . . ."

"I know. I can't help it. So who is this friend, Kevin?"

"A friend," she said, then hung up.

We were on a break, technically. Separated was a complex word. Seemed like we'd been on and off for a few years now. First it was the job, eating at me and making me hit the bottle like there was no tomorrow. And when I got clean, somehow I still managed to mess things up. The work that I did put my family at risk. I wanted to fix things, make us a proper family again once I got my firm off the ground and maybe take cases with less of a risk. Until then, we remained separated. If Christine wanted to date somebody, that was okay. Only it wasn't okay. Not by a long shot. She'd moved to her parents' place in the Hamptons to get Amy out of the city, and away from me. I seemed to have a habit of taking cases that somehow came back to bite me and those closest to me. So I decided it would be better if there was some distance between me and my family. For their own sake. After a few months Christine got a job as a litigator in a small law firm in Riverhead. She got her own place and seemed to be setting up a new life.

Kevin was definitely new. I didn't know the guy, and maybe he was just a friend, but even so I had a strong desire to put my foot through his face. I needed to go see Amy as soon as I could. She would tell me about Mom's new friend.

I put my watch back on and drew back the screen around my bed. Harry looked me over now that I was dressed.

"You could've brought me some underwear, you know?" I said.

"Eddie, I've done three tours in Vietnam, I was one of the first African Americans to reach the rank of Captain in the US Army, I've been pelted with rocks and spat on in a half dozen civil rights marches, I've conducted twenty capital murder cases, and I've lost count of the amount of death threats I've accumulated in my lifetime – but let me tell you, opening your underwear drawer is frankly beyond the limits of my courage," said Harry.

The laughter brought on a coughing fit, and Harry patted my back.

"Damn stupid thing you did, going in there."

"You would've done the same," I said.

He shrugged, and then adjusted the jacket of his suit. Harry always wore the best of clothes. A navy two-piece suit, pale blue shirt and navy tie with red diagonal slashes. Only his shock of white hair looked untidy. I knew that by ten o'clock that evening, the tie would be wrapped around a lampshade, the shirt would be open and Harry would have a drink in his hand. At least he always started the day looking his best. It goes with the territory – New York Superior Judges always turned themselves out well. Even though he'd showered, shaved, and put on his usual suave outfit, Harry didn't look so fresh. The bags under his eyes appeared to be bigger, and his voice was hoarse.

"What did you find out?" I said.

"Susan Howell is still suffering from smoke inhalation. Minor burns. She's okay. Same for the other guy, George Vindico. Nobody would tell me anything about Agent Harper, other than she got treatment and left early this morning. I got in contact with Agent Lynch, he wouldn't confirm Agent Harper's condition, but he said that everyone was accounted for and nobody was seriously injured in the fire. Still no word or sign of Leonard Howell."

I nodded. "And thanks for taking care of the hospital bill. I'll pay you back."

Harry waved away my offer. I'd found out this morning that my medical insurance didn't cover me if I ran into a burning building. And people think con artists are crooked. Harry had settled up for me, and I would pay him back, despite what he'd said.

I called Howell's cell. It must've been switched off. Part of me thought I should call the feds. What if Howell, McAuley and Marlon were lying in a ditch somewhere, dead, and the ransom missing? I swore under my breath, and decided to give him more time. Maybe it all went according to plan, but he had to hide out somewhere while things calmed down. I doubted that severely, but I couldn't rule it out. Not yet.

We took the elevator to the parking lot, and I climbed into Harry's British sports car. It was like an American sports car, except it went around corners without trying to kill you and it looked as though it had been built for people a lot smaller than me. My knees bit into the dash, and Harry took us out of the lot and onto the highway.

"You sure you want to go to Howell's?" he said.

"I want to talk to the feds. See what they've found out about the fire," I said.

Harry tutted.

"What's the real reason?"

I smiled, there wasn't much I could get past Harry. "If I stay close to the feds I might find out what really went down last night. The fire, the train station, it's all been carefully set up by somebody. I want to know who is pulling the strings here."

I tried to get Howell on his cell half a dozen times, without success. I needed to see him, to tell him what I'd seen in the video feed from the rail station. I'd asked Harry to check the papers, and the news channels, but there was nothing on the kidnapping story – it was all about the fire.

The shirt, with that slogan written across the chest.

Howell murdered her in the basement.

I'd spent only a short time with Howell, but from what I'd seen he was no murderer. He wouldn't touch a hair on his daughter's head. The shirt in the locker gave me chills just thinking about it.

The MG struggled to fifty-five on the freeway, and despite having the top down, the July humidity made us sweat it out in the car. This was particularly uncomfortable for me. My right hand was burning like hell, and the sweat made my forehead sting. I hadn't showered and every now and then I caught the smell of the fire from my hair.

"So while you were running into burning buildings last night, I thought about Max Copeland and our subpoenas. The original file is in your storage facility in DUMBO, along with the other dead cases. I went over there and paid a fortune to let the storage security guy give me access to the boxed files. Took me an hour to find the damn thing; didn't you ever think of having a filing system?" he said.

"Remind me to change my storage company," I said.

"Anyway, I looked over the file this morning before I came to get you; refreshed my memory. I made copies and left the original in your office this morning. You can deliver it to Copeland when this thing with Howell dies down."

"You get anything from the file?"

"Not really. Few things came back to me. Details about the fire, mostly. Julie was an addict. She'd been smoking crack. Fire marshal found a smoked bowl in a room, but that wasn't the source of the fire. The nursery was soaked in gasoline. The prosecution argued she got high and was going to burn down the nursery to make her daughter's death look like an accident, but somewhere along the line she couldn't go through with it and the fire got out of hand. Then she invented the story about the masked man to cover up her own crime."

"Sounds a little off, doesn't it?"

"The jury didn't think so. They took twenty-three minutes to return a guilty verdict," he said.

His voice dropped low. Those last words were nothing more than a whisper. This was still a painful case for Harry. Prior to taking up judicial office, Harry had practiced civil and criminal law. And he took me under his wing – helped me through law school, got me a job clerking for him, and when I wanted to open my own firm with Jack Halloran, Harry and his old partner gave us a start by finally winding down their practice, and handing us their few remaining clients. I owed him everything. One piece of advice that I'd always remembered from Harry: the victories are sweet and soon forgotten, but the mistakes stay with you forever.

He shook his head, and I saw him swallowing down a burst of emotion.

"Thinking about it now, we were beaten before we started. She had sustained a blow to the head. A severe one. Almost died herself. But she couldn't remember what had happened. Not all of it. She remembered seeing a man dressed in black. She maintained he was the killer. Only trouble was, nobody saw him. Police interviewed all of the locals – everyone they could find who might have been on the road that day and passed her house. She lived in a cottage, way upstate. Isolated, rural kind of place. No reports of an unfamiliar vehicle, or any non-locals. It came down to her word. And nobody took it."

"Except you," I said.

"Except me."

Both of us were silent for a mile or two. I didn't want to bombard Harry with questions. Talking about this case was difficult for him, but there were things I needed to know.

"Any idea why the appeal is suddenly happening now?" I said.

"No clue. Maybe new evidence? I don't know."

"You still haven't told me what convinced you she was innocent?"

He grew quiet, wrung his hands on the steering wheel.

"I'll let you read the file," he said, finally. Some things were too painful to be spoken aloud.

On the road to Howell's place, I told Harry a little of my involvement. There were some things I kept to myself. It made it easier for Harry – he was still a judge, after all, and telling him I'd helped my client obtain ten million dollars from the handcuffed wrist of an FBI agent seemed like the kind of thing I shouldn't mention.

Even if I'd told Harry everything – I knew in the back of my head that he wouldn't rat me out. He was the best friend I had. The age gap didn't seem to bother either of us – Harry could still drink me under the table when I was in the mood to hit the bottle. Thankfully those moods were few and far between these days.

Two or three miles from Premier Point, we could see the plume of smoke on the horizon.

My cell phone rang.

Howell.

"Are you all right? Did you get Caroline?" I said.

"No. Is Susan okay? The feds won't tell me anything. Are you still in the hospital?" he said.

His voice was raw, filled with tears and panic.

"Susan is okay, far as I know. Still in the hospital. I'm out, I'm on my way to your house. The rail station drop was more of a set-up than you bargained for, you know you called Lynch on a phone that had been stashed in a locker for the drop. There was a shirt in there too. Looked like the one Caroline was wearing on the day she disappeared. It had a message on it – 'Howell murdered her in the basement.' What the hell happened at the cemetery?"

He was silent. His breath quivered and buzzed down the line.

"We got to the graveyard. I was supposed to give the money to a man inside the Chrysler Memorial. McAuley was supposed to be watching my back and Marlon scouting ahead. There was no one around, no one in the memorial. Just two phone numbers written on a page and taped to the memorial wall. I called the first number and must've got Lynch. Second call just rang once then disconnected. I tried it again and the line was dead. That's all I remember. I woke up with the sun in my face. Somebody hit me from behind. McAuley and Marlon are gone. So was the page with the cell phone numbers, and so was the money."

"What! You think McAuley or Marlon set you up?"

"I don't know. I doubt it. I'm at the house. The feds are here. They're watching me close. They're thinking about arresting me."

CHAPTER TWENTY-THREE

Harry complained for the entire length of the single-lane road that led to Howell's property. The bumps from Harry's small tires leaping in and out of the holes in the asphalt sent hot shards of pain into my knees and my burned hand. He tried to avoid the holes but they were too many. It took a long time to make that drive. Beside us, in the field, I could see the heavy tracks made by Harper's Charger not that many hours ago. And up ahead, the fence lay in ruins where we'd busted through onto the driveway.

We came to the end of the road and Harry circled around, stopped and let me out behind the police cordon. An area of fifty feet around the perimeter of the house had been taped off as a crime scene. Two fire trucks waited patiently beside the property, one truck pouring the last of its water onto the charred ruins of the house. More cop and FBI cars had appeared overnight. SWAT was gone. Harper's Dodge Charger was still there. All attention was on the house. A man in a yellow hard hat walked slowly and carefully through the front door. I took a long look at the mansion I'd marveled at the night before. Black staining on the brickwork around the empty windows, the roof was partially collapsed on the right side, and the smell of smoke was still thick and all-consuming.

Sitting on a piece of broken fence, twenty feet away, I saw Howell. He watched me come closer. I saw one agent, keeping an eye on Howell from a distance.

"What's going on?" I said.

His eyes told me everything. There was loss, confusion, and a raw, nerve-shredding pain in that face. He swallowed, wiped away the tears streaking his face and ran his hands through his hair.

"Are you all right?" I said.

"The feds won't let me near the house. I called the hospital. Susan is going to be fine. George too. Nurse told me it was you who pulled them out of the house. Thank you."

"No need. In the end some firemen saved me and the female FBI agent, Harper, who got to Susan first. Why did the ransom drop go bad? What do you think?"

"Whoever took her . . . they're punishing me, Eddie. These bastards want me to live in hell. Why didn't they just shoot me? Why didn't they leave my daughter out of it?"

His shoulders hunched and shook as he broke down. I put a hand on his back, turned him and put my other hand on his shoulder. He didn't care about the money, didn't care about going to jail, or his house, or even his wife; Caroline was everything to this man. He'd been so close to getting her back – and now he had nothing. There were no words I could say to this guy. I made my living with language, and I had nothing to say – nothing that could give even a moment's comfort. Gently, he pushed me away and put his head between his knees. Howell had come to the conclusion that Caroline was definitely dead. I could see it on him like a black, misshapen creature clawing at his back.

I turned, something had caught my attention. An FBI agent, up at the house, running toward the front door. A shout rang out from the house and more agents and cops came up. I saw Lynch at the back of the pack, sprinting forward, pushing people out of the way. In a small group of feds, I saw the tall figure of Washington, and right beside him – Harper. Washington leaned on the hood of a dark sedan, his arms folded as he traded words with Harper. She had changed her shirt and looked to be in a lot better shape than me. They were both watching the front entrance to the house.

The man in the yellow hard hat was just visible at the threshold of the house. He was kneeling, and pointing downwards. He was soon lost to my view when the first few cops and feds surrounded him.

I ducked beneath the crime scene tape and walked past two other men in the same yellow hard hats and high-vis vests as the man at the front door of the house. As I passed the men I saw a logo on the vest – Gurley's Structural Engineers.

Nobody stopped me approaching the house. They were all too busy peering into the dark interior from the entrance hall. Politely, I elbowed through the crowd of agents and cops, until I could see a little way inside. I glanced back and saw Harper give me a wave. I nodded and turned back to the house.

Hard hat aimed a torch beam downwards. Lynch was on his radio, and listening intently at the mic in his ear.

"Are you sure it's blood?" said Lynch.

He listened. Waited.

The marble floor had collapsed. I could see right into the basement. Amidst the rubble and the white dust swirling in the torch light, I thought I saw something. Then, two crime scene techs in white hazmat suits and hard hats climbed out of the basement. They held a line and scrabbled up the rubble, right through the hole in the ground floor. One of them carried a large, clear plastic evidence bag. Inside I saw what looked like a long knife.

"That's it," said Lynch as he walked past me.

I held out a hand for one of the crime scene techs, he took it and I helped pull him up the last few feet of bricks until he came back to ground level.

"What did you see down there? Lynch said something about blood," I said.

The tech was sweating in his suit, and I'd turned away from him. I was within the crime scene boundary and nobody was throwing me out, not yet. My best guess was they were all too excited and probably got me mixed up with some of the engineers who were making sure what areas of the scene were safe to enter.

I could feel the tech looking at me, and I handed him a half-full bottle of water.

"Thanks," he said. "No body, but we got the next best thing – blood spatter on the walls. Looks like a lot of blood, probably from a major artery. She died down there. Nobody could've survived. We got enough blood from the wall for a field test. It tested positive for Caroline's blood type. And we've got what looks like the murder weapon," said the tech.

"Since when did this become a murder investigation?" I said.

"Since Howell faked the drop, stole ten million and tried to blow up the crime scene to hide the evidence," said the tech.

I spun around and began sprinting toward Howell.

Agent Lynch, and a couple of feds who I didn't know by name had almost reached the broken fence that Howell sat upon. They broke the news, and caught him as he doubled over, the scream tearing out of his lungs. He went wild, arms flailing and his face a horrific contortion. His mind and body were in shock, in freefall, and panic and pain were fighting to get control over him.

Agent Lynch didn't give a shit. He knew Howell couldn't hear him. The man was lost in a thick shroud of grief. It didn't deter Lynch. I knew what was coming.

Lynch raised his voice, almost shouting over Howell's cries. Loud enough for me to hear.

"Mr Howell, we made a call to your insurers after last night. The ransom was ten million dollars. We only got two. Mr Howell, I have no choice, you're under arrest for the murder of your daughter, Caroline Howell. You have the right to remain silent. You have the right to an attorney . . ."

I was ten feet away when it happened. One of the FBI men spun Howell to cuff him. Lynch and the other fed stood a few feet away, watching, with Lynch rhyming off Howell's Miranda rights.

Howell kept turning, he leaned into the spin and caught the fed with an elbow, sending him sprawling to the dirt. He came a full 360 and faced Lynch and the other agent.

Five feet away, and my lungs were drowning in gunk, my breath gone.

Somehow, I knew what Howell was going to do. I could see him spiraling.

A noise escaped from his throat; a raw, primal howl.

He reached behind his back.

Three feet away.

His hand came away with a gun. Lynch and the other fed dropped a little in their stance and made a move for their weapons.

But Howell was no threat to them.

The gun in Howell's right hand arced sideways, and then up, his bicep curling, his wrist turning the barrel toward the side of his head.

My shoulder hit him in the stomach and a shot rang out.

We both went sprawling to the dirt.

His gun landed beside me.

I scrambled to my knees, and saw him lying in the dirt, crying. Alive and unharmed. The shot went over his head. He was immediately flipped over by strong hands. His arms pinned behind his back and cuffed.

There are many ways to spot a liar. Emotion is real, it can't be faked. Love is real. Hate is real. Pain is more real than any of them. I knew what it was to be in pain. And I could taste that in the air around Howell. Losing a child is the wound that can never heal – that remains open and bleeding – always.

Pain was truth.

And that was good enough for me.

"My client has no comment to make at this time," I said.

Time.

Howell needed time to calm down. To think. To figure this out.

But time could be cruel. Time, it seemed, remembered all of your promises, even if you didn't. If the FBI was right, Caroline Howell was murdered in the basement of her own home.

Standing twenty feet away, I saw Agent Harper. We held each other's eyes, and then she turned away. No glory in this arrest. No victory. Right then I had a feeling Agent Harper and I believed the same thing: whatever happened to Caroline Howell was not at the hands of her father.

Knowing that and proving it, were two very different things.

PART
II

August 2nd, 2011

East Brother Island Hospital for the Criminally Insane,
New York

Julie Rosen never had a visitor before that day. Now two men had come to see her. The orderly took her arm and led her to the visitor's rooms while Julie shuffled slowly beside him, holding on to her drip for support.

Two guests waiting for her. Today was a good day.

They sat together, all three, in the family room overlooking the adjacent Rikers Island. For a long time Julie sat in silence. She wished she'd brought her hair clip. Every time a lock of hair fell over the left side of her face she carefully and quickly brushed it behind her ear. People didn't like seeing the scar tissue on the side of her head and she was careful to hide it with her long brown hair. Similarly, Julie always wore long-sleeve tops, to hide the burns. The tall man got up and stood at the window – watching the patterns of geese in the pale sky.

She was glad he'd moved away. The tall one frightened her. She thought his face was somehow wrong.

The other man sucked at a popsicle and said nothing. He'd brought one for Julie. Cherry flavor. Her favorite. He told her they sold candy bars, slushies and ice creams in the visitor's center. She thanked him and said she would save it for later. They sat, Julie talked. This man, this soft man, this gentle man. Julie liked him but she did not know why. Her medicine made her mind a little muddled sometimes. She told the man many things. She spoke of her fear that the hospital would close before she died. That would be the worst thing that could happen. Julie might not like her room in the new hospital. It would be different. It wouldn't be the same. This new room would have new corners, new shadows. And old things might grow in those shadows.

Merely thinking of it frightened her. The doctor had told Julie she should not dwell on anything that frightened her, or upset her. When she did, the orderlies came and tied her down, then pricked her skin to make her sleep.

The man removed the last of the frozen ice from the stick with his pale lips.

He took her hand in his and whispered to her.

"You sent me the letter," he said.

And she remembered. Two months ago, a letter had arrived for Julie. At first, she thought it strange, meaningless. But slowly, the words trickled into her mind. The dense, elegant, black script had woven itself through the damaged neural pathways, unlocking doors, and releasing dark misshapen figures. Demons that haunted Julie in her sleep. Only then did Julie realize these figures were not imagined – they were remembered.

And then, in the cold silence of her room, with the letter in her hands, she remembered it all. She had sent the letter to the gentle man. And now he had come.

And he had brought the memory roaring back, again. At once she knew all that she had lost. It was too much. Too much for anyone to lose, all over again, in the space of a breath. She saw the dark man in the nursery, smelled the gasoline, and felt heat from those terrible flames. But she'd learned not to trust memory. There were ghosts in her head and they made some things – strange. She had just taken a hit before it all happened. At least she remembered that much. What images of the day that remained were foggy. Misted in the smoke from a crack pipe, and the cloud of blood from a head wound.

Her eyes took in the room, as if awakening from a long, gray dream. The toys, the board games in the faded boxes, the smell of old silly putty, of paint. How she loved the vinegary, acidic smell of fresh paint. It was all suddenly there, and yet it had always been there. Only now, Julie could see and smell these things once more. Things that families used, that people used, that children used.

She had no use for these things. Soon, she would have no use for anything. The gentle man had been startled when he'd first laid eyes on her; she could tell. Her skin began to turn yellow last year. Then the stomach pains began. The doctors reassured her it was treatable with dialysis, but Julie didn't want that. Her time had come. Now, with the sweats, her skin looked almost golden. Even the whites of her eyes had turned yellow, like the eyes of a great cat.

She knew the orderlies were watching so she wiped away her tears, and held fast the hand of the visitor.

When she spoke her voice was stronger, clearer, and yet it was a sound that could have been whispered by a ghost – for it carried all the darkness and pain and rage of a life torn in half.

"Promise me," said Julie. "Promise me you will make them suffer."

The gentle man stood, and nodded. He promised her. He swore to her that he would do exactly as she had asked. And then he left the room with the tall man following.

The nice orderly, Sam, let her stay in the visitor's room while she sucked at her cherry popsicle. It tasted good. The ice cooled the sores in her mouth that came from biting her cheeks. It wouldn't be long now. She could feel her body giving up. Another day, maybe two.

It didn't matter. For all that Julie had endured, she knew that those who had wronged her would suffer more than she had ever imagined. She was sure of it. He had promised.

The gentle man did not lie.

CHAPTER TWENTY-FOUR

Six months after the fire at Premier Point

The offices of Max Copeland, attorney-at-law, were not what you might expect from a well-heeled lawyer. Then again, my own office doubled as my apartment – although clients never got to see the little bedroom in back. So I thought my office passed muster as a working legal base. Just.

Copeland's place was an exercise in minimalism. More like a waiting room in a Swedish euthanasia clinic. The receptionist wore a tight-fitting white dress. She sat in a white leather chair, behind a glass desk. A white laptop sat on the desk beside a white phone. Some white lilies flopped out of a glass vase, and the green stems were the only hint of color in the sanitized reception area. Visitors had a choice of sitting on a U-shaped white plastic bench – or a leather couch, which was also white.

The rest of the office looked like a maze of frosted glass.

I stood. For six minutes.

The receptionist didn't give me her name. She was blonde, and one of those women who was attractive but could've been any age. I guessed she was between twenty-five and forty-five. I heard the sound of metal tapping glass.

"You can go through. First on the right," she said.

I was relieved. Standing there I'd felt like I was making the place look untidy.

For almost six months, nothing had happened in the Rosen appeal. I'd wanted to confront Copeland, but Harry wouldn't allow it. He said just to let the appeal take its course, and don't provoke Copeland, as there was no guarantee he would pursue it to a hearing.

After all, plenty of appeals are filed and then withdrawn. Harry had seen it happen dozens of times. Then, three days ago, Copeland filed a motion to bring the appeal before the court for a full hearing as he'd completed his investigations. The case would come before the appellate judges in less than two weeks.

Now seemed as good a time as any to go see Copeland. Whilst nothing had happened in the Rosen appeal until last week, I'd been working flat out to prepare the Howell case and his trial was set to start this morning. Before I got into that, I needed to pay a visit to Copeland. Once the Howell trial got up and running later today, I wouldn't have the time for this. Howell needed every second I could spare if he wanted to stay out of jail. Thankfully, no one had figured out how Howell had got hold of the ten-million-dollar ransom that had been handcuffed to Agent Lynch's wrist. But that didn't matter much, not when it looked like Howell was going down for the murder of his daughter.

Harry's notion that the Rosen appeal might die away was proving ill-founded. I hadn't told Harry I was coming here, he would've stopped me. And Harry was probably right. Coming here was a bad idea, but I needed to let Copeland know there were no free shots against Harry Ford. Maybe I could make him think twice about the appeal.

The corridor of glass led me to an open door on the right. There were other doors up ahead, on the opposite side, but I ignored them and went through the first door on my right, as instructed.

This office at least had a window. I could see the Flatiron Building opposite, and the layers of snow on the roofs of the buildings beyond. The office itself was similar to the reception area. Acrylic sliding cabinets on one side, no doubt holding back a tide of case files, and on the other side I saw a glass-topped desk and Copeland behind it. His hand cradling his head as he scanned a pile of pages. He wore a jet-black suit, lilac shirt and black tie. A man in his late fifties, with a bushy white beard and bald head.

He didn't acknowledge me. Just kept on reading.

"Mr Copeland, I'm . . ."

"I know who you are. What do you want?" he said.

"I was thinking I wouldn't mind an office like this. Are you sure you're practicing law here? Looks to me like you and Mrs Personality outside could put on a couple of white coats and open this up as a laboratory."

That made him raise his head. His lips were drawn tightly together and he looked at me like I was a shit stain on his white Chanel rug.

"What do you want?" he said.

I walked toward the desk, slowly. Letting him see he couldn't intimidate me.

"I want you to drop the appeal in the Rosen case. Julie Rosen was found guilty, and maybe that's wrong or maybe that's right – but God rest her soul, she's dead. Torturing her lawyer, who fought hard for her, won't bring her back."

"There are those who see merit in an appeal. I'm one of them. If that is all you wanted to tell me then you should leave."

"Who exactly is giving you instructions in this case? Far as we know Julie Rosen had no relatives or friends. Certainly no one who could afford your services."

"Client confidentiality. Now if you don't mind . . ." He pressed a button on his phone console and a red light appeared in the corner of the digital screen.

"Why now? Why after all these years?"

"Maybe you don't understand, I don't have to explain anything to you."

"See, I think you do. Fighting for someone's innocence is a just cause, no doubt. But you don't have to burn a good man in the process."

"Harry Ford. Use the judge's name, won't you?" He leaned back in his office chair, folded his arms across his chest and for the first time I saw enjoyment spread across his face.

"Yeah, Judge Ford. He fought her case better than anyone could have. Think about what you're doing here. You've hurt a lot of people in the past. Way I hear it, a lot of murderers are walking around this city as free men because they paid you to handle their appeals. And you destroyed a lot of good lawyers in the process. I don't want you to hurt anyone else, especially not Harry Ford."

"If he did nothing wrong, then he has nothing to fear. But I think he neglected his duty to his client. She should never have stood trial. I'm going to represent her to the best of my ability. That is my duty to my client. If the good judge is ruined in the course of this appeal, well, that's just a bonus."

"What about your duty to the people of this city? You think buying a Goddamn clean room and working out of it is enough to take the shit off your shoes? Think again. There's representing your client to the best of your ability, and then there's what you do; getting child rapists set free because of a procedural fault with the evidence. We all owe a duty to this city. Our oath demands it. Don't go down this road with Harry."

The door opened behind me and a tall man in a black suit entered the room. He wore his hair in a buzz cut, which matched his hard features. Thin mouth, broad head, long thick arms with tattoos over his hands.

Security.

"And what will you do, Flynn? Write to the Bar Association? Complain to the cops? Go ahead, I'm not worried about them."

I reached his desk, leaned over and placed my hands on the glass. The security man came forward and stood beside me, ready to make a move if I even thought about grabbing Copeland.

"The only person you need to worry about is me. If you go after Harry, I'll come after you."

He didn't even blink.

"That would be foolish, Mr Flynn. And dangerous. You're a small fish, like all those other lawyers I took down. I'm a friggin' barracuda. You know why I target lawyers in my appeals? Because I need someone to blame. Prosecutors and judges usually withstand criticism. But a defense attorney? No one is batting for that team. And besides, the fewer defense attorneys that are around, the more business there is for me. Your involvement won't change a thing."

The guy was ice cold. Unshakable. I knew then it had been a mistake to come here. I stood up straight. My hands left moist prints on the glass. Copeland looked at the smears on the desk and tutted. He plucked the red, silk handkerchief from his breast pocket and began wiping his desk, furiously. When he was done, he stared up at me.

"You still here? Leave, or you'll be carried out. You don't scare me. I've faced great lawyers before. The best. Better men than you," he said.

"I'm sure you have, but I'll let you in on a secret – I'm *not* a good man. Not even close. Leave Harry out of this, or you'll find out how bad I can be."

Copeland looked past me at the tall guy with the buzz cut and said, "Introduce Mr Flynn's face to the sidewalk, would you, Bear?"

The guy's real name wasn't Bear. I'd bet my life on it. If you're looking to get hired as personal security it pays to have a name that either breeds intimidation, or fosters a sense of security. All personal security guys with an eye on the business were called "Bear", or "Snake", or "Tomahawk". Having to write out the personal name tags at a security convention was probably a whole lot of fun.

"That's it, you're out of here," said Bear.

He side-stepped, so he was right behind me. I felt his right arm slam across my throat. He locked his fingers to his left forearm, leaned back and started choking me. When he began walking backwards I had no choice other than go with him.

I'd made a total mess of this meeting. Instead of finessing Copeland I'd let him get to me through Harry. The man knew who I was, he knew what Harry meant to me.

A stupid mistake.

I pulled down on Bear's arm to get some air. Soon as he'd grabbed me I decided to let him take me out of the office. No point in making a bad situation worse.

"Make sure Flynn understands what happens to people who threaten me," said Copeland.

That sounded like more than just throwing my ass onto the street. Copeland's hired muscle hooked his right arm closer around my neck letting his left go free and I felt a sharp, stabbing pain from the rabbit punch.

"I'll make sure he understands," said Bear and I could tell he was smiling by the way he said it. This was a guy who clearly enjoyed his work.

I thought the situation would probably only get worse for me. No point in holding back any longer. First thing to do was break his grip. Easy. My thumb dug into the center of his palm. I squeezed hard and felt bone. Specifically, I felt two bones. Making sure my thumb was in between the bones of his middle fingers, I applied the last ounce of pressure and instantly his fingers relaxed and his grip weakened.

But I wasn't trying to break his grip on my throat. I just wanted him to open his hand a little. Which he did. Just enough to allow me to grab his little finger.

I don't care how big or how tough you are because when somebody who knows what they're doing gets hold of one of your digits – the fight is over before it even started.

The rabbit punch had pissed me off and I yanked too hard the first time.

There was a sound like a bag of popcorn bursting in a microwave. Except the popping and cracking sound came from the little bones, cartilage, sinew and ligament in the guy's finger.

I let go and turned around to face him. He'd turned pale, his mouth was open and he was shivering and sweat broke out on his forehead. He made a big deal out of not looking at his hand. Then when he did look at it, the unnatural angle of his finger poured the rest of the color out of his face and his legs began to wobble. He sat down in a chair in the corner before he fell on his ass.

I regretted hurting the guy. Even as I twisted his bones until they broke in my hand, I knew that in my head I wasn't breaking the security guys' hand, I was really thinking about hurting somebody else.

I made for the door to Copeland's office and without turning to face him I said, "Tell your pet to keep his paws to himself. This isn't over."

Before the door to his office closed, I heard him calling after me. "You're right, Flynn. This is just the beginning."

CHAPTER TWENTY-FIVE

I managed to beat my way out of Manhattan via the Henry Hudson Parkway, then the Saw Mill River Parkway to Yonkers where I found the Bronx River and another ribbon of asphalt. The snow on the side of the highway had turned black from the fumes and dirt from the passing vehicles. Traffic was busy but moving. It took me an hour and a half to make the twenty-five mile trip from New York City to the Westchester County Court, in White Plains.

On the way I had time to think about the last few months.

Couple of days after the fire at Howell's house, I went up to Riverhead and visited Christine and Amy. I'd called ahead, to make sure her parents weren't in the house. I had a great relationship with my in-laws; they bitched and complained to Christine that I wasn't good enough for her and I ignored them. Pretty perfect, actually.

Visiting Amy had been regular, once a week. Lately, Amy had begun to make good friends and some weekends disappeared for me because of sleepovers at her BFFs or camping trips – that kind of thing. Work got busier for me too. Folks don't have much consideration for their lawyer's social lives when they get arrested, so a lot of Friday and Saturday nights in police precincts meant that regular weekend visits gave way to a few hours here and there on Sundays. On that day, I was still coughing up black spit occasionally, and my hand still hurt like hell, but I'd enjoyed a full day alone with my daughter.

Christine and I talked on the porch after I dropped Amy off at Christine's parents' house. They were set to have a family dinner that evening. The word family didn't seem to include me.

Christine dressed in a white blouse and pale blue jeans. Here and there, silver streaked her long brown hair. She looked different. Older than the day we first met, but just as beautiful. And beautiful in a new kind of way. A way that made me think about how much of her life was passing me by. Behind her, Amy sat on the staircase and called one of her friends on the landline.

We got the small talk out of the way first. Her new job was going pretty well, she had interesting cases at the firm, and the managing partner, Kevin, was a tall divorcee with two kids of his own.

He'd been doing little odd jobs in the house, helping out Christine's dad. They got on like a house on fire, apparently. Christine had been seeing a lot of him, as a friend.

"You sure you're just friends?" I said, standing on the porch, my car keys in my hand.

At that moment, I couldn't get much of a read on Christine. She looked kind of sad. Her eyes were heavy, but her teeth and hands were clenched tightly, so I guessed there was a little anger and frustration going on too.

"Your job puts all of us at risk. You know it, you've said it yourself and even I know it now. We love you, but you're not here," she said, and by the time she'd finished her sentence any trace of anger had faded into a familiar disappointment. I was used to that tone.

A car pulled up in the driveway behind me. I didn't need to turn to know it was her parents, Bob and Diane – come to make sure I'd returned their granddaughter in one piece.

"You didn't answer my question," I said.

"Do I have to? Look, he's my boss. And yeah, I like to think we're friends. He's a good guy, you'd like him."

Somehow I doubted that.

"Okay, I gotta split. I'll see you next . . ."

"Amy's going to camp for the summer," she said, quickly.

Amy must've heard me when I said I was leaving. She put the phone receiver on the carpeted stairs, came out, pushed past Christine and gave me a hug.

"I hear you're going to camp?" I said.

She let go of me, and stared up into my eyes. My girl was turning thirteen, she was getting bigger every day.

"I was going to tell you. It's okay, Dad, I'll call you most nights, at eight. Like we used to. I get to see my friends and hang out and stuff. I can still see you when I get back," she said.

"It's fine, I'm happy for you. Call me when you can. I'll always be here," I said, trying to keep the emotion out of my voice. This meant I wouldn't get Amy for most of the summer. She gave me another hug, then ran back inside to finish her call.

I nodded to Christine and said, "I'll call you," turned and jogged to my car. No way did I want to speak to her parents. I just needed to get the hell out of there as fast as possible. I felt close to breaking down, and I didn't want Christine, Amy, or anyone to see that. The Mustang growled as I sped away, but I only drove two blocks, stopped and then banged the wheel for a full minute. The burn on my hand started bleeding and the pain became a welcome distraction.

Pulling off Main Street in White Plains, I drove past the courthouse and found a multi-story car park. I got out, grabbed my files and made my way back to the street, thinking about Bear's broken pinkie. I wasn't thinking about Bear when I twisted his finger, I wasn't even thinking of Kevin – I was thinking about myself and what a damn fool I'd been. These past few months I'd come to realize that I'd pretty much lost my family, and I couldn't see a way of getting them back. I hitched my coat around my shoulders and braved the cold on the way to the courthouse.

I'd never practiced in this court before, and I wasn't familiar with the staff, the judges, or the layout of the place.

The courthouse boasted a tower, reserved for administrative staff and the county Supreme Court, and an annex; a white stone, half-circle that wrapped itself around a courtyard that now separated the original building from the new build. A wall of curved glass on the top floor of the annex gave a great view of the snow-covered courtyard.

Whilst the glass wall proved to be a thing of architectural beauty, it was a pain in the ass when you were conducting a trial with any kind of media interest. The reporters, photographers, cameramen, TV anchors, bloggers, they could all see you coming a mile away thanks to that glass wall.

I could see a whole posse waiting outside the courtroom as the elevator dumped me onto the top floor of the annex. No way to avoid them. I kept my head down, pushed through the crowd, ignored the questions and the hands on my elbows. They were a persistent bunch, and they followed me inside.

"No comment," I said.

I ignored them and made my way to the defense table. There was no one else in the courtroom. Just me and the reporters. Over the years I'd gotten to know and like a handful of crime reporters in Manhattan. They knew that the best approach was a soft one. Most of the reporters who were still throwing questions at me, while my back was turned, were locals for small-town papers and the competing news agencies in White Plains.

I placed my files on the table, took out a pen and a legal pad. Sat down, and closed my eyes. It was a full two minutes before they stopped trying to get my attention.

I adjusted my tie, made the knot tight, and then swept my hand along the length of the dark fabric – smoothing it out. About four inches below the knot, I wore a small tie pin. It was an inch-long ceramic pin, which held the two halves of my tie straight. There was a plain black pin head, no bigger than a shirt button.

I'd bought the pin yesterday.

The trial was due to begin at eleven thirty. The judge had a sentencing first thing. That gave me over an hour before we officially began proceedings in The People v. Leonard Matthew Howell.

We had insisted on a speedy trial, and the District Attorney's office had lit a fire under the respective asses of both the FBI and the Police Department. There was no confirmation that Caroline Howell had been moved across state lines. Her body had never been found, but enough of her blood was found in the basement to make it murder. While the FBI made Howell's arrest, they couldn't prosecute him in federal court under the Federal Kidnapping Act. Instead the feds handed him over to county and became FBI prosecution witnesses in the state trial.

I thought of that morning after the fire. I remembered that itchy feeling I had; I couldn't wait to get this trial started and prove Howell was innocent.

Sitting at the defense table, with my head in my hands, and the trial about to start – I would've given anything to take back that eagerness to represent my client.

I knew in my gut he didn't kill his daughter. There was no actor in the world who could've faked the agony I saw in that man when the FBI told him they thought his daughter was dead and that he had murdered her. The suicide attempt, the cries, the clawing at the ground. All of that wild anger had nothing to do with the accusation of murder. It was the loss of his beloved daughter.

In a cell beneath New Rochelle district court, the day after his arrest, he told me to apply for bail so he could kill himself. He didn't want to live in a world without his daughter. His mental condition had deteriorated and I got him to sign a document giving me Power of Attorney – so I could look after his finances and promote a few people in his company in an attempt to keep the business afloat. I knew the practical business of living would help to keep him in the world.

"I can't go on, Eddie. She was everything. And somebody took her. She was special, you know. My first wife and I had tried for years to get pregnant. I was still in the marines, active on every tour, so it took a while. We tried IVF and it didn't work. She wanted a child so bad. She was worried too. In case something happened to me on the job. We tried IVF again, two more times. Last one was the charm. She was so happy. I remember coming home after my last tour, and there she was – this little pink bundle in my wife's arms. Caroline and I had a special relationship. More than just father and daughter, you know? My first wife could be . . . cold. She and Caroline didn't bond properly. Not like they should. Caroline was always closest to me. Now, both of them are gone. I can't . . . I can't deal with that . . ."

Nothing could balm this wound. Not time. Not alcohol, not drugs.

"Lenny," I said. He didn't hear me, and I took his silence as acceptance.

"You're forgetting something. Somebody did this to Caroline. And they're still walking around. Right now, the cops and the FBI aren't looking for them because they think that person was you. Help me out here. Where's Marlon and McAuley? Somebody hit you on the head. Think about this."

"I don't believe they had anything to do with it. Whoever took Caroline probably has McAuley and Marlon somewhere, or they've been shot, chopped and dumped in the Hudson."

His knuckles turned white, his fists tight.

"Help me, Lenny. Whatever you've got left, you gotta use it to keep going. You owe it to Caroline to find out who killed her. Give me some time. I'll get you off, and while I'm doing that we'll find out who really did this. We can do this together. I can't do it alone. I need you."

His hands fell across the table, and his arms and fingers were trembling.

"What if we don't find him? What if you don't get me off?" he said, not looking at me. His eyes could no longer fix on anything or anyone.

"I will," I said.

"What if you can't? I can't live with this, Eddie."

I nodded.

"I'll do it if you promise me something," he said.

"What?"

"Promise me if I get convicted, and we can't find who really took Caroline, you'll help me punch out."

I recoiled, instantly. The thought was repellant. But after the initial revulsion, it almost made sense. I knew how I would feel if something happened to Amy. Or Christine. They had been in danger before – real danger. And I knew if they were not in this world, I wouldn't want to be either.

"Promise me!" he roared.

The guard appeared at the window of the conference cell in the bowels of the district court. I waved him away and he moved off.

"I'll need something small – like a pen, or a pill. You could do that. You could give me something, slip it to me during a visit. I can give you six months if you swear to me you'll do this if we fail. I need to know there's a way out, Eddie, one way or the other. Swear it."

He wanted to hear the words. He wanted to look me in the eye and know that I meant it. There was no way I was going to let him kill himself, but I needed him to stay alive and if that demanded that I lie to him, I was prepared to do it.

"I swear to you, if we can't find the killer, and if you get convicted, I'll help you find a way out."

For a long time he stared at me, his ravaged eyes searched my face for any sign of a tell. He saw none.

Howell didn't make bail and I was relieved. At least on the inside he would be put on suicide watch. Although, six months inside hadn't let him mourn either. He was still a man who wanted to die. And in that six months there had been no word, no sign of McAuley, Marlon, nor the ten million dollars. If there were kidnappers involved other than McAuley or Marlon, they made no approach.

Sitting in the courtroom in White Plains, an hour from the trial beginning, I knew two things.

First, with all of the new evidence that came out in the last six months, Howell would probably be convicted.

The second thing I knew was that when the jury gave their verdict in a day or two, Howell would ask me for the ceramic pin. I'd shown it to him yesterday. He'd weighed it, tested the edge and pricked his finger by accident. He'd given it back to me and nodded, satisfied. It was razor sharp. There was no metal in the pin to set off the electronic detectors, and it was small enough to fit inside his cheek. He could hide it for a short time, undetected.

Would it be more humane to let him suffer, or let him die? I'd thought about little else. In the end, I wore the pin for show. It served as a convincer to keep Howell on this earth long enough to get to the end of the trial. If he wanted to die after the trial, that was his decision – but I wasn't going to be the one to help him. I knew I would never give him the pin. I'd lied to him to keep him alive. Eventually, I'd have to admit that to him. And he would hate me for it.

CHAPTER TWENTY-SIX

Howell sat beside me, dressed in a plain white shirt and dark pants. He had that faraway look which some defendants get on their first day of trial. They don't quite know where to look, so they stare off into the distance. The jury waited patiently, and the courtroom gallery boasted a good crowd. The judge sat silently, waiting for proceedings to begin.

Assistant District Attorney Michelle King got to her feet, walked around the prosecution table and stood in front of the jury. She wore a navy pantsuit, and a pale blue blouse with a hint of color from a red silk scarf around her neck. I'd checked her out with the local defense attorneys. She was talented, smart, went to a decent law school and was well respected by the local judges. Apparently, she had a penchant for those neck scarves. It was this modest fashion accessory and her smooth, confident delivery in court that had earned her the nickname "The Silk Hammer."

One defense attorney told me that it didn't matter if your client got crushed by a ton of silk or a ton of lead. The damage was the same – only King dumped the weight without you or your client even knowing about it.

She waited while the jury put down their pads and pens and looked at her. Jury selection had not gone too badly. During questioning there were at least four jurors who stated, in answer to my questions, that they would do everything they possibly could to protect a loved one in danger – including taking matters into their own hands. These four were all men, all in their early to late forties, who had manual jobs and families. Two of them were African American, one was Hispanic, the other white. They were my only hope in an unwinnable case as a jury, even if they believe the defendant committed the crime, can at their discretion return a *not guilty* if they feel like it. A big "the hell with you" to the prosecution.

Of the eight female jurors, two were ex-military and I thought they gave me the biggest problem. Folks who went through military training usually toed the line – they didn't question authority and stuck to the rules – even if it was life or death. Plus, they were army. They wouldn't look that favorably on an ex-Marine.

The other six women were a mix of White Plains middle-class ladies. A bank clerk, a grocery store owner, a manager in a car dealership, and three housewives. I'd already used up my juror challenges getting rid of three grade-school teachers, a retired stockbroker and a kindergarten teacher. Teachers tended to go with the authority figures. I needed folks who could at least envisage the bending of rules for a good cause. The stockbroker got canned because I hate stockbrokers, and so does everyone else.

If I had to guess, I'd say King had the better spread of jurors. My only chance was the four men, going with their gut and doing what any father would do. They might, just might be enough for a hung jury. There was one female juror who could be persuaded, but I wasn't sure. And my ace in the hole was juror four. The only white male and undoubtedly the only asshole in the group. I'd noticed him, looking down his nose at the female jurors and he wasn't too comfortable being the only white male on the panel. I picked him because he had an American flag tattooed on his arm – which meant he was pro-military, but by the way he slouched in the chair I could tell he'd never served a day in his life. The tattoo of the AR-15 assault rifle on his other forearm meant he enjoyed his right to bear arms. He'd sent a half smile toward Howell when he was brought in, and I knew right then I had this guy on my side.

One of the first things I'd learned about jury trials was never underestimate the power of an asshole. I'd rather have an asshole on my side than a nice guy who'd actually listen to the other jurors in the room. If the asshole is on your side you can pretty much guarantee he'll stay that way. Assholes lack the imagination to open their minds.

But there was a hundred miles of rough road between now and the jury retiring for their verdict, and unless things changed dramatically – or some of the prosecution witnesses didn't show – the vast majority of the jury would only go one way: Guilty.

"Ladies and Gentlemen of the jury. My name is Michelle King, I represent the People of the State of New York. It's my responsibility to present evidence to you, which we believe proves the case against the defendant, Leonard Howell."

She paused, took a step back, held her hands out wide.

"Your job is to evaluate the evidence. No one else does that but you. We say that when the evidence is presented and you've had time to consider all of it, you will believe, beyond all reasonable doubt, that the defendant murdered Caroline Howell. His own daughter."

Another pause. Let the jury look at the man who murdered his child.

I'd been through this with Howell; don't look at the judge or the jury, just focus on the prosecutor or me during opening speeches.

Either he'd forgotten, or he no longer had anything to lose. He stared at the jury. The asshole stared back, unafraid to look Howell in the eye.

"Some of the evidence that will be presented in this case is highly disturbing. There are graphic images which we have to show you. We don't do this lightly, members of the jury."

One of the ADAs at the prosecution table hit a button on a remote control. The two large plasma televisions that sat on either side of the judge's bench came to life. Some of the jury looked away – not wanting to confront the horror so early in the proceedings. But their fellow jurors tugged at their arms, reassured them, and got them to lower their hands from their eyes. On the screens were identical photographs of Caroline Howell, from her Facebook profile pictures. She was wearing a red and white striped top, smiling for the picture as she stood in front of her house.

"This is Caroline Howell. A beautiful girl with her whole life ahead of her. She was an A-grade student, well liked in her class and popular in the community. Her father, who was facing bankruptcy, led her to the basement of the house, he took up a knife and cut her throat. He lied to the police and the FBI, then conned his insurance company into giving him ten million dollars for the ransom. The money has not been recovered, and the ransom exchange never happened. The ten-million-dollar ransom has disappeared – along with two of the defendant's more trusted employees – Peter McAuley and Marlon Black. One of those employees ratted out their boss and wrote a note to the police on Caroline's shirt telling them that her father killed her in the basement. What did happen is that while the FBI were delivering what they believed to be the ransom money – Leonard Howell remotely triggered an incendiary device in his basement in an attempt to destroy the crime scene. He did this by using his cell phone to call a pager that triggered an explosive device in his basement.

The jury took all of this in while gazing between King and the image of Caroline on the screen.

"He has hidden Caroline's body, but despite his effort he could not conceal his crime. Our experts found bloodstains in the basement which match Caroline Howell's DNA. More bloodstains belonging to the victim were found on a pair of spectacles recovered from her car. Those spectacles belong to her father, the defendant. The murder weapon was also recovered from the blaze – a kitchen knife with Caroline's blood on it and the defendant's fingerprints. When federal agents arrested Howell for his daughter's murder, he attempted suicide. He did this out of guilt. The guilt that he felt for murdering his own flesh and blood for money. You too will see his guilt. Of that I have no doubt."

CHAPTER TWENTY-SEVEN

The judge presiding over the case turned her attention to the defense. Her Honor, Judge Patricia Schultz, was not well known to me. This was the first case I'd tried in front of her, but I knew her by reputation. When I discovered she would be trying the case, I'd called a few local defense attorneys who'd previously told me all about the silk hammer – King. Schultz was a respected justice with a fair, open mind and she liked to have as little to do with the trial as possible.

Some judges interfere all the time. Objecting to questions, asking questions, making remarks and demands. All that accomplished was to lengthen the trial and piss everybody off.

Judge Schultz was the opposite. She let the lawyers get on with it, but at the same time she had a keen mind. She was a good listener but if you wandered off course, or didn't play by the rules, she let you know about it – big time.

Harsh, but fair. I could live with that.

I stood and took up the spot in front of the jury, which had been occupied by King just moments before. Howell's glasses turning up in Caroline's car was a sure-fire winner for King. The blood spots on the lenses had been confirmed as Caroline's. I didn't have a way around that piece of evidence just yet. Instead, I decided to get the jury thinking about something else.

"Ladies and Gentlemen, for the record, my name is Eddie Flynn and I have the honor of representing the defendant in this case, Leonard Howell. You've listened to Miss King, and she has been fair in outlining her role, and your role in this case. But I'm here to tell you about what's not fair. It's not fair that Leonard Howell is sitting in this court as a defendant. He should be sitting here watching whoever kidnapped his daughter receive a lengthy prison sentence.

That would be fair. That would be just. Leonard Howell loved and adored his daughter. He sits here today as a man broken by grief. Broken by the loss of his child. You cannot ease that suffering. But you can give him half of what justice demands. You can acquit him. The evidence in this case, which Miss King briefly mentioned, is at best circumstantial, and at worst it is entirely false.

"Leonard Howell got a separate call from the kidnapper after they had contacted the FBI. He told my client that if he wanted his daughter returned alive he was to bring ten million dollars to a drop-off point. He was warned, if he told the police or the FBI about the real ransom drop, his daughter would be murdered. What would you do in that situation?"

I wasn't allowed to ask the jury anything, but this was rhetorical. For as long as I could, I stayed quiet, and let the jury ask themselves that question. I had to put them in Howell's shoes. That's the secret to winning a jury. Really, a jury trial was a psychological game. The prosecution wanted to put the victim right alongside the jury. And every defense attorney knew they had to take the jury out of the stand, and put them in the defendant's chair. Perspective was everything.

Judge Schultz saw through my play, but instead of calling me on it she cleared her throat and I took that as my cue to get going again.

"My client went to the ransom drop with two men. Peter McAuley and Marlon Black. His longtime friends and employees. At the location of the ransom drop were two telephone numbers. My client called them both. The first was answered by an FBI agent who picked up the call from a burner cell phone in his ransom location. The second call set off the explosive device in my client's home. That night, my client's wife and other members of his staff were in that house. He would not willingly put them in danger. Then, Leonard Howell was struck on the head from behind. When he woke up, the ransom, the note with the phone numbers on it, and his friends, were all gone."

I paused again. Let the jury roll this around in their minds. Let them get a feel for it.

"Miss King is right to say that it is your job to evaluate and weigh up this evidence. Because each piece taken individually, or the entirety of it taken as a whole, proves nothing. You will hear the prosecution theory that Leonard Howell was attempting to defraud his insurance company out of the ransom, and that the kidnapping had been set up by the defendant purely for the money.

"There's one problem with this theory; it doesn't make any sense."

I strode forward, slowly, closing in on the jury with what I hoped was the truth.

"Those of you who have children, those of you who have a loved one, those of you who know what it is to hold a child in your arms – ask yourself this question; would you kill that child for money?"

A shorter pause this time, because it was an easy question. With each moment I felt more jurors were psychologically moving toward the defendant. They were looking over my shoulder, imagining they were in that chair.

"In fact, is there any amount of money in the world which would make you harm a child? No. No parent could do that. None of us could even conceive of it. The prosecution will not be able to persuade you that Leonard Howell could do it, they will not be able to persuade you that he was motivated by money to do it. You know why they can't persuade you? Because I know, looking at each of you, that nothing could persuade you to harm your own child. And Leonard Howell is just like you. So, at every stage in this trial ask yourself – could this man kill his own child? I think you all already know the answer."

I backed up, turned and walked away to the sound of King raising an objection. The judge agreed that my last statement should be disregarded by the jury.

"Mr Flynn, I know you have a great deal of experience in the Manhattan district courts, but we do things differently here," said Judge Schultz. "In your last comment you invited the jury to prejudge this matter. Let me be clear that I will not stand for that kind of behavior from counsel."

I nodded, apologized. She turned to the jury and said, "You must ignore counsel's last remark. Do not prejudge any aspect of this case. First, listen to the testimony, understand all of the evidence. The time for evaluating and judging comes at the end of this trial, when you retire to consider your verdict. Not before. Are we clear?"

The jury nodded. King was pissed at me but refused to show it. The trouble with asking a jury to disregard anything, is that they're only given that instruction after the horse has leapt out of the barn and is galloping halfway down the lane.

I finished my summary, sat down and made a note, which I passed to Howell. He read it, slid it back across the table to me.

The prosecutor bent low over her desk, whispering to her assistants.

I'd already guessed her play. With an opening statement like that, King's first job was to ruin the defendant's credibility – make him look like a liar. Originally King was going to call Agent Lynch as the first witness, I'd seen her witness list and Lynch was a good call to start with – he could lay out most of the story for the jury right away, but she needed to ruin Howell first.

The note I'd written for Howell said:

> Don't react. The DA is gonna change up the witnesses. Better to get the worst over quickly.

Howell nodded. I patted him on the back, whispered to him to keep calm.

A male Assistant DA left the courtroom, presumably with a fresh running order for the prosecution case. He would gather the witnesses, give them the new list, get them coffee, tell whoever needed to know that they probably wouldn't be needed until after lunch.

Michelle King got to her feet and called her first witness. One of her best witnesses – somebody who knew Howell, who could paint him in a bad light for the jury. At least I'd worked it out, and I'd told Howell in advance.

The Silk Hammer was gearing up to hit Lenny with their best shot. "Your Honor, the People call Susan Howell."

CHAPTER TWENTY-EIGHT

The morning after the fire, Susan Howell remained in critical condition. Hospital staff had not permitted Howell to see her. He was told to wait. Instead, he came back to his smoldering home, where he was arrested not long after his return. The speed of her recovery increased after Howell didn't make bail. I'd checked with my client, and with the visitors log in Rikers Island – Susan Howell had not visited, had not called. Neither of them had exchanged a single word since the fire.

During one of our many legal visits in Rikers, about three months ago, we'd talked about Susan.

"The police arrested her, interviewed her and released her without charge three days after the fire. I've got her statement here," I said.

I slid the statement across the steel table in the legal visits room. He scanned it, pushed it back toward me.

"I'm not a naïve man. She was with me for the money. Always had been. She's beautiful, and she made me feel great. I thought she'd make a great mom for Caroline, but she took no interest in my daughter after we got married. When things got tough, financially, I could tell she was looking for a way out. Her eye started to wander, know what I mean."

My mind flitted back to the moment I met Susan Howell for the first time, and seeing her stroke Marlon's back. A touch that lingered too long.

"She's divorcing me," he said. From the breast pocket of his prison jumpsuit, he removed a folded-up letter. He slid it across the table. It was from Gore & Penning, one of the top divorce firms in the city. Both of those guys were Rottweilers. They'd torn apart half a dozen celebrities in recent years, and crippled some of New York's wealthiest men with alimony settlements that would take them the rest of their lives to pay off. The letter offered a settlement – 85 per cent of the assets in exchange for a quick, low-profile divorce.

"We'll put that on the back burner for now," I said.

"I honestly don't care, Eddie," said Howell.

Before he sank any lower, I changed the subject. I needed to get him thinking. Then at least he might start fighting and that would keep him alive.

"This is tough but I need you to hear this. The prosecution is claiming Caroline was murdered in the basement. They have a blood pattern analyst who says the west wall of the basement is stained with her blood. He says it's likely to be arterial spray. Somebody cleaned up the wall, but the staining remained visible with the application of luminol. And they found a kitchen knife, hidden in a box that was destroyed in the fire. The knife has your fingerprints on it. The photos of Caroline that came with the ransom demands could've been taken in your basement."

"I've no idea about any of that. You saw how dark it was outside – it's not supposed to be like that. We had fairy lights in the trees, spots and light features in the garden furniture. The power supply went through a meter box in the garage. I checked the lights, can't remember when, two, three days before the fire and saw the cable had burned through. I never got around to changing it. Could be somebody hurt her in the basement, then carried her out in the dark."

"From the time Caroline went missing, at any stage were you in the basement?"

"I can't say for sure. She never liked it down there. I used to do a little carpentry when she was younger. She would come down and watch me, but insisted I kept the basement door open."

"Was the basement kept locked?"

"No. It was always open," he said, and his eyes lost focus. I could almost see them shifting into darkness.

"Did the DNA test confirm the blood in the basement and the blood on my glasses belonged to Caroline?" he said.

"Yeah, it did."

He was no longer with me. His mind had shifted. I needed to bring him back.

"Susan has an alibi for the day Caroline disappeared. There was no physical evidence linking her to the basement, the fire, or Caroline's body. Reading between the lines, I get the impression the cops think she was in on it with you, but that they'll never prove a case against her. If they charged both of you, you would've been tried alongside her. Their lack of evidence against Susan could actually work in your favor if they had made the case you both conspired in the kidnapping and murder. They probably thought Susan could be put to better use a prosecution witness than a defendant. So apart from her confirming her alibi in this statement, what else could she say that might hurt us?"

"I have no idea," said Howell.

"And how come you haven't spoken to her since the fire?"

His eyes fixed on me.

"Looking at her, talking to her, even being in the same room as her, would only remind me of all the times she'd let Caroline down. Caroline's mom didn't bond too well with her. Post-natal depression, I guess. I thought Susan would've done a better job, but she messed up just as bad. They felt like small things at the time, and I didn't pay them any heed. Now . . . now that she's gone, they hurt. Every time she dismissed Caroline when she tried to talk to her new mom, every missed appointment, recital, cheerleader rehearsal, it's just too much now . . ."

He stopped talking, closed his trembling lips and fought down the pain.

"I hate her for that. I think my daughter hated her, and now I do too. And she choked in front of Valter. We almost didn't get the money."

"What about the explosive device in the basement?" I said.

"What about it?"

"Forensics said it was a pager, linked to a small blasting cap. Your cell phone registered a call to that number to trigger the device. It looks like you cleared everyone out of the house so you could destroy the crime scene. The basement was soaked in gasoline. When you were in the marines, did you ever learn how to set up a remote trigger like that?"

"No. But I saw plenty of them. Once you call the pager, the vibration completes a circuit and triggers the blast. I've never made one."

135

"What about the gasoline?"

"We had some in the garage. Couple of twenty-liter cans. Susan regularly ran out – she would never remember to fill up at the gas station."

I nodded, put down my pen and leant back my chair.

"You think Susan will back you up?" I said.

"I think so. She won't mention the ransom. No way. If she tells the cops she knew about it, she might get some kind of deal from them but the insurance company will come after her for the money. Other than that, I'm praying she'll tell the truth."

In the witness stand, Susan Howell looked every inch a scorned wife. Black pantsuit, white blouse, handkerchief already in her hand and her eyes, although still large and bright, were full of malevolence for Howell.

"How long have you and the defendant been married?" asked King.

"Five years now," she said. Her voice was different than I'd remembered it. In the courtroom it sounded softer, more demure.

"Is it a good marriage?"

"I thought so. We were very much in love. But the last year has been difficult."

"How has it been difficult?"

"Well, Lenny's business took a downturn. There were some contracts which didn't get renewed and we've been struggling financially. That adds pressure to any relationship."

King nodded at Susan Howell, then looked at her desk and turned over a page, read it, and laced her fingers together across her stomach. Any jury can understand that financial worries cause difficulties in marriage. She wanted the jury to identify with Susan, make them feel like she was one of them.

"And how did you both deal with the financial problems?"

"He became withdrawn, and devoted more and more time to the business. We had to make sacrifices – so the condo in Florida was sold, some of the cars. It didn't help. Eventually we were struggling to pay some of our staff, and Lenny decided to put the house up for sale before we got into serious trouble with the mortgage company."

"Have you any idea of the kind of debts that you both faced?"

"Yes. When we counted up the figures, it worked out at approximately ten million dollars."

Two male jurors blew air through their lips, with a pained expression. That was the kind of debt that could make people desperate and King was playing on it. She spent around ten minutes with Susan, breaking down that figure, cementing it into a detailed reality. By the time she'd finished this line of questioning several jurors were shaking their heads, or underlining figures in their notepads. This was the only real motive that the prosecution had, and they needed to play on it – hype it up any way they could.

"Was there any hope of turning the business around to satisfy some of these debts?"

"Not that I was aware of. I think Lenny managed to persuade two of the smaller insurance companies to come back with their kidnap and ransom work, but apart from one major client and the two he got back, Lenny had lost around forty per cent of his business."

"I want to move on now, Mrs Howell, and talk about the day Caroline Howell disappeared. That was July second. Where were you on that date?"

"In Hawaii, on vacation with some girlfriends."

"Did you speak to your husband that day?"

"I got a call from Lenny around seven a.m. That would make it around one p.m. in New York. I was still asleep when he called and left a message. I got up, had a shower and picked up his message at breakfast. He sounded agitated. So I called him back. He said he was in the office, in the middle of something and he would call me back. The girls and I went out hiking and then hit the spa. So it was later that evening when he called to ask if Caroline had been in touch with me that day. I told him she hadn't and he hung up. Later I found out she was missing and I got a flight home the next day."

"Why was your husband angry?"

"Objection, Your Honor, leading," I said.

A nod from the judge, "Sustained."

The prosecutor didn't argue. She focused on her witness and moved on quickly.

"How did your husband seem to you, when you spoke on the phone that day?"

"Unusual. I can normally tell when something is bothering him. He was short with me, and he didn't say goodbye at the end of the call, like he normally does. I thought he was anxious and pissed about something."

"Did you talk again, before you got home?"

"Yes. I called him from the airport. He just said, 'Get home.' That was it."

"What happened when you returned home after your flight?"

"I saw the police cars outside the house. Seeing that brought it all into perspective. At first I'd thought she must've met a boy and run off for a few days. Seventeen-year-old kids rebel – in one way or another. I did. But the police cars made me fearful. When I walked into the house I needed to get a stiff drink, to calm myself down, right away. I just didn't want to deal with something like that. I had my own problems – the mortgage, the creditors . . ."

I watched King nodding along to the answer, but I could tell that inside she was seething. Three of the women on the jury had taken a dislike to Mrs Howell. You could see it on their faces. Their chins were tucked in against their necks, eyebrows raised, heads turned to the side – it was a look which screamed *"I don't believe you just said that."* Here was a woman who could only see the disappearance and murder of her stepdaughter in terms of how that affected her, how that made her feel. As if it was selfish of the daughter to do such a thing.

"But you remained strong, for your husband?" said King.

"Objection, leading."

A look from the judge sufficed.

"What do you remember of those first days when Caroline was missing?" said King, lowering her voice and slowing her delivery in an attempt to inject some emotion into her witness.

"I tried to stay strong, for Lenny. It was tough. The house was constantly filled with policemen, federal agents and all of Lenny's people. And the reporters just wouldn't leave us alone. That was the worst of it, the press attention. I just couldn't abide it."

I wrote down her answer in full. Underlined it. This was my way in.

CHAPTER TWENTY-NINE

Before Mrs Howell did herself any more damage, King moved things along.

"During the nineteen days when Caroline Howell had allegedly disappeared, did you ever go into the basement of your property?"

"No. I think I've only ever been in there once, shortly after I moved in. I was looking for something. I don't like cellars, they freak me out so I never went back down."

"To the best of your knowledge, during those days when Caroline was supposedly missing, did you ever see your husband go into the basement?"

"Yes," said Susan, confidently.

I couldn't help myself. My head swiveled and Howell's eyes met mine.

"When did you see your husband go into the basement?"

"On the night of the fire."

"Tell us what you saw."

"It was sometime after midnight. I was in the kitchen, fixing a drink. A lot of people were leaving the house. Ahhm, I think it must've been like a shift change-over thing. Most of the cops left, and the FBI agents, or most of them, went outside too. I took my drink and headed back down the corridor, I was going to go upstairs and watch TV. Take my mind off things. Just before the stairs is a hallway to the left of the main corridor. I saw Lenny open the basement door at the far end of the corridor and walk down the stairs."

Her answer sounded good. It had been practiced, no doubt, many times. King would've asked her this question over and over, and made her put in as much detail as possible. Details artificially inflate credibility and King knew it.

She lowered her voice, almost to a whisper, and asked Susan, "Are you sure it was him?"

"I'm positive. I saw him from behind, he was wearing his black suit, and he walked down the stairs. He was carrying a large can of something."

"Could it have been someone else you saw?"

"No. I didn't think anything of it, at the time. I remember when I walked past and I got into the main hallway, I saw Peter McAuley and Marlon talking. There was no one else in the house that it could have been. The FBI wouldn't just wander into someone's basement, and our driver, George, he was a . . . well . . . he can't walk straight. So it wasn't him. It could only have been Lenny."

The Silk Hammer was cutting off as many escape routes as possible, nailing her evidence down.

"You mentioned he was carrying a can. Could it have been a can of gasoline?"

"I didn't see the can clearly, I suppose it could have been."

As much as some of the jury disliked Susan Howell, they sat forward for that last answer. Some made notes. Others swung their attention back to Howell. They were making that judgment – could this man have killed his own daughter?

"What happened after that?" said King.

"The house filled again, with the police and the FBI. I remember that the insurance guy came with the ransom. Then mostly everyone left. There was one FBI agent around, and George was downstairs. Around three a.m. the whole house shook. I'd managed to fall asleep and the noise woke me up. Then I saw that all the windows in the house had blown out, and George burst into the room. I don't remember too much after that, it's all a bit hazy. I tried to get out, but I fell and I must've hit my head. I knew though, on some level, that the whole house was on fire, but I couldn't get up. Maybe George tried to lift me, maybe. Then I blanked out. Next thing I remember was waking up in hospital."

A juddering breath escaped from Susan Howell, and she wiped her eyes with the tissue.

"When you were told that Caroline's blood was found in the basement, what was your reaction?"

"At first, I . . . I couldn't believe it. I couldn't get my head around it. Perhaps it was shock, or something still lingering after my head injury, but for a long time I just couldn't process it. Then I learned about the fake ransom drop in the train station, and that Lenny had gotten ten million dollars from the insurers, not two, like he'd told the FBI – and all of our financial problems over that year . . . It didn't take me too long to realize just what had been staring me in the face all along – Lenny lied to everyone so he could steal . . ."

"Objection, Your Honor," I said. I couldn't let the comment come out. Even so, the jury would be finishing her sentence in their thoughts.

Judge Schultz leaned over and addressed the witness directly. "Mrs Howell, you are here to give evidence to this jury regarding your factual recollection of events. You are not here to speculate."

"I'm sorry," she said, and then burst into tears with perfect timing – almost as if she'd been prepped to cry when the judge gave her a talking-to about stepping over the line.

"Mrs Howell, please take a moment," said King.

We waited while Susan apologized, dabbed at her eyes with her sleeve. Then King came forward and handed her a fresh handkerchief. It quickly became smeared with mascara. The prosecutor slowly moved back behind her desk, letting the jury watch the crying witness. The longer she sobbed, the greater the sympathy from the jury.

I sat back and looked at King. She shrugged her shoulders.

"Mrs Howell, I know how difficult this is for you, but I have one last question. Did your husband ask you to take part in his scheme to defraud his insurance company out of ten million dollars?"

"Yes. He asked me to distract agent Lynch when he came into our home with the insurance agent. I refused."

"Thank you," said King.

I thought back to my conversation with Howell in the cells three months before; no way was he expecting this from Susan. I turned to my client and saw he was deflated, but not yet defeated. His chin hung low over the table, and he couldn't look Susan in the eye.

I thought about what King had achieved with this witness. She wasn't likeable, but she painted Howell as a debt-ridden, angry, liar. The testimony that she'd seen Howell go down the stairs and into the basement with a can of gasoline was the main point, but I couldn't just jump into that – I had to go softly at first.

Before I stood to begin the cross, I felt a hand on my forearm. It was Howell.

"Go easy on her," he said.

From the corner of my eye, I saw someone stretch an arm over the rails that separated the gallery from the lawyers. I turned and saw it was Agent Harper. She was dressed casually – leather jacket, jeans, and her hair looked exactly the same as the last day I saw her – tied back in a ponytail. In her hand she held a small piece of paper and she was offering it to me. I hadn't seen Harper since Howell's arrest. She greeted me with a half-smile, but that disappeared as soon as she'd handed over the note.

I took it, unfolded the paper and read.

"Don't ask Susan Howell about the phone calls to Hawaii."

The paper held my attention for longer than it should. Was Harper playing me? Or trying to save me from a car crash that I hadn't seen coming? She sat back down, and I saw her scan the crowd. Agent Lynch folded his arms and gave Harper a look that said he wanted to strangle her.

I tore up the note, put it in my pocket.

Right then, I wasn't sure if this was a play; an act between Harper and Lynch to prevent me pulling at the sensitive threads of the prosecution case. From our limited time together that night of the fire, I knew Harper was skeptical about Howell's involvement. She'd worked out the drop at the train station was fake, and now Howell was testifying to that. Maybe she bought it? Maybe not. Either she was still unconvinced of his guilt and she was helping me, or she was setting me up. I made up my mind to ignore the warning. The phone calls weren't that relevant. I just needed to question her impression of her husband from that call. If there were any surprises coming out of that testimony I would've known by now. It was a risk, but a low one. And if it blew up in my face, at least I'd know whose side Harper was on.

CHAPTER THIRTY

"Mrs Howell, the prosecutor asked you about those initial days after Caroline went missing. Do you remember what you just said in response to that?" I asked.

"Not exactly," she said.

"Let me remind you, I took a note of it. You said, '*The reporters just wouldn't leave us alone. That was the worst of it, the press attention. I just couldn't abide it.*' Correct?"

"Yes, that's what I said. That was how I felt."

"So, the thought that your stepdaughter might have been kidnapped, raped or murdered wasn't your main concern at that time?"

Before I'd finished the question I saw the twitch. A small, fast movement of the head, a blink, a downturn of the mouth; all of it there and gone in an instant as she registered her mistake and sought to correct it.

"Of course she was my main concern. I was out of my mind with worry about Caroline. The added pressure from the media made it so much worse."

A flick of the hair – she thought she was back on track – panic over.

"You and your husband are estranged, isn't that right?" I said.

She didn't answer. Susan Howell merely knitted her eyebrows together and stared at me open-mouthed. I figured she didn't understand the question.

"Mrs Howell, you and your husband are no longer together. The relationship is over?"

"I can't see how it can continue," she said.

"So you'll be filing for divorce?"

"When this is all over, yes," she said, tugging a lock of blonde hair behind her ear.

"Who is your divorce lawyer?"

Her eyes popped open.

"Well . . . I . . . is that relevant?"

"Just answer the questions, Mrs Howell. I decide if something is relevant," said Judge Schultz.

Susan nodded, held her hands up and then crossed her legs.

"Jeffrey Penning, of Gore & Penning," she said, without further hesitation.

"Mr Penning handles celebrity divorces, doesn't he, Mrs Howell?"

"I believe so, yes. He's very successful."

"I'm sure Mr Penning explained to you that if your husband is convicted of murder, and spends the rest of his life in prison, that you would come out a lot better in the divorce?"

The same twitch of the head. It was almost like she was reeling from a jab. She said nothing.

King stood to object, but Judge Schultz was already shaking her head at the prosecutor before she'd opened her mouth. The jury needed to know if the witness was being impartial, or was motivated by a potentially large divorce settlement.

"Mrs Howell?"

"He might have said something like that."

"You mean he *did* say precisely that?"

She glanced at her shoes, stroked her thighs, and raised her head. "Yes. Yes, he did."

"If your husband is convicted of murder, the state will look after him for the rest of his life. He won't need any assets, or income to live. He has no surviving dependents. You would get, what? Ninety, maybe ninety-five per cent of the marriage assets?"

"Perhaps, I really don't know."

"You told the jury you and your husband are approximately ten million dollars in debt. Seven million of that is the outstanding mortgage, correct?"

"Yes."

"And what is the latest valuation of the family property?"

"I'm not sure."

I looked at the jury. Ignored the witness. A couple of the female jurors, and at least one of the male jurors, were nodding. They had probably been through divorce themselves. They knew that Mrs Howell

had prepared for this divorce like she was getting ready for war —
that's what happens when there's money to be split.

"Mrs Howell, your divorce lawyer asked you to prepare a complete
portfolio of marriage assets, did he not?"

"Ahm, yes."

"So you had your property, stocks, shares, cars, spoons, everything
valued, isn't that right?"

"Oh, sorry, yes, I remember. The real estate broker thought we
could get twelve million for the house. We won't get that now. The
house is in ruins."

I'd already asked Leonard Howell my next question and he was
sure of the answer.

"Mrs Howell, the insurance on the house is for fifteen million
dollars, isn't that right?"

"Ahm, I think so."

"You think so. The house is in joint names. Haven't the insurance
company paid you the compensation check already?"

Silence. She considered it for all of five seconds before deciding
she couldn't lie about this at all.

"Yes, they have."

I paused for effect, then said, "The fact that you received a fifteen-
million-dollar check almost slipped your mind for a second there,
didn't it?"

She shook her head.

"And the other assets come to just over four million dollars."

No reply. I kept going, she was on the ropes.

"And your debt, which you know to the penny, is ten million.
So there's fifteen million dollars in your account and another four
on the table for you in the divorce, Mrs Howell?"

She took some time to compose herself and think of a way out of
this; sipping water from a plastic cup, setting the cup back down on
the edge of the witness stand, leaning back in her seat and folding
her arms before she delivered her answer.

"To be honest, this is the last thing on my mind. I want justice
for Caroline. I've lost my stepdaughter, Mr Flynn," she said.

"You still haven't answered my question. Apart from the insurance money, if Leonard Howell is convicted of murder, you stand

to make almost four million dollars. If he is acquitted, you'll likely get around two million?"

"Yes," she said, loudly. "I still don't see what my divorce has to do with this?"

I had to move fast on that one. Judge Schultz was sliding forward in her seat, ready to explain to the witness that their job is to answer questions, not ask questions. I saved the judge the trouble, and handed the witness a document.

"Do you recognize this, Mrs Howell?"

A glance at the page and she nodded her head.

"It's my statement to the police."

"You gave this statement to the police after the fire at your property?"

"I did."

"At the bottom of page three is a signature, confirming the statement is both truthful and accurate. Is that your signature, Mrs Howell?"

The pages turned quickly, she found her signature on the copy and said, "Yes."

"And did you read this statement before you signed it?"

"I did."

"Mrs Howell, the jury will want to know why you lied in your earlier testimony. I want to ask you, is it because you think you'll do better in the divorce or is there some other reason?"

Open-mouthed, Susan Howell looked at the prosecutor and then the judge.

"I have told the truth," she said.

"Are you sure?"

"Of course I'm sure."

"Mrs Howell, in your earlier testimony you told this jury that you saw the defendant go into the basement carrying a can of gasoline on the night of the fire. You didn't mention this in your statement to the police?"

"No, I didn't think it was important at the time."

"Mrs Howell, you spoke to the police just after your house burned to the ground. You didn't think to mention to them that your husband went down into the basement just a few hours before the fire with a can of gasoline?"

She shrugged her shoulders. I didn't press for an answer – I was about to supply one.

"And you didn't mention to the police that the defendant tried to involve you in some kind of plot to defraud his insurance company. You didn't mention that either?"

There was no answer, only more tears.

"Mrs Howell, when did you decide to invent this story?"

"I did not invent this."

"You did not mention any of this to the police, three days after the fire. Did your memory suddenly improve when you were sitting in your lawyer's office discussing your divorce?"

"This has nothing to do with my divorce. I saw someone go down into that basement."

"Someone? So you're not sure who you saw?"

"I've already explained, it could only have been Lenny."

I paused. Checked my notes. It had gone as well as it could have. The jury doubted her – and that was all that I had to do – instill doubt.

One of the toughest parts of cross-examination is knowing when to shut the hell up and sit your ass down. Before you finish, there is always that nagging doubt. Did I ask the right questions? Was there some part of her evidence that's important which I didn't cover? Have I done enough?

Only with experience do you begin to get a feeling when the moment is right to stop. Leonard Howell's life was on the line – it was in my hands. That brought additional pressure, made me doubt myself more than I normally did.

One more.

"Mrs Howell, you described a voicemail message and a telephone conversation with your husband while you were in Hawaii, and around the same time as Caroline Howell's disappearance. You said your husband was angry, agitated. He denies this."

"He was angry."

"Mrs Howell, the defendant will testify that he was not angry, as you say. Is it possible you misjudged it and it was concern over his daughter's safety?"

I knew, as soon as I'd finished the question, I'd made a huge mistake. The witness wasn't looking at me – she was looking at King. I glanced at the prosecutor – saw that knowing smile.

What the hell had I just done?

CHAPTER THIRTY-ONE

"He was angry on the phone," said Susan.

I nodded, and sat down a couple of questions too late. Inside, I was screaming at myself – but I didn't let any of that show. If I did, the jury would pick up on it in a heartbeat. And King would do her level best to show it. She was walking toward the witness before I had time to pull my seat below the table.

"Mrs Howell, it has been put to you that your husband's demeanor was not as you described it. Are you sure your recollection is correct?"

"Positive," she said, again looking at me and with triumph in her eyes.

"Your Honor, I have a motion for the court," said King. The judge sent the jury out and called us both for a sidebar.

"What's the motion?" said Judge Schutlz.

"The motion is to introduce cell phone data, from the defendant and the witness," said King.

A cold sensation spread over my skin.

"This is an ambush, Judge. Any relevant information should've been handed over in discovery. And how did the police obtain this information? Was there a warrant issued, because I haven't seen one," I said.

"Your Honor, the defense opened this line of questioning with the witness. Mr Flynn put it to her that she was being dishonest in relation to her impression of her husband from those phone calls. We didn't know that was disputed and it so happens we have relevant evidence for the jury to consider in relation to that point. In fairness to the jury, they should have the full picture. We have the voicemail itself and the relevant cell data for the calls," said King.

I didn't argue back – the point was lost. Judge Schultz would allow the cell phone evidence.

"I'm granting the motion, let's get the jury back in."

If I'd pressed my objection any further I'd have risked alienating the judge – and it wouldn't have gotten me anywhere. So I nodded, turned and walked back to my seat like nothing had happened. It was the first time that I had an opportunity to get a full view of the crowd. Behind the prosecution table I saw their witnesses, spread out amongst the crowd. Funny, the prosecution witnesses normally sit behind the prosecutor, the defense witnesses behind the defense table; in many ways a criminal trial was like a church wedding that nobody wanted to attend. I saw the fire investigators, the experts, SAC Lynch, and George. Howell's driver sat with his head bowed, rubbing his knee. Poor guy – sitting on a cramped bench wouldn't do his leg any good.

Further back, close to the doors of the courtroom, I saw Harper staring at me. Disappointment writ large on her face. I should've listened to her. First chance I got, she and I would talk.

A face appeared behind Harper, straining to take a look. Bald, white beard, the face that I'd seen first thing this morning; Max Copeland. He probably wanted to check out his competition, size me up, and see how I handled myself in the courtroom.

If I was him, I wouldn't be too impressed so far.

"Your re-direct, Miss King," said the Judge. King removed two USB memory sticks from a wallet in the prosecution file. Handed one to me. The other she slotted into the port on the right side of the large plasma TV closest to the witness stand and swiped her hand across the lower half of the TV to switch it on. An ADA handed her the remote, and she held it behind her back.

"Mrs Howell, Mr Flynn has suggested that you are lying when you said your husband was angry in the phone calls he made to you. Can you confirm that you saved the voicemail he left you on the day of Caroline's disappearance?" said King.

"I did."

"Is this the voicemail?"

She whipped around and hit play. The screen turned a vivid blue, and I heard the beginning of a voicemail introduction.

"*Saved messages. You have one saved message.* It's me. I'm in the office, call me back."

"That's the message," said Susan.

For a second, I thought I was in the clear. The message was innocuous, and fair enough, he did sound a little pissed off.

But King wasn't finished. She returned to a file of pages that sat in a lilac folder on the desk. She flicked through it and came out with some copies of a report. I'd seen those kinds of reports before; the FBI Forensics logo sat brightly in the right-hand corner of the title page. She handed a copy to me, one to the judge, and one to the witness.

"Mrs Howell, this is a forensic analysis carried out by the FBI on the defendant's cell phone. The report catalogs points of origin for cell phone calls made in the United States by the cell phone number at the top left of the page. First of all, can you confirm that is your husband's cell phone number?"

"That's his number," said Susan.

King directed the witness to a particular page.

I was way ahead of her. I'd read the date on the relevant call, flicked forward to the map which they append at the end of these reports, and pushed the whole report in front of Howell. I expected my client to pick up the report and at least flick through it. He left it on the table, without picking it up or even looking at it. That wasn't good. It meant Howell knew what was coming, and he didn't care. My shoulders sagged and I felt as though a lead weight in my chest had suddenly sunk into my gut. The judge nodded, and the ADAs started passing out the reports amongst the jurors.

I looked at King. She didn't even bother pointing out the anger that came across in the voicemail. The jury had ears and they could pick that up on their own. No, King was winding up the bat, ready to hit one out of the park.

"Mrs Howell, please turn to the last page of this report. You will see the FBI have matched the geographic origin of this call to a cell-phone tower in Virginia. Do you agree?"

Mrs Howell studied the report.

"Yes, that looks like where the call was made from. The times match."

"So your husband left you an angry voicemail saying he was in the office and you should call him back, and this evidence indicates that your husband made the call from Virginia. Mrs Howell, where is your husband's office?"

"Manhattan. He was lying to me in the voicemail. He wasn't where he said he was."

"Mrs Howell, just one final question to wrap this up. You will see the map on the last page of the report has a blue dot and a red dot marked '1' close beside it. For the benefit of the jury, the blue dot is the location where Caroline's car was found, and the red dot is the rough location where the defendant made the call and left you the voicemail message. Mrs Howell, your husband seems to have called you on the day of your stepdaughter's disappearance, and left you that message, from a location half a mile from where your stepdaughter's car was eventually found – do you know why your husband would be in that area instead of in his office?"

"No, I've no idea."

"Any idea about why he would want to conceal his real location from you that day?" said King.

"To give himself a false alibi," said Susan.

I objected, the judge sustained it, and the jury were told to disregard the last statement of the witness. There was about as much hope of them disregarding the statement as there was of me winning the case. King had played it perfectly. I had no doubt that if I hadn't asked about the phonecall, King would've recalled Susan Howell in order to introduce this evidence. Her best play was to get me to open the door to this line of questioning – so the jury and the judge could see her slamming that door back in my face. I hadn't seen it coming, and the jury knew it. It made them doubt me, made them doubt my client. Great evidence is even better if you can make your opponent appear as though they'd brought it up. Trials are mind games. The prosecution would seek to undermine me and my confidence at every opportunity. They wanted me to question my tactics, make me afraid to ask questions.

No way was I gonna let that happen.

I ran my fingers over my tie, smoothing it down. It was a nervous reflex, and one that I told myself to stop. Every time my fingers touched that tie pin I thought about Howell. I would never hand over the pin. Not while we were both still breathing.

CHAPTER THIRTY-TWO

Howell slumped over the desk in the dull gray consultation booth, below the courtroom. Elbows on the table, fingers in his hair, as if he was about to ram his head into the pine desk.

My back was to the door of the eight-by-six room. A chair sat empty in front of me. I put my heel to the door, hands in my pockets and stared at the frayed, navy carpet tiles. Neither of us spoke. I couldn't win a case for a man who was bent on self-destruction, a man who lied to me, who kept things from me. When I set foot in a courtroom, knowledge is power. I had to know more about the case than anyone else. That was my thing. I just had my ass kicked because the prosecution knew more than me. This wasn't going to work. I checked my watch. We had five minutes before we were due back, and I needed to be able to rescue something from Susan Howell. I had one more bite of the cherry.

"Lenny, unless you tell me everything I'm going to walk. I can't represent you if you won't work with me. You want to die in jail? Fine. Don't bring me down with you. Don't hold things back. Remember, you called me six months ago. You wanted me in on this. So use me. If the jury had to make a decision right now, you'd get convicted for her murder and the real killer gets away. Do you want that?"

No movement. Blank eyes boring into the names of old felons that had been scraped into the flesh of the desk.

"Sixty seconds. That's all you've got. You talk, or I walk."

His left hand slipped from behind his head, and landed lazily on the table. His eyes closed slowly, gently, almost like the slightest movement caused him pain.

Fifty seconds.

I heard the soft *tap, tap, tap* of his foot beneath the desk. My breath, his breath, and the tap of cheap shoes on a thin, loose, carpet tile were the only sounds in the room.

Thirty-five seconds.

The soft whisper of the guard's key chain, distant and muted as he walked away from the consultation booth, and back to the security desk.

Twenty Seconds.

I kicked off the door, stood up straight. My hands dug into my pockets and I stared at Howell one last time.

"Good luck. I'm deeply sorry about your daughter," I said, turning to leave.

The door handle had turned a quarter inch when he said, "I was in a cemetery."

I froze. Thinking that it would be wise to crank the handle and leave Howell to his fate. I'd been so mad at getting nailed in the courtroom by King, I'd forgotten that I'd just given Howell an open question. God knows what he was about to tell me. If he told me that he'd taken Caroline – I wouldn't represent him. Shit. I wasn't thinking straight. I'd been treating Lenny with kid gloves when I should've been pounding him, getting him ready for the trial of his life.

"Which cemetery?" I asked, still holding the door handle.

"Green Pastures, in Virginia."

"What were you doing there?"

"Visiting a grave," he said.

I pulled the door handle down the whole way, cracked the seal on the door.

"Wait, please wait, Eddie. I'm sorry. I was visiting my first wife."

I let go of the handle and listened as the door sucked itself shut. His head was up, and his eyes were focused on me. Pulling out a chair, I sat down opposite Howell.

He nodded, leaned back, and took a photo from his pants pocket. It was a small picture – laminated to keep it from fraying in his pocket. He handed it to me. Howell's first wife had long brown hair that spilled over her shoulders. She wore a floral dress and sat on a clump of rocks looking out to sea. From her neck hung a silver chain with a butterfly pendant.

She was beautiful.

"I bought her that pendant on our first date. She wore it almost every day," he said.

"So, was it an anniversary of some kind? Is that why you went to the grave?"

"In a way, yeah."

It wasn't great. In fact, it was pretty thin, but it was a better excuse for being in the area than kidnapping your daughter and dumping her car. It didn't tell me why he lied to his current wife about it.

"And do you visit her on every anniversary?"

"I used to go there every week. But I stopped soon after I met Susan. She didn't like me spending time there. Somehow, Susan was jealous. Maybe because we had never broken up, and now that she was dead, we never would. One night, Susan told me that it was like I was cheating on her with my dead wife. God, why didn't I end it with Susan sooner?"

"So that's why you lied to her about where you were?" I said.

"Yeah."

"So why were you there that day in particular?"

"It's the day she passed. July second."

Nodding, I said, "Okay, but there's one thing I don't get. When you left that voicemail message you were pissed as all hell. Why?"

He didn't answer at first. His head fell, his breathing became fast.

"It's her family plot. For years it was just my first wife and her parents. But when I got to the grave that day, the soil had been turned over. Somebody else must have been put in the plot . . . on . . . on top of her."

He stood and began pacing up and down the floor, drawing in great gulps of air and letting it stream out of his nostrils. He looked ready to kill somebody.

"Lenny, take a moment. I need to know. This is important."

I sat in silence, giving him time. He had to wind down on his own. I'd read Howell's military service record. He was decorated, highly trained, and he'd left the marines and went straight to the police force with glowing recommendations. Those references helped when he left the force and set up Howell Security – the kidnap and ransom game was ripe for someone like him. He'd been on the inside, with the marines, the police, and the FBI. But for all his medals and specialist training, there were rumors from his days in the force. Rumors that suspects died from beatings, that fatal shootings weren't all as clean as IAB had made out. For the first time, I saw the old Howell. This was not a guy to cross. If you did, chances were that you'd end up dead rather than in jail.

"My first wife's sister died a few years ago. She was buried some-place else. At least that's what I heard. But the cemetery she'd been buried in had to be moved. A development commission were regenerating the land. I found out about it last year. I'd received a letter about it because I hold the papers to the family plot. I wrote back and told them to dump her body in the river. I didn't want it. They must've moved her anyway, put it in the last space in the plot with the rest of the family."

"You're not making much sense, Lenny. You're telling me your dead wife's sister got buried there recently – and that's what made you mad?"

I heard a dull crack from his neck as his head snapped in my direction. Eyes gleaming wet.

"She died *because* of her sister. I didn't want her stinking corpse anywhere near my wife."

I didn't know anything about this. Didn't know his late wife even had a sister, much less that she was responsible for her death. For the want of anything better to ask, I said, "I'm sorry. What was her name, your wife's sister?"

"Julie Rosen," he said.

CHAPTER THIRTY-THREE

I was careful not to let the name register in my facial expression. My mind felt as if it was rolling down a long hill, somersaulting and crashing into boulders and occasionally when it hit a tree, the spinning would stop, just for the briefest of moments and in that second an image almost formed in my mind, and then the world turned as the tumbling began again.

I was embarrassed to ask, I felt like I should've already known, but I managed to ask him to remind me of his first wife's name. Rebecca. Howell would say no more than that. I'd pushed him too far. He had retreated into himself, again. I thought about threatening to walk away, but this time I knew he would just let go – he had given me everything that he could at that point. Forcing any more out of him could damage that mind even more and there wasn't much left in him.

I got up and left the consultation booth.

Harry picked up my call on his cell. I was surprised he managed to take the call as I expected him to be in court.

"It's me. I need you to grab the Julie Rosen files and get up here to White Plains. Can you do that?" I said.

"What do you mean, can I do that?" said Harry.

"Well, don't you have a court list full of cases?"

Silence.

"Oh, oh that. Yeah, well I'm sure I can get another judge to fill in for a day. Where are you staying?"

"There's a hotel not far, just beyond the overpass closest to the courthouse. When do you think you can make it?"

"I can be there in an hour. Why? What's happened?" said Harry.

156

"I'll tell you when you get here. I'm just glad you can make it. How come? Did you have a case collapse on you today? I thought you were pretty busy."

I heard some mirthless laughter on the other end of the line.

"Thanks to you, Eddie, I've got a lot of free time. I'm on a leave of absence. It was that or get suspended. I got the call from the Judicial Complaints Commissioner about a half hour ago," he said.

"You were threatened with suspension? For what?"

"Tampering with an inquiry. Apparently you paid a visit to Max Copeland's office this morning."

My fist took a chunk out of the old plaster that peeled away from the corridor wall.

"I'm sorry, Harry. I just talked to him, I didn't threaten him. Well, maybe a little. And his security guy put his hands on me first."

"I know you thought you were doing the right thing. Doesn't matter, they were probably going to suspend me anyway. Copeland filed his final appeal brief this morning. He claims Julie Rosen had defective counsel, and that she was mentally unfit to plead."

"He's saying she was crazy?"

"Yeah. I had a psych report on Julie, but I only commissioned it after she was convicted. The psychiatrist died of a heart attack two years ago. So he's not around to defend his position and say she was fit to plead. What we know is that a year into her sentence she was declared insane. If Copeland can convince a judge she was mentally unfit to instruct counsel at the time she would automatically get a new trial. Because she's dead, she can't be tried again and would probably be acquitted."

"And what would happen to you?"

"If I was at the bar, I could lose my license. But because I'm a judge, I'm out. Think about it, it's prima facie evidence that my judgment is compromised. No decision of mine would stand after that. I'd be automatically appealed for every single decision I make because of this case. My position would be untenable. Career over. Everything I've fought for, every sacrifice just to get here . . . it would all be for nothing. The commissioner would insist I resign."

"It's not going to happen. I'll make sure of it."

"There's nothing you can do. Say, why do you need the Rosen papers now anyway? What's the sudden urgency?"

I debated what I should tell Harry on the phone. If he thought I might endanger the Rosen case appeal, he might refuse to come up here. But I trusted him, and the truth was more important to Harry than covering his own ass.

"There's a connection to the Caroline Howell case. My client was visiting his wife's grave on the morning Caroline Howell disappeared. He said his wife's sister was Julie Rosen, and that Julie had something to do with the death of his wife. Any of this ring any bells with you, Harry?"

At first he didn't respond, but I could hear his breath rush down the phone.

"I'm stunned. This is all new to me. I mean, I knew there was family, but Julie didn't talk to them, and wouldn't allow us to go near them. Julie never faced charges for anything other than infanticide and arson. Maybe it's a coincidence, maybe it's just the same name and not the same Julie Rosen?" said Harry.

He could've been right. I thanked him and said I'd see him in the courthouse. I headed back to the courtroom and saw Harper leaning against a pillar and sipping take-out coffee. Before I approached her I looked up and down the hall and made sure Lynch wasn't watching us. He wasn't around, or at least I couldn't see him. Harper nodded at me and I made my way over.

"You trust me now, Counselor?" she said.

"Why'd you warn me?" I said.

Harper took a sip of coffee and stared into the cup as she gave her answer. "I still don't think he killed his daughter. He wouldn't put her at risk for money. I don't care what the evidence says, I trust my gut."

"I wish your boss thought that way," I said.

"Me too."

"I have to say this is a strange position for a federal agent. You don't think he did it. I get that. But why are you willing to put your career on the line for Howell? You don't know him, so what's the play?"

"My boss didn't see the note. He never will. You asked the damn question anyway. There's nothing he can do. I'm still taking a risk, but it's a small one. And there's no play here, I don't want Howell's money. I just don't want to see an innocent man go down."

I detected something in Harper's voice.

"I kinda got the impression there was a little personal history between you and Lynch. Is this about him? Proving him wrong?"

"Between you and me, there's history but none of it is good. That still doesn't change what I believe and it's not the reason I'm doing this."

The clerk opened the courtroom doors, calling everyone back in. Recess was over.

"Why are you doing this?"

Harper tossed her coffee into the trash, stood up straight and said, "Whatever happened to just doing it because it's the right thing to do?"

Five minutes later, the judge and jury were reseated and I was back on the case.

"Mrs Howell, your husband went to that location, in Virginia, to visit the grave of his first wife, isn't that right?" I said.

She seemed more relaxed. Maybe she knew she'd already landed a few good punches during her testimony and didn't need to worry about it any more.

"I don't know for sure. Maybe," said Susan.

"He went there every year, on the anniversary of her death. Don't you remember?"

"Like I said, maybe he did, maybe he didn't. I wasn't there."

"Precisely. You weren't there, Mrs Howell, so you can't say for sure why your husband was there or what he was doing, correct?"

"Correct," she said.

I didn't dare ask anything further. With the way King had laid that trap for me, God knows what else I could've walked into. I decided to end the cross. And let Mrs Howell leave the witness stand before she did any more damage.

"Nothing further for this witness," I said.

Susan stood and as she stepped out of the witness stand, her eyes lingered on Howell. I found it hard to interpret the look for sure, it was probably a mixture of knowing she'd won and a bitterness that he'd finally seen through her – right to her core. The ugliness which lies at the heart of some people is their most closely guarded secret – they don't like others knowing about the beast that lies inside.

"How could you?" said Howell. He didn't shout it. Just said it, loud enough for the jury to hear.

His wife put her hand to her mouth, and at first I thought she was stifling a laugh. No, she was telegraphing his slight, so that the jury could see Howell's words hit her deep.

"Keep it down," I whispered.

The judge focused her attention on Howell, ready to strike down any further outbursts.

"Caroline always hated you," he said.

At this, Susan fell to her knees and wept as if she'd taken a gut punch. I heard a few gasps from the jury, and hushed whispers. I guessed the whispers might've come from TV casting agents, marveling at her performance.

The judge stamped her foot, "Mr Howell, you have a lawyer to speak for you in this court. Do not speak, except to your lawyer. I will not tolerate anyone being abused in my courtroom. That's your second strike. One more outburst and I will have you removed and the trial will continue in your absence. Do you understand?"

He said nothing. Simply stared back at the judge. A silence filled the room, spreading out from the bench and touching every person. Howell's eyes had gone, lost in a world of suffering that no man could take from him. There was pity in Judge Shultz's eyes. She could see this was a man who had lost the most important person in his life – and that aching was making him crazy.

"Lenny, stop it," I said.

His eyes reverted to the floor, and fresh tears came. He held them back. There was some kind of resolve left, and I hoped it would be enough to see him through.

The next prosecution witness got up in readiness for their appearance on the stand. King was about to call them, but she'd stopped and waited to let the scene with Howell and Susan play out before the jury. She was ready now, the moment had passed.

"Your Honor, the People call their next witness: Doctor Dallas Birch."

My client covered his face. I'd done everything I could to prepare him, but this would be beyond most parents. Doctor Birch was an experienced Blood Pattern Analyst. He'd examined the blood found in the basement, and made two conclusions. The first was that Caroline was beaten to death in that basement. The second conclusion was that she was beaten to death by her father. The details were almost too horrible to bear. I knew then, whatever Howell had left wouldn't survive the next twenty minutes.

May 2002

Upstate New York

A car pulled up outside the cottage. Julie heard the tires crawl through the gravel. It was almost four in the afternoon and she knew her sister was always early. Not rudely early, just a few minutes. Polite and punctual. Dependable, their mother had called it. Even her sister's punctuality became a source for comparison in Mother's eyes. The volume on the CD player had been turned down low – so she could listen for the car. For all the years of rivalry and mutual loathing that lay in their past, things had become better between Julie and her sister in the last year. Julie wanted to maintain that accord.

It was important.

She heard her sister's key in the front door. Smoothly, she covered the canvas with oilcloth, put down her palate knife and took off her overalls.

A month ago the overalls would've dropped to the floor and she could have simply stepped out of them. Not so, these days. Julie had to maneuver the overalls down, over her swollen belly. Careful that the fasteners should not catch on her jewelry. She threw the overalls in the corner of her makeshift studio, left the room, closed and locked the door.

"I've got all your favorites. All the good stuff. Chocolate chip cookies, raspberry swirl ice cream, popsicles – cherry of course. I got four bags of potato chips in the back seat. But you know it's a treat, right – you need your organic fruit salad first. The muesli . . ." said a voice from the kitchen.

It was Rebecca. Her arms were filled with brown paper sacks, brimming with pasta, French bread, and even the bristles of a pineapple poking over the edge of the bag. Her soft brown hair drooped over her face. That face. Clear, smooth, skin which looked almost golden in sunlight.

The contrast in Rebecca's appearance, as Julie remembered, came in the shape of her eyes. Julie knew Rebecca had her mother's eyes. They are hard, and quick to anger. And they sometimes robbed her of her natural beauty.

But not today.

Rebecca bent from the knees, placed the sacks on the table and exhaled. Julie watched her straighten up and stretch – her left hand pressing into the small of her back, and her right hand gently caressing the bump that made her maternity dress balloon out from her still slender figure.

Julie felt her own bump, and stared at her sister's belly.

They were the same size; the bumps. That was about it. Julie was smaller, and much heavier than her sister. Mother said Rebecca got the looks – but Mother always failed to mention what attribute Julie had received in return. As she grew older, Julie realized that while her sister possessed their mother's clear skin, high cheekbones and long slender frame, Julie had inherited their mother's sickening, spiteful tongue. As she grew older still, Julie realized that she had more in common with her mother than Rebecca ever would.

Julie had inherited her mind. And all of the twisted, thorny branches of thoughts that came with it.

The memory caught Julie unawares – and when she returned her attention to the present, she saw her sister staring at her. No. Not at her. At the bump.

Without speaking, without arrangement, or prompt, both sisters approached one another. They stood only a foot apart, and each of them held their hands on each other's stomachs. Running their fingers over the fabric of their clothes, feeling the smooth, roundness of each other.

Rebecca's eyes were clouded with tears.

The sound of another car on the driveway startled them both. They broke apart and each turned toward the large window in the kitchen that led to the drive.

"Who is it? Who could that be?" said Rebecca.

Julie knew who it was, but said nothing

"Don't tell me it's him. Don't tell me you called him," said Rebecca, backing away, shaking her head.

"Goddamn it, Becca, I was lonely up here. It's been months now, and I'm still clean and the baby is fine. I'm going a little crazy is all."

Her sister took another step backwards, angled her gaze to the corner of her eyes and was about to speak when Julie said, "Not crazy. Relax. Bad choice of words . . . it's just that I'm so lonely."

"But him. We talked about this," said Rebecca.

"He's changed. He's working now. Honest to God. It's not nine to five but he has money in his pocket, he's clean and sober and we're good. I'm being careful, trust me."

The back door that led to the kitchen opened and Scott stood in the doorway. He carried a clutch of shopping bags in his right hand.

"Rebecca, good to see you," he said.

She ignored him for a moment, and instead kept her eyes on Julie. Julie approached Scott and gently took his hand, leading him into the kitchen.

"You remember Scott Barker, Becca?" said Julie.

Rebecca nodded, and placed her hands over her stomach protectively as she eyed Scott.

"I remember the last time we met very well. Do you, Scott?"

He said nothing, looked at the floor and inhaled.

"I remember it very well," Rebecca continued. "I dragged Julie out of your apartment, covered in bruises and vomit and took her to the ER before she OD'd. She almost died. You were too stoned to notice."

"I'm clean now . . ." he said, but didn't get the chance to finish.

"So is Julie. So is her skin. When she was with you she got a lot of bruises, burns, cuts. You're clean and sober, I get that. But are you still beating your girlfriends?"

Scott said, "I got help for that too. I've changed. Julie's changed. We're both better now."

Julie folded herself into Scott's arms and watched her sister back away toward the hallway and the front door.

"Congratulations, by the way, on the baby," said Scott, in a dead voice.

Rebecca's fingers spread over her stomach, shielding it. "We'll talk later, Julie." And with that, she turned and slammed the front door on her way out.

Nuzzling into Scott's chest, Julie said, "Thank you. I'm sorry. I didn't know you were coming up this weekend. I could've warned you Rebecca would be here."

"It doesn't matter," he said.

"I suppose you're right. As long as we're together – that's all I want."

"I know, and we will be together. You, me, the baby. I have one more job — then I'm done," he said.

They kissed, and Julie tasted something familiar on Scott's lips. Something hot, and oak-like and sour. Whiskey. She took his face in her hands and said, "Promise me one thing?"

"What's that?"

"Promise me you won't tell her."

"I swear," said Scott.

CHAPTER THIRTY-FOUR

At least half a dozen jurors didn't know what Blood Pattern Analysis meant. They looked lost. When Doctor Birch explained that he analyzed bloodstains to determine how a violent crime was committed, a murmur floated around the jury. They knew the bad stuff was coming: the photographs, the details of how a young woman died, horribly. I could see some of the jurors steeling themselves; breathing in and out, rolling their shoulders, biting their lips. Two of the male jurors looked apprehensive. Especially the young guy in the white, button-down shirt with a row of pens in his breast pocket. The female jurors appeared to be better prepared for what was to come. The lady in the black top and jeans sat up straighter, her pen in her hand, ready to make notes.

"Doctor Birch, what qualifies you to provide expert testimony in this case?" said King.

The corner of his mouth curled, and Birch looked toward the jury. He was a man who enjoyed discussing his resume.

"For twelve years I was a serving police officer and I developed an interest in blood spatter analysis. It turned out that my interpretation of blood spatter, even while I was an amateur, proved decisive in a number of cases and led directly to arrests and convictions. This, I felt, was my calling. I left the force and trained with the Federal Bureau of Investigation in blood pattern analysis. After gaining my Blood Pattern Analysis certification, I set up my own consultancy practice and so far I've been involved in around three hundred cases in over fifteen years."

I made a few notes and watched the jury appraising Doctor Dallas Birch. He was an impressive man; physically large and with the personality to match. He wore gray pants, a white shirt and blue sports coat. His hair was short and neat. Just like his answers.

I'd done my homework on Birch. A few phone calls to local defense attorneys who were good enough to talk to me. It seemed that Birch was almost part of the furniture in this courthouse. His involvement in blood spatter analysis went right back to the time when the discipline was just starting to become a regular aspect of police investigation. And because he used to be a serving White Plains cop before he went into this field, he got all their blood spatter work. Cops look after their own.

Even though he'd prepared a ton of reports, all of them favorable to the police, he had only testified twice before. In most cases he wasn't required to testify because the perp pleaded guilty, or the defense didn't challenge his report and it just got read into the record. Even if this was all that happened, Birch still came to court to watch. Like the defense attorneys told me, Birch was part of the furniture around here.

King needed to get the expert testimony moving. She got right into it.

The first photograph on the screens was a wide shot of the house after the fire. Smoke was still rising, and part of the structure had collapsed.

"I was tasked by White Plains Police Department to undertake an analysis of the blood found in the defendant's basement, blood-staining on the defendant's spectacles and the blood found in the deceased's vehicle," said Doctor Birch, in an accent not far from Texas. Then again, nowhere is very far from Texas.

He continued, "According to the Fire Marshals, and the structural engineers, the fire had spread to the gas line, and caused the explosion in the basement which compromised the steel supports. Part of the ground floor marble slate had collapsed so I had to wait until the engineers propped the area and made it safe to conduct my examination."

With a flick of her wrist, King pressed the remote control and brought up a photograph of the basement. There was a clear blast pattern in one corner, but the remainder of the room appeared free from smoke damage.

"Talk us through this photograph, Doctor," said King.

"As you can see – the blast was localized to one corner of the basement. The rest of the walls still had some smoke on the surface, but they remained intact. The force of the blast was directed upwards into the remainder of the house. The white paint on the bricks of the basement wall is still clear and relatively bright."

A second click of the remote brought up a new photograph. This time the basement was not lit up with bright lights for the camera. It was in semi-darkness. Apart from the wall to the left of the photograph. A strange, blue smear was visible.

"And this photograph, Doctor Birch. What does it show?"

"The crime scene investigators used a bioluminescent product, such as luminol or some other substance, to search for latent bloodstains that have been cleaned up, and are no longer visible to the naked eye. The blue pattern you can see on the wall is in fact blood."

"And when you attended the scene, and you saw this blood, what exactly did you do?"

"I went through my investigation and evaluation procedures first. So I took some relevant information from the officers on scene, and I examined the spray pattern on the wall. Perhaps if I could see photograph five it would help?"

"Of course," said King, bringing up the photo on screen which was a close-up of the blue blood pattern.

"As you can see, this is a classic pattern. I examined the individual droplets within the pattern, measured them and determined their direction of travel . . ."

"Sorry, can I just stop you there? How did you determine the direction of travel of the blood on the wall?"

"It's quite simple. When a droplet of blood is travelling fast enough and at an angle when it hits a surface, it will create an instant droplet stain. A circle stain, if you will. A drop of blood that falls perfectly vertically will create a circular shape, with a soft serrated edge and a drop that falls at an angle will create more of a balloon shape, with the fat end of the balloon being the first point of contact between the blood and the surface area."

"I see, so you can tell, by the shape of the droplets, what direction they came from?"

"Yes, I used the stringing method to calculate the likely point of origin. Basically, I attach a string to the wall, tracing through the axes of travel to the stain. This allows me to determine angle and point of origin. In this case, the bloodshed event occurred six feet from this wall, and the blood source came from a height of five feet two inches above floor height."

In the short pause, I heard Howell's knuckles cracking beneath the table. His fists were clenched tightly, blanching the skin on his hands and fingers. I placed a hand on his arm, gently, trying to calm him without drawing attention.

King had paused to let the jury take this in. It was technical data that didn't really mean anything. Not until her next question, anyways.

"Doctor, do you know the height of the victim?"

"Yes, Caroline was tall for her age. She was five foot ten inches."

"Was . . ." murmured Howell, under his breath. To Howell, every word spoken in the trial brought her murder into the present, right into every breath he took.

"Tell us, Doctor, your analysis of this scene based on your scientific investigation, please."

I leaned forward, me and the jury and most of the folks in the courtroom. This was how all the blue patterns, strings and calculations added up.

"The pattern on the wall looked to be classic medium velocity impact spatter. The bloody knife, found in the basement with the deceased's blood on it, gives us a piece of corroborating evidence. In my view, the pattern is consistent with a knife or sharp edged instrument striking and severing the carotid artery. At first, the opening of the vein, with the blood under full pressure from the heart, forces the blood to shoot out in a high velocity arc, which then falls as the hole in the vein widens and blood pressure drops. The sweeping pattern of the stain is highly indicative of this type of injury. The victim's height, and my calculations of the point of origin of the bloodshed event match precisely with a fatal blow to the throat."

"How can you be sure of your theory?"

"I was able to reproduce the same spatter pattern in test conditions, using a syringe to simulate the bloodshed."

The screen beside Birch flicked to an image of a white room. The same pattern was on the wall only this time it was red. I'd seen this photo before, but only now did I see that there were a few spots of blood on the floor of the test area. I flicked through my file and found the photos of the bloodstains found with luminol. They were a match. Spray on the wall, but only a few drops on the floor.

"Are you aware, from your subsequent briefing, of the DNA profile of the blood found on the wall?" said King.

"Yes, I was informed that the blood matched the DNA control profile of Caroline Howell," said Birch.

"Earlier, you described the wound to the victim's throat as a *fatal* wound. How can you be certain this was an injury which resulted in a fatality?"

"The blood pattern is in the classic scythe shape and formation, from arterial spray. If someone opens your carotid artery you will bleed out in seconds unless there is a surgeon and full crash team standing by. Even then, it's likely you will die."

"No!" screamed Howell. He stood up, a wild look on his face.

I got to my feet and took hold of him, and I felt him grab my jacket. Our eyes met, and I thought that Howell looked like a man who was drowning. There was a desperate, primal aspect to his face.

His hands tightened, gripping my shirt.

"Get me out, get me out, I can't listen to this, get me out, Eddie . . ." he begged.

I was about to ask for a recess when Judge Schultz beat me to the punchline.

"That's your third strike, Mr Howell. I warned you. Security, please take Mr Howell to the cells. You'll remain there for one hour. When you return, if there are any further outbursts I'll hold you in a permanent state of contempt and you will not be in this court for the remainder of your trial. Take him."

He whispered an apology. He let go of my jacket, smoothed it down. My shirt too. He wept as he was led away. I didn't hear it, I was too busy arguing with the judge. She wouldn't listen, and the jury watched the scene in silence. The rumble of conversation that erupted in the crowd drowned out my voice. The door to the left of me that led to the cells slammed shut.

I took a moment to calm down, and wiped my lip. Doctor Birch smiled at me. He knew we were about to go at it, and he was feeling pretty confident. I had no blood pattern analysis defense expert, and now I didn't even have a client.

CHAPTER THIRTY-FIVE

The court calmed down after the ruckus created by Howell. King was done with Doctor Birch. She thanked him and sat down.

Like a tennis match, the ball was hurtling toward me and everyone in the courtroom thought I had no chance of reaching it, never mind batting it back across the net.

My hands felt hot and wet. From the corner of my eye, I saw a juror lean back and fold his arms like, *"What the hell are you going to argue with here, pal?"*

Doctor Birch had proven to be a convincing witness. His testimony was clear and the jury seemed to understand its importance and accept it. In reality there was very little that I could argue with.

But reality didn't matter. Neither did the truth. We were in a courtroom, after all.

I had my tactics all planned out, ahead of time. Even so, I could fall flat at any moment. Just because you know what punches you're going to throw doesn't mean any of them are going to land.

I got to my feet, moved out from the defense table and stood in the well of the court, right in the center of the space surrounded by the judge, jury, witness stand and prosecution. I didn't have a single note in front of me. Doctor Birch coughed, took a sip of water and fixed his gaze straight ahead. It was a basic tactic that some expert witnesses employed from time to time. The last thing any witness wants is to become angry under cross-examination. It's usually a sign that they've lost their credibility. Easiest way to avoid an argument is to avoid eye contact and focus on listening to the question and taking a second before answering. That way, you can't get drawn into an immediate answer and a combative approach. Even if Birch hadn't gotten a lot of real time on the witness stand during his career – he would've been prepped for testimony a bunch of times by a handful of prosecutors and most of them would pass on this tip. It's real simple, but highly effective.

"Doctor Birch, everything you've just told this court is total garbage, isn't that right?"

A beat. No eye contact from Birch. No objection from King – she didn't want to appear overprotective of this witness.

My gaze zeroed on him, but in my peripheral vision I saw a couple of jurors sit bolt upright. The judge dropped her pen and I could feel her hard stare. It didn't feel too friendly.

"No. That's incorrect," he said. His delivery had slowed; more measured, and his tone was lower to help instill his answers with greater authority. I'd seen some of these techniques displayed by witnesses before, but never all at once. It made me think Doc Birch had learned a hard lesson in the witness stand, and no way was he going to lose his temper again. Not if he listened to the prosecutor's tips on surviving cross-examination.

"You said, in your earlier testimony, that blood spatter analysis was your 'calling', is that right?"

A beat. Eyes on the floor.

"Yes. I am passionate about my work."

"You were a police officer before you opened your forensic consultancy practice, correct?"

The delay between question and answer shortened by half a second.

"Yes, and I left the force to pursue my calling."

"And you followed that calling to the FBI, where you trained in this discipline. That's what you told the court, right?"

Back to a full second delay. Thinking through his answer before he opened his mouth.

"That's right."

"Were your training and qualifications obtained from the Forensic Science and Research Center in the FBI National Academy in Quantico, Virginia?"

We waited, and he said, "The very same."

Now it was my turn to slow it down. I took one step toward the jury, faced them, stopped, and said, "Doctor Birch, at the FBI National Academy, what does the sign say above the entrance to the dining hall?"

His customary delay began. Two seconds passed. Five seconds. I didn't look at Birch. I watched the jury and the jury were watching him. At the ten-second mark the faces of the jury members began to change. What at first was benign interest became intense scrutiny on the fifteenth second of silence. There's nothing quite like that silence. It has a personality all of its own – a weight, a dense quality that fills everyone who swims in it with an increasing sense of unease. Two female jurors shielded their eyes with their hands, cringing at the silence, and looked away. The juror I pegged as the asshole leaned forward and put his elbows on his thighs, and the rest of the jury had moved beyond embarrassment. They were now curious: some were resting their chins on their fingers, the young lady in the glasses clicked the top of her pen and held her notebook ready for the answer, other jurors just stared at Birch. The creaking of King's chair broke the quiet. She had leaned forward, almost willing Birch to open his damn mouth and say something – anything.

"I don't think I can remember," he said, finally.

It was a bullshit answer and I turned on him, closing the gap between us as I said, "Are you saying that you don't remember what the sign says?"

His fingers were locked over his belly, but his thumbs tumbled over one another in a frantic circular pattern – like the wheels spinning in his head.

"I don't know what the sign says," he admitted.

"You don't know what the sign says because the truth is you have never been to the FBI National Academy at Quantico, isn't that right?"

His jaw worked silently – the muscle bulging at the side of his head.

"That's correct."

"So when you stated that you didn't think you could remember what the sign said, that was a lie, wasn't it?"

"No."

"If you have never set foot in the National Academy you would agree that you have never seen the sign, correct?"

"Yes."

"So you couldn't have forgotten what the sign said because you've never laid eyes on it?"

"Yes."

"So when you said you had a problem with your memory of the sign – that was a lie, Mr Birch?"

"No. It wasn't a lie. I simply misstated. And by the way, it's *Doctor* Birch."

His answers had become instantaneous, his volume increased and his pitch went up along with his blood pressure. I turned away from him and went back to the defense table. I grabbed a single page, held it in front of me so Birch couldn't see it, and said, "When you testified that you gained your Blood Spatter Analysis certification from the FBI, you really meant to say that you had completed an online correspondence course in Blood Pattern Analysis, BPA, which was developed, supposedly, with the FBI's assistance?"

"They did assist with course preparation materials," he said.

"Your actual qualification in BPA comes from which university?"

His answer was muffled and mumbled at first. I couldn't make it out.

"Say that again, Mr Birch, if you will?"

"Deboro University," he said.

"And where is Deboro University?" I said.

"I'm not sure," he said.

I was a lot closer to King than the jury. I could've sworn I heard her whisper "Jesus" under her breath. This was turning into a car wreck right before her eyes and there wasn't a damn thing she could do about it. Dallas Birch, part of the courtroom furniture. He'd been around so long that the DA's office no longer remembered, or cared, how he'd gotten to be there. I'd done my research. Blood Spatter Analysis was one of those grey areas of forensics, where opinion sat uneasily with science. And the longer the analyst had been in the field, the more likely it was that they'd never undertaken the more formal qualifications that existed now. His qualifications sounded great – but they unraveled as soon as I started to investigate them.

"I can help your memory, Mr Birch. Deboro University has its registered address as a Post Office Box number in Cleveland. That ring any bells?"

"You may be right," he said. This time I heard the arms of his chair creak and twist as he grabbed them. Although maybe the sound came from his gritted teeth. I didn't care which.

"That's where you got your doctorate from too?"

The "yes" came out in a short exhalation.

"The training you've received comes from a university without a campus, or a lecture hall or even a small tutorial room. You do a course online, and then you get emailed a diploma. That sound about right?"

He didn't answer.

"And if you want a doctorate, that costs an extra two hundred dollars, but doesn't actually require any additional work, does it?"

"I don't remember," he said.

"For two hundred bucks you can get a doctorate in Blood Spatter Analysis, or Physiotherapy, or Nutrition, or Hair Styling?"

"I don't know. I only did the blood pattern module," he said.

It was time to move on, while the jury were still shaking their heads.

"The information you received before you began your analysis included the victim's height and the fact that a knife was found with her blood on it?"

"Yes, that's correct."

"That was as far as your analysis went, wasn't it? You simply based your report on that information. Caroline Howell's height would give you an approximate starting point for the bloodstain emanating from the victim's throat – correct?"

"I carried out a full and detailed analysis and based my findings on those results," he said.

"During your analysis of the blood pattern, what allowances did you make for the variance in blood viscosity caused by red and white blood cells?"

A beat.

"None."

"You accept that it is widely held by all leading blood spatter experts that the viscosity of the blood can alter the pattern?"

"Yes."

"During your analysis of the blood pattern, what allowances did you make for Newton's law?"

A crack from Birch's chair startled two of the jury members. He'd almost broken the arm of the chair. He hissed, "I'm not sure what Newton's law is or what it has to do with my analysis?"

"I'm sorry, Newton's law is more commonly known as the law of gravity. I guess they didn't teach that in the PO Box in Cleveland. In any event, if a liquid is propelled through the air do you accept that gravity has some bearing on its travel?"

"I accept that."

"But you didn't account for it in your analysis. I could go on, but let me short circuit this. Mr Birch, you do not have any training of any kind in the areas of wound pathology, fluid dynamics, or physics?"

"No. I don't need to," he said.

"Then perhaps you've failed to grasp the *gravity* of the situation?"

He stood up, fast, his teeth bared and the arm rests and back of the witness chair came with him as they separated from the seat. He was still holding the arm rests. His face was almost completely red and he was about to launch into a verbal attack on me when King stood and said, "Objection". It was enough to close Birch's mouth. He dropped the remnants of the chair, looked around, and decided to remain standing.

"Your Honor," I said. "I wish to bring a motion to strike out the entirety of this witness's testimony. He is not an expert in this field—"

King cut me off before I could go further and we talked over each other for a good half a minute until King saw the jury glaring at her. She'd made a mistake by hiring a spatter expert who always delivered the results that fit the prosecution. Her hired gun had just shot a huge hole right through his own foot and into her case.

Before I'd even asked the judge to exclude the testimony, I knew the judge wouldn't do it. But the jury saw me call for it and I thought that maybe a few of them were thinking the exact same thing.

February 2003

Foley Courthouse, Albany, NY

With soft, tender strokes, Julie Rosen ran her fingers across the red, raised scar on her scalp. It still hurt. But the little jolts of pain kept her awake, kept her focused. The burns on her arms had healed well. They no longer troubled her and she could cover up the scarring. The wound to her head had muddled her thoughts and she had developed a habit of worrying the wound with her fingertips; prying it open and maybe hoping, on some level, that it would help her memory. She tried to focus on Harry. He believed her. She knew it. She felt it as surely as the ridge of scar tissue beneath her fingers. At times, during the trial, Julie had felt sorry for Harry. She was letting him down. They had been over that day so many times that it made Julie's head sore. She remembered the man in black. The gasoline and the kiss of the flames on her skin. But the images were fuzzy, and she couldn't remember the order in which those things happened, or how long the whole thing had taken. Sometimes she didn't remember the man in black at all.

When there weren't gaps in her recollection, and she talked about the intruder, her language let her down. She often said, "I don't remember, the man in black must've hit me . . . he must've started the fire . . ."

And that was the problem. During their meetings in preparation for the trial, Harry winced every time Julie said, "he must've", or "I can't remember, but that's what must have happened."

"Try not to say 'he must have', because it sounds like you don't know. If you're asked a question in court, then you say 'he did', or 'he didn't' because then you're speaking to what you remember, not what you think might have happened. Do you understand the difference?" said Harry.

Nodding, Julie understood. But in the witness stand she forgot. Or perhaps, she merely spoke the truth, for she could not remember what had happened that day. Harry had to be careful talking about the case. When he brought up the baby, Julie hugged herself and cried. The crying invariably became a wailing, rocking panic attack. Except on one occasion. Harry asked about Julie's relationship with baby Emily. Julie stayed silent for a long time, and scratched at the side of her head.

"I don't remember her face," said Julie. When she brought her hand away from her scalp her fingers were red with blood.

Now, Harry was talking to the jury and Julie was trying to listen. It had been a long time since she'd tried to concentrate so hard. Even with the best of intentions, Julie drifted off. While Harry spoke, she drew pictures of teddy bears, and bouncy balls, and empty cots on a legal pad. The pencil sketches gave the pictures a child-like quality.

"Members of the jury, the prosecution have no direct eye-witness testimony to challenge Julie Rosen's account of what occurred on that terrible day. This man who terrified my client, who burned down her house, who murdered her child, he has escaped. My client is not the perpetrator – she is the victim. She lost her baby. She deserves your kindness, and your sympathy, not your judgment."

When Harry sat down beside her, she placed a hand on his arm to comfort him. He had done everything that he could. And Julie knew that it would not be enough. In her deepest thoughts, she wanted to be punished. Her little Emily deserved more. She could have had more. A life, a chance to grow up in a nice house, with a nice family and a dog. And Julie knew that she had failed Emily. She'd lost her baby. She deserved judgment, punishment. It would help.

The jury retired, and as Julie stood to be manacled and taken back to the cells to wait, she turned around to look at the crowd behind her. Scott was not there. Several times during the trial she had felt his presence, but had never caught sight of him. He must hate me, she thought.

Julie waited in her blue dress in the cells. But not for long. The jury came back very quickly, within half an hour. When the guard broke this news to Harry, Julie saw his face drop. He knew the verdict instantly.

She followed Harry back to the courtroom, and drew perfect circles, freehand, as the jury read their verdict.

Guilty. On all counts.

Poor Harry looked broken by the decision. Julie felt relieved. And this time, when she left the court, she saw him.

He stood at the back, wearing a black coat. Scott. He was crying. But Julie knew that those tears were not for her. The tears were for Emily. Tears of relief, that her murderer would be punished. And Scott's tears soon dried up, and his eyes returned hatred to his former lover.

Julie prayed that, in time, he would forgive her.

CHAPTER THIRTY-SIX

There was no re-direct from King. She let Dallas Birch go lick his wounds and flipped over her notes. She was contemplating who she would call next. Her strongest witness would be Lynch, so it was best to leave him until last. We were getting short on time and it was likely that whatever witness she called wouldn't finish their testimony before the court closed business for the day.

Before she called her next witness, I tried to get the judge to let Howell back into the courtroom. The judge said he hadn't served his hour and he would be allowed to return tomorrow: he had to learn that he couldn't disrupt his own trial and get away with it. I returned to my seat.

"Your Honor, the People call George Vindico," said King.

Calling George was a real risk for King, but one that she couldn't afford not to take. She called him because he was in the house when it went up in flames. And he'd given a witness statement that confirmed Howell's finances were going down the toilet. I guessed that George's physical condition also played a big part in this. The prosecution didn't have a body – and therefore no focal point to pull on the jury's emotions. But if King let the jury see George hobbling along, and established that Howell knew George would be in the house when he supposedly triggered the explosive device – it gave the prosecution their next best thing to the real victim.

He shuffled along the center aisle, opened the small pine gate separating the lawyers and clients from the public and dragged that bad leg into the witness stand, the steel bar of his leg brace at the bottom of his shoe clicked on the tile floor with each painful and awkward step.

The short, blonde, female clerk handed him a Bible, and asked him if he wished to swear a religious oath or to affirm that he was going to tell the truth.

I felt for George. He looked like a man about to face a bullet. His back was bent slightly, and twisted because of the leg. His black suit jacket was buttoned at the waist, and his tie looked like it was strangling him. If he tried to stand up straight he wouldn't be able to stand at all.

He took the Bible in this left hand, and raised his right hand, as directed by the clerk.

The clerk said, "Repeat after me, I swear by Almighty God . . ."

George stared at the Bible in this hand.

"I swear by Almighty God . . ." prompted the clerk, again.

I looked at King, and saw that she wasn't paying attention. Her head was bent over her notes.

The clerk didn't know what to do. The judge, who'd been flicking back through the case papers, brought her attention to George, drawn by the awkward silence. I got up and approached King.

"Michelle, he's got a world-class stutter. Didn't you notice? I would've thought you might have warned the clerk; told her to take her time."

The skin on George's face and neck had turned pale. He was staring at the book in his hand, frozen. The stutter had utterly paralyzed George. It was difficult enough for him to talk one-on-one, but speaking in front of a busy courtroom was clearly beyond him.

"Sir?" said the judge.

"Your Honor, Mr Vindico suffers from a stammer. I would ask that we just give him a little time," said King.

"Of course. My apologies, Mr Vindico. Just take a moment to settle down. Take your time, we're not going to rush you," said the judge.

It was almost as if George didn't hear the judge. He lowered his right hand. I thought that holding his hand up for too long would make his back become painful. The twisted stance must have been agony – I saw the Bible begin to tremor in his left hand.

One of the ADAs sitting beside King covered his mouth and turned away from the witness stand. I saw his shoulders rocking with suppressed laughter. Some of the onlookers in the courtroom began to giggle. That stopped when the judge made a point of rising in her seat and peering out into the crowd, searching for the culprit.

I remained still, patient.

I watched George. Part of me wanted to cover my head in my jacket. It was painfully embarrassing.

His eyes were boring into the cover of the Bible that now shook violently in his hand.

The book stopped shaking.

His eyes closed.

He rolled his head on his shoulders, and stretched his back. He seemed to grow about two inches. His spine straightened.

But his posture didn't return to its former, crooked state. His back remained straight. He stood tall. Then he raised his right knee and placed that bound and braced leg on the seat in the witness stand. He dragged the leg of his pants over his calf, exposing the leather brace. With ease he unhooked the catch, and swept the brace off his leg, folded the straps carefully and placed it at is feet.

With his right hand he worked at his ankle, probing the muscles with his fingers. He raised his foot off the seat, swiveled it to get the blood flowing then put his leg down.

He stood straight and true. The years seemed to fall away from him.

His face had changed.

No, not his face. His eyes.

They were clear and determined.

He raised the Bible, held out his right hand and when he opened his mouth he spoke clearly, precisely and quickly.

"I swear by Almighty God that I will tell the truth, the whole truth, and nothing but the truth, so help me God."

The clerk stumbled back, the judge was wide-eyed. King stood still, her hands up and open – stunned into silence by the transformation.

"Please state your name for the record," said the clerk.

George put the Bible down, unbuttoned his suit jacket and said, "My name is Scott Barker. The lies have to stop."

CHAPTER THIRTY-SEVEN

The crowd had never seen anything like this before. Neither had I. A witness called to the stand and admits to being somebody else entirely. Someone we had no clue about. Every living soul in that room knew that something extraordinary was happening. Something unexpected and very, very wrong.

Shock buzzed in the air like static.

King stood, open-mouthed. Completely thrown. All of her preparation gone up in smoke. She didn't have the first clue what to do next.

The man who now called himself Scott Barker sat down, and I could see the tension working in his jaw.

He certainly wasn't George any more. He looked like a different man entirely.

Slowly it began to filter through my mind, chipping away at the wall of amazement that was blocking my thoughts.

George Vindico probably never existed at all.

Who the hell was this guy?

The judge's gaze fell first on King, and when she got nothing she looked to me.

My guess was that the judge and King shared my own feeling. I didn't feel like a lawyer any more. My part in this game had changed. So had theirs. We were no longer playing any role in what was happening. Instead we'd all become witnesses.

The world had tilted. The floors crumbled.

I put the brakes on.

"Your Honor, I must insist that my client is here for this witness's testimony. The integrity of this trial will not survive my client's absence any further."

She nodded. Judge Schultz knew she was pushing it, keeping Howell away. But now she had no choice.

"I'll adjourn to allow you some time to consult with your client. Bring him up to speed. We'll recommence here in half an hour."

Judge Schultz swiveled her chair toward the witness stand to address George.

"You have been sworn in, Mr . . . Mr Barker. You are now under oath. You will not speak to the prosecutor about this case, or discuss it with anyone until you have completed your testimony. I'm also placing you under subpoena as I expect that the prosecution may wish to treat you as a hostile witness. You will not leave the precincts of this courthouse until your testimony is complete."

There was no acknowledgment from the witness. Barker merely stared at the judge with a cold detachment.

The judge beckoned to a court officer, who went over to her and listened while she gave him instructions. I didn't need to hear what was said. The judge didn't like Barker one bit, and she was going to make sure that he didn't leave. The court officers would watch him closely.

I left my papers on the defense table and darted for the door that led to the cells as soon as Judge Schultz got up to leave. My hand was on the handle of the door when I heard fast heels approaching from behind.

"Eddie, is this something to do with you?" said King, an accusatory look on her face.

I opened the door, and as I went through I said, "I have no idea what's going on. I'm sorry, I need to see my client."

The small corridor had bare concrete walls and at the end was a single steel door painted dark green. I jogged the twenty feet to the door and banged on it with my fist. Nothing. I hit the door again.

A slot in the door opened and a pair of eyes filled the space.

"Who are you looking for?"

"Howell. He came through a little while ago. Judge says he's free to come back into the courtroom. I need to speak to him right away."

The slot slammed shut. An exchange of muffled voices on the other side of the door filled the cold corridor.

I heard the slot slam open. The eyes said, "Sorry, you'll have to see him tomorrow."

The steel plate slid across and I yelled before it closed, "Wait, I've got to see him. Let me talk to him."

"You can't. He's gone."

"He's what?"

"Prison van left a minute ago. The jailor thought Howell was done for the day, so we put him on the last transport van."

Slam, from steel on steel. I fought the urge to punch the door. It would do no good. I needed to calm the hell down.

I took a deep breath in and out. Cracked my neck. Smoothed down my tie.

Something was wrong.

Instead of my mind and my muscles winding down, I suddenly felt even more afraid, more anxious. My heart was thumping, my guts were turning over and I had the urge to run, to fight, to do something urgently but what the hell that was I couldn't tell.

The revelation from Barker had hurled me into a spin, but whatever had happened in the corridor, just then, had fed that unease like gasoline on a campfire. I pulled at my collar to loosen it.

Then my hand strayed. Something tapping a foot in my subconscious.

I smoothed down my tie again.

In a terrifying instant it hit me. I hadn't realized what it was at first. But in that explosive moment I knew.

The tie pin was gone.

CHAPTER THIRTY-EIGHT

My mind went back to Howell grabbing the lapels of my jacket in court before he got sent to his cell.

Somehow he must've swiped the pin. Yet I didn't feel it, didn't register it until now. I should never have worn it. I should've tried some other way to get Howell into the trial. Stupid. Stupid. Stupid.

Howell wanted to get sent back to his cell. He wanted to get into the prison van.

And during that journey from the courthouse to Sing Sing he was going to use the pin to open his veins.

I hammered on the steel door and this time the guard didn't open the slot, he threw open the door. He was big and bald and looked about ready to grab me by the throat.

"The van, you've got to call them. My client has a weapon. He's going to harm himself. You need to stop the van and get him out."

It took him a few seconds to absorb this.

He finally said, "We don't have radio contact. The van's run by the Department of Corrections, not justice. We don't have any way of contacting them in transit – you need to call the jail."

I turned and sprinted toward the court. The door clanged behind me as I ran back into the courtroom.

The jury were already gone, King was in conversation with her team and Barker remained in the witness stand, one hand on his chin in deep thought. I hurtled past the defense table into the center aisle and bundled through the crowd that were making their way toward the exit.

There were plenty of abusive comments, and angry stares as I pushed my way through the slow-moving crowd, scanning the faces as I went. I saw Max Copeland sitting impassively, scribbling in a black notebook. Ignoring him I spoke my apologies to everyone and continued to fight through the masses.

At the courtroom door I saw who I was looking for.

She was outside the court, in the oval glass-walled hallway, in hushed conversation with Joe Washington.

I called out to her, and sent a tall guy in a brown coat stumbling as I put my shoulder to his back to get him out of my way. I stopped, steadied him and when I got to the two FBI agents they were both looking at me quizzically.

"Harper, it's Lenny Howell. Somehow he smuggled something sharp into the court. He's in the van on his way back to Sing Sing. He's going to kill himself on the way. We need to contact the jail and get somebody to stop that van."

Washington reacted immediately, punching numbers into his cell phone as Harper asked, "What does he have?"

"I don't know for sure. But he's serious. You saw him try it at the house when they arrested him for murder. Those vans have single secure booths for prisoners. The guard and the driver won't know what he's doing until it's too late."

Holding the palm of his hand over his cell phone, Washington said, "This is going to take a few minutes. I'm waiting for a patch through to prison security. When did the van leave?"

"I'm not sure exactly, maybe only a few minutes ago," I said.

The feds exchanged glances.

"Come with me," said Harper.

CHAPTER THIRTY-NINE

One of the benefits of law enforcement is great parking. While I was in a multi-level structure half a mile away, Harper had left her Dodge Charger within fifty feet of the courthouse door.

Washington followed us outside, but didn't get into the car. He was a big man and the Charger didn't need any extra weight slowing it down.

"You two go get the van. I'll call you on your cell, Harper, soon as I get Corrections on the phone," said Washington.

"With me, Eddie. Somebody might have to talk Howell down," said Harper.

We got into the car.

It felt like I had an insect trapped inside my head and slowly but surely it was eating my brain. A black insect that you could call stupidity and guilt. I felt that thing bite into my skull as surely as I've ever felt anything. I buckled my seatbelt. Throwing the muscle car into reverse, Harper thumped her boot through the accelerator. One hand on the wheel, one hand typing on a satellite navigation system attached to the dash with a plastic bracket.

Horns and brakes met us and a brown station wagon swerved past, the driver thumping on the horn in the center of his wheel.

Harper ignored it all. She pumped the clutch, flicked the gear stick and ate the gas pedal. I chewed my knuckle and punched the dash. This was all my fault.

A call came in on her cell phone, and she hit a button on the steering console. A Bluetooth system took the call through the stereo.

"Prison transport can't raise the van," said Washington. *"The radio's been broken for a week, and they ain't got around to fixing it yet. They're trying the driver and guard's cell phones but nothing so far. All I got*

is a location from the tracker. They're headed north on the Tarrytown Road and in less than a minute they'll take the slipway for interstate 287, Westbound."

"Got it. Stay on the line," said Harper.

We blew through the intersection on Main Street and hooked a left onto Hamilton Road. My right foot buried itself in the floor as I willed the car on, faster and faster.

Traffic up ahead. A white van in the distance. My heart leapt. This could be the prison van. I sat up and regretted it as Harper swerved right to avoid a motorcycle, narrowly avoiding the crash barrier and then brought us back into the lane. The van was closer now and I swore when I saw that it was a camper van.

"Take it easy," said Harper. "We'll get there."

I didn't know this part of New York. The roads were unfamiliar even though I'd probably driven them before at one time or another. We were on a two-lane road. Speed limit fifty-five miles an hour. Harper hit ninety as we shot past the camper. I turned around when I heard the camper driver's horn. The whole side of the van was shaking from the wind displacement.

The Dodge lurched left, then right to correct and I was almost thrown into Harper's lap. Grabbing the door handle saved me and I managed to right myself in my seat.

"There's the slipway for the 287; where are they now?" said Harper.

"Hang on," said Washington.

We took the single-lane slipway far too fast. Harper feathered the brakes and we began to snake left and right, the back end wobbling and Harper fighting the wheel as the tail of the Dodge threatened to throw us into one of the concrete crash barriers on either side of the road.

"They're just passing the exit at the Pearson Center," said Washington.

The Dodge continued to fight Harper until we turned onto the 287. A three-lane expressway that moved fast and had little traffic. Speed limit was still fifty-five.

Nobody was doing fifty-five.

Acceleration pinned me to my seat and Harper took us past half a dozen vehicles, swerving in and out of the fast lane. Going through the bend, we saw the van.

"Any update on contacting the driver?" said Harper.

I bit my lip and prayed.

"Negative," said Washington.

The white van had two small windows at the rear, set high up. It sat in the center lane at a steady sixty. Harper took her foot off the gas and came parallel to the van. It was on our right.

"Put on your siren," I said.

"This is a personal vehicle. No blues and twos, no siren," said Harper.

The same small, square windows, high up on the driver's side of the van. Each one was reinforced glass and too high for anyone to see inside. Our only chance was to get level with the cab and flag down the driver.

As we leveled with the van driver Harper hit her horn.

"Take this," she said, handing me her FBI badge and ID.

I wound down my window, held out the badge and signaled to the van driver to pull over. The sound from Harper's horn drew the driver's attention.

He switched his gaze back to the road and the van sped up.

I called out to the driver but he couldn't hear me over the roar of the engines and the whipping of the air as we cut through it.

"Shit, did he see the badge?" said Harper.

"He saw it," I said. "Probably thinks it's fake and we're trying to bust somebody out of custody."

Increasing our speed to match the van, Harper angled closer, and told me to try again. Maybe the driver of the van would take a better look this time.

Same result, he sped up. Only this time he gave us the finger before he put his foot down.

Every second that passed, every slap of my hand on the passenger door of the Dodge, every inch I extended my arm to show the driver the badge – all of it felt like we were already too late.

"It's another twenty minutes to Sing Sing," said Harper, glancing at her navigation screen. "It's interstate virtually the whole way. We won't hit a stop light for another ten miles. You think we could wait that long?" she said.

I brought both of my arms back inside the car, and tried desperately to think of another way to get the guard's attention. I didn't need to decide if we could wait another ten minutes before stopping the van. I knew, somehow, that we couldn't wait another minute.

"We need to stop this van, right now," I said.

"How sure are you that he's going to harm himself?"

"I'm certain," I said.

"Any luck on the cell phones, Joe?" said Harper.

"They're trying. I've got a black and white en route and a paramedic. They'll be there in five," said Washington.

Harper slapped the steering wheel, "Hold on," she said.

CHAPTER FORTY

"What are you doing?" I said.

"I'm going to get the van on my side and then I'm gonna shoot out the front tire," said Harper.

She braked and let the van pass us, then slipped in behind it and followed through into the right hand lane and increased our speed so she'd be the closest to the van.

"You'll flip it if you take out a tire. At this speed you'll kill everyone," I said.

Harper reached into her jacket and drew a Glock. She placed it between her legs and lowered her window.

"Wait, come up closer and shoot above the tire, into the engine," I said.

"That won't stop it. I couldn't get through the engine block with a shot gun," she said.

"No, but you might hit the air intake or a distributor, that'll kill the engine instantly."

She glanced at me once, then the road ahead and drew level with the side of the van, just slightly forward of the cab. Right hand on the steering wheel. Her left grabbed the Glock and she extended her arm out of the window. Her head flicked quickly between the road and the sight at the end of the barrel. She increased the pressure on the accelerator.

Almost level.

"Wait! We got a guard, they're stopping," said Washington.

Sure enough, we flew past the van as the driver hit the brakes. Harper drew her hand back inside the car, steered right and took us onto the hard shoulder. I turned around in my seat and saw the van had followed us and was coming to a stop.

Harper brought the Charger to a standstill, grabbed her ID off the dash and threw open the door. She was faster than me getting out of the car, but my long stride caught up with her sprint just as we reached the van. A guard stood outside with a shotgun ready, the stock against his shoulder, finger on the trigger.

Harper held up her badge and I ran past them both, toward the back. The doors were open and I leapt inside. My heart catching in my throat. No other guards were in back.

Six reinforced doors to individual mobile cells.

I called out to the guard, "I need keys, which one is . . ."

My left foot slid out from under me and I thrust a hand out to steady myself.

I didn't need to ask which cubicle was Howell's any more.

A dark stain spread out from beneath door three.

"Get this open now!"

I felt the floor shift and dip with the guard leaping into the van, and I stood back to let him open the door. He opened the door just at the exact same moment his right foot slipped out from underneath him and he fell back. He got up and stared numbly into the open transport cell. He didn't dive in to help, didn't call for assistance, he didn't do anything. Pushing him out of the way I flung open the door and when I saw inside, I stopped being angry with the guard.

The sight was enough.

"Jesus H. Christ," said the guard.

A transport cell is a square, four-foot-by-four-foot box, with just enough room to sit down. They are normally painted industrial gray, with a ridged plastic floor and a steel seat. No seat belts.

The gray was gone. Words floated in front of my mind.

Red. Soaked. Dead.

The cubicle was a riot of blood.

Something inside me collapsed.

Howell wasn't moving. He'd slipped off the seat and fallen under it, his legs folded awkwardly beneath him. I slipped my hands underneath his arms and lifted him out of there and laid him on the floor of the van.

I checked for a pulse.

Barely, just faintly I detected the weak throb beneath his jaw. The guard was over the initial shock. He'd grabbed an emergency kit from the front of the van and was cracking open the lid. A bandage and gauze soon found its way to Howell's neck, where a strong, steady flow of blood was streaming from a wound in his throat. The guard told me to keep pressure on the wound. I pressed down on the right side of his neck as hard as I could. Howell's face was almost pale blue. He'd slit his wrists too. The guard grabbed the bandages, doubled them up and began tying a tight tourniquet on each arm, just above the elbow.

In the distance, I heard the wail of sirens.

I watched as the guard slapped Howell, peeled open his eyelids and shined a torch into them, shouting his name – trying everything that he could to wake him up.

In the corner of the little red cell, I saw my pin – shining, even in the blood.

With one eye on the guard, I kept one-handed pressure on Howell's neck, and reached across with my other. The pin was wet and sticky. I put it in my pants pocket. I glanced up. The guard was still working on Howell and Harper stood outside the van with her back to me, waving her arms to flag down the paramedics. In the distance I could see the flashing lights from the ambulance.

"He's going into arrest. Move over, keep the pressure up," said the guard. I shimmied round to give him space to work. He began chest compressions, and then slipped a rubber funnel with a paper cover over Howell's face so he could blow into his mouth without tasting blood.

I could feel Howell's blood soaking through the knees of my pants. There was blood on my shirt, and my hands. I kept thinking that I'd allowed this to happen. This was my fault.

The paramedics pulled up and Harper turned to face me.

She saw it then. The guilt was on my face as plain as the red stains on my hands. I couldn't hide it.

There was no getting away from this.

CHAPTER FORTY-ONE

The drive back to the courthouse took a lot longer than the journey out. Even though we had all that time, we said nothing until Harper made the right turn off of Main Street.

"What did he use to cut his throat, Eddie?"

"I don't know," I said.

"They didn't find anything in the van."

"Maybe he still had it on him, somewhere," I said, gazing out of the window at the courthouse as we drove past.

She had agreed to take me to my car so I could change into my spare suit and shirt.

"You know he's alive because of you," she said.

I didn't thank her. He was also almost certainly going to die because of me. He'd lost a lot of blood. It was all my fault for buying the pin. No way I would ever have handed it over, I just wanted him to see it so he would cooperate. I should've said no, I should've resisted.

Harper said, "How did you know he was going to try to kill himself?"

"I just knew," I said.

She nodded. "I guess sometimes you've got to go with what you know in your heart."

The pulse of the engine invaded the car, and Harper fell silent. Her eyes drifted across to the bloodstains on my knees, my hands, my shirt and jacket sleeves. The iron tang of blood in the air was so strong you could almost taste it.

"Listen, it's not every day a fed helps me out. I want to know why. Sure, you're not convinced Howell is guilty. I get it. But it takes more than that to risk your job by helping me. If there's another reason why you're helping, I want to know. I *need* to know."

Traffic backed up, and Harper touched the brakes, slowing us down to a crawl.

"I was out of the Academy maybe a year when I went on a surveillance job with Lynch. Two months of sitting in cars, vans and cold apartments while we stared at a house in Jersey. Any chance he got, Lynch would pair himself with me. It was his op, and I was the least experienced so I thought he was showing me the ropes. You know, keeping a close eye on the rookie in case I messed up."

I nodded, but said nothing for fear of interrupting her story.

"One night we were alone in the apartment when he made a pass at me. I made it clear I wasn't interested in anyone in the Bureau. He didn't take no for an answer. He grabbed me. Pinned me against the wall. It wasn't a good night."

"God, what happened? Did you report him?"

She checked her rear view mirror and took two deep breaths. It was almost as if she was steeling herself to look into her past.

"No, I didn't report him. I pushed him off me and I got out of there, fast as I could. I didn't know what to do at first. Talked to Washington about it. He had my back. Always has. We argued about it. Joe is like a solid granite statue of everything that's good about the Bureau. He spent two days trying to convince me to make a complaint, but I knew it was Lynch's word against mine. So I said nothing. Because I was going to say nothing, I then had to spend an hour talking Joe out of breaking Lynch's neck.

"The surveillance job turned into a bust the next week. My first arrest. We were expecting to find a cache of weapons in the house. Turns out all we got was an old .38 that belonged to the perp's late mother. He didn't have a license for it, so I busted him anyway."

Her voice slowed, and became clearer. I heard the crackle of leather on the steering wheel as she tightened her grip.

"Ever since that night, when Lynch and I worked together he's tried to pin something on me. He wants to ruin my credibility in case I ever do make a complaint. It's too late now. It's been eight years. I thought he would've let it go, but no. Twice now he's kicked me off an op because of an alleged complaint that never actually materialized."

"Like at Howell's house, the night of the fire. He said there'd been a complaint about you assaulting me."

"Exactly. It's bullshit."

"So one reason why you're helping me is that you think Howell is innocent, and the other reason is you want to get one over on Lynch?"

"It would be nice to prove him wrong, but that's not the real reason. The guy I busted on my first arrest for possession of his mom's .38, the guy who didn't even know there was a gun in the house, well he didn't make bail. Hung himself in prison six months later. That's on me. I could see it on his face when I showed him the gun: he didn't know it was even in the house. I still busted him, and it cost him his life. No way am I letting anyone else go down for something they didn't do. Not on my watch. I can't allow it. To be honest, it's maybe for selfish reasons because I'm not sure I could live through that again. No way. I would just quit."

I turned my attention away from Harper and watched the road ahead.

"You won't quit," I said.

"What makes you say that?"

It was obvious. Harper was five foot nothing, female, and tough as anyone I'd ever met. And here she was, at the frontline of the FBI still calling out her boss when he made the wrong decision without any fear of the consequences.

"You don't know how to quit," I said.

A warmth spread over her face. She sat up a little in the driver's seat and said, "Okay, my turn. I have a question for you about Dallas Birch and your cross about the sign over the mess hall at Quantico."

"Shoot."

"I trained at the Academy, I ate at that dining hall damn near every day and I don't remember a sign above the door. So what *does* it say?"

"I'll be damned if I know," I said.

"You don't know?"

"No. I don't even know if there is a sign. Until you mentioned it just now, I wasn't even sure there was a dining hall."

*

Harper took us into the multi-story parking lot and wound up three levels until I spotted my car. There was a space just opposite. She reversed the car into the space and I got out.

I'd driven into my space, the front of my car almost touching the concrete wall. Harper got out of her car and lit up a cigarette.

In the trunk of my Mustang I had a pale blue suit, a fresh white shirt and a couple of ties. Popping the lid of the trunk, I peeled off the bloodstained jacket and shirt, removed my cell from my jacket and dumped the clothes in a bag in the trunk. My cell had two missed calls. Harry Ford. He'd left a message to say he was in White Plains, in a jazz bar, and he'd wait for my call. I put the cell in the trunk and paused when I saw my hands. I hadn't washed them yet. Dry, ochre-red stains were ingrained in the grooves of my palm, my fingers. Blood sat thick and black beneath my nails.

Harper said, "You've got a lot of scars for a lawyer."

Dropping my hands by my sides, I turned my head toward her. She was looking at my chest, my arms, even scanning the scar tissue over my knuckles. When she realized I was watching her she quickly turned her back, coughed and looked at the painted concrete floor.

"Cuts, broken bones, even puncture wounds – they all heal," I said, taking the lid off a water bottle that I kept beside a tire iron. I poured the water over my hands, started using my nails to dig out the blood. In the last few years I'd had a few trips to the ER with injuries. I didn't care. What kept me awake at night was the blood on my hands that I couldn't wash away.

Harper's cell chimed – echoing around the parking lot.

She took the call, and stood close enough that I could hear Washington on the other end of the line.

"*Is Eddie Flynn still with you?*" said Washington.

"I'm standing right next to him," she said.

"*Get him over to White Plains PD. Don't go back to the court. We need him right away.*"

"What's going on?"

"*Scott Barker just dropped a hand grenade into the Howell case,*" said Washington.

CHAPTER FORTY-TWO

Washington waited for us in the lobby of White Plains PD. He shifted his weight from foot to foot, impatiently. He told Harper that the judge had pulled the case for the day. The trial was scheduled to begin again at nine a.m. It was almost five o'clock, so it was quitting time for the judge and jury anyway.

"What's happened?" said Harper.

"I haven't been briefed yet, but Lynch looked like he was about to burst a blood vessel in his forehead so it can't be good for the prosecution. All I know is there was an incident in the courtroom with Barker and he's been taken into custody. He's in the cells, downstairs," said Washington.

The lobby of the police department was fairly quiet. Half a dozen folks sat around on wooden benches – no doubt patiently awaiting their turn to lodge a complaint, or meet an officer about an ongoing investigation. Washington took us through a door to the left of the lobby and up two flights of monochrome blue stairs in a pale gray stairwell. The stairs led to a long corridor, painted white, with rows of thick pine doors on the right hand side. We walked past the first five offices and Washington knocked at the sixth door before opening it.

Inside was a long pale room with no windows and a pine conference table. Agent Lynch sat beside two police officers in uniform. Seated at the other end of the table was ADA King and her associates. One of the uniformed cops stood and offered me a hand.

"Mr Flynn, I'm Captain Powers, this is Lieutenant Groves, and I understand you know everyone else?"

I shook hands with Powers, a tall, good-looking man in his fifties with elegant fingers. Groves was short, rotund and had a wicked smile.

"Please take a seat." Powers gestured to an empty chair.

I sat down and Groves pulled a laptop toward him. The lid of the laptop was open and it was powered up. He tapped on the keys and began weaving patterns on the track pad.

"What's going on? There was an incident in the courtroom and you need me here, that's the message we got. Now I see the prosecutor is here . . ."

"Hi, Eddie," said King, with as much politeness as she could muster. She looked pissed but was doing her best not to show it.

"Hi, Michelle," I said. "Don't suppose you have any updates on my guy?"

"Actually, we just heard from the hospital. Your client is critical, but stable. He's still unconscious, but it looks like he'll live," she said.

My eyes closed as I raised my head to the heavens. The relief was bitter.

"I asked the prosecutor to be here," said Powers. "And you. Although, your presence was also requested by the man we have in custody."

"What man?"

"Scott Barker," said Powers.

I placed my hands on the table, leaned forward. If Barker had been arrested this could be good news for Howell. But arrested for what?

"You had better tell me exactly what's going on here," I said.

Powers gestured toward Lieutenant Groves, who swiveled the laptop around and pushed it toward Powers. In turn, Powers slid the computer toward me, the screen facing me.

"Look at this," said Powers.

The screen was security footage of the courtroom. It was from a camera mounted high on the southwest wall of the court, close to the ceiling.

"I didn't know the courtroom had a security camera," I said.

"It's disguised to look like an old fire alarm. There have been incidents in the last few years and most courtrooms now have clandestine cameras fitted. The rest will be installed shortly. It's protection for the judge and the jury. Jury intimidation is on the rise, so now we monitor everyone who uses our courts," said Powers.

There was no time stamp on the footage. The judge's seat was empty, but Scott Barker sat with his head low in the witness stand.

I could see a few people scattered around the public seats, and the court officers were keeping a watchful eye on him. I guessed that when this was happening I was tearing through the streets in Harper's car. The court wouldn't adjourn until they found out exactly what was going on and why I wasn't there, and why my client wasn't there.

Nothing happened for a few more seconds, then Barker's head whipped up in the direction of the door. He'd seen someone enter the courtroom. He got up and out of his seat, opened the half door of the witness stand and stepped lightly down the three steps. He strode confidently toward the nearest court officer – no dragging his foot, no limp, no arching of the back – he moved swiftly and confidently. The court officer was already moving toward him, hands up, making sure he didn't leave the courtroom. From his jacket pocket, Barker produced a white envelope and handed it to the officer. They talked for a moment. The officer called over his colleague. The officer with the envelope spoke to his associate, and Barker walked back toward the witness stand, opened the door, got back in and sat down.

The officer with the white envelope began walking toward the doors, while the other kept an eye on Barker.

The screen then shifted to a camera outside the courtroom. I saw the officer entering the hall with the white envelope in his hand before he gave it to a young woman in a cream suit.

I looked up. The woman in the cream suit was sitting at the conference table beside King. It was someone from her prosecution team.

I pushed the laptop away and saw King holding a clear, plastic evidence bag in her hand. Inside the bag was the envelope.

"We're showing you our chain of custody here, Eddie," said King. "I want you and the court to know that none of this came from us, that we've not withheld any evidence. This is the envelope that Barker handed to the court officer."

She put down the evidence bag, reached below the desk and came up with another evidence bag. Inside was a photograph. It looked as if it was printed on letter-sized paper, from an ordinary home printer. She slid the bag across the table to me and said, "We found this in the envelope."

Harper and Washington had remained standing at one end of the conference table, a little to my right.

Harper saw the photograph before I did. So did Washington. I could tell by their eyes, which widened and then instantly narrowed. Washington clenched his fists, Harper bit her lip and gave Lynch a look like she wanted to slam his head into the table.

"Don't say it. We don't know what this means," said Lynch.

"Oh, I'm going to say it. I'm going to keep on saying it, Lynch. You've got the wrong man," said Harper.

CHAPTER FORTY-THREE

The photograph came to me. I picked up the clear bag and examined it.

Caroline Howell's wrists were bound behind her with cable ties. Her feet too. She lay on her right side with her legs curled up, her knees almost touching her chest. She was dressed in the same clothes as she'd worn when she went missing – white shirt, blue jeans. No biker jacket covered in pins, though. Her hair appeared wet and slicked back, away from her face. The blonde, full hair that I'd seen in the other photographs of her now looked lank and greasy.

Her face angled toward the camera. In this picture she was bone pale, and her cheeks had a sunken, hollow aspect. It may have been an effect from the flash, but I thought she looked as though she hadn't been out in daylight in some time. Her mouth was parted, and her teeth bore a yellow scum.

So much had changed about her. She had lost a lot of weight. I could tell, not just from her face, but her clothes seemed to hang on her – baggy where once they'd been tight. The only thing that had not changed were her eyes. They were the same as the other photographs of her in the basement that Howell had been sent. Still brilliant, still blue, still roaring in terror.

I looked at the rest of the photograph – the surroundings. She was no longer in a basement. At first I wasn't sure if the photo had been shopped with some kind of software, because at first it looked as though there was a frame around the photo. A black tint around the edges that became a hard gray rectangle that contained the image of Caroline Howell in the center. Then, when I held the photo closer, I realized what I was looking at. The photographer was standing in an elevated position, probably on dark soil, and they were bending over to photograph Caroline as she lay six feet below them at the bottom of what looked to be a concrete grave.

I put the photograph down. Pinched the bridge of my nose and closed my eyes.

"What is Barker saying?" I said.

"Nothing, for the moment. We don't know when this was taken. We don't know by whom, we don't know where. There's a lot that we don't know. And he won't talk to us," said Powers.

I looked at the prosecutor. King was staring straight at me – waiting for the question.

"Are you going to pull the trial, withdraw the charges?" I said.

"No. Barker could be Howell's accomplice," said King.

"He's said he won't talk to the DA. Or us, or the FBI," said Powers. "He said he'll only talk to you or Howell."

"Me?" I said.

"That's right. This is all very unusual, Eddie. Ordinarily we wouldn't even contemplate it. But he's lawyered up and it's all been explained to him. At the moment he's been arrested for perverting the course of justice and withholding evidence. The only reason we're even thinking about this is because of what he said to the court officer," said Powers.

I thought back to the exchange I'd seen on the video.

"What did he say?"

Powers looked around the room before he spoke   there were no objections.

"After he told the officer to give the envelope to the prosecutor, he made a comment," said Powers, as he drew a notebook from the table, flicked through a few pages.

"He said – quote: 'Howell is guilty.'"

CHAPTER FORTY-FOUR

Washington and Harper immediately started arguing with Lynch who stood his ground. Powers and Groves both got to their feet and tried calming things down. King just looked at me.

I looked at her.

"I can't talk to him," I said.

No one heard me apart from King. She gave a false smile and a wink. Even in this shitstorm she was all about the win, all about the case, all about getting her conviction and covering her ass.

"I can't talk to him," I said, louder this time.

The cops and the feds stopped arguing and looked my way. I focused my attention on King, ignoring them.

"If I talked to him, Ms King would go straight to the judge and tell her that I'd spoken to a witness who is still under oath. That compromises the integrity of that witness's testimony, and that gives Ms King a mistrial. Right now, Ms King knows that calling Barker was a major mistake. It could derail her case. If there's a mistrial the prosecution get to start afresh – this time with Barker struck off the witness list. I'm not going to fall for it, Michelle. You want me to talk to Barker – fine. I need permission from the judge."

Lynch placed both hands on his face, drew them down over his skin. The action popped open his mouth and eyes, and he shook his head trying to stave off sleep.

When he spoke, his tone was heavy, strained – like every word was a struggle.

"Barker has been playing a game for a long time. Four years he's been working for Howell, apparently in disguise. We don't know what he has to do with this, but he's got a picture of our dead victim. I had an image tech take a look – and her guess is this photo could've been taken before the fire. Think about it – she was missing nineteen days by the time we found her. If she'd been kept in a hole with no food and little water – she could look like that. My theory is Howell faked the kidnapping, McAuley and Marlon helped him and they took off with the money. Barker was in on it too, but he was also planning something else. I don't know what. But he's involved in the kidnapping. We know that from the photo. He knows what happened and my guess is he knows where the money and the rest of the kidnappers are. And we have to know that too, right now."

"You said Barker lawyered-up, so who's the lawyer?" I said.

Powers nodded and said, "Max Copeland – I guess you've probably heard of him. We've been keeping an eye on them in the consultation booth. Neither of them have spoken to each other. They're waiting for you."

My mind was already reeling, trying to decipher Barker's actions – but this piece of information confirmed something for me. The Rosen case and Caroline Howell were inextricably linked. The feeling that I'd had earlier that there might be a connection was now proven.

The rule of three. Coincidences can throw you into wild theories. But having the same thing confirmed to you three times was more than a coincidence.

Howell's sister-in-law was the late Julie Rosen. Harry and I got served with subpoenas in the Rosen case the night of the ransom drop. Max Copeland represents the Rosen estate and Barker. There had been a fire at Howell's and at Julie Rosen's property. And Copeland had been in court from the very beginning of the Howell trial. I'd thought he'd come to check out my courtroom style, study me, look for weaknesses. Turns out he was there to watch his client.

I didn't say a word of this in the room. Harry was involved and I couldn't do anything until I'd spoken to him and made sure I wasn't landing him in the middle of something horrible. Second, I didn't trust anyone in that room, maybe apart from Harper. But it was too soon to spout theories – I needed more. I needed Harry.

At that moment, thinking about Harry gave me a feeling that I was missing something else – something I'd just been told. Or seen.

"Lieutenant Groves, can I see the video again?"

He skimmed the laptop across the table. I opened it on the frozen image of the courtroom, moved the cursor over the play icon and clicked. While I watched, the others resumed their conversations, ignoring me.

I was grateful for that.

On the screen, I watched Barker sitting passively in the witness stand. Then his head came up, and he moved off toward the guard with the envelope. I watched the camera shift to the hallway, and this time I saw Harry straight away. I was watching for him.

He was typing on the screen of his cell phone. His back to the court.

When Harry arrived, he would've gone straight into the courtroom, looking for me. When he discovered I wasn't there, he would've left the courtroom and tried to contact me on my cell.

I couldn't be sure, but I felt strongly that Barker's eyes locked on Harry when he came through the doors of the court. That's who he was looking at. And seeing Harry, even briefly, sent him out of the witness stand with the envelope. Another possible connection with the Rosen case. Or not. Now he wanted to talk to me. Somehow, I got the impression that we were always going to end up at this point and all of it arranged by Barker's hand.

I needed to change it up. Barker had been waiting for Harry and I had no idea why.

"Does anyone have any idea who Scott Barker is?" I said.

Lynch had turned away from Harper, put his back to her. He answered me, as Powers was too busy talking to King.

"We're running his fingerprints and DNA to make sure it's him, but he's got priors. Scott Barker is forty-four years old, born in Philadelphia. He moved around a lot after high school – so we've got convictions for possession of narcotics in a couple of states before he settles in New York and starts his own business buying and selling rare books and paintings. Seems he tried to set himself up as an art dealer. Last time he was arrested was for supply in 1998. And then nothing. The rest of his record is sealed," said Lynch.

"What do you mean, sealed?"

"I can't access the rest of the file – there's a court order sealing it. We're talking to Justice now and we should have it lifted soon."

I nodded, closed the laptop.

"Let's go see the judge right now," I said.

King nodded. All were in agreement.

"I'll see you there. I just need to make a stop first," I said.

CHAPTER FORTY-FIVE

Harper's Dodge pulled up outside a jazz bar, one of the few in White Plains. She'd agreed to give me a lift back to court and didn't mind picking up one more on the way. Harry Ford stood on the sidewalk, wearing a red sweater, tan pants, a gray coat and matching gray cashmere scarf. At first, he didn't approach the Dodge. He was still gazing up the street, looking for my Mustang.

"Is this another member of the defense team?" said Harper.

"Not exactly, but you can trust him. Harry might be able to help figure this whole thing out."

I wound down Harper's window and called out.

Harry stood with his back to the bar, silent and still, framed in neon and scotch. Under his left arm was a thick file of papers. The Rosen case.

I called again, louder this time.

He saw me, and came over. I got out of the car, shook hands, folded the passenger seat forward and climbed into the back of the Dodge. There wasn't much room in the back. There was a shelf that passed for a seat. I knew Harry couldn't fold himself into the back without incident – certainly not after a lengthy wait for me inside a jazz club. Harry threw the seat back, and it crushed my knees. He didn't notice. He just got in, closed the passenger door and introduced himself to Harper.

"What's going on?" said Harry.

As Harper took off into the two-lane, I filled Harry in on what had happened so far that day.

He didn't interrupt, just nodded every now and again while Harper took us toward the courthouse. With Harper present, I didn't mention anything of my theory that this case and the Rosen case were somehow connected. I didn't want Harper to know. Not yet. And Harry didn't react to the name Scott Barker. I'd leaned to the side, careful to watch his face in the vanity mirror when I said the name. It looked like the name was not known to Harry.

"This is delicate," said Harry. "I don't think the judge will let you talk to him. She can't. Any way you look at it, whatever you ask him is going to have an impact on the case, and therefore his testimony. If anyone talks to him about Caroline Howell outside of the witness stand it's an automatic mistrial. It's lucky he didn't say anything under police questioning. And do law enforcement know who this guy is?"

Harper told him they had agents working with the police on this, building a picture of Barker, but at the moment they had nothing to connect Barker to Howell.

We parked outside the courthouse. As I got out of the back, Harper took a call on her cell. Lynch, Washington, and the PD brass were standing outside the courthouse. At a guess, I'd say the call lasted close to a minute before Harper hung up, without having spoken a word.

A hundred feet ahead of us, outside the courthouse doors, Lynch reached into his jacket for his phone and I saw one side of his face light up as he took a call.

It could've been a coincidence, but I noticed Harper watching Lynch. Similarly, Lynch didn't seem to be talking. He ended the call and put his phone away.

New information. And Harper had made sure she got a call before the senior agent.

I stood beside the Dodge, hands in my pockets. After a few steps, Harper and Harry turned around, surprised that I hadn't followed them onto the sidewalk.

"What did you get on Barker?" I said.

Harper took a second to weigh up her options. I didn't flinch from her gaze while she decided if I'd made her. She stepped closer and spoke softly. Harry stood a little away from the two of us but close enough to pick up every word.

"Fingerprints threw up a couple more hits. Different IDs. He got pulled over on a DUI as Luke Pelley in West Texas, possession of narcotics as Scott Franklin in LA, and a different ID again in Westchester New York. Despite all the arrests, and different identities, Scott Barker has never done any time."

The agent had her hands in her pockets, her head to one side, and she'd been looking at the floor as she spoke. Only way you get busted and not go to jail is if you make a deal.

"Is he a professional snitch?" I said.

Her shoulders dropped an inch. She knew he was. A paid informant can take many forms. The pros make it their living to change identities and infiltrate criminal gangs. They're not cops and don't have to abide by the normal rules of an undercover, which means they can get deeper into the organization, and much faster.

"We don't have a clear picture on Barker yet. We're gathering everything—"

"But you suspect he's a pro snitch, and you already have something that's making you nervous," I guessed. "Come on, Lynch is going to tell the judge anyway – I may as well hear it from you."

She kicked at the ground, sighed and said, "From what I can gather he started off being a snitch, then went AWOL. Seems he had a talent for reinventing himself and disappearing. He was discharged five years ago. The cop who was handling him had to drop him after an operation went south and they did a psych profile on Barker. I'm getting clearance for it to be sent over now. He's a borderline sociopath, but – and here's the kicker – he's also highly intelligent. Like, seriously intelligent. He's got the IQ of a chess grandmaster. And he can become anyone."

"Is there any connection to Howell from his file?"

"We're working on it."

CHAPTER FORTY-SIX

Judge Schultz sat in a fat leather chair behind her desk in the judge's chambers, which were really just a large office, with two couches underneath the windows, and four swivel chairs arranged around her desk.

We filled up the whole place.

King, Powers, Groves and I sat in the office chairs, facing the judge. Lynch, Harper, Washington and the ADAs took up the couch space.

The judge leaned back in her chair and stared at the ceiling. She'd refused to look at the photo that Barker had produced to the court officer. I thought that was probably the right decision; Judge Schultz wanted to avoid any hint that she had prejudiced herself by examining something that wasn't yet admitted as evidence in the case.

But she listened to King as she laid out what had happened since the adjournment. The judge already had a lot of the story from the clerk who'd talked to the court officers.

"What do you have to say about all this, Mr Flynn?"

"Your Honor, my client is still in the hospital, so I don't have his view on this – but I don't see how anyone can talk to Mr Barker without compromising both his testimony and the entire trial."

She nodded. Took a good ten seconds to examine her ceiling fan. The soft burr of the fan blades cutting the warm air was the only sound in the room.

"Your Honor," said Powers, "We have arrest warrants out for Marlon and McAuley – Barker is very likely a co-conspirator. It may be that he will tell the court that the defendant arranged the kidnapping, or he may tell us where we can find our missing suspects and the ransom money. We don't know until we question him. But we absolutely must do so. And our twenty-four hours on the detention clock are ticking by."

"I appreciate the urgency of this matter," said the judge. "Mr Flynn, bearing in mind your client's condition, do you have any objections in relation to simply resuming the case with this witness, right now?" said the judge.

I thought it over. Howell had to hear this, but he was still unconscious.

"My client should be in court when this witness is questioned," I said.

The judge nodded and said, "I have to balance the prejudice to your client, with the urgency that has now entered this portion of the trial. In my view, this witness has to be dealt with quickly so that he can questioned by law enforcement. I'm also conscious that it appears to me that your client attempted suicide. He put himself in the hospital, Mr Flynn. It may be that his ultimate goal wasn't to kill himself, but simply delay the trial."

I opened my mouth to speak, but Judge Schultz held up her hand to silence me.

"At the end of the proceedings today – bearing in mind the strange statement made by Mr Barker – I expected the media to be speculating, wildly, about his testimony. That was a real concern to me – I had the jury sequestered."

King and I looked at each other. Neither of us knew about this.

"It was just for one night, initially. I wanted to see what the media were making of it and if there was a real risk of prejudice to the jury. So, in short, the entire jury is at a motel, right now. I imagine they're having dinner and we can probably get them all back into court within an hour. My ruling is we deal with this witness in open court, tonight. We resume in two hours."

Getting a doctor on the phone is like placing a call to the White House and asking to speak to the President. Eventually, after I threatened to get the doctor subpoenaed to appear in court the next day, I got thirty seconds with the physician. The news made me want to hammer my head into the desk in the small consultation booth two doors along the hallway from the courtroom. Howell should've been awake by now. But he wasn't. The reverse had happened. He was showing all the signs of coma. Apparently coma can occur in cases of heavy blood loss. The doc called it hypovolemic shock. Howell probably would wake up, but he could wake up in one hour, one week, or one month from now. Or possibly never. CT scans of the brain were good, a blood transfusion had saved his life but there was no sign of him regaining consciousness any time soon. We just had to wait.

Harry had spread out the Rosen case over the desk in the consultation room. He sipped at vending-machine coffee, made palatable with a splash of bourbon from his hip flask, as he read over the transcripts of the Rosen trial. We had some time before the case resumed and Harry wanted to refresh his memory.

I disconnected the call and tossed my phone onto a pile of documents.

"Howell is still out. It could be a coma," I said.

Harry nodded.

I picked up the last chunk of pages from the file and flicked through them. Nothing. I'd read the entire Rosen case from beginning to end. All of the witness statements, police evidence, and the court transcript. So had Harry. No mention of her sister, Rebecca, no mention of Howell or Barker. The last thing on the file was the booklet of photographs. I picked it up, watched Harry turn away. I didn't blame him. He had to look at those photos once, while preparing for the trial. He didn't need to look at them again. They would play like a reel of film in front of his eyes for the rest of his life. He'd warned me about the photos. Said there was nothing there. He was probably right, but I needed to make sure.

I flipped open the cover, scanned the photos of the blackened walls. The house had been totally gutted by fire. Sure enough, the nursery photos were there. And photos of the collapsed cot. I'd already read the forensic report. There was very little of the body left. Part of the rib cage remained, a partial thigh bone, and skull fragments. The rest was ash sitting on the metal springs of the mattress. When fire has an accelerant such as gasoline, the heat destroys everything. A human skull will fracture, flesh and sinew falls away, bone is reduced to powder. I closed the photo booklet, whispered a half-remembered prayer and closed my eyes as tight as I could.

"Maybe we're seeing this the wrong way," said Harry.

I opened my eyes, looked at him and said, "What do you mean?"

"Maybe it's not the case, but Julie Rosen herself. Something in her past that I didn't know about, or didn't know enough about at the time."

"The psychiatrist's report," I said.

Julie had pleaded not guilty to the murder of her child, Emily Rosen. The case took ten days and the jury considered their verdict for all of twenty-three minutes.

Julie Rosen was found guilty.

Harry had asked for a psychiatric evaluation prior to sentencing. The psychiatrist interviewed Julie, looked at all of her past medical history, her doctors and hospital records from birth, and found that she was suffering from a psychotic breakdown brought on by drug addiction and post-natal depression. She admitted smoking crack. The prosecution argued the drugs and the depression made her kill her child. The fact that she hadn't left the house or dialed 911 also led the prosecution and the psychiatrists to believe she was attempting suicide. They all believed Julie wanted to burn to death in that house, along with her baby. She was sentenced to life without the possibility of parole. After two years inside the prison authorities managed to move her to a facility for the criminally insane. At least there she would get treatment.

Both of us stood at the desk, moving piles of documents, looking for the psychiatric report.

"It's not here," said Harry. "I'll get a copy from court records." He got on the phone to his clerk and told him to get down to court and email him the record.

"We'll have it within the hour," said Harry.

"Howell told me that Julie Rosen killed her sister, his wife. You have any inkling of that when you represented her?"

"No. She told me there was no family. I'm not even sure I knew she had a sister before today. There's something in the back of my mind, though. I think I read something about her family. Maybe there's more detail on the family in the psych report."

Harry rubbed at the gray hairs on the top of his head that he could never seem to flatten down no matter how much hair product he used.

"Maybe we're looking at the wrong case," he said. "We need to go through every piece of the Howell case, from top to bottom, this time looking for Rosen and Barker."

"I don't think I missed anything but, sure, go ahead," I said.

Bundling up the Rosen case, Harry put it to one side as I handed him the files in Howell's case. Harry slipped on his earbuds, selected Beethoven on his iPod and started to read. He listened to classical music when he read. Said it helped the creative side of his brain: Bach for personal injury cases, Schubert for robberies, but it was always Beethoven for murder. When he wasn't working it was the Stones on vinyl. He said it was the only thing that helped him relax.

I got up, stretched, and left the consultation room in search of more coffee. The vending machine sat at the end of the hall. There was no one else around, and I heard my footsteps echoing as I made my way toward the machine, searching for change in my pocket. The sun had gone down and the ceiling lights made the place feel strange – somehow unfamiliar. Two of the lights were out at the end of the hall, making the small LEDs on the vending machine brighter and sharper by contrast.

Standing in front of the machine, I leaned toward it, trying to use the light from its electronic display so that I could see whether I had the correct change.

That's when I felt a hand clamping my mouth shut and a strong arm reaching over my shoulder from behind and pulling me toward a pitch-black alcove.

CHAPTER FORTY-SEVEN

My change clattered onto the floor, my heels bouncing along with the coins as I was dragged into the dark.

I felt myself being spun around, a palm flattened my lips and buried the back of my head into the wall. A fist shot out from the dark and into my ribs before I could get my hands up. Then someone gripped my tie and pulled it tight, choking me.

It took a few seconds for my eyes to adjust, but I saw who it was. There was no attempt at disguise.

Agent Lynch spoke quietly, but I could hear the anger and fear in his voice, rippling the tone and sending it high and then low.

"You listen to me, you piece of shit," he said. "I know it was you who switched the ransom money in the suitcase. I can't prove it, but I know. I won't let you destroy this case. The prosecutor is not going to ask Scott Barker any questions. None at all. Neither are you. He's going to be in and out of that witness stand in ten seconds and then I've got him. I can make him talk. If you start asking questions it might tip off McAuley and Marlon. I don't want that. Neither do you."

To emphasize his point, he pulled harder on my tie and slammed my head against the wall again. My vision blurred, but only for a second, and I could feel the back of my skull pulsing with pain. I scanned the corners of the hallway that were visible to me – no security cameras covering the alcove. Lynch had chosen this spot carefully.

"Don't worry. No one can see us. Now, do you understand me? When Barker gets on the witness stand you keep your mouth shut. If you mess up, I'll make sure you and your client will pay for it," he said.

I nodded and he eased the pressure on my face, then took his hand away completely and let go of my tie. He was out of breath, but his hands weren't shaking. He had let his anger get the better of him – he needed Howell to be found guilty to validate his handling of the investigation. He'd made the call on arresting the father of the murder victim and he'd been the one to lose the insurers' ransom money. If Howell turned out to be innocent then Lynch's career was finished.

My ribs were burning from Lynch's cheap shot, and I had to pull hard on my tie to loosen the tightened knot, letting me breathe again. I pushed off the wall, leaned out of the alcove and looked to my right, along the corridor. I knew there was at least one security camera halfway down the hall.

It was pointing in the opposite direction.

Lynch stood with his hands on his hips, watching me.

"Like I said, nobody can see us. Did you think the camera recorded me grabbing you at the vending machine?" he said, smiling. "Don't underestimate me. I had the cameras point the other way. Law enforcement sticks together, you know. Don't even think about running to Powers about this. It's your word against mine. This little conversation never happened."

His head turned to the left, to look at the camera; making sure it was still pointed away from us. He looked back at me, smiled and said, "Sorry to disappoint you."

"Oh, I'm not disappointed," I said. "I'm delighted."

Lynch wore a confused expression as my right hand folded his cheek in two. The snap punch caught him on the left side of his jaw, and his eyes closed as his legs folded beneath him. He landed on his back, and didn't move. I kept both eyes on the camera as I dragged him over to the benches that sat in front of the glass wall. His eyes were open as I put both hands underneath his arms, and hefted his ass onto the bench and laid him down.

His breath was coming fast, and his limbs were Jell-O.

I turned back to the vending machine, picked up the correct change from the floor and fed two bucks into the slot. By the time the second coffee had finished pouring, Lynch had managed to sit up. He was holding his jaw and staring at me.

I picked up the paper cups of coffee, one in each hand, and stood in front of the agent.

219

"You need to be more careful. Looks like you slipped on some loose change and fell. The cameras were pointing the other way. Your word against mine. Sorry to disappoint you."

He stared up at me, the rage returning to his gaze.

I turned and headed into the light.

I backed into the door to the consultation booth, letting it close behind me. I put Harry's coffee in front of him.

"What took you so long?" said Harry.

"I got into a fight with the coffee machine."

CHAPTER FORTY-EIGHT

Handing me a document from the Howell case, Harry poured a measure into his coffee from the silver hip flask as I read over the witness statement he'd fished out of the pile.

"We're missing something," said Harry.

The statement Harry gave me was from a PD tech who'd examined security footage from the New Rochelle rail station. I'd read it before. Twice.

It began by setting out the rationale for the footage search. The rail station only kept security footage for the last six months. The cell phone that had been found inside the locker was switched on and when the tech examined it, an hour after it was found, the cell retained a forty-three per cent charge. From the make and model the tech was able to discern that the cell phone held a charge, in standby mode, for around ten days. That meant that the phone had to have been placed in the locker around five days beforehand.

Yet, having gone through the entire footage for a full ten days, the tech had not seen anyone approaching that locker on the security footage.

"They've missed something," said Harry. "This is the only time frame that we know of where someone directly connected to the kidnapping was in view of a security camera. Somebody put the cell phone into the locker. They just haven't been able to see it."

I nodded.

"You're right," I said.

"Everything Barker has done has some meaning behind it. Four years of hiding in plain sight in Howell's organization. He has to be involved in Caroline's disappearance. There's something here that we're not seeing."

Harry's cell phone chimed. Dragging his thumb across the screen he squinted at the message and then handed the phone to me.

"My clerk copied the psychiatrist's report into an email. I can't read on these things – it's just too damn small. Tell me what it says," said Harry.

I didn't read the entire report, I scanned through it looking for the paragraph that dealt with the patient's history. There were long-standing mental health problems, exacerbated by drug and alcohol abuse. Family background was stable. Both parents were deceased. The doc noted that Julie Rosen lost contact with her sister about three months before the fire.

"Listen to this: '*When questioned about her relationship with her sister, Julie became agitated and then withdrawn. She said, "She hated me," and shrugged her shoulders. She refused to relate any feelings associated with her sister, and merely stated, "We weren't close," and repeated this answer when I put the question to her again. Ultimately I had to move on, as she became increasingly aggressive.*'"

There was no further mention of her sister.

"'*Julie stated to me simply, "I loved my baby. The man took her away from me." It is likely that no such person existed. Such thinking is indicative of paranoid schizophrenia, but there are deeper issues which lead to a more complex diagnosis. In all probability Julie has manifested sociopathic behavior for some time, which has gone untreated. She has an inability to express emotion toward her surviving family – her sister. The other possibility is a narcissistic pathology, consistent with sociopathy, which renders Julie incapable of empathy. This is evident by the matter-of-fact style of recall in relation to the death of her child.*'"

I looked up and saw Harry staring at the floor. The lids of his eyes looked as heavy as sacks of potatoes. There was a sadness in his face too.

He wiped at his eyes, and I saw tears glistening on the tips of his fingers.

"People aren't born like that. They are made. Drugs, sickness, whatever it is – Julie Rosen is a victim here too. Never forget that, Eddie. If she was lying about the man in black, then she's still a victim. No matter what kind of evil people do to each other – they harm themselves just as much as they harm others. Something broke inside Julie. No mother willingly harms their child. If she was telling the truth about the intruder, then I've let her down. I've failed her."

I nodded. I could've told Harry that there were no excuses for harming a child, but I didn't. I knew he wasn't making excuses for her. He was trying to do what we all do in the face of something bad, something evil – we try to understand.

Sometimes that works. Sometimes it doesn't because the act is so abhorrent that it can't be understood. In fact, it shouldn't be understood.

Placing Harry's phone on the desk, I then jotted down some notes, tore off the corner where I'd written a few lines and handed it to Harry.

"Think your clerk could find out a few more things for us?" I said.

Reading glasses hung from a fake gold chain around Harry's neck. He brought the half-rim glasses under his nose and stared at my notes.

"I'll see what I can do," he said.

Two knocks on the door made me turn. I got up, fist clenched, ready to lay out Lynch a second time if he tried anything.

It was Harper, with Washington standing behind her.

"The jury are here, the cops are on the way with Barker. His lawyer is here. He asked to speak to you and the prosecutor."

"What about?"

"Barker wants to make a deal."

CHAPTER FORTY-NINE

While defense lawyers had to make do with cramped, foul-smelling, and none-too clean consultation booths, the District Attorney's had a plush back office on the fifth floor of the courthouse. I'd left Harry in the consultation room, thinking and listening to Beethoven's Fifth. The elevator opened onto a landing with double doors ahead of us. There was a black pad on the wall beside the door, so that prosecutors could swipe their ID to open the doors. Harper went to the intercom that sat just above the swipe card reader and pressed the call button, igniting the LED that encircled the button.

More dull beeping, but faster this time, alerted Harper that both doors were now open. She pushed the right hand door and I followed her, Washington trailing behind me. There were an assortment of desks on the left, with ADAs typing on laptops surrounded by towers of paper. On the right, a bank of offices with glass walls and shades on the other side. Harper stopped at the last office, knocked on the door and went inside.

Another conference room, another polished wooden table surrounded by office chairs. Only this time the table was walnut, and the chairs looked as though they each cost as much as the conference table in the PD's office.

Sitting at the head of the table, Max Copeland laced his fingers together over the waistcoat of his tailored three-piece suit and gave me a hard stare. Bear was nowhere to be seen. My guess was Copeland figured he'd be secure in the courtroom without his minder. He ignored King on his right. I took a seat on Copeland's left so that together we formed a semi-circle. Harper and Washington closed the door and sat at the opposite end of the table. In the corner, I saw Groves and Powers.

Copeland checked his watch. Settled his hands on the table again and stared straight ahead.

"Agent Lynch will be here in a moment," said Harper.

For the sixty or so seconds that we waited in silence for Lynch to arrive, I didn't once take my eyes off Copeland. Not once in that minute did he look at me or break his gaze away from the blank wall in front of him.

The door to the conference room opened and Lynch came in fast. He'd slicked back his hair, and from the dark spots on his shirt I guessed he'd been in the john splashing cold water on his face and then running his fingers through his hair. Lynch acted like nothing had happened between us. He simply ignored me.

"We're all here. Let's have it," said King.

Copeland didn't react, didn't even acknowledge King. He waited for a moment, then drew back the cuff of his shirt revealing a gold Rolex. He gave the watch his full attention.

I didn't want to look away from this guy. He had an air about him – wealth, privilege, education, and all of the ruthlessness that you might expect to go along with it.

He let the cuff of his shirt slip back over the watch, bent down to his right and came back up with a lilac folder which he placed on the desk in front of him. With slightly chubby fingers, he adjusted the position of the folder, making sure it sat square on the table. He then turned to King and spoke.

"My client has now been in police custody for precisely two hours. At this time, I am authorized by my client to make an offer in relation to the possible resolution of this case, and other matters."

A black, gold-embossed pen seemed to appear in Copeland's hand and he made a small note on the front of the folder. I glanced at it and noticed he'd recorded the precise time, six fifteen.

"As you already know from the photograph of the victim supplied by my client, he is privy to highly significant, relevant, and credible evidence in relation to the kidnapping and murder of Caroline Howell. I am instructed to tell you that there is more than just the photograph; there's Peter McAuley and Marlon Black, and the ransom. My client will reveal all of the relevant evidence to the police and FBI in open court in exchange for the following: first, the conviction of Julie Rosen, now deceased, for murder and arson – will be declared unsound and her conviction overturned."

I looked around the room and saw confusion and surprise on a few faces. The raised eyebrows on King in relation to the audacity of such a request, but the rest of them were just confused at the mention of Julie Rosen; they'd never heard the name before.

"Second, full immunity from state and federal prosecution for my client in relation to his current charges and any part he may have played in the abduction and murder of Caroline Howell. This is my client's offer. It is final, and non-negotiable. This offer is on the table for the next thirty minutes. Once the time is up, the offer expires and there will be no further information from my client in court, there will be no further offers or negotiations," said Copeland.

Copeland just confirmed, beyond any doubt, that the Rosen case and Howell were connected. Only Copeland and I knew there was a connection. Now, everyone else would start piecing it together.

He removed a draft agreement from his folder, gave it to King. Raising his left hand, Copeland unstrapped his watch, placed it on the desk in front of him and waited. Everyone else got up and left.

I stayed.

CHAPTER FIFTY

"I heard you and your client didn't talk much at the precinct. Not at all, in fact. When did you get instructions to make this offer?" I said.

Copeland sat at the head of the table like a mannequin. Silent. Unflinching. Cold.

"Scott Barker, that's your client's real name, right? He wanted to talk to me I hear. Why is that?"

His big, bald head caught the ceiling lights as he adjusted his position, leaning forward on the table with both elbows on the walnut. The only answer was a sigh.

I got up, turned around to make sure the blinds were still drawn. They were almost fully down, but I could see the polished shoes of the cops and the FBI standing outside the room, and Harper's unpolished brown leather boots. The footwear disappeared as I pulled the shades down full. No cameras in the corners of the room, no view into any other offices. We were alone. Nobody could hear us. Nobody could see us.

For a smart guy, sometimes I do the stupidest damn things. Maybe it was the photos of ashen bones that had once been Julie Rosen's baby daughter; maybe it was the picture of Caroline Howell I'd seen in Howell's study where she wore a jacket just like my daughter's; maybe it was because I could still smell Howell's blood on my skin – maybe it was all of those things. Whatever it was, I lost it.

Without being immediately aware of it, I found myself whistling an old blues tune as I walked back to my seat, pushed my chair to one side, got myself two handfuls of Copeland's suit jacket and hauled him to his feet. His initial cries were drowned out by my high-pitched whistle. I didn't ask him anything. Didn't threaten him. At that moment I just wanted to hurt him.

He was too small to have been a football player, but he had the wide shoulders and barrel chest for the game. Powerful too. He grabbed my wrists and began to press down. His leverage and thinking were all good. I couldn't hold on to him for much longer – he was going to break my hold.

"Let go of me, this is assault," said Copeland.

His eyes burned in a way that I'd only seen before in cruel men. Those eyes were intense, almost lit from behind and yet wet. Like they'd been dipped in distilled hate.

The pressure was making my wrists ache. All I could think about was making Copeland suffer – like he'd made a lot of victims and their families suffer. I wanted him to get just a taste of what it was like to be angry, and know there was nothing he could do about it.

Every nerve in my body wanted to hurt Copeland. I fought down that urge, and let go. Backed up a few paces.

"An innocent seventeen-year-old girl is dead. Her father just tried to kill himself, and you and your client are playing games. This has all been carefully planned. Barker's arrest, this offer, the appeal in the Rosen case – all of it. I'm through playing games. You tell me what the hell is going on or I will finish you."

"You're the one who's finished," he said, drawing a cell phone from his jacket pocket. He held it up, swiped the screen. A graphic appeared of an old-time microphone.

"I've been recording the whole meeting. I've got you assaulting me on the record. Now get out," he said.

He was out of breath. The anger taking hold in his chest. I stood still, not letting him see that I was kicking myself. Grabbing him was a mistake. He locked the screen on his cell, put it back into the inside breast pocket of his suit and adjusted his tie.

I spoke slowly, keeping my anger in check, as I walked toward Copeland.

"This is bigger than my career," I said.

Another step toward him.

"This is bigger than your paycheck."

Close now. Another stride and I'd be on top of him. He took two steps backwards and his back hit the wall.

"You've crossed the line," I said.

"So have you," said Copeland.

I was in his face now. Almost touching him.

"You're right. I have crossed the line. So, if I decided to beat the hell out of you right here it wouldn't make much difference," I said.

We were eye to eye. Our faces inches from each other.

"I don't know why you're getting so upset, Flynn. You're a defense attorney – we're the same."

"Oh no, no way. I do my job, but I won't help a murderer, or a kidnapper, or anyone that I know is guilty beat the system. I've been down that road and I'm not going back."

"How do you know who is guilty, or who is innocent? You can't know, not for sure. Everyone lies."

"I can tell. I can smell it on them. Like I can smell it on you," I said.

I got the reaction I was hoping for. His lips curled into a look of disgust, and he put both hands on my chest and pushed me away.

Turning, I walked swiftly to the door, put his cell phone in my pants pocket and left.

CHAPTER FIFTY-ONE

Outside the conference room, in the corridor of the DA's office, the battle was already in full swing. King waved the agreement in the air, while Lynch battled with Harper and Washington. Powers and Groves were each on their cell phones.

The agreement was a lifeline for Michelle King. Her perfect prosecution case hung in the balance and it was her fault for calling Barker as a witness in the first place. She wanted control. The agreement handed the reins back to her and she would fight to get it. What Copeland asked for wasn't unusual. Most of the high-profile busts in the last twenty years came through snitches. Any decent snitch wanted his payday and his ticket out of jail in exchange for his testimony. That was the way the system worked. Law enforcement figured it was the lesser of two evils to let the middleman slide and do some real good by taking out the guy at the top.

If you're going to spill your guts about all the criminal acts you've witnessed, you can't usually do that without implicating yourself in those crimes, which is a direct violation of your right against self-incrimination. Instead of pleading the fifth, you get immunity for your own crimes first, and then you get to paint the full picture without fear of prosecution.

Immunity agreements were part of everyday life in the justice system.

But normally those agreements stopped short of payment. You talked, you walked. No cash. No new identity. If you were lucky you got a bus ticket and a pat on the back.

Copeland's client wanted a conviction overturned.

That's not so easy.

But the fact that Rosen was dead, the victim had no other family members and no father on the birth certificate, made it at least possible.

Copeland had already lodged the appeal – and the conviction could be overturned administratively by one signature from a friendly appellate court judge.

I was at the double doors that led to the elevator by the time Copeland opened the conference room door. "He assaulted me. He grabbed me," he said.

Before Copeland could speak, all the heads in the room slowly turned to look at me, accusingly.

"He fell. I was helping him up," I said.

I didn't stay for the argument. The release button for the door was on the left hand wall, and I slapped it and pushed my way out of there. A door closer slowed the swing of the heavy doors and I saw Copeland pointing at me and shouting at Powers and Lynch.

The elevator announced its arrival with a bright, perky chime. A hand caught the door to the DA's office and pushed it open again.

I was joined in the elevator by Harper and Washington. They stood either side of me. All three of us stared straight ahead as the elevator doors closed.

"They need to change the carpeting in that room," said Washington.

"Damn straight," said Harper. "I almost tripped over it myself."

The doors closed.

Washington said, "He'll want to press charges."

I shrugged.

"I can't see a District Attorney prosecuting a case for an assault against the most hated defense lawyer in the state. Particularly when that lawyer alleges he got assaulted in the DA's own office with the Chief of Police and the FBI standing outside the room. They didn't hear any kind of commotion. His word against mine. No, that case would be deeply embarrassing for Ms King, and I've got a feeling such a case wouldn't enjoy reasonable prospects of success."

"Don't bet on it. Copeland's not the kind of man to let this go so easily," said Harper.

My hands dove into my pockets. I brought out Copeland's cell phone, flicked my finger across the screen to bring it to life.

I was met with a ten digit number pad and a request to enter the password to unlock the device. A temporary inconvenience at worst.

The overhead lighting in the elevator felt offensively bright, and perfect for my purposes. I held the phone up, and angled it so that it caught the light. On the screen, I could see two groups of circular smudges in the top left hand corner and just below and opposite. In between was a long smear, made by Copeland's thumb scrolling through the phone. The groups of fingerprints on either side sat perfectly over the "6" and "1" on the password screen. I figured Copeland to be in his late forties, to early fifties. Year of birth could be sixty-six. I typed in 1-1-6-6 and the screen unlocked.

The menu icon sat in the corner of the screen. I selected it and disabled phone calls by activating airplane mode, I made sure he couldn't trace the phone by deactivating the location signal. In another app, I found the audio recordings. There were a bunch of them, labeled under different names. Client names, I suspected. The audio folder titled "Vindico" held three recordings.

By checking the time signatures on the recordings I found the one he'd just made, and deleted the file. I wanted to listen to the other two files, but they would have to wait.

I couldn't resist checking the rest of the phone. The text messages were mostly from "Office" and contained dates and times of cases for hearing, and names and telephone numbers for various people.

Like, "Taggart. Rape. November 30th Brooklyn, Court 4."

But some messages were more personal. He'd had an exchange of texts with his office about my visit that morning.

He thought I was fishing. His secretary thought I was too, but added that she thought I was cute. She didn't get a reply to that message.

July 2011

Premier Point, New York

The bright purples, reds, yellows and whites of Rebecca Howell's garden seemed pale and gray to her. She sat at the kitchen window, looking over the lawn, the flower garden and the lane beyond. Perhaps the tears that had flooded her vision all day were somehow filtering all color from her view. That's what she'd thought, at first. Today had been hard. Harder than most days and every single waking morning had been agony for her, for so long.

But today was special. It was okay to cry today.

One of Caroline's friends had invited her for dinner, and then study. School would finish soon, for the summer, and Caroline's last exam was next week. God, the thought of having her for another summer had made Rebecca feel physically sick.

Those first years of Caroline's life had been bliss. The night feeds, the early mornings, the crying, colic, toilet training, all of the difficult things that parents complain about had not bothered Rebecca in the slightest. She had her special baby. The child that she had longed for, for years and years. Her little miracle.

Rebecca had insisted that they move after the baby was born. She told Leonard that they needed a bigger house, somewhere quiet, somewhere far away. At first, Leonard didn't want to move, but the business with Rebecca's sister had proved to be the final straw. Her sister's trial brought attention. She wanted to leave, to get away, before the reporters found her. Rebecca hadn't gone back to work following Caroline's birth – she was still on maternity leave. The county employed a retired medical examiner to fill in during her absence. If the press found out her career could suffer, her new family could suffer. Our family is private, she had told Leonard. And for a time, their new life away from it all had been the happiest that Rebecca could remember.

But as Caroline grew older, things changed.

It was that first trip to the lake when Caroline turned seven. Watching her child splash in the shallows with her husband. Remembering her own childhood with Julie, when they had played in the same pools, and run along the same country paths.

Too much.

She spent less and less time with her daughter. Until, finally, she could not stand to look upon the face of her special child.

That was when she'd decided that she'd made a mistake. Later that morning, she dropped Caroline at school and visited the little stationery store a block up from the school gates. She bought writing paper and a pen, returned home and sat now in her kitchen, staring out of the window through her tears.

Rebecca took up the pen, and removed two sheets of writing paper from the cellophane wrapper.

Her pen flowed quickly over one page, then the next. She folded the second page, put it in an envelope, wrote "Lenny" on the front of the envelope and left it for him to find. The second letter she would mail.

Standing at her open front door, she looked around the house for the final time. At last, she grabbed her car keys from the bowl in the hall and left.

CHAPTER FIFTY-TWO

I knew the DA, the cops, and the FBI had agreed to meet Barker's demands before they officially came to tell me as I waited outside the courtroom. From the atrium window I'd seen a black Mercedes pull up outside, a white-haired guy in a navy suit get out of the passenger seat, sign a document held by a clerk on a clipboard, fold his old white ass back into the Mercedes and take off into the night.

Appellate court justice in full swing. Only it was usually the other way around. A lawyer could spend years working on appeals for a wrongly convicted man, only to have an appellate judge spend five seconds glancing at the papers before deciding not to bother reading it, and that the guy was probably guilty of something and deserved to rot away in a cell for the rest of his life.

The clerk ran back into the building.

I knew this was bad. Scott Barker was getting everything he wanted. His game was playing out exactly as he'd planned.

The corridor lighting threw my reflection onto the glass. My tie was undone, hanging loosely at my open collar. I looked like I'd aged a year in a day. I felt it too. My legs were sore, my back and my neck. And my ribs were still smarting from Lynch's shot.

I rubbed at the fleshy muscle at the top of my shoulders, working my fingers deep into the tissue.

"They were always going to take the deal," said Harry.

His reflection joined mine. Seeing both of us in the glass made me realize how much weight Harry had lost. The Rosen appeal was eating him.

"I figure if the appeal is granted without a hearing, you won't face the same kind of criticism," I said.

"Don't bet on it. I was informed by the Commission on Judicial Complaints, in no uncertain terms, that if the appeal was granted I would be expected to resign. The pleadings Copeland has lodged have already created a stink." said Harry.

"And are you going to resign?"

"No. Not like this. Copeland knew the appeal would ultimately go this way. It has been planned, very carefully. I won't bow down to that son of a bitch. No way. I was never going to be Supreme Court Justice anyway."

"I'm glad to hear it," I said.

"I'm a small part in a clever man's game. You know, in many ways, it's easier predicting what an intelligent man will do than what a stupid man will do. Don't you think?" said Harry.

I said nothing. Just stared at the glass, our image framed in the lukewarm glow of halogen lighting and the night sky.

"There's often meaning, or at least significance behind every act conceived by a great mind," said Harry.

"What do you mean?" I said.

"Well, take the fake name, for example. George Vindico."

"What about it?"

"It has meaning," said Harry, with a sigh.

"Means nothing to me."

"I think it will, in time. George could be from Saint George. One of the most famous saints. He was a soldier. Legend says he slayed the dragon that cut off the water supply to a village, and that in later life George became a martyr when he refused to renounce Christianity."

"That's a bit of a leap, Harry. Could be he picked the name George because he's a boxing fan or he's got one of Foreman's grills at home."

Harry didn't laugh.

"I don't think so. Not when you consider the last name – Vindico. It's Latin. It means 'revenge'. I think Scott Barker created his fake identity to get close to Howell so that he could take revenge for Julie Rosen. He's getting her a posthumous acquittal. He's making her a martyr."

I considered what Harry had said.

"If that's true, then who is the dragon he's trying to slay?" I said.

Harry shook his head.

"That's what you've got to find out," he said.

The courtroom doors behind us swung open, and Michelle King stood in the open doorway. She held a signed document in her hand. She was smiling. She'd got what she wanted.

I knew in my bones that the only person who'd gotten what they wanted was Scott Barker.

"We're starting in five minutes. We've made a deal with Barker. Full immunity. He'll reveal everything on the stand. We learn about the truth same time as you," said King.

I nodded.

"Be careful in there, Eddie," said Harry.

CHAPTER FIFTY-THREE

I'd been practicing as an attorney for a good many years. I was still young, but I had put in my time in the courtroom. I knew a few tricks. I'd seen things. During a complex mail fraud trial I'd seen a juror fall asleep right in the middle of the prosecution's opening statement. Couple of years ago, a juror in a robbery homicide case had not looked at me, or any of the witnesses, or the judge or the prosecutor for the whole two weeks of the trial. He'd stared at the ceiling the whole time.

I thought I'd seen everything.

But I never saw a jury so pissed off in all my life.

Every single one of them.

I folded my arms, scowled at the judge and the DA and made a point of looking pissed too. I kept the jury in my peripheral vision as they took their seats. A couple of them nudged the juror next to them, then subtly hinted in my direction.

See, he's just as angry as we are.

Any chance I got to get into bed with a jury, I took it. Little things sometimes make all the difference.

A cop in uniform followed behind Scott Barker as he made his way back to the witness stand. The cop stood to the right of the jury, and let Barker make the last few strides to the witness stand. Seeing him walk normally told me a lot. His back was straight, feet fairly wide apart as he walked, and his arms swung loosely by his sides. He gave the appearance of a man on his way to do some serious damage in a fight; he was always in perfect balance and control.

A hand on my shoulder. Harper.

The judge was arranging her papers on her desk, King was whispering to her assistant and the jury were being handed their trial folders by a clerk.

"What is it? Not much time here," I said.

She knelt down, and I could feel her breath on my neck as she whispered.

"I've just heard, somebody from the Justice Department is on their way here, right now. Guy called Alexander Berlin. He has information on Barker . . ."

The clerk had handed out six trial bundles to the six jurors in the front row. She stepped up to the back row and gave out another six.

"No time, just tell me what you've got," I said.

"He started out as a drug runner. Got caught by the DEA and turned snitch. He brought down the whole organization. But Justice kept him on a leash and sent him out to do the same thing again. This guy has been in some of the toughest holes in the US, getting cozy with the hardest, worst people you can imagine. Somewhere along the line, he forgot he was supposed to be working for the good guys. Berlin suspects Barker has killed to get inside these organizations, but they can't prove it. It's confirmation – this guy will do anything to get what he wants, including murder."

All of the feeling disappeared from my fingers. Like I'd just held them in an ice bucket for a half hour. I turned, and saw Harry a row back, watching Barker.

"Jesus, and he's been with Howell all this time," I said.

"I know. Just watch yourself."

"Does the DA's office know this?" I said.

Harper shook her head, got up and walked away to take a seat in the row behind Harry.

Judge Schultz cleared her throat, and began explaining to the jury that there was essential testimony which had to be given in this trial, that it was time-sensitive due to another unrelated matter, and that the jury should hear it tonight. At least three audible groans from the jury could be plainly heard in the courtroom. When the judge told them they'd get an additional payment for the late sitting, it brought the jurors to life, and made the most belligerent of them shut up.

Judge Schultz finished her address to the jury.

Michelle King got to her feet, opened her notes and asked the witness her first question.

"When we were last here, you had indicated that your real name was Scott Barker, not George Vindico. Why did you take a false name?"

The question seemed a little alien to Barker. His eyes took on a fixed stare, and he ignored the crowd, much thinned thanks to our late proceedings.

"I created the identity of George Vindico for my own purposes. To get close to Leonard Howell and his daughter."

Everyone within a twenty-foot radius of Michelle King heard her neck crack as her head snapped in the direction of the jury stand. The jurors were confused, shocked, palms raised, mouths open.

"Your Honor . . ." said King.

"No way, Ms King," said the judge. Barker's answer was not what King was expecting. He was hinting that he was the one who'd targeted Caroline Howell. I knew King had been about to ask the judge for a mistrial. An unexpected statement like that could prejudice any jury. But Schultz was having none of it. Not yet.

King had to regain control or go down in flames. From the defense table, I saw the veins pulse in her throat, her neck and cheeks turning from pale pink to deep, violent red. Everything she'd ever worked for hung on the strength of her next question. Her eyes suddenly took on a sharp focus, and I knew she'd found something to anchor Barker's testimony.

She turned, picked out a document from the top of the pile on her table, and handed it to the clerk. The clerk gave it to the judge. Schultz skim read the ten-page agreement. Handed it back to the clerk who swiveled in her chair and returned it to King.

As King's high heels echoed on the floor, I thought I could detect a new confidence in the rhythm and determination of her stride. She slapped the document onto the small shelf in the witness stand, spun away and backed up ten feet. Without picking it up, Barker glanced at the document.

"This document is an immunity agreement, which you signed, in the presence of witnesses, not ten minutes ago, correct?"

She was leading the witness, and I could've objected, but Schultz would not have sustained my interruption – she was prepared to give King some leeway with this guy.

"Yes," said Barker.

The jury looked as though they were on a rollercoaster that was sailing up the incline, the wheels slowly clacking along, their apprehension building the closer the car got to the drop.

"Mr Barker, this agreement grants you immunity from prosecution in relation to your part in the kidnapping and murder of Caroline Howell in exchange for your testimony in this case against the defendant, isn't that correct?"

"Not quite," said Barker.

"Excuse me?" said King.

"Not quite," said Barker, again. Louder this time.

The flush returned to King's neck, and she clasped her hands together tightly, the whites of her knuckles standing out against the backdrop of scarlet nail polish.

"The agreement is very clear, and was explained to you by your lawyer before you signed it, Mr Barker."

"Oh, I agree. The wording of the agreement is plain and clear," he said, picking up the document.

He flipped over a page and his lips moved quickly and silently as he read through the document looking for a particular passage.

"I refer you to clause five, sub-paragraph one," said Barker.

One of King's assistants grabbed a spare copy of the document and held it out to her boss. King snatched it, turned over one page and found the clause.

"I shall read it to you, if you like," said Barker. "The above-mentioned immunities, and all of them, are conditional upon the following. Sub-paragraph one states: The detainee shall testify as a prosecution witness in the trial of Leonard Howell, and shall provide truthful testimony detailing the involvement of Leonard Howell in the kidnapping and murder of Caroline Howell."

The wording of the agreement was unusual. Not standard fare by any means. Nothing about this case was standard, and the prosecution wanted Howell so bad they jumped into Max Copeland's agreement without thinking twice about it. Even so, the meaning of the clause was clear – tell us Howell did it, and you get off.

"Correct, Mr Barker," said King. "As per the agreement, you are here to testify against the defendant, Leonard . . ."

"You still don't get it, do you? I'm here to, and I quote, 'provide truthful testimony detailing the involvement of Leonard Howell in the kidnapping and murder of Caroline Howell.'"

Losing the case, or getting fired and watching your career slide into a dumpster – all of these fears faded into the background for King. She'd had enough. Barker had pushed too many buttons. She practically spat the next question at him.

"Then let's have it, Mr Barker. Detail for us Leonard Howell's involvement in the kidnapping and murder of his daughter."

It could only have been four or maybe five seconds of silence in between the question and Barker's answer. Not a long time, really. But in a courtroom full of people, with a question like that, it was an age. It reminded me of the slow-mo replays on the mega screen at Yankee Stadium. The pitcher throws out and the camera slows down time itself. We see the ball spinning as it breaks through the air and, simultaneously, the batter starts to unwind from the hips, twisting his torso, turning his shoulders and heaving that bat toward the ball. In the distance between them, we can see all possibilities – strike three and you're out, or home run and the visitors take the game at the bottom of the ninth.

King's question may as well have been an underarm practice throw, and Barker was Babe Ruth.

"None," said Barker. "Leonard Howell had no involvement in the kidnapping of his daughter. To my knowledge, he never harmed a single hair on her head."

CHAPTER FIFTY-FOUR

"Your Honor, I have a motion at this time," I said, getting to my feet.

Schultz said, "Not so fast."

I was going to ask her to stop the trial and direct the jury to return a verdict of not guilty. It maybe was a little premature – but I bet a half dozen judges in the same district would've granted my motion and made Howell a free man.

Not Judge Schultz. At that moment she was more interested in what the DA was saying. Because while I was getting to my feet, King had already made a second request to treat her own witness as hostile. Schultz said, "Absolutely," and we were on.

"Mr Barker, your agreement . . ." King trailed off. Re-reading the clause, her forehead creased and her left hand came toward her mouth. The index finger of that hand settled on her lips and she read the clause again. Her arms dropped by her sides. The agreement was at once clear and yet open to a number of interpretations. On one reading, it hinted at Howell's involvement – on another, it stated Barker would speak to Howell's involvement but the agreement itself was silent on the extent of that involvement.

"Mr Barker, are you stating that you murdered Caroline Howell along with the defendant?"

It was a Hail Mary of the worst kind. Either King got results, or the whole case collapsed. And I was waiting.

"No. I did not kill Caroline Howell. Neither did her father."

"Then who did?" said King.

A huge risk. The question was wide open and Barker could say anything. I guessed King was hoping to get some wild theory – about aliens or extremists – and she could then expose Barker as a loon, so that nobody would believe him. That was her only play now, she had to destroy her own witness's credibility.

"No one did. You've been lying to this jury, Ms King. So has your expert witness, Birch. Caroline Howell is not dead."

A smirk appeared at the side of King's mouth, but she quickly forced it away. This was what she was after – the more ridiculous Barker sounded the better.

"Mr Barker, Caroline Howell's arterial blood was found in a crime scene that the defendant attempted to destroy. DNA doesn't lie. You're the one who's lying, isn't that right?"

"I am many things, Ms King. I've lied to many people, for many years. But I have my honor. I take my duty very seriously. When I stepped into this witness stand I took an oath on the Bible. I will keep that oath and speak the truth. Caroline Howell is alive."

"And how do *you* know this? How do *you* know she's alive?"

"Because I have her. Leonard Howell should think of me as his priest. And unless he confesses his sins, she'll be dead in twelve hours."

PART
III

CHAPTER FIFTY-FIVE

I'd never seen a statement from a witness punch an entire courtroom like that. It was a shockwave. The jury recoiled, like they'd been blasted by an explosion. I heard gasps, and one woman in the gallery even had to stifle a scream. King had unleashed a Goddamned tornado that ripped through the room.

She just stood there. Stunned.

In that moment, while every living being in the room tried to process this statement, Barker reached under the small shelf in the witness stand that held the microphone and served as a half desk for any exhibits that the witness may need.

A sound like tape being torn: something adhesive being pulled away. His hands came up with a strip of tape, and something small and black. He pulled the item away from the adhesive tape, reached up and slotted it into the TV that sat beside the witness stand. Only then did I see it was a flash drive. He'd arrived in court with this drive, and taped it under the shelf of the witness stand before he showed the court officer the photo of Caroline Howell and got himself arrested.

The TV came to life automatically as its hard drive loaded up the flash drive. An image appeared on the screen – identical to the photo Barker had earlier. Caroline Howell curled up at the bottom of a concrete grave.

"What are you . . .?" King's words died as she looked at the screen.

Whatever had happened, I'd missed it, as my attention had shifted to King when she began to speak. I looked back at the screen.

That's when I saw it.

This wasn't a photo.

Caroline's feet moved.

This was a video. A hand came into shot, up close, it held a copy of the *Washington Street Journal*. The date was yesterday. The headline devoted to the Middle East peace summit that was set to begin yesterday morning. The hand flipped over the paper, displaying the text below the fold. There was the lead article on the Caroline Howell case beginning today in White Plains, NY, and a picture of Leonard Howell.

The hand dropped the paper into the grave, and its pages fluttered open and landed on Caroline like a paper blanket.

A man stepped in front of the camera. It was Barker.

I managed to tear my eyes from the screen and I looked at him and saw he was the only person in the court not looking at the TV. He wasn't watching me. His eyes were not on King, or the judge, or the jury. He was staring into the crowd. I turned and saw Harry Ford. He was standing up in the middle of a row, some guy behind him was asking him to sit down but Harry ignored the guy – his eyes were locked on Barker.

I looked up at the screen just as it went blank and the video ended with a close-up on Barker's face. Then Baker's voice echoed around the room. But not from the video – he was standing up and addressing the court.

"I give this warning to everyone in the room – do not test me. I will not tell you what Howell has done. I need to hear his confession from his own lips. Then, and only then, will I let his daughter go. If he doesn't confess in twelve hours – she dies."

Judge Schultz hammered the gavel, and stood, shouting, "Court adjourned." She made toward her chambers, her hands over her mouth, and her shoulders heaving.

The jury were led out of the court by the bailiff, suddenly snapping to life, and he had to yell at one of the male jurors who was pointing and swearing at Barker. Half of the jury were in tears, the others didn't know what the hell was going on.

Agent Lynch, followed by two cops, marched past me, headed for the witness stand. Barker was lifted from behind by a big, bald cop, and thrown over the witness stand, knocking the mic to the ground. He was handcuffed, and led out of the court, Agent Lynch removing the flash drive and placing it into an evidence bag.

Michelle King had to be restrained by her assistant as Barker was led past her.

For the first time in my career I had no clue what the hell I was supposed to do. My neck craned back and I looked at the ceiling and felt like I wanted a drink more than oxygen. I needed Howell. I needed answers. With Howell in a coma, I had nothing.

Harry shook me, and I came out of it, I couldn't hear him calling me. My mind was spinning like a carousel.

"Eddie, I need to talk to you. I think I know what this is about," said Harry.

CHAPTER FIFTY-SIX

Harry would have to wait.

The judge called me and King into her chambers. Both of us knew exactly what the judge was going to do. The probable outcome suited King just fine. She'd been played by Barker. Just like he'd played everyone.

Grinding a large eraser in between her fingers, Judge Schultz spoke with barely contained rage.

"Ms King, I realize this is probably not your fault. I'm not apportioning blame here – but there's no doubt in my mind. This witness has twice brought evidence that was not in the prosecution's possession into a live trial. No one has the slightest hope of knowing how authentic or otherwise this evidence is – and I'm certainly not going to let the jury consider it. It's not fair on your client, Mr Flynn, but this trial has become a total circus. I'm declaring a mistrial. The jury will be released and we'll empanel a new jury in two weeks. Hopefully your client will have recovered by then, Mr Flynn. And Miss King, hopefully you'll have had time to consider the evidence that Barker has provided. Maybe he should be on the indictment along with Leonard Howell? Or maybe the prosecution have made a terrible mistake here. Think carefully about this, Miss King."

I thought I saw King's eyes tear up. She shook her head and said, "No, Your Honor. Mr Barker will not be a defendant. He has an immunity agreement. And the prosecution are convinced that this was a stunt by Mr Barker, to have the defendant acquitted."

"You can't be serious?" I said.

She swallowed and said, "Our position remains. We have her life's blood on a wall, confirmed by DNA analysis. She's dead. And her father kidnapped and murdered her."

Prosecutors operate through blind faith in the system. Not the justice system, of course. No, the prosecutorial system. If you spend all day, every day, putting people away for years and years, you've got to believe that what you're doing is right. The cops bring you the case, you look at the evidence, maybe ask for a little more, and then you run that bull through the court straight toward a conviction – every time. If a smart defense lawyer manages to get the defendant an acquittal, it eats at your very soul. That was wrong. You're right. You see the prosecutor's mind laid bare in the court of appeals. Maybe the Innocence Project have new DNA evidence that makes it clear, beyond any reasonable doubt, that the convicted prisoner is in fact innocent. How many prosecutors look at that evidence and say, "Okay, we got this one wrong. Open the doors and let this guy out." Very few would even contemplate it. They fight. The defense is wrong. They're right.

King had already been sucked into that vortex of opposition. She was smart, but if you put blinkers on every day, soon you won't be able to see anything.

Judge Schultz couldn't even bring herself to look at King. The judge knew this was prosecutor blindness. Nobody who'd seen that video could doubt it.

"Get out, both of you," said the judge.

"No," I said.

The judge froze. She didn't speak, just held out a finger pointing toward the door.

"If you declare a mistrial then Barker is no longer under oath. He can walk away and come back for the new trial. And if he's telling the truth, Caroline Howell will be dead by then. He's given us a window to save her. It might be bull, but it might be true. If it is true and you declare a mistrial – you're killing that girl."

"But the trial has been broken, irreparably," said Judge Schultz.

"I know that. You know that. Miss King knows that. But Barker and the jury don't. My client is in a coma and whatever Barker wants from him, well, he's not going to get it from Howell. Give me some time. Let me cross-examine. A seventeen-year-old girl's life could be at stake."

King nodded and said, "As long as we agree, right now, that this is no longer a real trial. So the public and the press are barred, and Barker's testimony is sealed."

Judge Schultz tapped her pen on her desk. I could hear the soft crunch of her teeth grinding together.

"Can't you arrest this man?" she said.

King shook her head. "The immunity agreement. I don't want to be the first prosecutor to get her victim killed during the trial of their murderer. We can play along for twelve hours. Then one way or another, we'll know the truth. If it's all lies – we've lost nothing. But if it's true and we let this man walk out of here . . ."

"I get it," said the judge. "We'll lock down the building. The jury and court staff stay, defense, prosecution – and no one else."

"What about Barker?" said King.

"The holding cells will do for now. How much time do you need, Mr Flynn?"

King and I didn't speak as we made our way out of the back offices. The clerk led us out, back into the courtroom which was now completely empty. The jury was in their holding room and would remain there for the next four hours. I couldn't face Barker without knowing exactly what was going on, what Howell had supposedly done, and without knowing exactly how I was going to play it.

Four hours. That's the time Judge Schultz had given to me. If I couldn't unravel this in that time I would have to start asking Barker questions anyway. The feds and King would help get as much information as possible. King didn't want this – but she couldn't ignore Barker.

Our feet echoed loudly on the hard floor of the deserted court-room. The silence felt strange after so much noise, so much incident.

It felt like a bar, or a house, straight after the meat wagon took a corpse away in a body bag. There was a presence in the room. Like a stain brought about by sudden bloody violence. You could taste it, feel it.

I gathered my files and made my way out.

Harry was waiting for me in the corridor. He had a bundle of pages under his arm, and a worried expression on his face.

"I know who George's dragon is," he said.

CHAPTER FIFTY-SEVEN

The cops, the FBI and the prosecution team disappeared upstairs into the DA's office for a crisis meeting. From the hallway window I saw Copeland, wearing a pair of handcuffs and being folded into the back of a patrol car. I'd hoped that Powers would arrest him. That was a good call. He was in on it with Barker and Powers was gonna lean on him hard. Both of them would be in custody now, but Barker had a golden ticket out of there.

My cell rang. Harper.

"What's happening?" I said.

"World war three. Everyone's blaming each other. Lynch is getting a lot of fingers pointed at him. PD have taken Copeland back to the precinct, but they won't be able to hold him very long. Barker is in the cells and is refusing to speak to anyone – says he'll only talk in court, under oath. We heard back from legal – that Goddamn immunity agreement is watertight. Even if he's really got Caroline, he could blow her head all over the pavement in the middle of Times Square and legally the only thing he could be arrested for would be littering. This is so messed up. We're going to map out a possible search area for Caroline and get boots on the street – FBI, PD, even firemen and traffic wardens. We think that if he's got her, she's probably not being held too far away. We could really use Howell right now. What are the chances of him waking up anytime soon?"

"I talked to his doctor a few minutes ago. They don't know. There's a chance he could wake up, but we need to work on the basis that he won't. Barker wants a confession from Howell, we need to figure out what he thinks Howell has done."

"Is this something to do with the Rosen case that Copeland mentioned in the deal? We're pulling the file."

"I don't know for sure yet. I'm going to talk to Harry. See if we can figure things out. I'll call you in an hour and if we come up with anything, you'll be the first to know."

I disconnected, and joined Harry in the consultation booth.

"Maybe we should get out of here for a little while. I can't sit in this courthouse any longer – it's not helping. Plus, looks like it's going to be a long night. I say we go get a drink and talk this over," said Harry.

I checked my watch. Coming up on seven o'clock.

"Sure, I could use a drink," I said.

Harry drove us for all of three minutes before we found a suitable spot. The bar's proximity to the courthouse was about the only thing it had going for it. The sign above the door was a three-foot-by-ten-foot board, but the paint had long since faded away making the bar anonymous. Didn't matter. The spotlights above the sign had blown out and because nobody could read the sign anyway it at least saved the owner the hassle of changing the bulbs.

Inside, it was dark, warm, and smelled of men, grease and hops. My kind of place. A short L-shaped bar on the right with a short L-shaped bartender behind it. He was in his sixties, grizzled and bent over with age and a good deal of booze, probably tequila. "What'll it be," he asked, and I almost asked for a slice of lemon – so powerful was the smell of tequila on his breath.

Harry ordered two doubles of Irish, and told me to take a seat in back, where one lamp burned over a table in the corner. Two or three hardened drinkers studied their folded newspapers on bar stools, but apart from that, we had the place to ourselves. I put my files on the table and went in search of seats.

By the time I'd found two stools to go with the table, Harry arrived with the drinks. He put two lowball glasses of whiskey in front of him, and pulled an open bottle of Pepsi from his coat pocket and put it in front of me.

I wanted a real drink.

My problem was that I wanted a lot of real drinks.

I took a slug from the bottle of Pepsi. It was warm.

"No ice? No glass?" I said.

Harry examined a greasy fingerprint on the inside of the first glass of Bush and said, "You're probably safer drinking out of the bottle. I'm thinking of canceling our food order."

"You ordered food in this place?"

"Sure, I'm hungry. I ordered pizza off the menu. The bartender made a call. He's ordering in. I'm probably being charged double for a bacon and mushroom pizza from the place on the corner. Still, at least it wasn't cooked here."

He took a long sip, smacked his lips, set his drink down then went fishing through the papers on the table. It took a few seconds, but eventually he drew a police report out of the pile of papers. I could tell it was a police report because of the badge logo in the corner of the first page. He handed it to me.

"I already read the report in the Rosen case," I said.

"You haven't read this. I got it faxed to the court office. A cop I know in the precinct did me a favor. You told me Howell hated Julie Rosen because he held her responsible for his wife's death. This is the police report into the suicide of Rebecca Howell."

CHAPTER FIFTY-EIGHT

Some cops put down the facts in their reports and nothing more. Some tell you what happened, then they tell you what they think really happened.

The cop who'd investigated the incident was Officer Theo Cruz. He was the type to let the DA know what he was thinking in his reports. It was a subtle art, learned on the job and perfected with years of experience.

A long-distance truck driver called Al White had called in the accident over his CB radio. That part of Upstate New York where the accident happened had no cell-phone coverage, as Al discovered when he'd tried to use his cell to call 911. He was on a twisting, mountain road and came around a right-hand corner to see a silver, family SUV in his lane. He hit the braking sequence on the rig and pulled the horn.

Al said the car didn't move, it stayed in his lane and drove straight for him. He even saw the woman driving the SUV. She looked calm, relaxed even.

At the last moment the SUV swerved out of his lane and went straight through the crash barrier on the opposite side of the road and over the precipice.

Al got the truck stopped, radioed in the accident then climbed down out of the cab and ran to the crash barrier. Below him was a sheer drop. Maybe a thousand feet to the bottom of the canyon. A river flowed fast below, and he saw the SUV, upside down just before it sank beneath the depths.

He waited for the paramedics and the cops.

Officer Cruz was first on scene, ahead of the ambulance and mountain rescue. He spoke to Al, and surveyed the crash scene.

He noted Al's description of the calm demeanor of the SUV driver, and the fact that they didn't get out of the way of the truck at first, even after it had sounded its horn. In his statement, Officer Cruz recorded that the crash barrier which the SUV penetrated was a temporary barrier of wooden construction. Apparently a cattle truck went through the steel barrier some weeks before after a collision with another vehicle.

On a separate sketch, Cruz traced the path of the SUV from the marks on the road. Although the SUV had only braked briefly as it turned, the angle of the tread was enough to determine that the driver had hit the barrier head on, at speed. The lack of skid marks before the barrier meant the driver didn't try to brake at this point.

Cruz underlined that although this barrier was on a bend, it was a gentle, sweeping bend.

The last line of the report laid out the important facts of the accident, not as a finding, but letting the DA know Cruz's mind.

"It was almost as if the driver moved into the lane of oncoming traffic to create the perfect angle to hit the damaged barrier head on, so as to ensure her vehicle passed through the safety barrier and into the crevasse. The driver, Rebecca Howell, was found inside the SUV by county divers in the Terracotta River."

Appended to the report was the medical examiner's verdict: Suicide. The ME confirmed Rebecca Howell took her own life, by vehicular accident, in July 2011. Confirmed by both the circumstances of the accident – and the suicide note, which was found by the deceased's husband in their bedroom.

The ME recounted the contents of the suicide note in its entirety.

"Dear Lenny, I love you. I can't live with this any more. You know, deep down, something is wrong. I did that. What we had was special and I broke it.

I thought I knew what I wanted, what we wanted. The price was too high.

I thought I could forgive Julie. I couldn't. When I think of her I feel like she's already dead and that gives me comfort. We deserve to die, Julie and me, for what we did.

I can't go on living with this pain. Too many lives have been ruined by me, and I won't let that happen to you, or to Caroline.

I love you, always."

Case closed.

Only, it never really closed. This was it. I could feel it. Everything stemmed from this.

"You see the link?" said Harry.

I scratched my head and said, "Something happened between them. Something really bad."

"Look at the incident date. Rebecca Howell committed suicide six weeks before her sister died in an asylum," said Harry.

CHAPTER FIFTY-NINE

"Lay it out for me, Harry. I want to know if we're thinking along the same lines here," I said.

He slugged back the first whiskey, placed the glass back down on the table, twisted it around and stared at the second glass.

"Julie Rosen was a gifted painter, and suffered serious psychological problems for most of her adult life. She had several convictions for possession of narcotics, did some probation, some community service and eventually a short stint in rehab. It didn't work. She had a string of lovers, she told me that herself. Different guy most nights. She falls pregnant. Baby is born in July 2002 with no father's name on the birth record for Emily Rosen. Emily and Caroline Howell must've been around the same age?"

"That's right. The *Washington Post* gave Caroline Howell's date of birth as May 24th, 2002."

Harry nodded.

"August 2nd 2002 Julie says she discovers a man, dressed in black, in her daughter's nursery. The place is soaked in gasoline. The man either attacks her, or she falls and sustains a bad head injury. She's also high. Fire fighters drag her out of the burning house."

"But she doesn't mention the man who supposedly did this?"

"That's right. The prosecutor hung his case on that fact. Julie was arrested and tested positive for crack cocaine and that sealed her fate. Nobody in the area saw a man in black, or any unusual cars. He disappeared. Or he never existed in the first place. The head injury really fuzzed her memory – she had problems with long-term recall. She kept saying there must have been a man, but at that stage she couldn't remember much at all. I think she was beginning to doubt herself. I told Julie we didn't have a hope of proving there was such a man – and it would go easier for her if she told the truth. She said she couldn't remember what happened, not really. I fought for her. Hard as I could. But it was hopeless."

Silence invaded the conversation. Harry drained the second whiskey in one gulp, spread his lips over his teeth and sucked air.

"Maybe there was a man in black? Maybe Howell went to her house that day to settle a score. Something happened between Julie Rosen and Howell's wife, Rebecca," said Harry.

I rubbed my chin, raised the warm cola bottle to my lips, thought better of it and set it down on top of the papers on the table. I thought over Harry's theory.

"Lenny Howell wouldn't harm a child. I can't be certain, of course, but that's my read. It's not in him. You saw Barker in court just now. Does he look familiar?" I asked.

"He is familiar. I think I've seen this man before, but I can't be sure. It was a long time ago, but I remember a man came to almost every one of Julie's court appearances. He never spoke to me, never spoke to Julie. He was there for the trial, every day. I think I remember approaching him once, and he left before I could get to him. Thinking on it now, it could've been Barker."

"Scott Barker was Emily Rosen's father?" I said.

"That's the connection. Must be. He must believe the man in black was Leonard Howell," said Harry.

This time the silence didn't have to invade, we sat back in our own thoughts and let it in willingly. Only this time the silence wasn't as pure. I could hear the TV, the volume turned low on a news channel. I heard one of the old-timers flipping over a page of his battered newspaper, take a hit from a bottle of Sam Adams and smack his lips at the same time as the ass of the bottle hit the bar.

I glanced over the table at Harry. He looked tired. Slumped a little on his stool, head heavy, shoulders slouched. He wasn't a young man, and the day had taken a toll. You might've thought Harry was about to fall asleep if you weren't able to see his eyes. They were ruby-brown, but dulled through age, and they moved rapidly. The pupils moved in short, fast flits – seemingly without focusing on anything for more than an eighth of a second before they moved on and on. I knew him well enough to know that Harry wasn't looking at anything. He was thinking. It was like watching a graphic of a swirling half circle as a computer loaded a program – accessing and activating thousands of lines of code in seconds. Harry's brain was doing the exact same thing – running the theory over and over in his mind – examining it for holes or inconsistencies.

Unconsciously, Harry began to rub the top of his head.

"Why now? If we're right, why would Barker wait till now to do anything about Leonard Howell's crime?" he said.

I found myself picking at the corner of the label on the cola bottle. Peeling it away in chunks.

"I don't know. We could be way off here."

"And why keep Caroline alive? Why not kill her? Only reason I can think of is that it's not about Caroline – it's about Howell himself. This is some kinda game, Eddie. That's for sure. Nothing is what it seems. That video. Maybe it's been faked. Doctored somehow, I don't know, with computers. If she's alive how do you explain the blood on the wall?"

It was my turn to lean back and rub my head. I ran my hands over my face.

Stopped.

"You could do it exactly the same way as Dallas Birch did it," I said.

"What?"

"Take blood from Caroline, then use the syringe to simulate the spatter . . ."

I trailed off, a thought that I'd had earlier that day popped back into my head and stayed there.

"The blood droplets on the basement floor matched the blood droplets on Birch's reconstruction," I said.

"So?"

"So if somebody has their throat cut with a knife, and there's arterial spray, there's also probably gonna be a huge blood pool if they bled out. No pool of blood in the basement. Just a few drops. Harry, I think Caroline is alive."

"But why?" said Harry.

No sooner had he asked the question, than he shot forward and his eyes burst open wide as his mouth.

"Let's assume Emily Rosen is Scott Barker's daughter. Let's assume he and Julie Rosen had a relationship. What if your wife was an innocent woman, tried and wrongfully convicted for killing her own child? Is there a more fitting revenge that doing exactly the same thing to the person who set it up?" asked Harry.

I nodded. It fit.

"That's it, Harry. That's exactly it. Barker wanted Howell put on trial for murdering his own daughter. That's why he set up the fake ransom so it looked like Howell was defrauding the insurance company. That gave him motive. Then there's the blood, the explosive device to make it look like Howell was trying to destroy the crime scene, the fire, everything. It was all set up to put Howell on trial – exactly like Julie Rosen."

"But not convicted, why's that?" said Harry.

I looked at the floor, thought about Amy and how I'd felt when I thought I'd lost her.

"The only thing worse than losing your daughter is losing her twice. Imagine it, you're on trial for your child's murder and some maniac says she's alive, he has her, and if you don't admit to some crime he'll kill her. I think Barker is going to kill Caroline, and make Howell blame himself for it. Even if Howell could confess, my guess is Barker will do it anyway. That's the ultimate revenge."

"Sick bastard," said Harry.

My cell phone was ringing. Harper.

"We've got a crisis response team inbound and we're setting up an incident room at the precinct. The SAC wants to talk to you and Judge Ford," said Harper.

"We don't want to talk to Lynch," I said.

She sighed. "We have to pull together on this. As much as it pains me. We need you. And you need us. We're going to hit Barker's apartment – and we want you both there."

CHAPTER SIXTY

Harry drove while eating lukewarm pizza. I sat beside him and complained about his driving while I ate lukewarm pizza. Stuffing a slice into his face as he overtook two cars was the highlight of the ride. Somehow we made it to the precinct. Harry parked up and we made our way inside.

The Bureau had set up a crisis response base on the second floor. There were around twenty agents either hauling paper, on the phones, working on laptops or pinning maps and photos to a sheet of glass that sat in the center of the room. Washington was drawing a timeline on the glass with a fat, orange marker. Meanwhile Harper directed the agents as to where the timeline would take them next. On the glass I saw a floorplan of Howell's home, another plan this time of the rail station at Rochelle, and photos of all the relevant players – Leonard Howell, Susan Howell, Caroline Howell, Terry McAuley, Marlon Black, and a big red circle around a picture of Scott Barker.

"You're not authorized to be here," said a tall, male agent wearing a sickly green necktie over a bright, white shirt.

"I'm not authorized to be anywhere," I replied. "And whoever authorized your tie should be fired."

"Wait, he's with me," said Harper.

The tall agent backed away, glanced forlornly at his tie and went about his business. We made our way toward Harper.

There were no pleasantries from Harper. She motioned toward a set of table and chairs to her left, we sat and she got straight down to it.

"Max Copeland is saying nothing. Barker won't say a word, either," said Harper.

"Does Barker know that Howell's in a coma?" I asked.

"No, and we want to keep it that way. Who knows what he'll do if he realizes that? We have to figure out what Barker thinks Howell has done. Meanwhile we're retracing our steps. Going over everything in the Caroline Howell case. Maybe we can find her ourselves."

"Has the case been re-opened then?" I asked.

"Not officially. We're officially investigating Barker. I'll have a search warrant for his apartment in the next ten minutes. I called you both in because we have to figure out the connection to the Julie Rosen case. That's what we're missing here. And we don't have much time," she said, and pointed to a digital clock affixed to the wall above us. The digital readout on the clock counted down from eleven hours and four minutes. Almost an hour gone. Three hours until I was back in court, with not much to show for it. If Howell couldn't give Barker his confession, I would have to do it, and pray he let the girl go.

"Give me what you have," said Harper.

Before the four remaining minutes of the hour were up, Harry and I had told Harper all that we knew and all that we suspected had really happened in the Rosen case.

"There was no evidence of this man in black. No mention of him at all until Julie was in a hospital bed and being asked questions by two homicide detectives. No one had seen a car, or a man fitting that description on the road leading to her house or anywhere close to it. Julie was high when she was brought in. She maintained this man-in-black theory until the trial. I'd told her the jury might not believe her."

Harry paused, swallowed down the emotion threatening his voice. Out of every lawyer, judge, or cop I'd ever met – Harry was the one man who'd believed in the justice system. He had to. He'd been a part of it for forty years. And in that time as a lawyer he'd never betrayed a client, never misled the cops, and always told the truth to the judge and the jury – he'd kept his oath.

I could see the tears threatening the corners of his eyes. He cleared his throat, stared at the desk.

"Even if the man in black was real, you still wouldn't have been able to prove it in court. You fought the case, you did the right thing," I said.

264

"It doesn't feel right any more," said Harry.

I knew how he felt. I'd been there. Being a lawyer is one of those professions where you can do a hell of a lot of harm simply by doing your job.

He tried to say something, but the emotion rising at the back of his throat wouldn't let him. He wiped at his eyes. Guilt, anger, regret – call it what you want – it was beginning to tear at Harry with its black claws.

I took over the conversation with Harper.

"Howell had a reputation for dispensing his own brand of justice, but I don't believe Howell would've intended to harm the child. He's got a strange sense of morality – he might kill Julie but the thought of harming a child would be repulsive. That's just my reading of him."

"I could believe that," said Harper, "But why attack Julie Rosen?"

"We don't know. I still don't believe he was involved. There's something deeper here," I said.

Flipping over the pages in the police report into the suicide of Rebecca Howell, I found the page with the suicide note and handed it to Harper. She read it slowly, her fingertips brushing her lips as her eyes scanned the script.

"So Julie and Rebecca did something. Something bad. Howell found out about it maybe? I suppose it's possible. What do you think Julie and Rebecca did?" she asked.

"I've got no idea. In terms of a connection, we think it's possible Barker was Emily Rosen's father and maybe he's trying to frame Howell," I said.

"Rebecca Howell is the key here. Any theories?"

"I'm not sure. Not yet. I need to see Rebecca's medical records. I've dealt with a few suicides and it's rare for one to occur without some pre-existing psychiatric problems. Rebecca Howell's note confirms something happened between these sisters and I think it goes back a long way. Maybe there are counseling records or something like that which could shine a light on this. If Howell was the man in black, we might just be able to find the real reason. It has to be about Rebecca; something to do with her."

"Getting her medical records won't be easy," Harper said.

I pulled a document out of my file and gave it to her.

"Her next of kin is Lenny Howell. This is the power of attorney Howell signed allowing me to act for him. This will be enough."

Harper called over a young male agent and told him to go get Rebecca Howell's medical records even if it meant waking the damn doctor out of his bed. A call was coming in on her cell. She answered it, hung up.

"That was Lynch – he's coordinating the search area. Meanwhile he just got us our warrant for Barker's apartment."

CHAPTER SIXTY-ONE

The Dodge Charger couldn't accommodate all of us, so we took a dull gray/blue Crown Victoria and tore through the streets to Barker's apartment – sirens and blues the whole way. I sat in back beside Harry. Washington was up front with Harper in the driver's seat. Harry didn't want to come along. I knew it, but he didn't say it. Washington had insisted we ride along because of the clock – if there was anything in the apartment that could be relevant to the Rosen or Howell cases, Washington needed to know right away. Harry was the only person who had known Julie Rosen, and I had a working knowledge of both cases, but the FBI didn't want me. They wanted Harry.

Only reason I was in the car was because Harry insisted on it. Another Crown Vic, of a similar indeterminate color, came behind us. In that car were two feds who would act as the entry team – both were white males in their thirties with light hair. They both wore sunglasses, blue tees and blue jeans. One was called Beck, and the other Allen. The FBI were made up of thinkers, drinkers and door-kickers. I guessed that Beck and Allen fell into the latter category. In the back of the second car was a forensic tech called Kit, a small guy in glasses and a Pearl Jam tee-shirt. I looked over my shoulder and saw Beck, or it could have been Allen, struggling behind the wheel as they tried to keep up with Harper.

"You do know that having me come along for this could cause serious problems for the DA if they decide to retry Howell?" I said.

Angling in his seat, Washington spoke to me over his shoulder.

"I'm not worried about the Howell trial right now. Our tech's looked at the video Barker played in court. They're saying either it's the best fake they've ever seen or it's real. Right now, we're working on the assumption that Caroline might still be alive. Better that way. If it's a scam, we've lost nothing but some overtime."

We pulled up outside a small apartment building ten minutes from the precinct. The Crown Vic that had followed us, pulled up on the right. The occupants quickly got out and made it to the building before us. I got out of the car and looked around. It wasn't a bad area but it wasn't great either; a convenience store, a taco joint and a bar were in the same block as the apartment. I saw a school across the street and a park nearby. The building itself didn't look that old. Probably went up in the early nineties. Harry and I followed Washington and Harper into the lobby.

Black and yellow tiles in a zig-zag pattern on the floor, and monochrome white on the walls. An unmanned security desk sat across from a bank of elevators. A set of double doors ahead of us must've led to the stairs. Beck, Allen and Kit waited in the lobby.

"Where the hell is the building super?" said Washington. He made a call on his cell. It didn't look like he got an answer.

"Apartment seventy-three is on the eighth floor. I say let's go and to hell with the super," said Harper.

A nod from Washington sent Beck and Allen racing up the stairs, their side-arms drawn and held low in front of them. Kit stayed in the lobby with the rest of us.

"I'm not climbing eight flights of stairs," said Harry.

I nodded.

"We'll take the elevator. We just need to wait until the entry team is at the front door," said Washington.

I hit the button to call the elevator, checked my watch.

On Washington's belt was a small, black radio receiver. I saw him take a set of earbuds from his overcoat, plug one end into the receiver and place the other in his ear.

"Check, Washington. Command serial . . ." and he rhymed off some sort of standard radio code to connect with Beck and Allen. I glanced to my left and saw Harper doing the same.

The elevator arrived, Harper got in and held the doors open.

The echoes of federal boots on the stairs dwindled away the higher they got.

I looked around the hallway. Two security cameras were mounted high on the walls. One in the northeast corner, above the security desk, and another in the southwest corner. I made my way around the security desk to the door behind it. I tried the handle and found it open. Inside was a luggage rack, a mop and bucket that hadn't seen much action lately, and a small table that held a bunch of half-empty cleaning products. Nothing else in the room.

I came out, closed the door behind me and made my way to the acrylic plan of the building tacked to the wall beside the elevator. Fire exits and rally points were highlighted on the plan in red.

On the eighth floor there were a dozen apartments. It was also the top floor. Apartment seventy-five was hatched in green. I checked the key and saw it meant this was the building supervisor's apartment. From the plan, the supervisor lived directly across from apartment seventy-three.

"The super's apartment is right across the hall from Barker's," I said.

Joining me beside the elevator, Washington checked the plan. He nodded and tried the super from his cell, again. Nothing.

A buzzing of soft static, then Washington placed a finger over the receiver in his ear. I guessed the entry team were outside Barker's front door.

Washington pressed a button on his mic, and said, "We don't have the super. It's a hard entry. Go for it. We're coming up."

A pan-pipes version of "Love In An Elevator" played in the elevator car while it slowly ascended. Nobody spoke. Kit tapped at his aluminum suitcase, out of time to the music. Standing beside me, Harry rubbed at his chin. It was almost as if a weight was descending on him, slowly crushing him. Harper and Washington exchanged a glance. They needed a break in the case – something that might lead them to a half-starved seventeen-year-old girl in a concrete grave. They were desperate. I could smell it on them. And I knew why, too. Because if we didn't find something in the apartment then the feds were pretty much out of ideas. There were no more leads. With the time remaining, even if Harper had ten thousand men they wouldn't be able to locate Caroline in time.

I turned away from the others and watched the lightbulbs on the brass floor-display flicker on and off as the elevator made its way to the top floor.

269

The doors opened and we came out to a brightly lit corridor. To our left was another set of double doors with a pull handle on each door that led to the stairwell. On the right was a long corridor leading to apartments on either side of the hall. I saw Beck, or it could've been Allen, standing at the open door of apartment seventy-three. The fed was waiting on Washington. As we reached the open door to Barker's apartment I saw the name tag on the fed's vest read Beck. He holstered his weapon and slipped his thumbs through the belt eyelets on his jeans.

Beck spoke softly in a Southern accent that helped slow down his speech. There are few fast talkers in the deep South. He said, "It's clear. Looks like we were expected."

CHAPTER SIXTY-TWO

It was a small, clean, well-kept apartment in an otherwise average apartment building in White Plains, lit with a single bright ceiling bulb. All four walls were covered in a cream wallpaper with faintly patterned horizontal stripes. A thin beige carpet on the floor. A tidy kitchen area to the left. Ahead, a couch in the middle of the floor and opposite the kitchen was a single bed. A door to the left of the bed must've led to a bathroom, probably with just enough space for a toilet and a shower. A small bookcase to the right of the bed looked to be the only source of entertainment in the room.

That was all.

No TV. No pictures on the wall.

Sparsely furnished, but in reality there wasn't much room for any more furniture.

Beck and Allen were slowly turning the place upside down. Opening cupboards and emptying out the contents, overturning the couch, rifling through the bookcase. Allen found a piece of paper slotted between the pages of a hardback like a bookmark. Carefully he unfolded it and began reading.

We were all inside the little apartment now, and there wasn't much room with the bodies standing around. I moved beside Allen and read over his shoulder. The letter was addressed to Julie Rosen and written in the same hand as Rebecca Howell's suicide note.

> Julie,
> I made a mistake. I thought I could trust you. You promised me and you lied. But you were right, I'm not a good mother. I'm sorry for what I did. I hope you are too.

Goodbye,
Becca.

I was lost in that letter. The words were floating around my head like ghosts in an old house.

Washington tapped Beck on the shoulder, "You said you think we were expected?"

"Yeah, check it out," said Beck. He stopped ripping open the couch, walked past us, slammed the front door shut and went back to the couch. At first, I didn't notice it. I stood beside Washington next to the kitchen. Harper and Harry stood on the opposite side of the apartment in front of the bed.

I only saw it when Washington started forward, headed for the door.

There was something on the back of it. Letters had been carved into the plain, varnished wood with a sharp knife. Each stroke had been repeated many times with the blade, giving it a frenzied appearance. Like each letter had been clawed into the wood.

It was a message. For us.

You will never find her. Daddy must confess his sins.

Washington drew out his cell, hit a button on the screen and held the phone to his ear while he slowly walked over and stood before the door. He ran his finger along the letters, and jerked his hand away when he got a splinter.

"The Goddamn building super must have heard this being done. Where the hell is he?" he said and he took the phone away from his ear to look at it in anger while the super failed to pick up his call for the third time.

"Shush, quiet," said Harper.

Everyone stopped. Washington sucked at his finger and moved close to the door, his nose almost touching it. I thought he was maybe trying to figure out what kind of knife or implement had been used to draw the message.

"Do you hear that?" said Harper.

"I do," said Kit, laying down his suitcase.

We listened. I didn't know what for. Then I heard a cell phone ringing. It was faint. Without making a sound I moved toward the source. It seemed to be coming from close to the door.

Washington ended his call.

The ringing stopped.

In that same second a lot happened all at once. Harper, Washington and I came to the immediate conclusion that the ringing sound belonged to the super's phone. I knew Harper and Washington realized this too because both of them reached for their side-arms and Harper took a step toward the door. The phone was probably in his apartment, across the brightly lit corridor.

Immediately after I realized the super's phone was probably in his apartment, I came to three conclusions.

The first was that in all likelihood, the super was dead.

The second was that Washington was standing in front of the door and examining the message precisely because that's what Scott Barker wanted him to do.

Before I could wrap my head around the third thought, Washington flew past me, backwards, in a cloud of splinters, noise, dust, blood and light that shone onto his ruined chest from the five-inch hole in the center of the door.

CHAPTER SIXTY-THREE

It's in those long, excruciating moments of unexpected violence that you really get to know somebody. You get to know who they are on a basic, primal level. Washington's body hit the upturned couch, knocking it over. Before the couch landed, Harry was kneeling in front of Washington, pressing a cushion into the hole in his chest. The turquoise couch cushion quickly turned red.

In that same moment, Beck and Allen dove for cover behind the small kitchen island. Kit was on his hands and knees, crawling toward Harry and Washington.

Harper was a whole other story. Her gun was in one hand and the other was outstretched, about to grab the handle and throw the ruined door open.

And me? I was thinking. I guessed that whoever was on the other side of the door had hidden in the super's apartment and watched Beck and Allen make their entry – then saw me, Harper, Washington, Harry and Kit follow the entry team into Barker's apartment. The large hole in the door could only have been made with a shotgun. I didn't hear another round being racked into the chamber so I assumed this was a Mossberg Riot gun – which could fire repeatedly.

One shot, straight through the center of the door had caught Washington full in the chest. Nine inches above the hole in the door I saw a peephole. I imagined the shooter watching us walk into the apartment through the peephole in the super's door.

And when he came out of the apartment opposite with the shotgun in his hands, he could watch the peephole in Barker's door from the corridor. The light from the hot ceiling bulb in Barker's apartment would be a speck of light. When that single point of light was extinguished it meant that someone was standing directly in front of the door – blocking out the light.

The perfect time to shoot.

Harper's gun was raised, ready to snap into a shooting position once she opened the door. But opening that door only had one outcome. The shooter would still be there, waiting for another target.

I couldn't call out – it would just send a useful signal to the shooter.

We stood across the apartment from one another. The door was on my right. And Harper's left. If I wanted to save her I would have to dive across the open space. Which meant diving across the path of the next shotgun blast to go through the door.

I crouched, bunching the muscles in my calves, ready to spring low and hard and grab Harper's knees, bringing her down before the shooter could take her head off.

But I didn't jump.

Didn't need to.

Harper had seen everything I had. I knew it. Because she pinned her body to the wall, angled the weapon and emptied a clip through the door at head height.

More bullet holes appeared in the center of the door, and I saw Beck, Allen and Kit following Harper's lead. The noise was deafening. Three firearms discharging fiercely in an enclosed space, tearing the wood to shreds. I dropped to the floor and covered my ears.

Clips slid out from their handguns, to be replaced smoothly by fresh, full magazines. I glanced at Harry and saw the strain on his face – his full weight now on Washington's chest, trying to stop the blood.

Washington made no sound.

When I lowered my hands the ringing in my ears felt like a monk banging a church bell inside my head. It hurt and I staggered a little as I got to my feet.

The apartment door was open.

And Harper was gone.

CHAPTER SIXTY-FOUR

Before I followed her, I saw Beck and Allen assisting Harry. One of them spoke to Washington, while the other lent his weight to the compression on the wound and Kit got on his phone – called for backup and a paramedic.

"Agent down. Shotgun wound to the chest. Urgent medical assistance required," said Kit.

The door opened on Harper's side, so I stepped smartly past the door and flung my back at the wall so I could get a look at the corridor.

I couldn't see Harper, nor anyone else.

I waited a beat.

No shots.

Then I heard Harper swearing, loudly. I kept low and moved quickly into the hallway, looking in all directions. Nothing on my left, just open corridor. Straight ahead I saw the super's apartment. His door was open and I could see him sitting in an armchair facing the hallway.

He was dead. A dark stain had soaked his shirt and his head was thrown back, exposing a gaping wound in his throat from a knife that had cut him to the bone and almost taken his head clean off. There were bullet wounds in his legs, stomach and under his chin. Clearly postmortem and from the feds firing through the door. I checked my right and saw Harper.

She stood at the double doors that led to the stairwell. She was still swearing. I saw her raise her gun, then bring it down hard on the door. A metallic clang and nothing else. I ran to her and saw that a U shaped bolt held both handles of the doors closed. It looked like a lock for a motorcycle. A single piece of steel, in a horseshoe shape looped through both door handles then locked in place by a steel bar across the bottom.

Harper hit it again.

"Son of a bitch locked the doors and took the elevator," she said.

She stepped back, then kicked the doors hard. They didn't budge. Whoever shot at us must've called the elevator, and slipped the lock on the doors before they opened fire.

Harper swore once more, then lowered her head and breathed hard.

She ran past me, and I knew where she was headed. I'd seen it on the building plan in the lobby. I followed her and almost knocked over Beck, who came charging out of Barker's apartment.

"Fire escape," cried Harper.

Beck and I followed her into the super's apartment, past his corpse and saw her standing in front of the window with a chair raised above her head. There were two bullet holes in the glass already, high up in the corners. More strays from the feds blind firing. The chair flew through the window, hit the iron railing of the fire escape, tumbled over it and fell to the street.

Harper put one boot on the windowsill and leapt onto the black, wrought-iron fire escape. The floor was fine, black iron with a steel mesh. She landed lightly. Beck placed a foot on the windowsill and launched himself out of the broken window.

In the half-a-second that he was airborne, a cold panic hit the back of my neck like a bucket of iced water.

The shooter had planned this. All of it.

He knew we'd come to Barker's apartment. He'd planned on killing the super. He'd planned on lying in wait for us. He'd planned the lock on the stairwell doors, the shot through the door, and making his escape in the elevator.

I was about to lean out, to warn them. There wasn't time. In the instant that Beck's weight hit the fire escape, the entire section of floor twisted in a scream of metal on metal. Beck was thrown back, toward me, but low, and his head hit the bricks and he disappeared. The floor had twisted on its diagonals which meant Beck went down and the section of floor Harper stood on, went up, throwing her high and in the same direction as Beck.

Glass bit into my left hand as I grabbed the frame of the broken window, and stretched out my right hand toward Harper.

Fast feet behind me. Either Allen or Kit were almost at my back.

I caught the collar of Harper's jacket, and her right hand grabbed my elbow, but the force of Beck tilting the floor so violently meant Harper had significant momentum and I couldn't stop her hitting the wall to the right of the window. She dropped and I held fast.

The glass shards left in the window frame had cut my palm, making my grasp slippery. I held on.

But when Harper reached the bottom of her drop I couldn't hold.

The window frame broke in half, and Harper's weight pulled me clean out of the window, head first.

CHAPTER SIXTY-FIVE

My thighs and knees raked across the remaining shards of glass that protruded from the bottom of the frame. I felt my pants rip and my shoe come off. Probably Kit or Allen making a last-ditch grasp and only succeeding in relieving me of my footwear.

Harper landed feet first on the iron stairway one floor below us. The momentum of her fall took her all the way down and her back thumped into the stairs.

I ducked my head and closed my eyes.

The top of my shoulders landed on something before my legs swept down and my heels found the iron stairs with terrible force. My left foot had lost a shoe so the impact was much worse without the cushion of the heel. The pain shot right up my leg, into my shin.

The pain felt good.

It meant I was alive.

I turned and saw that I'd landed on Beck's stomach. I got up onto my hands and knees and saw Harper on the stairs above him, her mouth open in a moan of somebody who just fell one story and landed on a set of iron stairs. She was in a shitload of pain but alive.

Beck was dead. His head was almost tucked behind his right shoulder. He must've broken his neck when the back of his head hit the bricks and he fell through the platform.

The surge of adrenaline that hit me in the fall began to subside, and I started to feel the burning in my legs. I glanced down and the pain doubled. My thighs were torn from the glass, and I reached down to peel away the rip in my pants and see how bad it really was, when my hand started to burn. I turned over my wrist and saw a glittering stripe of broken glass in my palm.

Somehow, I registered the sound of a car; the engine revving high, tire squeal and a horn below me. Only thing I saw in the street below was a set of headlights disappearing into the distance – headed for the freeway. The shooter, making his escape.

But who the hell was he?

Another sound made me look in the opposite direction. Somebody tapping on glass. I swung around and saw an elderly couple standing at the window of their apartment, gazing out at me. We were now on the seventh floor.

I heard Harper swearing again, and I swore too.

But I didn't call out a cuss word, like she did.

I made a promise.

A promise to Beck, to Washington, to Howell and to myself.

I swore that when I found out who was responsible for this I would personally put them in a pine box.

Then the pain dissipated and I caught my breath. I was aware of Allen and Kit above me, calling down to see if we were okay. I ignored them. I ignored the confused couple opening their window to help us. I ignored Harper kicking the stairs with her heels and roaring in frustration. I ignored the pain.

My mind was on other matters. The letter from Rebecca to Julie. I was beginning to get an inkling of what it really meant.

CHAPTER SIXTY-SIX

We lost a full hour at the scene.

Senior FBI staff were swarming the place. And the old spook from the justice department had arrived: Alexander Berlin. He had brown hair cut short, blue suit, white shirt, red tie, but I couldn't tell the color of the rod that was jammed up his ass. I guessed the rod was at least as old as he was – maybe late sixties.

With some pleasure, Lynch and Berlin spent a full half hour laying into Harper, Kit and Allen. It didn't matter that they'd just been shot at, didn't matter that Harper's partner took a shotgun blast in the chest, didn't matter that Harper's back was probably bruised to the bone.

Only thing Lynch and Berlin cared about was that they'd taken two civilians, in the shape of Harry and me, not only into the heart of an ongoing investigation but straight into the middle of a firefight. Agent Beck was dead, and Washington was fighting for his life. A civilian was also dead – the super. This was messed up.

Underneath the super's bed, the feds found an acetylene torch and an angle grinder. The son of a bitch had burned and then cut the iron supports at opposite diagonal ends of the iron frame that made up the top platform of the fire escape. He'd left the support bars hanging in place by a thread of metal. Harper's weight on it alone had been insufficient but as soon as Beck's boots hit the floor the final threads gave way and the platform bucked and twisted.

He'd planned ahead.

All security camera footage had been wiped. There were no cameras on the street. Nobody saw the car pull away from the building.

We had exactly zero.

After the lock on the stairwell had been cut through, I sat on the floor of the landing, with my pants around my ankles as a

281

paramedic put steri-strips onto the cuts in my thighs. The bandage on my hand felt tight. He'd picked the glass out of it as best he could. He then placed two pads on each of my thighs and asked me again to go with him to the hospital to get the cut on my hand stitched. I declined, again. He gave me some painkillers which I swallowed dry.

Berlin's rant was cut off by a call on his cell. He made his way into Barker's apartment to take it. I hadn't heard all of the conversation with Harper. He'd taken her aside for some of it.

Now that Berlin was out of the way, Harper dropped the mask. She'd declined to go to the hospital too, but now I saw the pain on her face. She put her hands over her head, slowly, and stretched her back muscles.

She swore like a longshoreman throughout the manoeuver.

"What now?" I said.

She checked her watch. I checked mine. Under two hours until I was due back in court.

"Basically, we're shut down and shut out," she said.

Harry walked down the stairs with four bottles of water in a paper bag. He handed one to me. Harper and Kit declined theirs. Harry put the bottles on the floor. As he bent down he noticed the bloodstains on his cuffs and the spots of blood on his suit. He took a handkerchief from his pocket, spilled some water on it and began to dab at the stains.

"Any update on Agent Washington?" he said.

Without looking at him, Harper shook her head. She was staring at the floor, her hands on her hips.

"I'm headed to the ER now, nothing else I can do here," said Allen, and he and Kit shook hands with Harry and me and left.

"What's happening, Harper? Talk to me," I said.

"It's Berlin's show now. Lynch has got him on board and as far as they are concerned the shooting tonight may not be related to Caroline's case."

"You're kidding me," said Harry.

"He thinks Scott Barker is full of shit. That he's playing a game to mess with Howell. The official FBI position has now changed. There is no credible evidence to the contrary so our position is that Caroline Howell is dead. We are still actively pursuing Marlon Black and McAuley as accomplices in her kidnapping and murder."

"You think one of them was the shooter?" I said.

"Maybe. The problem is we're now looking for that shooter instead of looking for Caroline Howell."

"What the hell is this? I thought the feds had re-opened the case," I said.

"Washington did. But he's no longer on the case. This is politics. Did you notice who signed Barker's immunity agreement on behalf of federal law enforcement?" she said.

"No, I haven't seen it," I said.

Harper pointed at the open door of Barker's apartment and said, "Patrick Lynch. He's in charge and he doesn't want it on his record that he made a deal to let a kidnapper and murderer go free. They signed the agreement because they thought Barker was going to bury Howell. We know how that turned out. So, all agents are now pursuing Marlon and McAuley. Berlin is on his way to talk to Barker right now. If Barker won't talk to him, and he probably won't, Berlin can say he fully explored Barker's credibility. If she is alive and she dies in the next eight hours – Berlin and Lynch have clean hands. Every law enforcement officer who signed that immunity agreement is praying that Caroline is already dead. They don't want her found."

"What are you gonna do?" I said.

"Head back to the precinct and see if I can get into the crisis room."

My cell phone hummed in my pocket. I drew it out, didn't recognize the number but I took the call. I listened, thanked the caller and disconnected.

"Harry and I need a lift," I said.

"Where to?" said Harper.

"The hospital. Lenny Howell just woke up."

CHAPTER SIXTY-SEVEN

Before we got in the car, Harper persuaded a medic to dose her up on muscle relaxants and ibuprofen. After ten minutes she was good to go and insisted on driving. Said she was fine. Harper reminded me of a quarterback who'd taken a big hit and dosed up to finish the game. Damn, she had a lot of heart. She drove the midnight streets of White Plains while I talked. Harry was up front beside Harper and I sat in back so I could stretch out my legs while I waited for my painkillers to kick in.

We headed downtown, winding through the streets in the Crown Vic. The sharp, burning sensation from the cuts in my legs and hand began to ease off as the first drip of pain relief began to seep into my system. No one spoke during the ride. I thought Harry and Harper felt just as numb as I did. Yet, there was hope in that car. The one person who might know the truth had just come back into play. Now, more than ever, Caroline Howell needed her father.

We parked outside the hospital and walked briskly through the paramedic's entrance to the ER, with the help of Harper flashing her badge to security. On the way in we discussed how to handle things with Howell.

"Maybe we shouldn't tell him every little detail about what's happened. We can talk about Scott Barker, try and find out what we need to know, but we don't tell him that Barker says he has Caroline and she is alive. What if Barker is lying or worse, what if he's telling the truth and we don't find her in time? This man just tried to punch out. If he finds out she's alive and he loses her again . . ."

They both nodded. A staff nurse directed us up one flight, and we found Howell's private room easily enough in the long, pale corridor. His room was the only one with a correctional officer and a cop stationed outside.

Again, Harper's badge got us inside.

The room was illuminated by a sickly desk lamp that sat on the nightstand. The lamp was bent over, almost like it was about to collapse. Whatever nicotine-colored light came off the bulb made Howell look terrible. His forehead shone with sweat, and I couldn't tell if his skin had become jaundiced or if it was the fault of the yellowed light bulb cover. A stick-on bandage, about the size of a pack of cigarettes, sat on his throat. His wrists were heavily bandaged. He stirred from a deep sleep and tried to turn his head but the bandage caught his movement, stopped it, and he winced. His eyes closed and moments later, he began snoring softly.

I heard the rattle of cuffs and saw a bright pair attached to Howell's ankle. One end on Howell's right leg, the other attached to the bed rail. It was as excessive and unnecessary as most of the practices in the US penal system.

"He's waking up," said Harper.

We approached the bed, and I watched Howell fight awake. He looked like he'd been given a strong shot of something for the pain.

"Lenny, it's Eddie. I'm here with a friendly fed and a buddy of mine. Can you talk? It's important."

"It didn't work," he said.

His voice sounded like a rusty chainsaw. I took his hand in mine, careful not to touch his bandaged wrists.

"I'm glad it didn't work. Something happened. The trial has changed. George Vindico isn't . . ."

"Jesus, poor George. How is he?" said Howell, struggling with every word.

"His name is not George Vindico. He's been lying to you, Lenny – for years. I think he had something to do with Caroline's disappearance. His real name is Scott Barker. That name mean anything to you?"

"What?" he said, drawing up his elbows, trying to lever himself into a sitting position. His arms slipped on the sheets and his head dropped back down with a cry, and a grimace.

"Take it easy. I just need to know who this guy is and how he connects to you, or your late wife, Rebecca."

Something stirred inside Lenny, and his gaze became clearer, his face more animated. His words tripped out faster and with greater precision, but his throat still sounded raw.

"I know the name. I remember it, but I never met the guy. I was on my last tour of Afghanistan. I'd saved up to open my company when I got home. Rebecca was pregnant with Caroline. Her sister, Julie, was pregnant at the time too and Rebecca had given her some money to set her up in a rental cottage outside of town while she had the baby."

He took a coughing fit that spread fresh agony across his face. I held a cup of water out for him and he sipped at it from a straw. Satisfied, he licked his lips and continued.

"I didn't think we could afford it, but Becca insisted it was the least we could do to support Julie. Her sister had problems and this was the first time she'd been clean in years. My wife thought it was important to support her while she was pregnant, as much for the baby as Julie. I think Becca was afraid that without support Julie would start using again – hook up with her old friends."

He wanted to say more, but his throat gave out. I offered him more water but he waved it away, and took a moment before he continued.

"Becca called me one night, while I was on base. Told me Julie's old boyfriend Scott Barker had come back into her life. Becca was afraid of this guy. He was bad news. At one time Becca dragged Julie out of Barker's apartment – he was beating her. Anyway, I said I would get a couple of buddies to watch the house for a while and maybe go have a talk with this Scott Barker – make sure he knew to stay in line."

He fell silent. His mouth was dry and his tongue was no longer able to wet his lips. I gave him another sip of water. He drank little, but it was enough to grease his pipes.

"She didn't want that. Said it would come back to bite us. So I didn't. A month later Caroline was born, and two months later I came home to my new baby girl . . . our miracle . . . docs . . . docs said we couldn't have kids. She was so beautiful."

Those words pulled at him as surely as if they were yanking on his stitches.

"And what happened with Julie?"

"I don't know. When I came back she was already in jail. Becca cut all ties with her. Next time her name was mentioned was in the note Becca left for me when . . . after . . . she took her own life. I guess, some part of Becca blamed herself for what happened with Julie. I guess she felt she could've done more, and maybe that terrible thing wouldn't have happened and her niece would've still been alive."

"And you don't know if Julie and Rebecca had a fight, or a falling out?"

"I'm not sure. Becca told me Scott was Emily's father. But even so, she didn't want him around. Maybe they fought over that? I don't know for sure. She didn't like to talk about it. Is Scott the man who took Caroline?" said Howell.

"I think so. We're working on it. Scott Barker seems to think you need to confess something to him. Any idea what that might be?"

He shook his head.

We talked for a couple more minutes, until the drowsiness overcame him. And then, quietly, we left the room.

"We're due back to court in an hour," said Harper, as we left the hospital, headed for the car.

Something was eating at the back of my mind. I was so close to this, I thought that now and again I caught glimpses of the truth, but then those ideas drifted away. Time was almost up.

The drive to the courthouse took no time at all. I could tell Harper and Harry were just as tired as I felt; their feet dragged along the sidewalk as we made for the courthouse entrance. Most of the building was in darkness and the lobby lights were only half lit. Lynch waited at the doors, his arms folded and a scowl on his face.

I stopped dead. Harry and Harper shuffled on another few feet before they both realized I was no longer keeping in time with their steps.

They turned toward me.

Something Howell had said was somersaulting through my brain on a loop.

The cloud in my mind was beginning to clear, at last. I had a theory. One that made sense of all of this. But I needed evidence – something to show Scott Barker.

"I think I know what's happened. Caroline is alive. I can find out exactly where she is but I need a few things first," I said, tossing my car keys to Harper.

"Get your best tech to go and find my car. Hopefully they can do something with that shirt."

"What shirt?" said Harper.

"My shirt. The one in my trunk that's covered in Lenny Howell's blood. But that's not all. I'm going need some paperwork and time alone with the tech."

"What is it?" said Harry.

"I don't know exactly – it's just a theory, for now."

"And how is all of that going to tell you where Caroline is being held?" said Harper.

"It won't. It's ammunition. Once I have those documents, and the results back on my shirt, I'm going to question Scott Barker. If he wants a confession, I'll give him one. Then I'm going to hear his."

CHAPTER SIXTY-EIGHT

I folded the pages away in a manila file. Rebecca's medical records contained very little in relation to mental illness, or depression. She'd changed physicians in 2002, and her new doctor thought she might have post-natal depression. Rebecca told the doc, some years later, there were "bonding issues" between her daughter and her. There were no further records on this – just a prescription for anti-anxiety meds that was not repeated. I'd read the file in twenty minutes, cover to cover. I took it to the defense table in court one, and sat quietly reading it again before anyone came in. Only when I closed it, placed my hands on top and shut my eyes did I know for certain what had happened all those years ago. There weren't many pages in the file that were relevant. It felt thin and insubstantial. Yet it would have to do. I kept telling myself I had enough. There were bullets in that file that I could shoot at Barker. Some would miss. Some would hurt. But none of them were enough on their own.

Over the last ten minutes, as the judge, jury, and the witness came into court, I'd been trying to order my questions. What would I open with? What should I hold back?

I became conscious of my breathing. Deliberately, I slowed everything down. Let my heart rate drop, my chest slow, in the hope it would help to stop the tornado of information and questions in my mind.

It helped. For about two seconds.

My eyes snapped open and I saw that every single person in the courtroom was silent and looking at me. Judge Schultz was tapping a pen on her desk. My opponent, Michelle King, mouthed "Good luck" silently. In that moment, we almost ceased to be opposing counsel. King had let a wrecking machine into the courtroom, and somehow, if Caroline Howell was found alive, at least King would know that this mess had amounted to something good. This was beyond a case now.

This was life or death.

The others wore worried faces. Captain Powers, Lieutenant Groves and Harry looked at me like I was about to take control of a plane locked in a terrible nosedive toward the ocean. Only Harper held up her chin and had hope in her eyes.

I thought I would have more ammunition. Something to break Scott Barker.

Standing, I told myself that I would have to make do with the cards I'd been dealt. Someone on the jury coughed, but I didn't look at them. The jury didn't matter now – they were just props for show. There was no one else in the courtroom apart from the key players and King's assistant. No press, no audience. Just us.

The room felt strangely empty.

I looked at Scott Barker, silent and still in the witness stand, and I thought about my father. He played cards on an amateur level. He never won big, but he never lost either. One night, sitting on a bar stool in MacGonegal's I asked him how he always got so lucky at poker.

"Luck has no part in it. It's not about the high cards, son. Any hand can be a winning hand. Doesn't matter if it's the best hand at the table or the worst. It's all about how you play it."

My father thought card cheats were the lowest of the low. He never cheated at cards his whole life. Not once. He played the game.

Now it was my turn. Except I didn't have a full deck.

So I figured it was okay to cheat.

Before I opened my mouth, I paused and looked again at Harper sitting in the row behind me, right beside Harry.

Harper whispered, "A chopper's standing by. Good luck."

I nodded. Everything we'd discussed was ready. I just hoped I got something out of Barker that we could use.

"Thanks," I said.

Scott Barker had loosened his tie and lost the suit jacket, but other than that he looked well. No fear. No doubt. His face was a marble god in a museum; solid stone. Motionless. Dead. And yet his eyes were full of life and hate, and they reflected the inferno inside him. He didn't look at me. Just stared straight ahead.

"I have some questions for you," I said.

Still without making eye contact, Barker said, "It was your client I wanted to see. Not you. Bring him to me and I'll hear his confession. It's the only way to save his daughter."

I didn't acknowledge him. The first move was key. Whoever came out on top would likely dominate and determine the outcome. I needed that person to be me, but I couldn't show it.

"My client tried to take his own life. He's in the hospital. Stable but critical. And he's in a coma. There is no way to talk to him. You have to talk to me," I said.

"I don't believe you," he said.

"Can I ask you some questions?" I said.

His face became empty again. Shutting down. He had said his piece. There would be no more talk.

"I can give you my client's confession," I said.

Nothing.

"The way I see it, we can help each other. I want to know where you're holding Caroline Howell. You want to know, for sure, what happened all those years ago with Julie and the baby. And the man in black."

His eyes remained still. Like twin pearls of glass in a doll's face.

"You have other questions too. I can help you," I said.

A flicker at the corner of his mouth.

"You're probably thinking that I'm bluffing. You're wrong. I'll play. How's this to start?"

I removed a single page from the file. It came in via FBI request. Old records from the Department of Corrections.

Holding up the page I said, "The last time you saw Julie Rosen alive was August 2nd, 2011. Not long before she passed away."

Instantly his head came up and those blue orbs of his locked on to my face.

"The visitors log for Julie Rosen, patient of East Brother Island Hospital, only has one entry. Two names. Two visitors. Two false identities – Alan Marsh and Tom Bell. One of them was you, wasn't it?"

He didn't move. Didn't speak.

"Julie wrote to you. You came to see her. During her trial, you watched from the sidelines. You didn't support her when she was facing a murder charge because you thought she'd murdered her child. Your child. But she wrote to you in 2011 and told you otherwise. This letter was recorded. One piece of correspondence mailed to Scott Barker, at a PO Box in Jersey?"

No answer. But this was no longer a criminal trial. Judge Schultz was giving me any kind of leverage I needed. I could see it in the way she leaned forward – she wasn't going to interrupt, neither was King – they were both willing the truth to emerge by any means.

"You came to see Julie under a false name. You came because something in that letter changed your mind about Julie's guilt?"

He nodded.

"Julie's memory was shot to hell from a head injury. She didn't just suddenly remember exactly what had really happened, did she?"

Barker had one thing going for him – his patience. He'd sat in his web for years before he'd struck. Caroline didn't have time.

"You don't want a confession. You want to know the truth because Julie couldn't give it to you," I said.

"No," he said. The answers were coming and I didn't dare stop. I needed this man to open up and talk.

"You want answers, Scott. I've got them all. You just need to talk to me about Julie. She got a letter from her sister, Rebecca Howell. Right before Rebecca drove through a crash barrier on a mountain road, right?"

He hesitated. This was not what he'd planned. He wanted Howell on his knees. He wanted to enjoy that power. I couldn't give it to him. So I had to sell him something else.

"The letter, it was Rebecca's confession, wasn't it?"

Barker's breathing quickened. He'd been planning this for so long. I knew he wanted to talk, he needed to talk.

"Let's give the court Howell's confession together," I said.

"It was all Rebecca's fault," he said. "She admitted that she thought Julie was an unfit mother. And she wanted to take the child, my child, away."

I removed a photocopy of the letter that was found in Barker's apartment and read it aloud.

"*Julie,*

I made a mistake. I thought I could trust you. You promised me and you lied. But you were right, I'm not a good mother. I'm sorry for what I did. I hope you are too.

Goodbye,

Becca."

"Julie wasn't lying about the man in black, was she?"

"No, she wasn't. It was Howell. He murdered my child. Burned her to death as she slept. I want him to know what that feels like," said Barker.

"You're wrong. Julie got it wrong too. Or haven't you figured that out yet?" I said.

He was on the line: hooked into this story. He leaned forward slightly.

"Julie got a blow to the head, she was high, disoriented – fighting for her life. It wasn't a man in black – it was a woman," I said.

Barker's jawline tightened, his eyes narrowed.

"Rebecca dressed in black and came into the house with her spare key. She was going to take Emily and burn down the house, so no one would know the child had been taken. People would believe that junkie Julie got high and torched the house. No witnesses, no one would come looking for the baby. That was the plan," I said.

Barker's cheeks reddened, and he gave his response fast. "She was in on it with her husband. Howell has to pay for what he did. Julie disturbed him, and my daughter paid for it with her life. He kept silent when Julie was convicted. He knew his wife had caused all of this and he did nothing."

"Leonard Howell didn't know anything about the fire. Records show he was on active duty at the time in Afghanistan. You've got this all wrong, Scott," I said.

CHAPTER SIXTY-NINE

The air smelled stale. I knew there were around twenty other people in the courtroom; ADAs, cops, feds, all watching and listening with great intensity, but it didn't feel like it.

It was just me and him.

There was something new about Barker. Ever since he'd thrown off the act, I found it hard to look at his face. Occasionally, I thought I could see George, but then the cold, hard edge drew itself back into his features. But since I'd mentioned Julie, there was some kind of tension and anxiety at work deep inside Barker. His fingers seemed to tremble slightly, until he noticed and corrected the problem by locking them together; and the dead stare had an aspect of hope in its lost, lingering shine.

I shook my head and said, "You've been playing a game for five years. Plotting out the perfect kidnap, the perfect frame-up. Rebecca Howell was already dead, so you wanted Leonard Howell to go through exactly what Julie went through – a murder trial for a child they did not kill. But you don't know the whole truth. You tell me where Caroline is, who is holding her and how we get her out, and I'll tell you what Julie kept from you."

"She kept nothing from me. She told me she remembered. When she hit her head, it all became twisted, but the letter made her remember the way it really happened. I need your client to admit it. Otherwise, all of his suffering, all of Caroline's pain, all of *this* was for nothing."

"That girl has suffered enough. We don't have time for   "

"Trust me, there's time. Time still to save her," said Barker.

"I'm not saying Julie lied to you. Julie has been acquitted. Her memory has no stain upon it now. But there are things that Rebecca

294

and Julie kept secret and which I'm sure Julie forgot. I can tell you but you have to tell me where Caroline is. What do you say?"

"Julie told me everything," he said.

"She didn't tell you it was her sister in her house, dressed in black. She didn't tell you Emily's secret," I said.

He gripped the armrest, turned away from me and looked at the ceiling. The anger, the pain running through Barker was clear on every inch of his face.

"Tell me where Caroline is, and I'll tell you about Emily," I said.

Barker hadn't planned for this. His eyes darted around the room, his face contorted in indecision. For a long time, he said nothing. He wrestled with it. I didn't dare push him.

He finally turned toward me, "Tell me about Emily first," he said.

I stayed quiet for a long minute. As did Barker. I needed to make it look like I was sizing him up – making my judgment call. The truth was that I needed him to believe that I was reluctant to tell the story. That he'd made a small victory.

It was time to play the first card. I leaned over, flipped open the file and brought out a single document. I placed it on the table, swiveled it around and slid it toward Barker. He glanced at it. He'd seen it before. He knew exactly what it was and what it said. Emily Rosen's birth certificate.

"Your name is not recorded beside the entry for 'Father', why not?"

"Julie and I discussed it. My line of work at the time was – risky. I wouldn't have wanted it recorded that I was a father. Certain people could use that against me."

"Sounds as if keeping your name off the record was a good decision. But it wasn't your decision, right?"

"Julie wanted it blank. Said she needed time to think. I had to go away on a long job and thanks to Howell we never got around to it."

"So I'm right. It was Julie's idea in the first place."

I got no reaction to this. Cold, detached, Barker listened with no expression on his face. That was okay. For now, all I needed was him to believe that I knew what I was talking about. Layering fact upon fact. He knew it all to be true.

My one hope of finding Caroline alive rested on this man believing every word I said.

Picking the file up off the floor, I put it on the desk, selected the next single page and handed it over. As he read it, I readied another document. This one was three pages long. I couldn't show this to him yet. I needed him to read the first page. Study it. Then hit him with the second document.

He looked at the first page closely. I knew this was something he hadn't seen before. The skin around his eyes curled into deep wrinkles.

"This is Julie's last bank statement. The FBI got it for me a few minutes ago. This records deposits into Julie's account. August 2001 – ten thousand dollars. June 2002, same week that Emily is born – another ten thousand."

"So?"

"The deposits were made by Rebecca Howell."

"I met up with Julie again in around June 2001. A couple months later she moved upstate into a cottage her sister rented for her. She mentioned Rebecca helped set her up after rehab. What has this got to do with anything?"

Another card. Another single page document – this time from Rebecca Howell's records.

He read it with a confused expression, threw it aside.

"This is a report from Rebecca Howell's obstetrician. It confirms that due to cell damage – Rebecca Howell could not conceive naturally."

"I think I remember this. Julie talked about her sister's miracle pregnancy. Her sister had been trying for a child for a long time. Guess they got lucky," he said.

"No, they didn't," I said and handed him a two-page report and attached photograph. The report had been prepared by the FBI lab in Manhattan within the last hour.

"Leonard Howell is no angel, Scott. But he loves Caroline. Loves her more than you will ever know. His devotion to his child is something that you could never have."

His nostrils flared. I was standing on a nerve here. Deliberately. It was Barker's messed up emotions of loss, love, revenge and hate that had driven him to these extremes. This was a man who would kill for love. These were the emotions I needed to play upon.

"See the photograph at the back of the report. That's my shirt. Leonard's blood is all over it. He didn't want to live if his daughter was dead. There was no point. She was his life. He opened his wrists and his throat with a sharp object. You couldn't do that. But Howell could because he loved his daughter."

"Howell and his wife burned my child to death!"

His voice reverberated around the room, and it was not until the last echo faded that I spoke again; softly and quietly.

"You're wrong. Rebecca Howell did something worse."

I took up the letter Rebecca had written to Julie and read aloud. *"I made a mistake. I thought I could trust you. You promised me and you lied.* Julie made Rebecca a promise: In exchange for twenty-thousand dollars, Julie would give her baby to Rebecca. The first ten thousand was paid just after Julie got pregnant, the next after she gave birth."

With quick, violent motion he shook his head.

"The document in front of you is a DNA analysis of Leonard Howell's blood, taken from my shirt. It compares it to a control sample and there are no genetic marker similarities."

I saw him stiffening in his chair, his eyes becoming wider, more alert.

"The control sample is from Caroline Howell."

I was aware of other people in the room for the first time in several minutes. I heard the gasps.

"I've been through all of Rebecca Howell's medical records. She changed physicians in September 2002, so she could have a fresh start with a new physician, maybe one who wouldn't know the real reason for the omission in her medical records. See, there's a gap. A maternity gap. There is no record of Rebecca Howell ever becoming pregnant, never mind having a baby. No blood tests. No scans. No ante-natal appointments. No pregnancy. There's a note in the file made by her new doctor who states that Rebecca told him her old records were lost. Maybe that was enough for her new doctor. It's not enough for me. The maternity notes aren't there because there never was a pregnancy."

I let the silence build in the room. He was lost in terrible thoughts, his eyes moving rapidly, hoping and praying that the truth was somehow false. I watched his face crumble, his lips move silently.

"Rebecca Howell faked her pregnancy. Leonard was in Afghanistan. His last tour. She probably wore padding for months – making it appear to friends and neighbors that she was with child. There was no pregnancy. And yet, Leonard Howell came home to a baby girl. Your baby girl."

Shaking his head, he listened and buried his fingernails in his scalp as he began to rock back and forth. The weight of his mistake taking full grip in his mind.

"My guess is Julie changed her mind after the baby was born and broke her promise to her sister. Rebecca had paid money, she was months into the lie. That fake pregnancy was now real and a huge part of her life. Rebecca's last day as a county medical examiner was twenty-four hours before the fire."

I took one more piece of paper from a stack in front of me, gave it to Barker.

"That's a cremation order for an infant called Jane Doe. She was found in a dumpster, and was not more than a couple months old. No one claimed the body. The order is signed by Rebecca Howell. It's the last thing she did as a medical examiner. She never returned to that job. Know why? She filed the order away in the case notes, and she took that child's corpse away. She went to Julie's house to steal the baby, and burn the house down to make it look like the child perished in the flames. But no child died. Rebecca put Jane Doe's body in the cot and set it alight. And she left with Emily."

I'll never forget the sound Barker made. I'd heard it before. Howell had made the same sound when he'd stood on the driveway of his ruined house and learned that his daughter was most likely dead. It sounded like a soul being ripped in two.

"Tell me where your daughter is. We can still get her out alive. Tell me!"

"The tomb of the unknown artist, in Sleepy Hollow Cemetery. Marlon will shoot her at seven a.m. if you don't stop him."

CHAPTER SEVENTY

I'd never been in a helicopter before, and once we'd landed in a field to the rear of Sleepy Hollow Cemetery I promised myself I wouldn't ever set foot in a helicopter again. I had no idea how long we were in the air. It felt like an hour, but it could've been ten minutes. My eyes were shut the whole time and the only thing I could concentrate on was gripping the support straps that hung from the ceiling. The landing was a little rough, and I'd been holding on so tightly that I'd managed to pull one of the fabric straps from the ceiling. It hung loosely around my head.

The FBI tactical team shook their heads at me. Lynch whispered to them, and then shot me a condescending look. Harper told them to knock it off.

I checked my watch. Six forty-five. In fifteen minutes Marlon would put a bullet in Caroline.

We got out of the chopper, and my feet sunk into deep, wet grass. Keeping my head low until we were well clear of the blades, I ran, hunkered over, to the crop of trees that separated the cemetery from the field.

I hung at the back of the pack, with Harper. Lynch led the tactical unit, who carried automatic rifles and wore black helmets and Kevlar. Lynch wanted me there. We couldn't spare the time, and Lynch envisaged that Marlon would hear the chopper coming so it was likely there might be a hostage situation. In that case, I was to get on the phone to Barker and use him to talk Marlon down. Barker still wouldn't talk to the feds so they needed me here, as liaison. What I knew might come in handy. Might not. But they wanted me there all the same. Harry stayed behind.

I'd asked Barker if he had any way of contacting Marlon – via a cell phone or secure email. He said no. Marlon had been paid the ransom for his work – and he would fulfill his obligations to the letter. I'd asked him how certain he was of this.

"I swore an oath to Julie. To clear her name. To make the ones who hurt her suffer. I paid Marlon well to do the same."

It seemed that Barker had first encountered Marlon in LA. He'd tried off-loading two antique shotguns with no bill of sale, or provenance for the weapons. It took Barker all of three minutes to find out they'd been stolen two weeks previously from a house in Beverly Hills. Some money had been taken from the house, a car, and the guns. But not before the weapons had been tried and tested. Marlon had emptied both barrels into the elderly male owner of the house before he'd left.

Trained to exploit an opportunity, Barker had turned Marlon into an asset. Someone who could do wet work for him. And he'd done plenty. He'd put two in the back of McAuley's head at the ransom drop six months ago. Barker also confirmed Marlon had been responsible for the set-up at his apartment. He'd shot Washington, and killed Beck, and the super

Lynch ripped open the sleeve of his shirt on a thorn bush as he pushed his way through the line of trees to get to the cemetery. By the time I had to climb through, the branches had been pushed down by the team ahead of me.

The only light came from the small beams attached underneath the tactical unit's rifles. Sunrise was still a good forty-five minutes away and the hill ahead of us was still cloaked in heavy darkness. Lynch covered his small flashlight with his palm as he stood in the north corner of the cemetery and consulted the map.

He looked around, but didn't scan the torch light in his direction of view.

"Six hundred yards up the hill. It's one of those walk-in tombs. Looks like a little house. This part of the cemetery is closed to the public, so if you see a male – they're hostiles. We go, two-by-two cover. We'll come up on the left until I say break, then B team will flank from the right. Wait for my signal before we go in. Flynn, you stay at the bottom of the hill," said Lynch.

The grass was knee deep. Ahead of us the rows of tombstones, statues, and railed-off graves began. Many of the stones and ornate figures were covered in lichen, they were crumbling and here and there the stones themselves had tumbled over and broken in two. I watched the four-man team, with Lynch at their head, as they filed up the hill. A low mist looked like a blanket of cobwebs that covered the ground.

Harper and I waited for them to get ahead, then she started up after them, through the dead, toward the tomb at the top of the hill.

It was still full dark. The sun had yet to threaten the skyline, and I checked my watch. Coming up on six fifty. Ten minutes to go. It was possible that Marlon may not even be here. Maybe he would stay away, and only arrive at seven, when it was time to put the girl down. It's not easy killing someone. Some can do it without blinking. Some are compelled to murder, be it through circumstance or psychosis. For others, it's part of the job. I got that impression from Marlon. And even though it was a simple task, it couldn't have been easy. It would be especially difficult to sit in the room with the girl, and count down the hours, the minutes, and the seconds until it was time to pull the trigger.

I'd met Marlon, briefly. I didn't think he could easily sit beside a teenager for the night, then shoot her in the morning. That takes a special kind of killer. My guess was Marlon wouldn't do it that way.

I was wrong.

The silencer helped. But no silencer on the planet can render a gunshot mute. The explosion of primer and gas has to make a sound. It's still pretty loud. And the action on the ejection port of any automatic weapon is also bound to create noise. The slam of the steel port opening, and then closing as it ejects the spent cartridge. It's like a soft hammer fall. Audible, but not loud. Imagine that happening twice per second, for three seconds.

The other sound came from the rounds peppering Lynch's Kevlar vest. And then I heard something else. The sound of someone choking on their own blood. I saw Lynch a hundred yards ahead of me. He'd turned away from the shots and held his hand toward the blood gouting from his throat.

I looked around. Standing at the bottom of the hill, in the grass, with no cover, I decided I was in the worst place possible. I bent low and moved up the grassy bank, toward the tombstones.

A hand on the back of my head slammed me to the wet thick grass. I hadn't heard Harper come up behind me, but I knew it was her. The hand on top of my head was small, but the force used to put me face-down was considerable. She grabbed the back of my shirt and together, we crawled behind a raised clump of grass. My legs were bleeding again and the pain caused me to clamp my teeth together to stifle a groan.

The return fire from the tactical unit was deafening. It seemed to come from all around.

"Did you see where the shot came from?" said Harper.

"No," I said.

She leaned out, stared up the hill.

"He has to be at the top. Laying down with a rifle. He's got the perfect firing position. High ground, and the right weapon and enough elevation to see the whole graveyard," she said.

"What're you going to do?" I said.

"Quiet. Don't make a sound. Stay here," she said, then rolled over three hundred and sixty degrees, back onto her stomach, then crawled forward.

I moved forward too. Every inch of that crawl sent waves of pain through my torn legs. I got close enough then turned and put my back to the tombstone. It was just as well. Huge clods of earth and grass from the same flattened area where I'd been lying suddenly leapt into the air as rounds struck home.

The tactical unit ceased firing. They were taking cover.

I felt the cold seeping through my shirt. I was soaking wet, again. And the cold only served to heighten my panic, my heart beating against my chest and my breath was like the exhaust from a car engine – great, fast, steady plumes of frozen breath drifting up above my head.

I heard cracks and felt small stones landing on my belly and legs.

Marlon must've seen my breath and he was peppering the tomb-stone with rounds. I heard the cracks from bullets bouncing off old stone. I controlled my breathing, put my head low so any fog from my breath would mingle with the low-lying mist on the long grass.

This old part of the cemetery really was a hollow, until you got to the top of the hill. The echoes were strong and deep. I heard the same sound of metal impacting stone at high velocity all over the place. It was like being in a movie theater with surround sound. Lethal volleys of suppressing gunfire were resounding in my ears from every angle.

I worked up the courage, and got my feet beneath me and quickly whipped my head around the tombstone and back again.

I saw the tomb on the hill, but I didn't see any of the feds or the shooter.

But I could hear the feds all right. They returned fire with their assault rifles. And I heard a single command.

"*Covering.*"

More shots, both silenced and loud. Then just the *phut phut* of the silencer on the rifle.

"*Man down, man down.*"

Silence. No wind. Not even a puff of air through the trees. If Marlon had put someone else down, that left three tactical agents, plus Harper. A terrible thought came to me. Saying "man down", didn't necessarily mean it was a man. What if Harper had been the last one to get hit?

More silenced shots and the sound of shells eating old tombstones.

It took me a few seconds to realize my cell phone was buzzing in my jacket. My heart was thumping so hard I didn't notice it at first. My back hard against the tombstone, and covering the light from the screen with my jacket, I checked the phone.

A text from Harper.

The assault team can't move. They're pinned below the shooter. Can you get to Lynch's gun? I need a distraction.

Slowly, keeping as low as possible, I peered around the tombstone. Lynch was thirty feet away. Unmoving. His gun in the grass beside him. With the pain in my legs, and the view that Marlon had of the cemetery, Lynch's gun may as well have been in Kansas.

I texted her back.

I can't make it to the gun.

I checked the time again – five minutes to seven. I let thirty seconds pass. In that time I thought about Christine and Amy. They would be all right. In time, Christine would have a new man. Amy would have a new dad. They didn't rely on me financially. Christine was in a good job – her father would take care of them. It was a sobering thought, they didn't really need me.

Right then, the girl in that tomb needed me more than anyone else on this earth.

I took a breath and called out.

"Marlon, it's Eddie Flynn. I'm unarmed," I said.

I stood up, hands in the air above my head. Marlon was lying flat on the bank at the top of the hill. He was moving slowly to his right, toward the entrance to the tomb. His gun was aimed at me, and I knew that before he got up and went into that tomb he would shoot me dead.

"I've got a message from Scott Barker," I said.

Marlon stopped moving. His head bent low so that he could look through the telescopic sight on the rifle, taking aim right at me.

I closed my eyes and said, "Scott wanted you to know he told us the truth."

Three rapid single shots.

My heart thudded in my ears. I didn't dare to breathe. I knew if I took a breath the pain would take over, the shock would hit me and I would fall. I felt numb from cold. Maybe I wouldn't feel the rounds tearing through my body. My head swam and I felt dizzy. I wanted to grab on to something, breathe and take the hit all at once but fear froze every limb. I couldn't move. A burning started in my chest. My hands shook and I couldn't hold on any longer.

I took a breath. Opened my eyes.

At the top of the hill, lit by the flashlights on the feds guns, I saw Harper with her pistol aimed at the ground. I looked down at my chest. No blood. I filled my lungs with the freezing air. It felt good. My legs burned as I ran up the remaining three hundred yards of the hill, and saw Harper standing over Marlon. She'd snuck up from the right, and came upon him from behind.

Marlon was dead.

Two of the tactical unit members were working on Lynch, tying gauze to his throat before lifting him and running back down the hill toward the chopper. But I knew it was too late for him.

When I turned around, Harper was nowhere to be seen. And the heavy iron door that led to the tomb of the unknown artist lay open.

CHAPTER SEVENTY-ONE

Standing outside the tomb, with the door ajar, I could see light spilling out and cutting through the early morning gloom. I followed the indentations of Harper's boots where she'd trodden down the grass while making her way inside.

I peered around the door. The first thing that hit me was the smell. It was mold, and shit, and something else. Something old and foul and dead. I gripped the iron door to prise it apart further so I could go inside. Harper had only opened it so far; just enough to squeeze her small frame through the gap.

The door moved surprisingly easily. I'd braced my feet ready to have to push like the devil to open the thing. But Marlon must have oiled the hinges, and when I got inside I saw he'd put rollers on the bottom of the door to take the weight off the hinges. I stepped onto old concrete.

An oil lamp burned in the corner of the stone room. Harper knelt beside it. She was working at something on the ground.

It took a few seconds for my eyes to adjust to the light.

"Get help, we need to lift this," said Harper. I looked down and saw she was using a crowbar, working at what I thought at first was the floor. Turns out it was an inch-thick steel plate that covered the floor in the center of the room.

I hollered outside, and seconds later two feds came in. One of them had another crowbar, and he managed to work it underneath the plate.

Marlon had been a truly huge man. Only someone of his size could've slid this plate across the floor on his own. Just below the edges of the plate, was a layer of soil and dirt to make it easier to move.

"To the left, on three," said Harper.

She counted three, pulled the crowbar down, and we pushed with our hands and feet and slid the steel plate to the side.

The flashlights aimed at the hole in the ground.

Over the course of the night that I'd first met Agent Harper, and in the last twenty-four hours, I'd come to admire her. She was smart, and hard. Brave too. If I really thought about it, she was one of the toughest people I'd ever met.

It didn't stop the tears covering Harper's face as she stared into the depths of that hole. Not that I could blame her. Staring down, I only had one question in mind: How? How is it possible for a human being to do that to a seventeen-year-old girl?

It was beyond my understanding. In fact, it was one of those moments when I was pretty sure I shouldn't understand. There was no sense in it. Only evil.

CHAPTER SEVENTY-TWO

I waited in the conference room of the White Plains PD office. It was coming up on nine a.m. Adrenaline can only keep you going so far. My legs were agony. I couldn't wait to get home, take off my pants so they wouldn't rub against the cuts. Captain Powers had extended me some courtesies. Use of a laptop and printer. I was waiting for him to bring me Copeland so I could tie up a few loose ends.

Alexander Berlin came in to the room. The man from the Justice Department. He still had that stick up his ass, and the only question on my mind was whether he was going to take it out and beat me with it.

"I won't take up much of your time. I know you're tired and awaiting a guest, but I want to have a little talk about your tie pin, Eddie. We've checked the courtroom security cameras. Seems you lost that pin right before your client tried to take his life. The guard in the prisoner transport van says he saw you pick up a pin off the floor of Howell's transport cell."

I said nothing. Berlin took a seat beside me.

"Here's what I think, Eddie," said Berlin. "Captain Powers could arrest you. But I don't think that's fair. Your client was in pain. He wanted a way out. Maybe you gave him one? Maybe he swiped the pin without you knowing it when he grabbed your shirt in court?"

Neither of us spoke.

"Here's the thing, Eddie," continued Berlin, "I used to have a dog. I found him in a bad place and I took him home. I fed him. Protected him. Trained him to go out into the world and help us find the other bad dogs in the neighborhood. But see, sometimes that dog just can't change its nature. It'll turn up years down the line and it'll try to bite you – it turns rabid.

"Justice demands we take care of rabid dogs. Barker will go down for the murder of McAuley. He'll also serve time for conspiracy to murder. There will be further charges relating to agent Washington's wounding et cetera. Suffice to say, I've got my dog back under control and I'm putting him away for good."

"I'm glad to hear it," I said.

"Now, about that pin . . ." said Berlin.

"What pin?" I asked.

"Exactly. Right now, I've forgotten about that pin. My memory comes and goes. The thing about a good dog turning bad is you still need to replace the dog. I've heard your name mentioned before. Can't say where. The cases you've been involved in sometimes cross our radar. Right now, you're a puppy. When you grow up, I might have need of your services."

I didn't like this. I was nobody's dog. Good or bad.

"And what if I said I wasn't interested?" I said.

"Then, my memory might improve drastically. Don't worry. I don't need you now. Maybe I'll never have need of you. But if I do, I'll whistle. And I'll expect you to come running."

Without another word, he stood and left.

The conference room was empty and cold. The heater hadn't come on yet and the central heating system was playing up. I put my hands underneath my arms to keep them warm. My suit was still damp from the grass at the cemetery. The thought of that place, and what I'd seen when we pulled back the steel plate . . .

I shook my head, trying to get rid of the memory, popped the tab on a coke and took a long, long drink.

A knock on the door, then it opened and Harper led Max Copeland into the room. She told him to sit at the other end of the conference table, well away from me, and then she left and closed the door behind her.

"What's the meaning of this?" he said.

Other than advising a client during questioning, Copeland had never spent the night in a police station. He certainly hadn't spent a night in the cells before. He'd loosened his tie, undone his top button and he carried his jacket draped over his right arm. He let the jacket fall to the floor and folded his arms.

"I'll be suing the police for wrongful arrest," said Copeland. "I'll file the suit soon as I get out. Oh, and I'm still suing you for assault. Don't think I'd forgotten about you."

The urge to cave in Copeland's head hadn't left me from the first moment I'd met the man. I reminded myself that there were better ways to do things.

"The police and the feds are still considering charges, Copeland. This isn't over. Far as I'm concerned, you helped a man kidnap and murder a seventeen-year-old girl."

"Prove it. And who says it's murder?" he said.

My eyes found the dark wooden knots on the desk, and lingered there.

"A few hours ago, it became murder," I said. "But this can all go away, Max."

I took his iPhone out of my pocket, skidded it across the table.

"So it was you who stole my phone."

"I found it. Right here in the corner of this room. Must've fallen out of your pocket. Anyways, I didn't know who it belonged to so I checked the messages, and the voicemail . . ." I paused to watch the color evaporate from Copeland's face.

"And the voice recordings," I added.

I watched his big fingers swipe at the phone. He was going to delete the recordings. I took out my own phone and started playing one of them.

"You can't do that," said Copeland.

"I already did. You go ahead and delete them. I've got a few copies. One for the cops, one for the feds too. They only listened to the first session. The vanilla meeting. I listened to both recordings. You knew your client was going to be questioned about the murder and disappearance of a young woman, he gave you the name Caroline Howell, and he helped you draft the immunity agreement. You came into this precinct with that thing already done. You knew about this before Caroline was reported missing and you did nothing. How's the bar disciplinary committee going to view that one? More to the point, how's a jury going to look at that?"

The man's porcelain-white face began to shudder as the tremors took over. I could feel his fear howling around the room like a cold draft.

"It doesn't have to be like this. I could help you," I said.

His thought processes split in two. He wanted me to help him, but he sure as hell didn't trust me. Because he was in such a state, he wasn't thinking as clearly as he should have been. The decision came down to time. If not now, then soon. But in the very near future Copeland's fear would eventually get the better of him and he'd ask for my help.

In the end, I didn't have to wait more than a few seconds.

"How could you help me? And why would you do that?"

"You're not a bad person, you've just been led astray. Could happen to any lawyer. You think you're doing something in your client's best interests. That's all that the job requires, really. But then you start getting close to the line. Sooner or later you leap over that line and there's no going back. It's easily done. I've done it myself."

He said nothing, but a glint of hope appeared on his face.

"How could you help me?" he said again.

"I could make the recording disappear, together with all the copies. That's the only thing that ties you down to any wrongdoing in this case. You want it gone? I can do that. But you gotta do something for me."

"I have money. I could cut you a check for—"

"I'm not interested in money. You'll do two things. You'll sign this affidavit first."

I took the printout of the affidavit I'd typed that morning, got up and handed it to Copeland.

"This affidavit withdraws all of the allegations you've made against Harry Ford in the Rosen appeal. All of them. In fact, you're going to state for the record that Judge Ford performed his role at the original Rosen hearing according to the best traditions of the New York Bar. You'll also see the affidavit stipulates that you did not have a reasonable belief that Harry Ford had acted negligently in the presentation of the Rosen case."

"I can't do that. If I sign this I'm saying to the court that I lied in my earlier affidavits. I'll be disbarred."

"Of course you will. That's the whole point. Or would you rather take your chances in court and face a conspiracy to kidnap and murder charge?"

He read the affidavit again.

"You've got about ten seconds before I call Powers in here to arrest you," I said.

Copeland had made his money already. He didn't need to work – he just enjoyed it. I took some pleasure in taking that away from him. He rubbed at his bald head in frustration, took up a pen and signed the sworn declaration.

"That it?" he said.

"No, there's one more thing."

"What's that?"

"Second thing is easy too, all you have to do is deliver a message."

"What kind of message?" he said.

"A personal one."

CHAPTER SEVENTY-THREE

"What happened? Did you make it? Is she alive?" said Barker.

He sat in a chair across the table from me in a police interview room. Copeland remained standing. He didn't take up the other seat at the table beside me. Instead, he looked at his shoes.

"Well? Did you get her?!" screamed Barker.

My voice was slow, soft and heavy.

"We got to the cemetery by chopper. It was the only way we could be sure to make it there before time ran out. Marlon must've heard the helicopter landing in the adjacent field. Before we got up the hill to the tomb, he opened fire with an assault weapon. Killed the lead agent. The FBI took out Marlon and we got into the tomb."

The more I spoke, the deeper Barker's breaths became. His chest was heaving now. His mouth was open and his expression searched every word, every minor intonation – looking for the answer.

I could've just told him, but I wanted to drag it out. He deserved it.

"We pulled back the steel plate. Put a flashlight in the hole."

I hung my head.

"What?"

"We figure that when he heard the helicopter, Marlon opened the chamber, and shot Caroline in the head. Closed it, and went out to meet us, head on."

"I'm sorry," said Copeland.

I stood up just before the fit took hold of Barker. He bared his teeth and sprung to his feet. There was no panic alarm in this room. But I didn't need one. His anger wasn't targeted at anyone else in that room but himself.

His fists pounded the steel table. Over and over again. The noise was deafening. And he said, "No, no, no, no, no . . ." again and again as his fists began to bleed.

It took Copeland well over five minutes to calm him down. To get him back onto his seat. Tears pooled in the indentations on the table, and mixed with the blood from Barker's knuckles as he whispered Emily's name.

I sat down again, and listened while Copeland spoke to him, gently.

"You can never make up for this," I said. "But there is one small thing you can do to try and make things right. It's the only thing you can do. I'm going to ask you about the night of the ransom drop. You almost died in that fire. I have some questions, and you're going to give me straight answers," I said.

Copeland gave Barker a Kleenex. He rubbed Barker's back, tried to console him. This was the message I asked Copeland to give to Barker.

Cooperate.

The two men looked at each other. Barker nodded. Copeland nodded.

They had an understanding.

After that, Barker calmed down a little. He gave me his attention and said, "Tell me what you want to know."

"Everything. I want to know everything."

CHAPTER SEVENTY-FOUR

Ten minutes later I left Copeland and Barker alone in the consulting room. The look on Barker's face wasn't exactly calm. I could see the anxiety, the sheer tonnage of guilt that now pressed upon him, but he was not concerned about the jail time ahead of him. No, Barker didn't care about it. He was in hell now, and he'd no choice but to stay there.

Harper stood at the end of the corridor, leaning against the wall. Her arms were folded across her chest and not for the first time, I noticed how big the gun looked on her hip in comparison to her light, short frame. The morning sun streamed through windows behind her, masking her in silhouette.

I put my back to the wall and heard the door to the consultation room open. Copeland came out, shut the door and gave me a slight nod.

"Are my release papers complete yet?" he said.

I pushed off the wall, looked behind him at Harper who hadn't moved.

"They'll be ready in a few minutes. I believe Agent Harper is processing those papers now," I said.

He turned and looked at Harper. Swung back to me and said, "She looks like she's in a real hurry too."

"That's how it goes. The wheels of justice take time. Ten minutes should be enough," I said.

I resumed my position with my back against the wall. I closed my eyes and let the information that Barker had just told me sink into my mind. He'd cut the power lines to the outside lights of Howell's property the day Caroline went missing. He'd tracked her car, abducted her, taken her blood and planted it in the basement.

He'd set up the explosive device with Marlon's help. Marlon had killed McAuley and buried the body, on Barker's instructions. He'd played it perfectly. But this wasn't over. There was a time and a place for tying up loose ends. And today was not that day.

The silence of the corridor was routinely broken by Copeland's heels on the hard linoleum floor. He paced up and down.

"Are we done yet? What the hell is the delay here?" he said.

I checked my watch. Nine minutes had passed. I waved at Harper and she stood up straight and walked away. It was only Copeland and me in that corridor.

"It's time," I said.

Copeland looked puzzled. "Time for what?"

He was standing directly in front of the consulting-room door, his hands raised and a puzzled look in his face.

Captain Powers came around the corner, a pair of handcuffs swinging from his fingers. Before Copeland could react, Powers slammed him, face first, into the wall, grabbed his arms and put the cuffs on his wrists, tight.

"Max Copeland, you are under arrest for conspiracy to commit kidnapping, and murder," said Powers, before reading Copeland his rights.

"What the hell is this? We had a deal!" he cried.

"Not with me. We got everything Barker said on tape. He confirmed Caroline Howell's kidnapping was planned, to the last detail. We also have video of your consultations with Barker after his arrest. You don't show him that immunity agreement, you don't say a word. With Barker confirming the plan, and you coming into the station with that agreement already written, we can prove you knew what your client had done. Now, you're done."

"Let me give you a little piece of advice. Defense attorney to defense attorney," I said. "The recordings you made of your client were illegal. He didn't know he was being recorded. You did it to protect yourself from him. Smart. But you couldn't get past the fact that you'd recorded Barker illegally. I have to tell you, whether the recording was illegal or not, doesn't change the fact that it's attorney client work product. It's part of attorney client privilege. Doesn't matter if I found that phone, or if I stole from you. Without a warrant from a judge I can't listen to that recording or use it. The fact of the matter is, you couldn't have been prosecuted on the strength of that evidence because it was obtained, by me, illegally. It would never see the inside of a court. But when you got your client to talk about the plan, just now, he waived privilege."

Copeland fell against the door. His hand reached toward his heart.

"I want you to know this, Max. The phone could never have been used against you. You were gonna walk out of here, free and clear. Now, you're screwed. I want you to think about that."

"No, no, no . . ." he said, lunging toward me. Powers hauled on the cuffs, pulling him back.

"Come on," said Powers, taking him away.

As I watched Copeland being led away I couldn't stop a shudder running through me. There but for the grace of God go I.

I'd lied to Copeland. I'd lied to Barker.

I had crossed the line too. And there was no coming back.

CHAPTER SEVENTY-FIVE

Three days later, Harry and I were led into a private room on the fourteenth floor of the White Plains General Hospital. Lenny Howell sat up in bed, staring at the ceiling. We'd been told by the sister that her nurses had removed the heavy bandage around his throat the day before. He'd made good progress since he regained consciousness, but he was still weak.

"Some friends to see you," said the nurse who'd showed us to his room.

He didn't react when he saw me, but he looked puzzled at seeing Harry.

"How you feeling, Lenny? This is a friend of mine. Judge Harry Ford. You met him a while back, but you were still a little out of it. You can call him Harry," I said.

Only when Howell tried to raise his hand did I see exactly how weak he remained. Harry took his hand gently, and nodded.

"Eddie," Howell said, "I appreciate you coming to see me, but I don't want to hear about the trial right now."

I looked around the room.

"Notice anything?" I said.

"Nothing particular," said Howell.

"Well, maybe the clue is who is not here. There are no correctional officers in your room, nor are there any outside. Your ankle isn't chained to the bed any more, either."

He sat up just a little and looked around.

"You're right. How come?"

"Because your trial is over. Technically it was a mistrial, but the DA is no longer pursing any charges against you. You're a free man," I said.

I told him everything that had happened since the suicide attempt. He got the full story – unlike Scott Barker. It was unfair of me. The back of his head hit the pillow like I'd just socked him in the mouth.

"I want you to know that I lied to Scott Barker. The DNA test was false. In fact, it was never performed. Harper got the lab to write a false report. It wasn't a real trial any more – we needed Barker to cooperate. Plus, I was holding back something important."

Laying a single page in Lenny's hand, I said no more and let him read it. It was from the IVF clinic. Being a soldier on active duty, Lenny had signed a release for the clinic – his wife could use his sperm at any time without his permission.

"What does this mean? He said.

"It means Caroline is your blood, your daughter. But her birth mother was Julie Rosen."

Harry moved to the door of the private room, opened it. Howell closed and then opened his eyes and looked at Harry. I leaned over the bed and pinched Howell's cheek between my finger and thumb.

"Oww," he said. "What did you do that for?"

"I just wanted you to know, for sure, that you're not dreaming," I said, moving aside so he could see the door.

Caroline Howell held a walking stick, and was still unsteady on her feet. Harry took her other arm and walked her gently into Howell's hospital room. In a matter of days, she'd regained a little of her color, put on maybe five pounds, and her physiotherapist felt that Caroline would regain some of the muscle in her legs that had wasted away in those six horrific months.

When she reached the bed, she gave Harry a kiss on the cheek, and placed both hands around her father's tear-soaked face.

"Daddy," she said.

They wept together. Her long blonde hair stuck to his wet cheeks, and he smelled her, and held her, and kissed her and she held on to him. They cried together for the time that they had lost, for the suffering that they had endured, and for the promise, however faint, of a possible return to normal life.

Watching that scene, I tried not to think of Scott Barker. I tried not to think of his face when I lied and told him Caroline was dead. I wanted to hurt him. I wanted him to know what pain he'd caused – I wanted him to feel it and I wanted it to rip him apart.

Caroline didn't know that she was really Emily Rosen. When or if she ever found out was nothing to do with me. It would've been hard for Howell to see Caroline in the first few days after Harper dragged her out of the hole. She was dehydrated, skin and bone, and sick. Her hair had begun to fall out. It was one of the hardest things I ever did – just watching that girl, curled up and bleeding in a concrete hole in the ground.

How she must have suffered. How she must have begged Scott Barker to let her go. For months she must've prayed and begged and cried.

When I thought of that, I didn't feel so bad for lying to Barker. He was happy to torture a child in this way, just not his own child. And he had heard every word of her pleas and ignored them.

I breathed out, rubbed my eyes and felt a strong urge to go visit my daughter. Right then I wanted to hold her.

"Let's go, Harry."

Before we left, I remembered something else.

"Thank you, thank you!" said Howell.

"You don't have to thank me. I just need you to employ me, one last time. There's still the little matter of your divorce."

CHAPTER SEVENTY-SIX

The offices of Gore & Penning epitomized everything that I despised about lawyers. Maybe it was the combination of oak paneling and glass. Or the bowl of free gold-plated pens that they had in reception. The pens were embossed with the company logo. I was the opposition, here to try and negotiate a financial settlement between Lenny and Susan Howell. I even wore one of my better suits, and I carried a file and an iPad. I still got a disapproving look from the receptionist who probably spent more on manicures in a week than I spent on food.

She told me to wait. I took a seat, grabbed a bunch of free gold pens and set about scraping the company name off the side. They let me wait for a long time. Maybe a half hour. In that time I'd managed to get the name off five of the pens, which I stashed in my jacket pocket. A gold pen is a gold pen, after all.

A tall, blonde young woman in a striking, figure-hugging green suit came up to me and asked if my client would be arriving anytime soon.

"No. It's just me," I said.

She looked puzzled. Then she asked me to follow her. I walked for a long time, through wide, air-conditioned corridors jam-packed with young expensive lawyers in young expensive suits, as they talked on the phones, or tapped at laptops or hauled paper.

We arrived at a glass-walled conference room. She opened the door and ushered me inside. This was a corner office, massive, and boasting a tremendous view of the Manhattan skyline. It was a little after nine, and the ten lawyers on the other side of the table, with their backs to the view, were all sipping coffee from Gore & Penning branded mugs. In the middle of the group was Susan Howell. Five lawyers on her left, five on her right. Beside their decaf macchiatos and slimline lattes, each lawyer had a leather, company branded document folder and an iPad.

Pausing in front of my chair, I waited to see if any of the assholes on that side of the table would stand up and shake my hand. None of them did.

I sat down in a seat in the middle of the conference table, facing Susan. She wore fat, oval, dark sunglasses and didn't register my presence.

"Can I get you anything?" asked the young blonde woman in the green suit.

"No, thanks. I'm not staying that long," I said.

On either side of Susan Howell sat Gore and Penning, respectively. Two middle-aged, sharp-faced divorce lawyers.

I set my file on the table, with the iPad on top. I took a moment to look at all of the faces of my opposition. This meeting alone was probably costing Susan Howell ten grand an hour. The rest of the lawyers were male. Clean, short-back-and-sides haircuts, dark suits and sensible ties.

"Are all these people going to be talking?" I said.

"Not all of them," said the lawyer on Susan's left. "I'm Jeffrey Penning. I'll be leading this negotiation," he said.

I leaned back, laced my fingers together and placed my hands behind my head.

"Are you comfortable enough?" said Jeffrey.

"Pretty much. Say, why do you guys sit at that side of the table? Why don't you sit at this side so you can see the view?"

No one spoke.

"When is your client arriving?" said Jeffrey.

"He's not. You deal with me," I said.

Jeffrey shook his head, tutted. I wasn't surprised when several of the young lawyers on his side of the table watched him do this and then joined in. I've seen some sycophantic behavior before, but nothing like this.

"You don't practice much in the field of divorce, do you, Mr Flynn?"

"Not really," I said.

"You see, if you had a little more experience you'd know that we bring our clients to these conference negotiations so that we can discuss settlement. If we're going to have a meaningful negotiation maybe we should reschedule."

"That's not necessary. I'm not here to negotiate. There won't be a negotiation. Ever. I've got one offer to make. It's my final offer. Either your client accepts it, or she doesn't. Either way, we're not negotiating," I said.

Gore started the laughter rolling around the table. Through a smile he said, "We've heard that one before, Mr Flynn. There's always another offer. You've seen our initial proposals. We think they're fair. Eighty-five per cent of all assets. Bearing in mind that we're negotiating, we'd be prepared to recommend seventy-five per cent to our client."

Silence. I leaned back, closed my eyes and stifled a yawn.

"Are you sure we can't get you anything?" said the lady in the green suit.

"Actually, I like your pens. The ones you have in reception that you give out for free. I'll take a box of them, if you don't mind. But could you scrape off the Gore & Penning logo first?"

Nobody laughed. She looked dumbstruck. Then she turned on her long heels and left.

"Can we be serious for a moment?" said Jeffrey.

"Good idea," I said. "I'd like to speak to your client in private."

"Not a chance," said Jeffrey. The nodding dogs in two-hundred-dollar ties started up.

"Oh, don't worry, gentlemen. We're not discussing the divorce," I said.

"You're not discussing anything alone with our client," said Jeffrey.

"Really. That right, Susan?" I said.

She hadn't moved. For a second I thought it might be a mannequin behind those glasses and leopard-print dress.

"It doesn't really concern you guys. You see, Susan, I want to discuss a locker in New Rochelle train station."

Her hands shot out and gripped the forearms of the men either side of her.

"Leave us alone," she said.

She didn't need to say it twice. The commanding tone of her voice was enough. Gore and Penning stood, reluctantly. Their team did likewise, but Jeffrey Penning was wary. He didn't want any off-the-books transactions, because it meant those assets wouldn't feature in the official financial settlement and he couldn't claim his percentage on those assets.

"Nothing under the table, Susan. We agreed that," he said.

"Get out," she said.

One by one, the legal might of Gore and Penning left the room. Jeffrey was the last to leave. Before he exited I said, "Oh, I meant to tell your receptionist – my assistant will be joining me any minute. Make sure you show her in, right away."

"Why of course," said Jeffrey, sarcastically, and he slammed the door on his way out.

"This room feels a lot bigger now, doesn't it?" I said. I flipped open the iPad and fired it up. Susan said nothing.

I turned the screen around and stood it up vertically on the stand that was built into the protective cover.

I said nothing, just hit play.

The video was from the train station, date stamped a week before Caroline Howell went missing. The feds had been through every inch of security camera footage. They weren't able to see anyone approach the locker that contained the cell phone that Lynch found during the fake drop.

I knew, somehow, this was important. I don't like loose ends. When someone takes the trouble to so perfectly hide their activity, it meant there was a damn good reason for hiding it. It had been a month since Caroline was reunited with her father. I'd spent three days solid with the feds, going through the footage. At first, the FBI tech told me there was no point. How would I be able to see something that they couldn't?

I'd told the tech I wasn't looking for someone placing anything in the locker. He didn't understand that, but he was curious enough to let me trawl the footage with him.

I'd found it on the third day. The camera that covered the lockers was normally static, but it did have a limited range of movement. That was the first discovery I'd made and it helped me narrow down what I was looking for.

Two separate teams had viewed this footage. They were looking for somebody opening the locker door, placing the phone inside, dropping fifty cents in the slot, closing the door, turning the key to lock it, removing the key and walking away. They saw no one at the locker.

But somebody had to have taken that key. Somebody did go to that locker because Lynch found the locker key in the toilet cistern.

The feds didn't see anyone take the key on the video – fact. So I was looking for the reason the feds didn't see anyone taking that key.

I was looking for the distraction.

On the third day of searching I saw the first move. It played now on the iPad in front of Susan Howell. A kid, wearing a black hoodie, took something out of his pocket, pointed toward the ground and kept walking. He put the small item back in his pocket without breaking stride. Thirty seconds later an elderly lady passed in the same direction as the youth in the hoodie, and when she reached the spot where he'd pointed something toward the ground, her feet went out from under her like she'd hit black ice. Her toes went right up over her head and she landed on her back – her shopping bags spilled their contents over the floor and three passers-by came running to see if she was okay.

The kid had used a slip bottle. A small, 50 milliliter squeezy bottle containing water mixed with a little olive oil.

The camera shifts to focus on the fallen lady. All attention is on her. At the top of the screen you can see the lockers but you don't get a full view. If someone had been standing at the locker you'd see their legs and midriff – no more. Nobody at the interesting locker. However, the locker immediately opposite just got occupied. A tall man has opened that locker, placed a bag inside and he's there for a full five minutes with his arms deep within that locker. He closes it, and as he leaves he walks toward the camera. It's the briefest of glimpses and has been slowed down in this footage.

I watched Susan carefully as the footage went into slow-mo. She tried not to look at him. But she couldn't help herself. This man had been her lover, after all.

It wouldn't stand up in court, but it sure looked a lot like Marlon.

The old lady has been helped to her feet, her shopping recovered and placed back into her bags. She stumbles forward, toward the locker. She reaches out and puts a hand on the locker door, just to stop herself falling. The hand is on the door for a few seconds. Then she stands up again and goes on her way. The door didn't open. She put nothing in the slot. The footage is too grainy to tell, but I knew she got something.

She got the key.

"This is actually very clever. These lockers sit back to back. Marlon uses the locker which has a balsawood backing. On the other side of the balsawood is the locker that the feds opened the night of the drop. We know what the feds found in there – and now we know Marlon knocked down the balsawood partition between the lockers, placed the phone inside from the rear and replaced the partition. He got into the drop locker from behind. He also put the fifty cents in the slot. So you don't need to open the locker and place a coin inside. All you need to do is twist and pull out the key – which you did, when you steadied yourself after your fall."

"That's not me. You'll never prove it."

"I don't have to, Barker told us about your involvement. It wasn't his idea. Marlon fell for you, just like Lenny did. You figured out he wasn't who he said he was, and he cut you in for a share of the ransom."

A vein pulsed in her throat.

"Look, I know you married Lenny for his money. Nothing else. You were happy as long as he was rich, but when money started to get tight you needed to take whatever you could get and blow out of town. I've talked to two of your ex-husbands. They don't speak highly of you. I'm not surprised. You never told Lenny you'd been married three times. He just knew you were a widow. Your last husband died from carbon monoxide poisoning and if the feds find out about this I'm sure they'll look at your late husband's death a lot closer. Your might have gotten away with this too, but you got greedy. With the fire, you got a bigger payout on the house from the insurance company than you would've achieved had the house actually sold. But here's the thing – you're not getting one cent from Leonard Howell. That rock of an engagement ring you got sitting in a safety deposit box – it's time to hock it. That's what you get. You'll settle this case now, with no payout, no alimony, zip. You walk away with what you have. If you push this divorce – everything I told you will come out in a public court."

I pushed two copies of an agreement across the table. And followed it with one of my new anonymous gold pens.

"Sign it and get the hell out of here. The feds will put this together soon enough. You don't want to be here when they do," I said.

The paper had come to a stop in between her outstretched arms. She drew back her hands, letting her nails scrape the tabletop.

She signed it through gritted teeth, both copies, pushed them back toward me and stood.

The door opened and Jeffrey Gore said, "Your assistant is here."

"Your *assistant*?" said Harper, as she strode into the room.

"Sorry, I didn't think I should mention the FBI in here. Susan might not have signed the paperwork otherwise."

"What paperwork?" said Jeffrey.

I handed him a copy of the document Susan Howell had just signed and watched Jeffrey's face collapse as he read it. His client didn't seem all that surprised to see Harper. She hung her head, and waited while Harper read her her Miranda rights, cuffed her and walked her out. Jeffrey balled up the agreement and threw it at my back as I left.

"I promise you, this isn't over," he said.

"Don't make promises you can't keep," I said.

Outside the downtown offices of Gore & Penning, two feds waited in an unmarked car. Harper delivered Susan Howell into the hands of her colleagues.

"Take her in," she said.

One of the agents began to take off the handcuffs around Susan's wrists.

"Leave them on," said Harper.

"We got our own. Don't you want your cuffs back?" said the agent.

"No," said Harper. She reached into her jacket, removed her piece, and shield and gave them to the agent.

"Deliver these and my cuffs to the SAC. Tell them I quit," she said.

The two agents stood dumbstruck for a moment, before tucking Susan Howell into the back seat, getting into the car and driving away.

"I didn't expect that," I said.

"Neither did I. Washington was the only thing keeping me going in this job. He's being retired on an ill-health pension. Says he wants to buy into a private investigators firm on the Upper West Side – needs a partner. I'm thinking about it," she said.

"Good for you."

Her stance became awkward. She opened her arms, as if for a hug, thought better of it and held out her right hand. I shook it.

"See you around, Eddie," she said.

Her Charger was double parked across the street. She tore up the ticket on the windshield, got in and lay down an inch of rubber before joining the traffic.

I looked up at the blue sky, the clouds weaving above the skyscrapers. I thought about my family – Christine and Amy. I decided to sack the rest of my week, drive up and spend some time with them. Amy was growing taller by the day, it seemed. And I'd missed a lot of that growing. I walked a block, got into my car and stared the engine. Let it purr for a few seconds. I put it in gear and eased out just as my cell went off. The Bluetooth system picked it up.

"Eddie?"

"Yeah, Eddie Flynn. Can I help you?"

"Desk Sergeant Barnes here at the twenty-first precinct. Got a client for you."

I pulled up at a red light.

"You there?" said Barnes.

"I'm here," I said.

A mother and daughter passed me on the crosswalk. Kid was around Amy's age. The woman was wearing a red coat that flared open in the wind.

"You want the case or not?" he said.

The young girl broke free of her mother's grasp just before she got to the pavement, and ran into the arms of a tall brown-haired guy. He swept up the child in a twirling, joyous hug.

"What's the charge?" I said.

"Triple homicide," said the desk sergeant.

The woman stepped onto the sidewalk and kissed the man holding their child. I couldn't take my eyes off them.

My light changed to green.

"Eddie, you still there?" said the desk sergeant.

The car behind me hit the horn to get me moving. I ignored it.

"You want the case or not?" said the desk sergeant.

A couple more cars joined the chorus of horns. I let go of the steering wheel and watched the girl skipping away as she held her father's hand.

Acknowledgements

As ever, this book would not be in your hands if it wasn't for Euan Thorneycroft at AM Heath. He has guided me and put a lot of work into this novel. For Euan, Helene, Jennifer and all at AM Heath, I am eternally grateful.

The Orion Publishing team have been invaluable in kicking this novel into shape. I am particularly grateful to Jemima Forrester, Jon Wood, Francesca Pathak, Bethan Jones and Francine Brody for all of their incredible insights and hard work. Each of them have contributed in remarkable ways to making this book so much better.

To my family and friends, for believing in me. To John Ross and Son for their support and understanding.

And the greatest debt of gratitude is owed to my wife, first reader, and Pickle point picker, Tracy, who has helped me enormously with this book. I couldn't have written it without your support and ideas. Thank you.

Ask Steve Cavanagh . . .

Q. Eddie's journey to becoming a lawyer is so interesting and is a key part of his character. Can you tell us a little about your own journey to becoming one?

A. Quite a lot of people become lawyers because they have a strong, innate sense of what is right and wrong. They want to be Atticus Finch, defending the freedom of the poor and oppressed. They want to fight for truth and justice. I became a lawyer by mistake. I'd always thought of the law as something that I could probably turn my hand to, if needed, but I didn't really fancy all the hard work. I knew it would be a good profession and so I put it down as one of my choices of degrees at university. Eventually, I was accepted into university and had the choice of business studies and marketing or law. I thought I'd be better suited to business studies and decided to go and register my place on the course at matriculation. However, the night before matriculation day I found myself in a bar. It was a very pleasant place to be at age eighteen. The next day was not so pleasant. I was suffering my first ever hangover, and I had to complete what seemed to be an endless parade of standing in long queues, handing over forms, and the general malaise of registration day at university. After that, I went to my marketing lectures, but couldn't find my name in the list for tutorial groups. I spoke to a very nice lady at the University help desk, who couldn't find my name on the business and marketing course. But she did find it on the law course. In my fragile, hungover state, I'd brought the wrong forms with me to register and I'd signed up for law. My grant for the fees had been paid. I could take a year out and come back and do marketing, or I could stick with law. I decided to stick with the law course. Eventually, I became a lawyer. All because I'd essentially joined the wrong queue at one stage.

Q. Why did you make Eddie a defence attorney, rather than a prosecutor? Some might say that defending people who are implicated in a crime is far worse than trying to take them down…

A. The justice system doesn't really work like that. Everyone is innocent until proven guilty. I could never prosecute. I don't have it in me. I grew up in a working class family in Belfast during the troubles. Maybe because of that, maybe something else in me, I have always been on the side of the underdog; the ordinary citizen. I believe in people. I don't necessarily believe in the state. Growing up I heard about internment, and people in my community, from both sides of the divide, who were wrongfully convicted or murdered. I suppose, at a young age, I developed a healthy disrespect for the law.

Q. Eddie always seems three steps ahead of everyone else, particularly when he's cross-examining witnesses. Can you tell us a little bit about how you approach cases? And why do you think a con-artist like Eddie makes such a good lawyer?

A. A good cross-examination, as Eddie says, is like daylight robbery. You go in fast, you get what you need, and you get the hell out of there. But a great cross-examination is a burglary. You go in and get the answers you need without the witness even knowing you were there. You're picking the pocket of the witness. You have to think of a case as a story. There are always two sides of the tale. Whoever tells the best story in court usually wins. Every con-artist is a story teller. So is every lawyer. Also, con-artists and lawyers share the same skills – misdirection, manipulation, distraction and persuasion.

**Eddie Flynn has had his fair share of explosive cases . . .
Find out more in Steve Cavanagh's novels
The Defence, *The Plea* and *The Cross*, all available now.**